Billy and Me

Billy and Me

GIOVANNA FLETCHER

PENGUIN BOOKS

PENGUIN BOOKS

Published by the Penguin Group
Penguin Books Ltd, 80 Strand, London WC2R ORL, England
Penguin Group (USA) Inc., 375 Hudson Street, New York, New York 10014, USA
Penguin Group (Canada), 90 Eglinton Avenue East, Suite 700, Toronto, Ontario,
Canada M4P 2Y3 (a division of Pearson Penguin Canada Inc.)
Penguin Ireland, 25 St Stephen's Green, Dublin 2, Ireland (a division of Penguin Books Ltd)
Penguin Group (Australia), 707 Collins Street, Melbourne, Victoria 3008, Australia
(a division of Pearson Australia Group Pty Ltd)
Penguin Books India Pvt Ltd, 11 Community Centre,
Panchsheel Park, New Delhi – 110 017, India
Penguin Group (NZ), 67 Apollo Drive, Rosedale, Auckland 0632, New Zealand
(a division of Pearson New Zealand Ltd)
Penguin Books (South Africa) (Pty) Ltd, Block D, Rosebank Office Park,
181 Jan Smuts Avenue, Parktown North, Gauteng 2193, South Africa

Penguin Books Ltd, Registered Offices: 80 Strand, London WC2R ORL, England

www.penguin.com

First published 2013
008

Copyright © Giovanna Fletcher 2013

The moral right of the author has been asserted

Set in 12.5/14.75pt Garamond MT Std
Typeset by Jouve (UK), Milton Keynes
Printed in Great Britain by Clays Ltd, St Ives plc

A CIP catalogue record for this book is available from the British Library

ISBN: 978-1-405-90995-2

www.greenpenguin.co.uk

MIX
Paper from
responsible sources
FSC
www.fsc.org FSC® C018179

Penguin Books is committed to a sustainable
future for our business, our readers and our planet.
This book is made from Forest Stewardship
Council™ certified paper.

To Tom, for being my best friend,
for believing in me and encouraging me to write,
and for making me laugh until I snort.

Me

When I was four years old, all I ever wanted was to have a weeing Tiny Tears doll. I'd never been into dolls really, but when my best friend was given one for her birthday I decided that a doll that cries actual tears and wets itself was exactly what my life lacked. After hassling my parents for a few weeks they eventually caved in – although, if I'm honest, it captured my attention for about a week and then the poor thing was left in a puddle of her own mess (oops!). I have no idea what became of her, but I'm guessing my mum sold her at a car boot sale or something similar.

When I was eight years old all I ever wanted was to appear on Live and Kicking *and dance with Mr Blobby. There was something about that big dopey pink and yellow spotted blob that had me entranced for hours. Sadly, my desire never came true – but I still hold my Mr Blobby cuddly toy as one of my most treasured possessions and he happily accompanies me to bed every night (despite his missing eye).*

When I was ten years old all I ever wanted was to be a Spice Girl. I used to drive my mum and dad crazy, running around the house, shouting out the lyrics to Wannabe *whilst performing a little dance routine I'd made up. I was constantly putting my hand on my hip and swinging it out to the side, making a peace sign with my other hand and shouting 'Girl power!' as loud as I could. I loved them so much that I even named my goldfish Ginger after*

Geri – my favourite Spice. I was devastated when she decided to leave. The Spice Girls with no Ginger just wasn't the same, and so my passion to become one of them simply ended (after crying my eyes out for hours, of course).

At some point that extrovert little girl who used to sing to anyone who would listen and dance without a care in the world, became painfully shy and bashful. I suddenly became less confident at school and around other people – preferring the company of a good book to an actual human. It's bizarre how everything changed; at primary school I was the girl everyone wanted to befriend, but by secondary school I had become awkward and tried my best to avoid everyone. I hated attention, people asking me questions or putting me in the spotlight; I preferred to blend into the background unnoticed. I felt safer that way. On the odd occasion that anyone would attempt to hold eye contact with me I'd usually end up shaking like a leaf or turning bright red, causing me to stare at the floor for the rest of the day. Actually, I did have one friend, Mary Lance, who was equally as socially inept as I was. I say we were friends – but in reality we hardly ever talked to each other, so I guess she was more like a silent partner. It was just nice to have someone by my side at lunchtimes or in class, someone who wouldn't pry into my life. I think we took comfort in the fact that we weren't alone.

At the end of my A levels, when the rest of my year had either secured a place at university (Mary went off to study dentistry at Sheffield) or planned to take a gap year so that they could travel the world, I was still unsure of what I wanted from life. I decided to join those taking a gap year, although not to travel. Wandering aimlessly around the globe and experiencing what the world had to offer did have its appeal, but I just wasn't quite ready to leave my home or my mum at that point. I was simply going to stay in my home village of Rosefont Hill, deep in the Kent countryside, and get a little job to tide me over until I decided what I wanted to do with my days.

I started my job hunt by dropping off my CV in the village shops – there weren't and aren't that many to target. We have a bank, a library, a post office, Budgens, a florist, a few clothes shops, a hardware store, a café and a teashop . . . hardly the most riveting high street ever! The last place I entered was Tea-on-the-Hill, perched on the hill's peak, with great views over the rest of the village.

As I entered the teashop, my eyes wandered over the seven tables covered in mismatched floral print tablecloths, each surrounded by two or three chairs – all different shapes and designs. The cups, saucers and teapots being used by the customers were also contrasting in their patterns. Absolutely nothing matched, but bizarrely it all fitted together perfectly. The smell of freshly baked scones filled my nostrils and 1950s jazz played softly in the background. I was staring at a secret little den for women – why had I never been in here before?

Flying around the room was a woman who I guessed was in her sixties. Her grey hair was set in a big rollered quiff at the front, with the rest of her curls held in underneath a net. I watched her dart between customers – taking orders, bringing out food and stopping briefly for a little natter here and there. She continued to keep a calm smile on her face, even though it was clear that she was running the shop alone.

I stood at the counter and waited for her to come over, which she eventually did whilst wiping her hands dry on her pink floral apron, which covered a glamorous light blue dress underneath.

'Hello there, dearie. Sorry about the wait. What can I get you?' she asked, with a broad smile and kind blue eyes.

In the previous shops I'd walked into I had just wanted to throw my CV into the manager's hands and then bolt for the door, instantly feeling uncomfortable as panic started to consume me, but there was something about this woman that had me rooted to the spot. I even held her eye contact for a few brief moments and almost felt comfortable doing so.

'Actually, I came to drop off my CV,' I said, as I fumbled through my bag and pulled out a freshly printed one. The lady took it from my hands and casually glanced over it.

'Have you ever worked in a shop before?' she asked, squinting at the paper.

'Yes, a florist's,' I said quietly.

'So you already know how to greet customers with a friendly smile?'

I nodded politely as I felt her scrutinize me from head to toe, the smile still plastered on her heavily wrinkled face.

Perhaps I should have told her at this point that I'd spent most of my time there washing dirty buckets in the back room out of sight and not with the customers at all; but before I could speak up she'd moved on.

'How many hours are you looking for?' she asked.

I hadn't thought this far ahead, but one glimpse around the room told me that I'd gladly spend a lot of time here. 'As many as you can give me.'

'And – one last thing – do you like cake?'

'I love it,' I said, giving her a nervous smile.

'Good to hear! You're hired. You've come in at a very good

time actually, my last waitress unexpectedly quit yesterday – with no explanation!'

'Really?'

'Sadly, yes . . . although she was a grumpy chops so I'm not too bothered. I'm Molly, by the way.'

'I'm Sophie.' I offered my hand for her to shake but she looked at the hand, grabbed it and pulled me in for a warm hug instead. I can remember actually gasping at the intimacy, as it wasn't something I was used to. At first I felt rigid and stiff but once the shock had subsided it became strangely calming and pleasant.

'Now, do you have any plans for the rest of the day?' she asked softly, releasing me from her embrace.

I shook my head and shrugged my shoulders.

'Great, let's class this as your first day, then.' She slid a tray with a pot of tea and a cup and saucer in my direction. 'Go take that to Mrs Williams, the lady in the cream blouse with the purple rinse to the left – the one with her nose buried in Bella. I'll go dig you out an apron.'

Picking up the tray I made my way over to Mrs Williams and carefully placed the pot of boiling tea in front of her. She lowered her magazine and peered up at me over the top of her glasses; I instantly recognized her from out and about in the village.

'You're new here,' she stated.

'Yes, I've just started. Literally.'

'You live in Willows Mews, don't you? Your mum's that lovely lady at the library.'

'That's right,' I nodded, shyly.

'Aw, she's ever so kind – always helps me take my books

home. I've got greedy eyes when it comes to books, you see!' She let out a childlike chuckle and screwed her eyes shut. 'Send her my love then, won't you, darling,' she said, whilst pouring out a cup of tea and stirring in two sugars.

'Will do, Mrs Williams,' I said, as I walked back to Molly at the counter.

'You're Jane May's daughter?' Molly asked.

'That's right,' I said, with a slight nod.

'I thought so. Well if you're anything like her then I'm lucky to have you on board,' she said with a kind smile as she held out her hand and gave me an apron.

My first day working in the teashop whizzed by in a blur — there was one hairy moment when a plate managed to slip out of my hand, fly through the air and smash rather loudly into a billion pieces, causing me to blub dramatically — but other than that it went quite smoothly.

My gap year flew by before I'd even had a chance to think about what I wanted to do next, and so I extended it to two years . . . then three years . . . then four, until I suddenly realized that I had no desire to go to university at all; I was happy where I was, and am still just as happy eight years later.

Although I'd started as a waitress, Molly put a lot of faith in me and taught me all she knew about baking cakes and service with a smile. Every day we bake fresh scones, muffins and cakes, and experiment with new recipes, whilst putting the world to rights. At sixty-six years old Molly is continually being told by her doctor that she should be slowing down and starting to take things easy — but she's not one to listen.

I didn't just find a passion and career path when I stumbled *upon Tea-on-the-Hill that day; I also found a best friend. Look-ing back now, I know Molly had an inkling of who I was as soon as I walked into the shop. I also believe that, knowing who I was, there was no way she would turn me away without helping me, because it's in her nature to help those in need of healing; and I certainly needed some of that.*

PART ONE

I

It's now the beginning of April and after a dreary winter the village has started to come back to life with wild daffodils, tulips and other bright flowers coming into bloom. Different colours burst from the ground, bringing with them a sense of hope and optimism. Rabbits gaily hop across the path in the distance, happy to have the sun shining on their backs once again, and the birds in the trees seem to be chirping louder than usual.

I pull my red woollen coat in around me to keep out the crisp spring air that threatens to chill my bones. My cold button nose is buried deep inside a battered copy of *Wuthering Heights* as I make my way down the tree-lined alleyway that leads to the quiet High Street. Yes, I admit – I'm one of those annoying people who walk through life oblivious to my surroundings, while spying any impending dangers in my peripheral vision, thanks to my literary obsession! I still manage to keep up the obligatory nod of the head or polite 'Good morning' to the people I pass, whilst continuing to stay in the world of Cathy and Heathcliff. Having said that, at this time of the morning on a Wednesday, there are only a few other people milling around, mostly preoccupied shop owners, so I can allow myself to sink deeper into their tragic love story.

Taking strong strides as I make my way up the hill, I spot Molly in the shop, on the phone with her nose pressed up against the window. She gives me a slight wink and a wave, and then continues with whatever she's up to.

'Are you sure she's heading this way?' she quizzes the person on the phone as I come in the front door, putting my book in my bag. 'I can't see her yet . . .' Molly squints her eyes to the point where they're almost shut and then widens them in surprise. 'Oooh, June,' she coos, excitement making her voice go squeaky. 'There she is now! Gosh, what on earth is she wearing that for? She looks like she's in a banana suit!'

I follow Molly's gaze and find that she's looking at Mrs Taylor, who has decided to venture outside today wearing a tight, bright yellow two-piece. Oh, the scandal! I roll my eyes and walk over to the oven to start baking. I can still hear Molly wittering away on the phone while I tie on my red-and-pink spotted apron.

'You know what it is, don't you? It's her birthday next week – her son phoned up and ordered a cake. I suspect she's having a meltdown over that . . . Sixty-five! Hmmmm . . . Yes . . . Well yes, June – she never got over Robert leaving her like that. What an awful thing to happen to her . . . Ooh, June, I'd better go – she's heading this way . . . Yes, yes! Call you later.'

Molly hops away from the window, pops the phone back on the counter top and manages to look preoccupied with rearranging the counter display before Mrs Taylor enters the shop. I find myself rolling my eyes once again as Molly turns to welcome her with a beaming smile.

'Hello, Mrs Taylor! Ooh, I must say, you're looking rather colourful today . . . yellow really suits you!' Ahh, the friendly two-facedness of village life, I think to myself. I block out the conversation and concentrate on the Victoria sponge I'm whisking up.

A short while later, once Mrs Taylor leaves, Molly joins me by the oven.

'Come on,' she quips.

'What?'

'Out with it!'

'Huh?'

'You've been banging around for the last fifteen minutes. Why?'

This is news to me as I thought I was hiding my frustration quite well, so I can't help but look a tad sheepish (old habits and all that).

'I'm sorry, it's just . . .' I'm at a loss for words.

I've been 'that talked-about someone', and there's nothing worse than seeing those curtains twitch as you walk past someone's house or hearing conversations stop as you walk into a room. I could tell her that it annoys me the way everyone in this village thinks they have a right to gossip about everyone else's business. I could tell her I dislike it when she's mean about others. And I could tell her that there's got to be more to life than her constant gassing over the downfall of the locals. But I don't. Because I know that in truth Molly doesn't have a bad bone in her body. Surely she's allowed to vent every now and then? Especially if it's only over something as insignificant as the colour of someone's outfit?

'I'm sorry,' I say, letting out a sigh as I rub my head. 'I didn't sleep a wink last night. I've got a bit of a headache.'

'Oh, deary,' she coos, feeling my forehead to check my temperature. 'Do you want to go home? Try and catch up on that sleep? I'll be fine here on my own.'

See? She might have a loose tongue occasionally, but that will never overshadow her kind heart.

'No, don't be silly. I'm probably just dehydrated,' I say, as I pour a glass of water and down the lot in front of her. 'I'll be feeling better in no time.'

She looks at me like I've lost my marbles, but eventually my beaming smile wins her over and we both start icing the cupcakes she baked earlier, which have been left to cool.

At the end of my shift I drop in on Mum at the village library, which is several doors down from the shop, towards the bottom of the hill. Being council-funded, and only small, it's not the most luxurious library you've ever seen. It has ten rows of battered books, two old computers (which both take about five minutes to get online), a working area with wooden tables and chairs and a chill-out area with multicoloured beanbags scattered around. It could be a little on the depressing side, but Mum takes great pride in the place and makes sure the rows of books gleam to perfection, that her wall displays are always fun and inviting, and that she is quick to order in anything requested that they don't have in stock.

I find her on her knees restacking magazines, which I've never seen in here before.

'Hello, you!' Mum says as she gives me a tired smile and lets the magazine she's holding rest on her lap. It's clearly been a long day. Her hazel eyes have dark circles beneath them and they look as though they're struggling to stay open. Her hands go up to her chestnut-coloured hair, which is pulled back into a tight, high bun. She slides her palms along it to check that it's still neat – she hates it when wispy bits fly into her face or get into her eyes.

'Hello, Mum,' I say, bending down and giving her a kiss on the cheek. 'What's this?' I say, gesturing at the magazines in front of her.

'Oh, we thought it might encourage more young-sters to come in here.'

'By providing them with gossip about their favourite celebs?'

'Why not?' she asks, frowning at me. 'I've already spotted some very interesting articles while I've been unpacking them.'

I pick up one of the glossy titles from the shelf and flick through it, scanning the images of flawless men and women on red carpets being compared to their more natural-looking bodies while semi-naked on holi-day. 'Do you really think you're going to encourage people to read books by showing them pictures of celebrities looking fat or thin on beaches?'

'Keep your voice down,' she whispers, glancing over her shoulder. 'Reading is reading – no matter what the material. It's all about getting them in here – they might pick up a book or two while they're at it.'

I can't help but think she's being too optimistic as I put the magazine back on the shelf but, looking at Mum's hopeful face, I instantly feel guilty for slamming her idea.

'We've also had some new books delivered,' she continues, as she picks herself up from the floor, brushes dust off her knee-length black skirt and removes bits of fluff from her black shirt. 'Including a brand new copy of *Jane Eyre*,' she continues. 'So you no longer have to battle with those loose or missing pages!'

'Brilliant! Although to be honest it's probably my fault they've fallen out – I must've read that book about a hundred times.'

'Well, yes. That and the schoolgirls who leave it in their bags to be bashed around . . .'

'True.'

'I also heard a little bit of news today.'

'Mum, I don't want to hear any gossip!'

'Oh, Soph, it's not gossip! Anyway, you'll like this. Mrs Woodman from Cavalier Hall came in this afternoon. She's been visited by a location scout or something from a film company. They want to use the hall as the setting for one of their films.' She grins at me, knowing that I'll want to hear more despite my protesting.

'What film?' I quiz.

'This is the bit I think you'll like . . .' She pushes her glasses up her nose with one finger and pauses for dramatic effect. '*Pride and Prejudice!*'

'No!'

'Yep!'

'Another one?' I cry in disgust. Mum looks at me bewildered.

'I thought you'd be pleased. You love that book.'

'Yeah, I love the book – it doesn't mean I enjoy it when film companies come along and butcher it.'

'Oh, I'm sure they won't do that,' she says dismissively. 'According to Mrs Woodman the film's got a huge budget and cast. They wouldn't tell her who was involved, but – '

I interrupt her with a huge gasp. 'I wonder who'll be playing Darcy!' My mind ponders all sorts of possibilities, but only one man stands out to me as the one I'd love to have here in Rosefont Hill – Jude Law.

Unsurprisingly, Mum isn't the only person Mrs Woodman has decided to share her exciting news with. The next day when I get to work Molly is again on the phone to June, this time speculating about how much Mr and Mrs Woodman would've been paid for the use of their home. The news doesn't stop spreading there. In fact, it seems to be the hot topic with everybody in the village as I overhear snippets of different conversations throughout the day.

The shop has slowly become the 'cool' place to hang

out, attracting grannies and mums in the daytime and then schoolgirls from four o'clock onwards. There are a few different groups of girls that come in on a regular basis, but this afternoon we are joined by Janet, Ella and Charlotte – three fifteen-year-olds who simply love talking boys, make-up and gossip whilst sipping their pot of peppermint tea and picking at their skinny blueberry muffins.

As I sort through the cake orders for the next day, I can't help but listen in on their chatter as they mull over the rumours of who might be attached to the film.

Janet, a feisty brunette who's clearly the leader of the group with her bossy ways, is the first to divulge.

'I saw on *getcluedup.com* that Bobby Green is going to be playing that Mr Darcy guy.'

'Who's that?' asks Ella with a confused expression on her pretty face, her wild curly blonde hair sticking out all over the place uncontrollably.

'You know,' sighs Janet. 'That dude from this year's *Big Brother.*'

'The one who peed in the pool?' Ella squeals. 'And had a threesome in the garden?'

I chuckle quietly to myself at hearing the young girls talk so candidly about sex – a topic I'd never have been able to talk so openly about at their age.

'That's the one!' nods Janet.

Ella lets out a huge groan at the confirmation.

'But he's not even an actor! That would be crap!'

I vaguely remember hearing the girls talk of this Bobby Green character over the summer. To say I'd be disappointed if this 'lad' were to turn up instead of a serious actor would be an understatement. In fact, it would turn something that could be incredibly exciting into something decidedly naff!

'That's what I read, though,' sulks Janet, looking deflated that her findings hadn't impressed her friends more.

'Yeah well you can't believe anything you read . . .'

Charlotte, the quiet redhead who seems to quiver in the very existence of these two girls she calls her BFFs, pauses for a moment before deciding to speak. 'Actually, I heard that Billy Buskin might be doing it.'

I watch as Janet and Ella whip their heads around in disbelief and just stare at their friend.

'OMG!' squeals Janet. 'I would, like, love that! Where did you read that?'

Charlotte instantly becomes introverted, the attention of her friends making her look uncomfortable, a feeling I can easily relate to. She slowly continues to share her knowledge in a quiet voice that I struggle to hear.

'I didn't read it. I was told it,' she mutters.

'By who?' says Ella, who already seems sceptical.

'Lauren Davenport.' Before the other two can query the source she continues swiftly. 'Her mum is going to be giving horse-riding lessons to the cast, you know – the ones who have to ride. She said his name was on a list she was given. Although Lauren told me not to tell anyone –'

'You're so gullible, Char! I can't believe you fell for that,' says Ella interrupting her in a belittling tone, chilling my insides. 'As if Billy Buskin would bother doing a film about some old book. He has just done a load of blockbusters. Why would he bother?'

'But he has just done that war film,' argues Charlotte.

I've no idea who they're talking about and so zone out and think about Jude. Imagine walking through the village and bumping into him every day! That would be absolute heaven! Of course, he'd obviously bring lots to the role too . . . charm and charisma. I don't just want him here to ogle at – honest!

I'm not entirely sure where my Jude obsession has come from, but I think it started when Mum brought home a copy of *The Holiday* for us to watch one night a couple of years ago. One look at his playful smile, smouldering eyes and dashing good looks and I'd fallen under his spell. Embarrassingly, I actually feel myself smile back at him onscreen sometimes, as though his romantic words are meant for my ears only. Yes, sad I know, but he just sucks me in. I'm not a big film buff, not by any means, but quiz me on a film that Jude's been in and I'll be able to give you the right answer!

2

Rosefont Hill is a tiny little village, one where everybody knows everything there is to know about everyone who lives here. Nothing newsworthy usually happens, therefore you can imagine what an impact a film crew rolling into town has on it.

Four weeks have passed since the news of their visit broke and the village has continued to be a buzz of excitement. Each shop has had a spruce up, hoping that they'll gain some new trade. The local WI, of which Molly is the head, has examined every potted plant on the High Street and made sure they're watered, pruned and spruced to perfection. Each of the street lamps lining the main road now has a basket of colourful spring flowers dangling from its side. Even the local primary school children have been allowed to contribute by making a huge welcome banner. The large sign, made up of the children's tiny painted handprints, has been proudly strung up at the start of the High Street, ensuring it's the first thing our visitors are greeted with. It seems like every member of the community has done something to get the village prepared for its newcomers, and their hard work has paid off as it looks nothing less than idyllic!

I have to admit that despite my momentary scepticism

early on, I've joined them in their excitement and now find myself looking forward to it all – especially now that trucks full of equipment have roared their way through the village, as well as a few dozen members of the crew. Slowly, strangers have started milling around the village, although most of them seem busy setting up Cavalier Hall for the start of filming, which is apparently due to kick off any day now.

It seems like quite a lot of the village folk have been tarting themselves up somewhat for the event (with the possibility of A-listers and VIPs coming into town they want to look their best). I'm not entirely sure what they're hoping will come of their freshly dyed hair or their new cardis from Marks and Sparks, but looking good certainly seems to be important to them. For instance, I notice now, whilst looking at her from across the counter, that even Mrs Sleep from Pemberton Way has decided to apply a bit of lippy which she certainly wasn't wearing before the film crew arrived. I, however, am the same as usual – wrapped in a red apron, wearing chunky black boots, skinny jeans and a plain white vest top. My frizzy brown hair is whipped up and pinned underneath a massive red polka-dot hankie with a big roll of hair sticking out of the front (I'm still in keeping with the fifties look that Molly loves, I'm just slightly more low-key with it). The finishing touch to my look is a nice dusting of flour from the morning's baking session. Yes, forever glamorous. The white powder sticks to my clothes and my already pale skin and refuses to budge no matter how much I wipe myself down. It's a look

I've grown accustomed to over the years, even if I do appear quite ghostly. My relaxed state is not because I don't care about the starlet arrivals – it's just that looking after my appearance is a bit tricky when I'm baking and stood in front of a hot oven for most of the day. If I were to bother applying make-up in the morning before heading into work, it would simply melt away from my brown eyes within the first few minutes. It would be a waste of time!

'Oh, Sophie,' says Mrs Sleep whilst squinting her eyes and sieving through the loose change in her hand. 'How much did you say that was?'

'Three pounds fifty, please, Mrs Sleep.'

'Ahh . . . do I have that here, dear? I've forgotten my glasses.' The eighty-four-year old holds her hand out for me to look through and I can see that she doesn't have enough money to pay for the pot of tea and slice of Victoria sponge that she's already scoffed. I quickly glance around to check that Molly is occupied elsewhere, then lean across the counter and whisper to Mrs Sleep, 'You're forty pence short . . . but seeing as you're my favourite customer I'll let you off!'

Mrs Sleep chuckles like a cute little schoolgirl being told to keep a secret, with her hand over her mouth. Her eyes light up. She's still smiling to herself as she grabs her shopping trolley and wheels it out of the shop.

I pull two twenty-pence pieces out of my back pocket and toss them into the till straight away, knowing that I'd forget if I left it until later on.

'You'll end up skint if you keep giving away money like that.'

The stranger's deep voice startles me. I look up to see a man, about my age, gazing at me with a smile on his face . . . Now, we don't see many men in the teashop, we're far too floral and twee for them to cope with so they usually opt for the café down the road instead, therefore the arrival of this man (and a rather good-looking one at that), makes my heart momentarily stop and my cheeks instantly burn in surprise. He is jaw-droppingly attractive, with brown hair swooped up in a stylish quiff, a healthy tan and deep brown eyes which twinkle as he smiles.

'Sorry, I didn't see you there . . .' I somehow manage to say, softly clenching my jaw and forcing myself not to revert into the old, socially inept me. I've come a long way from that little girl who quivered at the attention of others, but I think a large part of that has been down to the safety of these four walls and Molly's time and care. Every now and then, especially when I'm caught off guard, I have to use every ounce of self-control I possess to keep calm. Of course, with this stranger there's the added element of him being drop-dead gorgeous, so I have no choice but to let my cheeks continue to blush.

'That's OK, you were busy . . . with your favourite,' he says with a slight smile. 'Don't worry, I've already checked my pockets and I definitely have enough cash on me.'

'Glad to hear it . . . I can only have one favourite a day.'

At this the stranger throws his head backwards and lets out a huge laugh. It's quite unsettling as I'm sure I didn't say anything funny enough to warrant such a grand reaction. I feel my cheeks flush further.

It's as if the sudden release of laughter has shocked even him and he quickly becomes quite uneasy as he picks up a menu from the counter and hides his face with it as he browses through it. I look away and give him a couple of moments before I ask, 'So, what can I get you?'

'I'll have a pot of coffee and a piece of lemon drizzle cake, please,' he says, with less confidence than before.

'Would you like to sit in or have it to take away?'

He looks around the room. There are only a few other customers in the shop and they're all quietly reading or nattering away.

'In, please.'

'Great, just take a seat wherever you like and I'll bring it over.'

'Thanks.'

I watch him as he turns away from the counter with one hand buried in the back pocket of his faded blue jeans. He ponders over which table to sit at before eventually choosing a table in the corner, away from the window. As I start to make up his pot of coffee, Molly appears at my side.

'Tell me everything!'

'What do you mean?' I ask, still flustered at the new arrival.

'Who is he?'

'I've got no idea!'

'Where did he come from?'

'Seriously, Mol, I've got no idea. I've never seen him before.'

'Really? He looks a little familiar to me. He's not Mr and Mrs Williams' grandson, is he?'

'Maybe, but I don't think so. Wasn't he in the Army? And ginger? I do think I've seen him somewhere before, though . . .'

'He must be something to do with the filming. Just look at him,' she says, glancing quickly over her shoulder. 'Oh, if I was ten years younger!'

'Just ten? Make that forty!' I joke.

'You cheeky little . . . I could show him a thing or –'

'Excuse me?'

We both stop talking immediately and whizz around to find the handsome stranger stood at the counter again. Unsure of what he has heard we stand in silence for a few seconds, quite startled.

'Sorry there, my love, can I help?' says Molly, jumping into action and going back to the sweet and welcoming lady that she is, dropping the comical cougar act.

'I just realized I'm hungrier than I thought,' he says while childishly rubbing his tummy. 'Any chance of getting a ham and pickle sandwich as well?'

'Of course. I'll bring it over when I'm done.'

'Thanks.'

As he walks back to his seat Molly turns to me and pretends to faint, causing me to stifle a laugh which makes me snort instead, much to my embarrassment.

A short while later, when Molly has popped out to get some shopping from Budgens, Miss Peggy Brown beckons me over to her table. I've noticed that the seventy-five-year old has been looking at the newcomer for quite some time, with a frown plastered on her worried face.

'Do you know who that is, dear?' she asks while nodding in the stranger's direction.

'Not the foggiest, I'm afraid.'

'Hmm . . . I'm not sure he's all the ticket.'

One thing I do love about the elderly ladies in the shop and around the village is their bluntness. There's no beating around the bush with them, they simply say whatever is on their minds. It's a quality I've come to admire, even if it does mean that they regularly point out that they don't like my new haircut, colour, or the jeans that I'm wearing.

'What makes you think that, Miss Brown?' I ask, suppressing a smile.

'He has been looking at that same page for the past hour and has been continuously muttering to himself.' As if to clarify the lunacy of his actions, she widens her eyes and adds, 'Talking to yourself is the first sign of madness, dear!'

I follow her gaze and watch as the man reads, then

covers his page and mutters to himself – sometimes with his eyes closed or other times staring at the ceiling. He continually taps the heel of one of his purple Converse trainers against the front leg of his chair. His face is alive and animated, as if he's in conversation, or twisted with concentration. I've never seen anything like it – no wonder Miss Brown has been frowning at him!

'It might be worth you going over and checking if he's all right!' she adds.

'Me?' I ask, with my pitch several tones higher than before.

'You wouldn't send a little old lady like me to go and talk to some lunatic would you, dear? I'll keep an eye on you from here and shout if he suddenly attacks. I'll have another tea when you're ready too, please.' she says with a nod, a wink and a firm shove in the newcomer's direction.

As I hesitantly walk towards him he has his eyes tightly screwed shut, his arms and legs crossed, and is tapping his fingers on his forehead in frustration.

'Sorry,' I start.

He stops and looks at me in a mixture of confusion at my interruption and continued frustration at whatever he was doing, the frown still buried deep in his brow. Now that I have his attention I'm overcome with nerves and am tempted to run back to my safe haven behind the counter. I look over my shoulder at Miss Brown and see her eyes widen at me, encouraging me to go on. I can feel my cheeks burning again and I have to drop my gaze to the floor so that I can continue.

'I'm so sorry to interrupt – it's just that Miss Brown, the elderly woman who is sat behind me and glaring at you, is a tad worried about your mental health,' I say, in what I hope is a light and jokey manner. Although, is there ever a jokey way to bring into question someone's mental health?

I briefly look up to see the frustration leave his face and watch as it's replaced with a look of intrigue as he sneaks a peek behind me in Miss Brown's direction.

'Really? Why? Have I done something to offend her? Did I eat with my mouth open? Slurp noisily on my coffee?' he asks, clearly amused.

I hear the elderly lady loudly tutting behind me.

'Actually she's worried about the fact that you've been talking to yourself for the past hour,' I force myself to continue. 'According to her it's the first sign of madness . . .'

Suddenly he breaks out into another huge laugh, making me look up from the floor and take in his joyful face – causing a smile to spread across mine uncontrollably. Once he has composed himself, he leans forward, lightly holds my forearms, pulls me towards him slightly and looks into my eyes as he continues in a calm and quiet voice.

'Please tell dear Miss Brown that I'm sorry for upsetting her. There's no need to call the men in white coats yet. I'm just lear—'

I stop listening.

Something jolts within me and I'm suddenly light-headed and shaky. I can't stop the fear mounting. I can't tell my brain that it's ok. I can feel the panic rising through me, causing my mouth to go dry, my breathing to shallow and my mind to get momentarily lost. I'm rooted to the spot.

'Are you OK?' he asks, concern breaking out over his face.

'I'm sorry . . .' I try and say, but no sound is coming from my mouth.

'Hey, you're shaking. Here, sit down!'

Before I can try to protest he leaps from his chair, pulls out the one next to him, gently takes me by the shoulders and lowers me into it.

'Can I get you something? A camomile tea?' he asks calmly before running behind the counter and rummaging around.

The noises he makes pouring and stirring are intensified in my head. SWOOOOOOOOOOSH. CLANG. CLANG. CLANG. PLOP. TING. TING. TING.

'Here, drink this,' he says coming towards me.

I take the tea and slowly sip at it, attempting to concentrate on the hot liquid as it works its way down through my body, trying to ignore the irrational terror that bubbles away inside me.

I'm aware of the stranger as he pulls his chair next to mine and reaches out, taking one of my hands in his, gently rubbing the inside of my palm with his thumb. Instead of freaking me out further, it has the opposite affect; it feels soothing and calming, reminding me I'm safe.

I'm grateful that he isn't staring at me. Instead both of us sit and look at our hands. Mine in his.

We sit in silence like this for a few minutes.

Slowly the fear leaves me and the nice feeling of calmness rises within me, causing me to sigh heavily in relief.

'Better?' he asks, his hand stopping the rubbing motion but continuing to clasp mine.

I nod slowly. Instantly feeling stupid, I keep my eyes on the cup I'm holding, too humiliated to look elsewhere.

'How embarrassing!' I say, closing my eyes.

'No it's not. Don't be daft.'

I look up at him with another sigh. For the last five minutes or so I'd turned into a trembling idiot. It's more than embarrassing. It's humiliating.

'Hey . . . it's OK,' he says, giving my hand a squeeze along with a sympathetic smile.

I glance over at Miss Brown and find that, thankfully, she seems to be preoccupied with a crossword puzzle. She's probably even forgotten sending me over in the first place – little does she know the drama she's sparked.

'At a guess, I'd say you were having a panic attack,' he continues cautiously.

I close my eyes and let out a groan.

'Oi! I said don't be daft,' he says, squeezing my hand again. 'Does that happen a lot?'

'They used to. They've not happened for a long time, though . . . and never in front of anyone before. I'm so sorry.'

'Don't be. I know what it's like.'

'You do?'

'Yeah,' he says, glancing around the shop.

He doesn't add any more so I don't question him further. It's enough to know that he understands in some way and that he doesn't just think I'm a nutter or some freak.

Closing my eyes, I try to focus on the calmness. Enjoying the steadiness that comes with each breath.

I can still remember my first panic attack. I was eleven years old.

I guess you could say I was in a fragile state — my world had fallen apart overnight, huge changes were happening at home and I was experiencing feelings I'd never felt before. Despite this, I was made to go back to school straight away. I think my mum thought it would help, perhaps make me forget the troubles at home. Or maybe she wanted me out of the way so that she could deal with her own thoughts. Her own heartache. Whatever her reasons for making me go back, I couldn't help but feel sent away. Banished because she couldn't bear to look at me.

Waking up that day I managed to take comfort in the normality of putting on my school uniform: a pleated grey skirt, white t-shirt and green jumper, white socks to my knees and black buckled shoes, the same as it had always been since my first day at Rosefont Hill C of E Primary School. It was familiar. However, walking into the school gates, through the main door, down the corridor and into my classroom made me more than aware that things had changed. I felt like an alien, different to everyone else in the room. I could feel everyone's eyes on me as though they were surprised to see me, their looks scrutinizing my face. Judging me. Looking for clues of my torment or guilt.

Unable to cope with the unwanted attention I kept my eyes on the ground as my feet shuffled along to my desk. I sat down and stared at my pencil case, trying to ignore the fact that I could hear them all whispering and feel them all continuing to watch me.

My skin started to itch, I felt uncomfortable in my own body – I wanted to get out, away from their goggling eyes.

I sat still and silent, wanting to disappear.

My teacher, Mrs Yates, a tubby woman with rosy cheeks and a love of pastel-coloured clothing, entered the room with authority, causing the majority of the class to go to their tables straight away.

'Morning, everyone. Can get you get into your seats quickly, please. Hush, hush,' she chimed, sweeping her long blonde hair from her face. 'Now, later on we're going to be starting a new painting project, but, before we do that I'd like to us to continue with the Tudor work we were doing last week. Jamie, this is a warning – stop faffing with Luke's hair and sit down,' she barked, causing the classroom to fall silent as the work commenced.

I was pleased. I liked the Tudors – all the anger, tragedy and passion that surrounded them. I managed to pull out my text-book and continue with my summary of the Tudor period that I was working on – I'd just got to the interesting bit about Henry VIII making up a religion just so he could get a divorce. I worked away, immersed in their world, blocking out the hub-bub of the rest of the class.

It didn't take long for Mrs Yates to make her way over and kneel beside me, placing one hand on my back and the other on my writing hand, stopping it from moving along the page, pulling me away from my solitude.

'Sophie, look at you working away. You're such a good girl,' she said softly.

I glanced up to see her looking at me with such big sad eyes and had to look away, unable to cope with her pitiful expression.

'I just want you to know that if at any point you want to talk about what's happened, then I'm here for you. To help in any way I can.'

To help in any way she could . . . it was sweet, but she couldn't give me what I wanted. She couldn't change what had happened, so why would I want to talk to her?

I didn't speak. I just nodded my head slowly and turned my attention back to my work.

She lingered for a little while, probably unsure whether or not to push the matter further, before standing up and walking off with a sigh.

It wasn't long before I had another visitor at my desk; this time it was Laura Barber, my bestest friend.

'Is it true?' she asked bluntly, terror stamped across her face. 'About what happened with your dad?'

I didn't know how to answer. I opened my mouth but no words came out.

Luckily Mrs Yates saved me from the conversation. 'Laura, back to your seat, please. Unless you want to continue your work in your break time instead?' she asked.

Laura gave my arm a tight squeeze and ran back to her desk.

I felt relieved.

At lunchtime I didn't want to join the other kids in the playground. I didn't want to run and prance around joyously and I

34

didn't want to have to answer anyone's questions. I didn't want to talk to them. So when everyone else had left the class to go play I lingered behind, deciding to do a bit more work on my Tudor project.

They'd all been collected and stored in the class walk-in cupboard earlier in the day so that we didn't carelessly spoil them when we were painting.

I was in the cupboard, reaching up for my book, when my whole body tensed up and an overbearing feeling of devastation took hold of me. I gripped hold of a shelf in front of me for support, sure that the whole lot would engulf me and swallow me up.

I was going to die. I was sure of it.

Slowly I crouched to the floor, squeezing myself into a ball as my head started to feel woozy, spinning uncontrollably.

The silence around me appeared deafening.

The small space seemed to slip away from me, growing in size. Giant books and folders loomed over me, threatening to tumble and squash me.

White light flooded in, causing me to squint my eyes in agony at its brightness.

The end was coming. I knew it was.

Death was coming for me.

Yet, just as instantly as the feeling had started, it left. Replaced by a feeling of warmth and peace.

I remained scrunched in a ball with my knees up to my chest, trying to make sense of what had just happened.

I was unaware of how much time had passed, but the sound of people entering the room and chairs being dragged around the floor told me that lunch was over.

'Are you OK, Sophie? You look a little pale,' Mrs Yates *observed as I stumbled out of the cupboard.*

'I want to go home,' I pleaded.

Given the circumstances they could hardly protest.

I didn't want Mum to have to come and collect me, I was perfectly able to make my own way home, especially as I came in on my own every day, but they wouldn't let me. So I sat in that hallway, my eyes skimming over the various displays of children's work, and waited.

Mum took a long time to come. When she finally arrived she didn't look at me. Her blotchy and puffy red eyes, no doubt caused by fresh tears, darted around the room in a troublesome manner. She mumbled something to the receptionist, signed me out and then walked out of the door. I followed silently behind, in the shadow of the broken woman in front of me.

I vowed never to make her collect me again. It would do no good to add to her worries.

In hindsight, it's clear that the episode in the cupboard was my first experience of a panic attack, but I didn't know that at the time. All I knew then was that I wanted to be as far away from other people as possible. The only person I cared about was Mum . . . but she was the only person, it seemed, who didn't want to talk to me.

A loud bang at the door and the commotion of Molly walking in with her hands filled with carrier bags brings my attention back into the room and to the fact that I'm meant to be working. Flustered from my thoughts, I begin getting up to go over to her when the stranger nudges me back into my seat.

'You stay there. I'll help her,' he insists, as he strides over to Molly.

Her eyes widen as he approaches her and takes the bags from her hands; she's clearly happy of the help. However, then I spot the worry start to cross her face as he starts talking to her. He's speaking too quietly for me to make out his words, but one look in my direction from Molly tells me all I need to know. He's grassing me up.

Surprisingly, Molly doesn't come over and fuss over me, instead she ushers the stranger behind the counter and gets him to help her unpack the shopping where they continue to whisper.

I'm not permitted to do anything for the rest of the afternoon. Molly would love me to go home and pop my feet up but, for once, I don't want to be home alone. I want to stay here. I spend the rest of the afternoon (once the handsome stranger has said his farewells), perched at a table with an endless pot of camomile tea, while Molly sends over a steady stream of cakes and naughty treats – which I happily pick away at.

3

Lying on my bed that night, my mind wanders off as I look around my bedroom at the pale pink walls with photo frames hung on them. Full of photos taken years ago, when we were a happy family unit. I've never redecorated – I've not even changed a photo in a frame. Occasionally, I might Blu-Tack a poster or something on the back of my bedroom door, but nothing more than that. Nothing that can't quickly be removed; letting me know that what once was is never too far away.

I can still vividly remember the three of us in B&Q and me being given the choice of what colour I wanted my room to be. As soon as I said pink my Dad grunted and moaned that I'd be sick of it in a few months and that he'd have to repaint it, but he let me have it anyway. As always. Being an only child I generally never heard the word 'no' when asking for something. In hindsight he was right of course; pink might have seemed like a fun idea at the time but as I got older it seemed too girlie and childish. Still, I would never change it. Not after the fun I recall us having as we turned it into my little den.

I can remember the excitement as we bought throwaway overalls and dustsheets then went home to decorate the very same day. Opening the tin of paint, mine and Dad's jaws dropped as we gasped at the brightness of the colour, although Mum reassured

38

us it would be less garish once it was up on the walls. Plus, she said, it would fade over time. We all giggled to each other as we dipped our brushes into the bright paint and started applying it to the walls, carefully lining all the edges before joyously using rollers everywhere else. Pink paint flew everywhere as we laughed our way through the task; I can remember purposely getting a blob of pink on Dad's nose (with Mum's encouragement) and then having him run around the room trying to get me back, which he obviously managed, prompting me to chase him again. It turned into a very messy game of tag, so by the time we'd finished painting we were as pink as the walls. I was ordered to have a bath to wash away the paint that had made its way into my ears, up my nose and into my hair, while Dad went out and bought us a family bucket from KFC – fast food was a rarity in our household and only eaten on special occasions. We ate the treat whilst sitting in the middle of the floor in my freshly painted room, looking around at our handiwork. It was such a great day.

When I came home from school the following afternoon I walked into my room to find Dad banging nails into one of the walls and hanging up thick wooden photo frames, all in various sizes. He'd carefully worked his way through the photo albums to select special pictures of us on days out in parks feeding ducks, on holiday or simply snuggled up at home. The three of us. Before it all disappeared. How I have wished over the years that I could jump into those frames and relive those little moments. Moments that I didn't realize were so special until they were no longer attainable.

*

I've hated change. Hated moving further away from something that I treasure so much. Something that seemed so perfect. However, lying in my room now, for the first time in years, I feel excited by the possibility of something new. Thrilling thoughts whirl around my head of the handsome man who walked into the shop today.

Once I stop cringing at the fact that I had a near panic attack in front of a complete stranger, I can't help but grin to myself at the thought of his smile, his touch, even his smell. Just thinking about him is enough to make my insides flutter. I've never experienced a feeling like this – I'm giddy and full of what I think is hope.

I managed to avoid company for the latter part of my childhood and have since been surrounded by women every day, so it's fair to say I don't have much experience when it comes to male interaction, other than saying hello to the local men I pass in the street. There's been the odd fleeting relationship or blind date set up by a few of the elderly women customers at the shop, who on occasion try to pair me off with their grandsons, but none of them have been that successful. So I'm baffled by the feelings stirring inside me.

I find myself replaying tiny bits of the day in my head – his hand smoothing out his hair, my hands in his as he rubbed them with his thumbs to calm me down, his concerned smile as he said goodbye . . . I'm a complete loser. What makes it worse is that I know nothing about this handsome stranger. I have no idea what has brought him to Rosefont Hill, although I'm guessing

Molly's right and that he has something to do with the filming. The thing I find most irritating is that I don't even know his name.

Will he be back in the shop soon, or is that it? Has he disappeared to wherever he came from, never to return? I spend the night rolling around my bed unable to sleep as questions about the newbie fill my brain.

After lunchtime the following day, just as I start to lose hope of the stranger ever coming back, in he walks. I can't help but smile at him.

'Hello, you. Feeling better?' he asks.

'Yes . . . although I still feel like the world's biggest plonker,' I admit.

'Really? Hopefully these will cheer you up a little bit, then,' he says, holding out a bunch of multicoloured tulips.

I'm shocked. No one has ever bought me flowers before.

'You didn't need to do that,' I say, as I reach out and take them from him, gazing at their beauty.

'Oh it's nothing. I was walking past the florist and saw them sitting there,' he says with a shrug and a smile. Batting away the idea that it could possibly mean anything more.

'Well, thank you,' I say. Unsure what to do next, we stand in silence for a few seconds. 'Are you staying for some coffee or having something to eat?' I eventually ask.

'Ah yes, please. A coffee would be great.'

'Lovely. I'll bring it over.'

'Thanks,' he says as he turns and heads straight to the same table he sat at yesterday.

While his back is to me I let the excitement over his reappearance cause a massive grin to spread across my face; it takes a ridiculous amount of effort to stop myself from jumping up and down and cheering with joy.

The stranger has his head buried in some papers again when I head over to him with his coffee, and on seeing me he closes the pile of papers and pops it down onto the table. I can't help but read the writing on the front as I lower the coffee in front of him.

'Ah, so you are working on *Pride and Prejudice!*' I exclaim.

'I sure am. Hence all the talking to myself,' he says as he raises his eyebrows. 'I've been learning lines. Well, trying to.'

'So your odd behaviour makes sense, then! Miss Brown will be thrilled to hear that.'

'Good,' he smiles.

My eyes widen and almost bulge out of my head as a thought dawns on me that he must have some insider's knowledge.

'You'll finally be able to end all the rumours then – on who's playing Mr Darcy?'

'Well –'

'All the schoolgirls that come in here have been harping on about this teen hot-shot bagging the role, apparently he did some big trilogy thingamabob –

not my cup of tea really, never seen it. Erm, Billy something . . .?'

'Oh?'

'Mmm . . . but me, I'm hoping for Jude Law,' I declare.

'Really?'

'Yep . . . I know it's a long shot but he'd be much better at it than some newbie heart-throb who probably doesn't know the first thing about romance or desire. So, do you have any idea if you'll be joined by the one and only Mr Law?'

He stares at me for a few seconds before saying, 'Actually I'm not on set until tomorrow, so hopefully I'll find out then.'

'In that case you'd better come back and tell me everything!'

'I'll be sure to,' he smiles. I can't help but smile back.

'Right, I'd better get back to work.'

He says nothing, just simply continues to smile back at me.

As I get up and walk away I'm in shock that I managed to stop being such a nervous buffoon and hold a conversation with this stranger, even if I did become a tad giddy. I have no idea what came over me. Perhaps I'm more excited about this film being made than I thought, or perhaps it was something to do with the concern on his face yesterday, and the fact that he came back. With flowers.

I can feel the stranger's eyes on me as I start baking muffins for the after-school rush. Every time I look up he is watching me intensely but looks away abruptly as soon as my eyes find his, rubbing his fingers against his forehead as if deep in thought, as though he wasn't looking at me after all. Usually attention like this is the sort of thing I try to avoid, as it tends to make me feel uneasy and want to disappear, but there's something about this guy that I find intriguing. I want to know more about him. Unfortunately those feelings still don't stop my cheeks from turning a deep shade of pink at the realization that I'm being watched!

I've only just placed the muffins on a plate when the door opens and in walk Janet, Ella and Charlotte with a few of their friends, all nattering about the latest teen drama.

'Well, I heard that Matthew only said he liked Michelle to make Sarah jealous,' declares Ella in a know-all tone.

'I wouldn't be so sure,' says one of the girls I don't recognize. 'He's taken her to the park to hang out. So he must like her.'

'We'll see . . .' says Ella with a smug smirk.

I can't help but sigh at the drama of it all.

'Hiya! Can we have a pot of peppermint tea and muffins for six, please?' asks Charlotte politely as they all gather around the counter.

'Of course,' I say. I start to make up the pot of tea while they all choose their muffins.

'They are all skinny muffins, aren't they, Sophie?' enquires Janet with a suspicious glare. A few months ago I accidentally gave them normal muffins (much to their horror), and this has led Janet to continually double-check that I'm not serving them a fat-infested treat instead.

'Yes, Janet. I made them es—'

I'm interrupted by Ella, who unleashes the loudest and shrillest shriek I've ever heard.

'AHHHH! IT'S BILLY BUSKIN!' she cries.

Luckily I've put the pot of boiling water down on the side before the rest of the girls join in with her madness. It's the handsome newcomer who is making the girls act in such a bizarre way. Janet instantly pulls out her mobile phone and starts taking pictures of him, Ella runs over and almost rugby tackles him to the ground, and one of the girls I don't know actually starts hysterically crying . . .

Oh. My. God.

I feel like shrinking behind the counter and hiding until they all leave as it suddenly dawns on me that he is the Hollywood hotshot that they've all been raving about. He is Billy Buskin – the one they've all got posters of pinned up on their walls. Why didn't that possibility even cross my mind? And why didn't he tell me? He listened to me harping on about blooming Jude Law and let me continue to talk about how I thought that this 'Billy Something' wouldn't have the first clue about passion or desire. So, basically, he was ridiculously kind to me yesterday, bought me flowers today and then I insulted him in a roundabout way by saying I thought he would be rubbish in the role. Crap! Oh what a nitwit!

I focus on finishing the girls' order as I attempt to compose myself, which isn't easy to do when I can feel my cheeks getting redder by the second and am having to fight the urge to burst out crying with embarrassment.

Billy, on the other hand, is a dream. He's more than welcoming to the school rabble as he signs their school books, has photos taken with them, and speaks to one of their absent friends on the phone. He even laughs politely at their jokes and answers all their intrusive and personal questions.

Eventually, the girls start to calm down when I take the pot of tea and muffins over to their table, although they continue to act in peculiar ways. Janet tries her best to sit in a seductive fashion (legs crossed, chest forward) whilst pouting her lips, Charlotte and Ella can't help but sit and stare in silence, and the sobbing friend continues to sniff away – they're all still in disbelief at having stumbled across their heart-throb in their local teashop.

It comes as no surprise when Billy decides to pack up and leave following all the excitement. As he comes up to the counter to pay his bill I struggle to make eye contact and am all too aware that my burning cheeks have caused me to resemble a flaming tomato. Even though I'm not looking at him I can make out the smile on his face as I hand him his bill.

Ten seconds of excruciating silence follows before he hands over some cash, leans in and quietly says, 'So, turns out I'm the newbie heart-throb you mentioned.'

'So I see . . .' I mumble.

'And I do happen to know who's playing Darcy . . . I would've said, I was going to – it's just that once it was clear you favoured Jude for the role I didn't quite know how to break the news.'

'Well, I'm very disappointed,' I say, whilst raising my eyebrows and shaking my head.

'That the teen hotshot is playing Mr Darcy?'

'No . . .' I say, finally looking him in the eye. 'That I won't get to meet Jude Law.' This causes him to rock his head backwards and let out another almighty laugh, which this time he is happy to let boom around the shop and doesn't try to cover up, even though it causes the girls to turn around and gawp some more.

'I've got to say, service in this place is a little peculiar, you're either having mini episodes and causing customers to wait on you in some twisted weird role-reversal thingy, or you're insulting them. Very strange approach to customer service, but it must be working because I can't wait to see what'll happen next time I'm in.' Then he quietly adds, 'Although it'll have to be during school hours of course.' With a quick wink and a broad smile, he turns away from the counter, shouts a quick good-bye to his star-struck admirers and walks out of the shop. Leaving me to stare after him.

As soon as he is out of sight, Molly rushes over, 'I told you I recognized him!'

'Oh, Molly . . .'

'What, pet?'

'I've just made an absolute idiot of myself!' I say, burying my face in my hands.

47

'As if!'

'No, seriously . . .' I quickly fill her in on our exchanges, all the time getting hotter with embarrassment, whilst my eyes prickle with threatening tears. Molly stops me and holds both my shoulders so that I'm looking straight at her.

'Soph, that young man came in to see if you were feeling better and bought you flowers. He hasn't been able to take his eyes off you since he came in – and I noticed that before I knew he was some blooming fancy film star! I'm telling you, he'll be back before you know it.'

'I doubt that, Molly!' I blub, as I give up and let the tears stream down my face.

'Well, I guess only time will tell!' she says, as she guides me into her arms for a warm embrace.

4

I don't read on my journey to work the following morning. I'm not in the mood. Whereas the night before I suffered from a lack of sleep due to excitement, last night I was left staring at the ceiling all night as I was burdened with the overwhelming sense of dread and humiliation. So, instead, on today's walk, I kick at little stones and fallen branches on the pathway, releasing some of the anger I feel towards myself.

As I walk out from the alleyway onto the High Street I'm surprised when I look up the hill to see a figure standing on the doorstep of the cafe, peering through the windows. It doesn't take me long to realize it's Billy. A wave of nervous excitement rushes over me as I continue to walk towards him.

'What are you doing here so early?' I ask.

'Ah, Sophie! There you are!' he says, blowing onto his fingers in an attempt to warm them in the crisp spring morning air. 'I wasn't sure when you opened.'

'Not until eight, so you've got quite a wait.'

'Really?'

'Yep.'

'Bugger.'

'I would invite you in but I can't offer you anything

49

hot until everything's heated up. So no coffee, I'm afraid.'

'I don't mind something cold until then! I couldn't just perch at a table and work on my script while you bake or whatever, could I?' he asks with pleading eyes.

I know that Molly won't mind. In fact, I know she'll be beside herself and bursting to point out that she was correct about him coming back.

'Ok, come on in, then.' I sigh, unlocking the door and letting us both in.

'Thank you. I've got to be on set at nine anyway, so I won't stay too long.'

'You're still working on your script, then?'

'Well, I guess you could say that I keep getting distracted,' he says with a glimmering smile in my direction. 'I think I'll blame Miss Brown for kicking it all off with her suspicious mind.'

And me, for a variety of things, I think. 'Well, I don't think she'll be doing that again – not now that she knows she's in the presence of greatness. In fact, I bet she's been on the phone all night to everyone she knows gushing about you. She'll have been telling anyone who'll listen that she knew there was something "special" about you from the start.'

I swear I can actually see Billy's cheeks redden as he mumbles, 'I'm sure she hasn't.'

I find myself taken back by this bashful side of him. After all, he's a Hollywood superstar; aren't actors meant to have huge egos and think incredibly highly of themselves? Surely he is used to better praise than that.

'Right,' I say, aware of the time. 'I've got to crack on with the baking.' I nod towards the oven. 'Can I get you anything?'

'No, no, no. I'm fine. Just . . . act like I'm not here.'

I give him a slight smile before heading behind the counter to the ovens where I whip up the morning batch of muffins, cupcakes, bread and a special carrot cake for Mrs Wallis who has her family over for the weekend. I'm almost finished when I hear Molly swing through the door at seven forty-five, ready to knock together her signature scones. I watch her stop in confusion when she sees Billy sat at a table, and then break out in a smile. I know instantly what she's thinking.

'Back again already, Mr Buskin? I didn't expect to see you so soon. At least not until opening hours anyway.'

'I wasn't sure what time you opened, but thankfully I was let in to get on with some work.'

'Hmm. Sophie's good like that. I'll leave you to get on with it. Let us know if you need anything.'

Molly's still smirking when she comes behind the counter and removes her coat. 'Good morning, my dear,' she says to me, before giving me a big wink and mouthing the words, 'See? What did I say?' I can't help but blush.

Having finished my contribution to the morning load I watch Billy, who is still looking increasingly wound up at the papers in front of him. In an attempt to make up for my appalling behaviour, I decide to say thank you and sorry by taking him a pot of coffee and some freshly baked breakfast muffins. He looks up in surprise when I place the loaded tray onto his table.

'What's this for?'

'It looked like you could do with it. Your frown lines have been getting increasingly worse for the last hour – not good news for someone who's face regularly gets blown up to the size of a house!' The words spurt out of my mouth before I have a chance to sensor myself. 'I mean in cinemas, because the screens are so big. I'm not saying you have a big head or anything.' I'm aware of myself rapidly turning into a bumbling buffoon, but Billy takes the comment the way I originally intended and he begins laughing out loud uncontrollably, yet again.

Once he has calmed down he looks down at the pages in his hands and whimpers, 'It's just these lines I'm trying to learn . . . Actually,' he says as his eyes twinkle with an idea, 'I don't suppose you could sit and go over them with me, could you? It's just so much easier to do if you have someone to read out loud with.'

I contemplate saying no, but somehow Billy's pleading eyes win me over.

'Hand them over,' I say, holding out my hand. 'I'm no professional but I did do my fair share of amateur dramatics when I was younger.' A slight white lie; I've only ever had one experience of acting, and that was when I played the Wicked Witch of the East in a local children's production of *The Wizard of Oz*, when I was nine. You know, the one that dies as soon as she appears? I think the part is usually just a pair of stuffed stockings, but seeing as I'd been paying two pounds a week to be part of the club they had to do something with me. Mum and Dad said they'd never seen the character played with such enthusiasm, which I took for a compliment at the time.

Billy smiles as I pull out a chair, sit down and join him. 'Thank you. Are you sure I'm not distracting you from your work?'

'Sadly not,' I smile. 'Our regulars won't start coming in for at least another half hour. Now, where should we go from?'

With a huge grin, he says, 'Let's go from the top of the page, from "Come, Darcy". Do you know the book at all?'

'Yes . . . it's one of my favourites,' I admit.

'Ahh, so you know what's happening.'

'Yep. Ok . . . here goes. "Come, Darcy,"' I put on a deep and manly Mr Bingley voice as I start, causing Billy to laugh. 'Oi, you can't laugh at me!' I say, pretending to be offended by his outburst.

'Sorry!'

I keep up with the silly voice, but with less gusto than before, as I continue, '"Come, Darcy, I must have you dance. I hate to see you standing about by yourself in this stupid manner. You had much better dance."'

'"I certainly shall not,"' starts Billy. '"You know how I detest it, unless I am particularly acquainted with my partner. At such a . . . gathering"?' His face squirms as he looks at me for confirmation or a correction.

'Assembly.'

'Right, sorry – "At such an assembly as this, it would be insupportable. Your sisters are engaged, and there is not another woman in the room whom it would not be a punishment to me to stand."'

'"Up with" . . . there's an "up with" at the end of that.'

'Ah . . . "whom it would not be a punishment to me to stand up with."'

'"I would not be so fastidious as you are for a kingdom! Upon my honour, I never met with so many pleasant girls in my life, as I have this evening; and there are several of them you see uncommonly pretty."'

'"You are dancing with the only handsome girl in the room."' Something about the way he slowly says the last part of the line, as his eyes penetrate mine with such meaning, catches me by surprise and renders me breathless, causing me to momentarily forget what I'm doing.

'Errr . . . sorry, lost where I am,' I say, flustered as my eyes search up and down the page. 'Oh yes. "Oh! She is the most beautiful creature I ever beheld! But there is one of her sisters sitting down just behind you, who is very pretty, and dare I say, very agreeable . . ."'

We work our way through the scene a few times, followed quickly by two others, before customers start coming into the shop and Molly starts to look snowed under, meaning we have to stop. To be honest, I'm glad to step away as I kept finding myself getting more and more muddled, whereas Billy seemed to be getting more confident with his lines and blowing me away – causing more awkward pauses.

As it nears nine o'clock Billy turns to me with a whimsical smile as he makes to leave.

'Thanks for that.'

'Oh, it was nothing,' I say, shrugging my shoulders.

'Seriously, you really helped.'

'No worries.'

'You might have just given yourself a little problem, though,' he says, raising his eyebrows and making his face look grim with concern.

'Really? What's that, then?' I ask, intrigued.

'Well, you've proven yourself to be very useful, so I'll have to keep coming back in now and hassling you for more! You're never going to get rid of me. Honestly, I'll be following you around everywhere trying to get you to spend every last minute with me and my script.'

'Oh . . .' I'm left speechless, unsure of how to respond.

'Bye, Sophie,' Billy chuckles, as he sweeps out of the shop, leaving me to stare after him with bright-red-blushed cheeks – yet again!

I don't see Billy again for a few days and it's torture. Although my mind is giddy over the mere recollection of his smile, I can't help the doubt that starts to seep through in his absence. Of course, if I were being rational I'd probably assume that he's just been busy on set and hasn't had time to pop by. But I'm not rational and feel increasingly anxious as more time passes. Have I somehow managed to put him off? If so, what did I do wrong?

I'm surrounded by cake mixture and dozens of tins, for a sixteenth birthday party order, when Billy finally walks back through the shop door. Instantly, the fear that has been mounting melts away. My tummy starts jumping somersaults and a huge wave of excitement causes a massive grin to appear on my face. He is here. He has come back.

I decide to say a quick hello while Molly serves him . . . I can't resist it!

'Hey! How have things been on set?' I ask, walking over with a glass bowl in my hands, mixing together some sugar, butter and eggs.

'Great! Well, actually, it's been quite full on, which is why I've not been in.'

'I see – we thought maybe you'd been replaced by Jude Law,' I quip.

'What, a real actor? No such luck,' he says with a smirk.

'Shame! Good to see you back.' I grin, returning to my workstation.

As I continue to whip, whisk, fold and beat I look over at Billy, who seems agitated with his script once again. I notice him dramatically sighing heavily at the page in front of him, the frown lines on his forehead appearing deeper than ever. I feel as though he is willing me to step out and offer to help him again. I'd love to, but today I don't have time.

After popping the last batch of cakes into the oven I look up and see a red-faced Billy striding over towards me.

'Sophie, I know I haven't known you long. But I just wanted to say that I've really enjoyed spending time with you over the last week and I'd really like it if you'd come out for dinner with me tonight . . . on a date. To say thank you.'

Shock is the only explanation I can give for the laughter that shoots from my mouth. My hand quickly flies up to cover it but it's too late, he has heard it. Billy registers the laugh, looks around at Molly, Miss Brown, Mrs Sleep and a few other customers in the shop (who are sat staring at him open-mouthed), and then turns on his heels and rushes out of the door, knocking over a stand of cards in his haste.

I immediately feel horrified at my reaction and so whip off my apron and run out after him.

'Billy! Billy! Stop!' I shout as the gap between us closes. 'I'm so sorry I laughed – but that was the last thing I was expecting you to say.'

'Really?' He turns round to face me and I notice he looks like a hurt little boy – wounded and embarrassed.

'Yes! Believe it or not, it's not often guys come waltzing up to the counter and ask me out.'

'They don't?'

'Strangely not. It's rare to even have men in there.'

I look down at the floor, not quite knowing what to say now that I've managed to stop him from running off.

'I didn't waltz. More like sauntered,' he says quietly

with a smile, as he brushes his foot forwards and back on the pavement. 'So, fancy dinner tonight?'

'Actually I can't –'

'Right, look, don't worry about it,' he interrupts, turning to leave, his mood changing instantly.

'Oi! Will you stop being so bloody dramatic?' I shout, causing him to stop and turn back to look at me again, his face full of surprise at my sudden outburst. I take a few deep breaths to compose myself before continuing. 'What I was saying was that I can't make tonight as I've already got plans with my mum.'

'Oh!'

'Yeah, but if you were to ask me out another day, one when I'm free, then . . . I might say yes.'

'I see,' he says, his eyes flickering with excitement. 'When's your day off?'

'Sunday.'

'And do you have plans this Sunday?'

'Not at the moment.'

'Perfect,' he beams.

I walk back into the shop with the biggest grin on my face, pretending to ignore the fact that Molly and all our regulars have had their faces pressed up against the glass of the window for the last few minutes, trying to make out what was going on. The shop is deadly quiet and everyone just stares at me, waiting for me to spill the beans.

'Come on then, out with it! What blooming happened?' Molly suddenly snaps, causing the room to erupt with laughter.

'Well, my lovely ladies, it appears I've gone and bagged myself a date!'

The ladies cheer in excitement, Molly rushes over to sit me down and then brings out a huge pot of tea and a carrot cake. The next hour is spent with us all sat round, nibbling on cake and slurping down tea, while my audience ooh and aah as I divulge all the details of our romance so far.

The house is still in darkness when I return home after work, so I'm surprised to find Mum curled up on the sofa in the living room with her eyes shut. Switching on a small lamp beside her I notice the damp tissue scrunched in her hand. Her eyes slowly flicker open and take me in. Confusion fills her face, then disappointment that I've found her like this once more.

'Hello, love . . . I'm sorry, I must've dozed off,' she explains, as she hastily glides one hand over her hair to check it's still in place.

'Don't worry, Mum.'

'But I haven't even made a start on dinner yet,' she says, starting to panic.

'Mum! It's fine. I'll make us something. Or we can get a takeaway if you like?' I say, trying to relax her.

'That's a good idea. Give us both the night off!'

'Exactly. Chinese?' I ask.

'Great.'

I reach for the phone to make our usual order of sweet and sour chicken, egg fried rice and chilli shredded beef.

'So, how was your day?' Mum asks once I've placed the order and made us a cup of tea each, which we decide to drink while snuggled up together in the living room on our worn-out teal sofa.

'Good.' I nod.

'Anything interesting happen?' she quizzes with a faint smile on her face as she gives me a slight nudge with her elbow.

'You've already heard!' I shriek in surprise.

'Oh, Soph, do you really expect news like that to stay quiet here?'

'True, but it would've been nice for me to tell you myself. Who snitched?'

'Miss Brown.'

'Now there's a surprise!'

'And Mrs Williams, who'd bumped into Mrs Sleep . . . and then June Hearne who had just got off the phone to Molly.'

'News really does spread like wildfire, then,' I say as we both sit and chuckle at the absurdity of it.

'You know, I met your dad when I was at work.'

For a moment I'm stunned into silence, Mum never brings up Dad. Ever. I clear my throat with a mouthful of tea before I can respond.

'Really?'

'Yes . . . I was working in the newsagent's at the time. First thing in the morning he came in to buy a paper, half an hour later he came back in to buy a bar of chocolate, five minutes later a can of Coke, then some cigarettes.'

'I didn't know Dad used to smoke,' I say, shocked by this tiny nugget of new information.

'He didn't. Turns out that each time he came in he was trying to pluck up the courage to ask me out. He was about to ask me when he chickened out and saw the cigarettes behind me, so asked for those instead. It was after that, when he came back in for some chewing gum, I think, when he finally got round to it.'

'What did he say to you?'

'Oh, I can't remember exactly . . .' she admits sadly. 'He and a group of his friends were planning on going to the cinema that weekend, so he asked if I'd like to join them.'

'And did you?'

'A good-looking boy like that asking me out on a date? Of course I did.'

Before she can reveal any more the doorbell goes, letting us know that dinner is here. The moment of sharing is broken as we both reach for our purses and squabble over whose turn it is to pay.

I've already admitted that I don't have much experience when it comes to men and that I've only been on a few dates, but perhaps it's time to reveal the full extent of my dating history. My first date came when I was nineteen and was with Mrs Sleep's grandson James; a short, blond guy, who walked like a mini rhino with his wide swagger and stocky build. James took me to the cinema to watch *Pirates of the Caribbean: Dead Man's Chest,* and then spent the whole film throwing popcorn at the people in front of us, and sniggering at how funny he thought it was. I managed to somehow ignore him and watch the film, which I thoroughly enjoyed. However, at the end of the night, when he sloppily licked his lips and plunged towards me with his slimy pout, I couldn't get home quick enough. The image of it in my head was enough to make me shudder for days. Mrs Sleep still asks (after all these years) when we're going to have a second date – it doesn't surprise me to hear James is still single.

The next date, which came a couple of years later, was encouraged by Mrs Wallis and was with laboratory assistant Russell, her grandson, who was of average height, had a pretty face and jet-black hair. He decided to take me to one of the local restaurants for dinner, which was a bad idea – it seemed we had nothing to talk to each other about. It was a disaster and full of awkward silences throughout with us both sat looking at the tablecloth or eating in silence. It could've been that Russell was just quiet by nature, but I had a feeling he'd simply been coaxed into taking me out by Mrs Wallis and couldn't be bothered. He dropped me off back home after the meal, without attempting to kiss me. Thankfully. Mrs Wallis keeps me up-to-date with the goings-on in Russell's life, and I believe he is now engaged to a fellow lab assistant. Good for him.

After those two experiences with dating I wasn't keen on going on any more – especially ones that were set up by the guys' grandmas. However, it was walking down the hill one day on a delivery, juggling with a load of boxed cakes that were threatening to topple over, that Shane came to the rescue. He kindly grabbed half the load and continued with me to my destination, which was a couple of minutes down the road. As a thank you I agreed to have coffee with him straight away afterwards. Perhaps because there was no build-up to it and no mention of the word 'date', that led me to be relaxed in his company – or perhaps I let him in because he was so sweet to me and softly spoken – his face rounded and trustworthy. We started to see more of each other as the months went by.

Looking back now I know I saw him more as a friend than anything else – he was the first person my age who I'd enjoyed spending time with in years. It was that fondness for him which led me not to grumble when he started to call me his girlfriend, or when he kissed me . . . or when he placed his hand under my top to unhook my bra and cup my breast . . . or when, at night-time, he'd led me into the park on numerous occasions, where he'd guide me under one of the giant willow trees and we'd have sex in the darkness. No, I didn't object to any of that. It was when he started to say that he loved me that it all got too much. He was the second man to ever tell me he loved me. A fact I couldn't cope with at the time. Molly and Mum thought I was mad when I suddenly ended things with Shane for no real reason. He was devastated but moved on quickly. Within months he was engaged and is now married with twin boys and has moved away from Rosefont Hill. Even now I wish I had been braver with my feelings.

This means that, like any single girl out there, my love life has been unsuccessful in many respects. Cringeworthy dates followed by a relationship that failed because the poor guy loved me can hardly be classed as victorious. So, although I'm on a high after the day's events, later when I get into bed the reality of the situation starts to sink in. I'm about to go on a date with someone quite special, someone who I think I really like, and I don't want to screw it up like I've been known to in the past.

Predicting another sleepless night, I decide to grab my laptop to do a little bit of pre-date research. I'm sure this will get me slightly more prepared to spend time in Billy's company, and what harm can it do? As I type his name into Google, glamorous pictures of him on the red carpet and in magazine shoots appear. His infectious smile and glistening eyes make me feel giddy as butterflies dance around in my tummy. I let out a laugh as I feel myself grinning back at his image on the screen like an idiot (he certainly has something of a 'Jude Law Effect' about him).

My eyes wander down the page as I find a list of all the films he has been in on *imdb.com*. It's huge! Honestly, it's no wonder Molly recognized him the first day we saw him. In fact, I'm surprised I didn't recognize him too as I've seen a couple of these films – albeit the ones from earlier in his career where he had smaller roles.

Continuing to inspect the Google search results, I find a link to his page on *Wikipedia*, which I click on without hesitation.

Billy Buskin

William Andrew Buskin is an English actor and model. Born in Surrey, Billy started his acting career with a small part in *Eastenders* and later took on many projects as a child actor. At nineteen years old, a chance meeting with Hollywood producer Alfred Higgins led to him securing the lead role in the film trilogy *Halo*, based on the best-selling book by Matilda Sutton, playing Sid Quest.

Early Life

Buskin was born in Surrey, England. His father Clive is a plumber. His mother Julie was a sales assistant, but stopped working when she had Billy and his siblings. Billy is the middle child and has older twin sisters and a younger brother and sister.

Wow! Big family. As the section on his upbringing and family life is quite bare I'm guessing he must be quite a private person when it comes to his home life, which is admirable as not a lot of celebs are. I keep scrolling down the page, skimming over details of his career since *Halo*.

I stop flicking through when I get to a section called 'Personal Life'. I pause before reading on; even though I know I should end there, close my laptop, and never look at the page again. There it is. Billy Buskin's dating history. I'm too intrigued to look away now. I take a few deep breaths before reading on.

Personal Life

Whilst working on *Halo*, Billy started a three-month relationship with Brazilian model Ariane Salvador, whom he met at the MTV Movie Awards. The relationship ended abruptly when she left him for veteran actor Hugo Miles, 47 years her senior, although she later regretted her actions, saying in an interview, 'Billy is the guy I should've married, but I was young and foolish.' Despite being devastated over the break-up, Billy soon found comfort from his new *Halo* co-star Heidi Black, and they became a couple off-screen as well as on. Once filming was complete on the trilogy, however, the relationship appeared rocky, with continuous reports of the couple arguing, splitting up and getting back together. They decided to take a clean break from each other but have reportedly remained friends ever since.

Although Billy has not had an official 'girlfriend' for the past few years he has been linked to numerous actresses and models including Sarah Atkins, Ruth Yates, Makaela Truce and Betty Sugar, to name but a few.

His serial dating has caught the attention of numerous tabloid papers – especially the *Daily Dawn*, which has crowned him their Womanizer of the Year for the past four years.

Needless to say, I can't stop myself from clicking on the names and letting photos of one dazzling woman after another appear on my screen. Ariane Salvador has the body of a goddess, Heidi Black is a beautiful blonde with a very curvaceous body, Sarah Atkins has the most perfect skin I've ever seen . . .

The number of girls that he has dated, had flings with, or simply been linked to is extensive and it feels as though every hot, desirable woman in showbiz is on that list. Obviously, it could all be a load of rubbish, just speculation and gossip with no truth behind it. But it shows me one thing. These are the women who have filled Billy Buskin's life and who surround him on a daily basis. They're beautiful, glamorous and spellbinding. What could I possibly have to offer him that they don't? After depressing myself by clicking on more images of these beautiful women, I eventually close my laptop and stare at the ceiling for the rest of the night, not managing to sleep a wink. My earlier excitement has left me and given way to anxiety and trepidation.

The following day I'm an absolute wreck at work. I burn three cakes and drop two plates before Molly eventually pulls me to one side.

'Darling girl, what on earth is the matter?' she asks softly.

'What do you mean?' I say, as I struggle to keep my tears at bay and from blubbing loudly.

'Oh, Soph. You've not been yourself all day. It's not like you to be careless or clumsy.'

'I know, it's just . . .'

'You're worried about your date?'

'Oh, Mol!' I sob. 'I'm just normal. I'm just boring old me!'

'Oh, petal,' she coos, as she puts her arms around me and holds me tight. 'Don't be like that.' She lets out a soft chuckle. 'Have you thought that maybe that's what he likes about you? Huh? Maybe boring old you is exactly what caught his attention and attracted him. Because – face it, duck – he has been mesmerized by you from the moment he laid eyes on you.'

'But I'm just me! What will I have to talk to him about? What could we possibly have in common?'

'Sweetpea, there's more to him than just being this Hollywood Adonis or whatever . . . he is a real human being, you know. And for once, will you stop selling yourself short! He might have all these fans, or what-ever, but they don't actually know him – they just have this fantasy version of him in their heads. Whereas you are adored by every single person who knows you and that is saying far more.' Molly then pulls me away from her and forces me to have eye contact with her. 'You know what else, little lady? He's blooming lucky to be going on a date with you – he should be thanking his lucky stars. Because you are the most special girl in the world, and I have never been so proud to know someone.'

Needless to say, I sob harder.

5

When my alarm goes off at eight o'clock the following morning I wake up in a panic, realizing I've not picked a date outfit yet – what a thoughtless omission! I have absolutely no clue what Billy has planned for today as he wanted to surprise me, although with hardly anything to do in Rosefont Hill it will be interesting to see what he has come up with.

As I don't know where we'll be going or what we'll be doing, I have no idea what will be appropriate to wear. Should I glam myself up in a pretty dress? Or should I go with my skinny jeans and boots for comfort in case we're doing something adventurous? I dart around the room picking up floral dresses and colourful skirts before discarding them immediately for being too flouncy. Clothes of all shapes and colours fly through the air as I anxiously root around for the perfect get-up.

After trying on everything in my wardrobe at least three times it dawns on me that Billy has only ever seen me in an apron and covered in flour – so whatever I choose to wear will be a big improvement! Therefore I decide to stick to my usual jeans and boots combo, but team them with a cute little pink blouse to dress it up slightly. At least I'll be comfortable this way and not pulling at a skirt hem or tugging up my tights all day.

After showering, I blow-dry my hair into some nice bouncy waves, pluck my eyebrows into something more agreeable-looking and carefully apply some make-up in the mirror (oh yes, today definitely calls for some foundation, bronzer and a touch of mascara).

As I finish with my make-up my head goes all dizzy and light, forcing me to stop and sit on the toilet seat with my head in my hands. I know it's the nerves creeping up on me once again and so I try to breathe through it. Just as I start to feel calmer there's a knock on the bathroom door.

'You OK, Soph?' asks Mum.

'Yeah . . .' I say as I lift myself up off the loo seat and unlock the door, flashing her a nervous smile.

'You look beautiful!'

'Thanks . . .' I say, biting my lip.

'Oh no! Look at that face!' she laughs as she wiggles my nose between her fingers.

'I'm just a bit nervous . . .'

'There's nothing to be nervous about. It's only a date.'

'I know . . .'

'Well, then! Just go and have fun,' she says, as she nudges me playfully on the arm.

With one last look in the mirror I give Mum a kiss goodbye, run into my room to grab my bag and coat and fly out of the door.

*

Billy's already standing outside the shop when I turn from the path onto the High Street. He has his hands behind his back, a purple rucksack slung over one shoulder and a huge grin on his face, looking gorgeous. I'm pleased to notice that he is also in casual clothes, wearing faded jeans and a burnt orange hoodie with a white zipper running up it. Interestingly, though, he's also wearing a pair of black wellington boots.

When I eventually join him at the top of the hill, he leans forward and gives me a kiss on the cheek, which instantly causes my insides to leap and dance around.

'You look beautiful,' he whispers in my ear.

I smile back, nerves getting the better of me as I feel my cheeks already turning pink.

'Right,' he says, his tone changing to a more commandeering one. 'These are for you,' he smiles, handing me a pair of pink and blue floral wellington boots he's been hiding behind his back.

'What are these for?' I ask, nervously laughing, taking them from him.

'Well, I know it's not been raining lately, but I thought it would be best to be prepared, we don't want to end up knee deep in a muddy puddle now, do we? I've popped some socks in there, too.'

I stare at him, flabbergasted. This is not what I was expecting at all. 'I've heard of girls being given flowers on first dates, chocolates even, but never wellies!'

'I've already given you flowers,' he says, raising his eyebrows. 'Quick, quick. Pop them on.'

'Hold on. How on earth did you know my size?' I quiz, eyeing him suspiciously. 'Are you stalking me?'

'Gosh, my cover's been blown already!' he smirks.

I lean against the shop wall and change into them in silence while Billy watches me and pops my discarded boots into his rucksack. Once I'm in my new footwear, and have stomped around a bit, Billy grabs my hand. 'Come on,' he says, as he pulls me along the road.

We turn the corner where I discover two large horses tied to a tree, waiting for us.

'Meet Tony and Connie,' he says.

'Wow!' blurts from my mouth before I can stop it as I take in the horses. The one Billy pointed out as Tony has a dark brown coat with a diamond-shaped white patch on his forehead and white socks; he's busy munching on some leaves from Mrs Wallis's garden. Connie, however, with her grey coat and black mane, is looking straight at us.

'I hope you don't have a fear of horses or anything.'

'No, no. I used to ride all the time actually, but I haven't been on a horse in years!'

'It wasn't a big fall or anything that stopped you from riding, was it?' he asks anxiously.

'Funny you should say that. I fell off and broke my wrist when I was ten. Back then I wanted to be a show jumper, but the fall meant that I couldn't go out for months. By the time my wrist had recovered I'd moved on to some new dream.'

'So you're not going to be worried getting on this

73

one?' he asks, grabbing hold of Tony's reins, letting me know that Connie is my ride.

'Absolutely not!' I declare, as I excitedly mount Connie with a huge leap. I'll admit, I'm quite chuffed with the way I just hop on up like an old pro, with only minimal grunting sounds. I adjust the stirrups and then sit and watch as Billy attempts to mount his horse – without success. First he tries to hoist one leg up but it can't quite reach the stirrup and then he tries to pull the horse towards the fence so that he can climb on from there – but the horse isn't having any of it. Each time Tony decides to go with him to the fence, he cheekily walks forward a few paces by the time Billy's perched on it, ready to mount.

'I've been doing this perfectly all week and now I've got company I can't get on the blasted thing. TONY!' he shouts as once again the horse fails to do what he asks.

'Calm down, cowboy,' I joke as I jump off my horse to go and help him. I grab Tony and guide him back to the fence, holding him tightly by the reins so that he won't wander off as Billy jumps on. 'There . . . finally!' I say, grinning at Billy before handing back the reins and mounting Connie again with ease.

'What an awful start!' he says.

'Oh, shush you. It's good to know you're not good at everything, Mr Big Shot!'

'Believe me – there are many things that I'm utterly crap at!'

'Good! Now, where are we going?'

For the next hour we hack through the local woods, which are covered in a thick purple blanket of blue-bells. It's beautiful. I find it thrilling to be back on a horse again after so long and I enjoy getting Connie to alternate between a trot and a canter, much to Billy's dismay, as his horse just wants to copy whatever my horse is doing. It's clear that although he is comfortable to sit on top of a horse, he isn't an experienced rider. I decide to ease the pace, though, when I can hear him struggling to catch his breath and turn to see him bouncing up and down painfully on the horse's back.

'Sorry,' I shout. 'Got a bit carried away there!'

'No, I'm glad you're enjoying yourself,' he calls back breathlessly, with a contagious grin on his face. He is ridiculously handsome, even in this haggard state.

'Would you like to stop for a bit? We could get off and walk if you like?'

'Actually, I think there's a big lake if you carry on going down this path.'

'I know the one.'

'Of course. Well, let's keep going until we get down there and then we can stop for a bit.'

'OK, sounds like a plan. You can lead the way this time,' I say, forcing Connie to stop so that we can let Billy and Tony through, much to her annoyance.

We ride at a leisurely pace down to the lake, stopping under a large oak tree, which we tie the two horses to.

'Are you getting peckish?' Billy asks, wiping his hands on his jeans.

'Actually, I'm starving,' I admit.

I was feeling sick with nerves this morning and running around in a panic trying to get ready, and forgot to eat before I left. Now that food has been mentioned, I realize I'm famished!

'Me too. I was too anxious to eat this morning.'

'Really? Why?'

'I had a date with a gorgeous girl planned.'

'Haaa! I'm so glad they give you lines to say in these films you're in, otherwise you'd be in trouble,' I say with a giggle.

'Thanks. Anyway, back to the subject of food . . . Close your eyes.'

'What? Why?' I laugh.

'Please?' he begs.

I smirk and roll my eyes, doing as he asks, instantly feeling very exposed and vulnerable at the unknown. My cheeks start burning as his warm hands engulf mine and he slowly leads me further into the woods. Excitement and nerves cause my skin to feel tingly and sensitive. I have to fight all urges to open my eyes to see where he is taking me. Somehow I manage to keep them closed as I listen to the sticks and leaves as they crackle beneath my feet while Billy guides me with ease.

'OK . . .' he says, placing a hand on my shoulder to tell me we've reached our destination. 'You can look now.'

I open my eyes and gasp in shock as I take in what's in front of me. Masses of twinkling fairy lights spiral up the thick trunks of a circle of trees, with thousands more hanging from their tall branches and dangling down, making a starry sky above us. A huge, thick, black sheet encompasses the whole lot, which seals it off from the outside world, and allows the lights to sparkle more in its darkness. Beneath the canopy of stars, a blue-and-purple-checked picnic blanket has been laid out, surrounded by a ring of bluebells, with tubs full of food, glasses and bottles arranged on top, along with a bunch of scattered fluffy cushions. The whole thing is like a den or a fort you might make as a child to play in, but it's far more magical. It's breathtaking.

I stare opened mouthed at the display in front of me. No one has ever gone to this much effort for me before. Ever. I'm so overwhelmed by it that I can feel tears threatening to burst out of me, so I have to tense my jaw to keep them at bay.

Billy, who has been stood beside me, watching as I take in the space around us, squeezes my hand – probably because I've been stood gawping at it all and not vocalized a reaction yet.

'Wow!' I manage to say, my eyes brimming with tears.

'Two "wow"'s in one date, hey? I believe that's a good sign . . .'

'It really is. How did you do all this?'

'Ahh, now that would be telling. Come on, let's sit down,' he says, guiding me by the hand to the blanket, where we both struggle to pull off our muddied wellies before parking ourselves on top and getting comfortable.

Billy picks up one of the bottles, unscrews it, pours its contents into two goblet glasses and hands me one.

'I figured we'd be thirsty after the hack, so I thought orange and cranberry juice would be nice, rather than wine or something.'

'That's my favourite drink!' I say in surprise, taking a gulp.

'Who knew?' he says with a smirk.

It's only as we start opening the tubs of food and I find one containing scones that things start to become clearer.

'Scones?'

'Yep,' Billy says, keeping occupied with a tub of ham sandwiches.

'They look delicious.'

'Mmmm . . . yummy.'

He continues to avoid my gaze by opening another tub, this one containing a tomato salad – so I poke him jokingly in the ribs.

'Ouch,' he laughs.

'Did you make these yourself? Or did you have a little helper?'

'I did make them myself actually, but under the supervision of a more experienced cook!'

'Molly!'

'How on earth did you guess that?' he asks in a high-pitched squeal.

'How on earth did she keep this a secret?'

'She said she's found it very difficult!'

'I'll bet! Are you aware how much of a gossip she is?

This would've killed her,' I laugh. 'So when did you do all this?'

Billy lets out a huge sigh, gutted that his cover has been blown and knowing that I won't give up until he gives me all the answers I crave.

'I guess I can tell you now . . . this morning. I met Molly in the shop at eight and she helped me make it all. She was great – especially when it came to all your favourite foods.'

'But who put up all this, then?' I ask, looking around at the enchanted forest that has been erected around us.

'A few crew members from the film helped out. I came down here with them before I went to sort out the food.'

'Sounds like you've had a very busy morning.'

'I have, but I wanted to make a good impression.'

'Well, you've certainly managed to do that.'

'Good.'

We both sit there beaming and giggling at each other as we start to tuck into the food in front of us.

I have never felt so relaxed and giddy all at once. Billy has a way of making me feel comfortable and safe in his company, but at the same time my body churns out a mass of desire and longing. He is electrifyingly charismatic . . . breathtakingly so.

Once we've stuffed our faces with all we can manage, we lie back on the blanket with our heads together on one of the pillows and gaze up at the lights twinkling above us. I'm acutely aware of the fact that our shoulders are slightly touching, allowing me to feel the heat coming from Billy's body, which sends shivers of nervous apprehension running through me.

'What's your favourite book?' I ask after a moment of silence.

'Oh dear.'

'What?' I ask.

'Well, I could lie and make something up, but the truth is I've never read a book from cover to cover in my life.'

'Ever?'

'Nope.'

'Blimey.'

'I know. Gosh, I feel like I've just been busted,' he says, bringing his hands up to his face in embarrassment. 'What's yours?'

'*Jane Eyre*,' I declare, without hesitation.

'Jane who?'

'It's a classic.'

'I'll read it some time.'

'Yeah, right! Hold on, does that mean you haven't even read *Pride and Prejudice*?'

'So, what did you want to become after you lost interest in horses?' Billy asks, changing the subject, and making us both cackle with laughter.

'A writer, then a doctor and eventually a florist. For a while.'

'How come?'

'I love flowers.'

'What made you stop wanting that?'

'I got a job at the local florist. Not a proper job or anything, I was only young. But I spent every Saturday cleaning out dirty buckets and then getting a whole fifteen pounds for doing so. Their stench and slime put me off eventually.'

'Sounds nasty.'

'Hmm, it was. Although I'd still like to do something with flowers at some point.'

'Really? So, what do you want now?'

'My own teashop.'

'To put Molly out of business?' he asks, nudging me.

'No, no, no, I'd never do that. Molly's getting older – whether she likes it or not she's not going to be able to run the shop forever,' I explain. 'In fact, she has a son called Peter who moved to Australia several years ago and she's always going on about possibly moving over there and being with him. Since her husband died she's been on her own. I think she'd like being with family. With that in mind, my plan is to save up as much as I can and then buy it off her when she does decide to move out there and sell it.'

'Seriously?'

'Yep. I hate to tell you this but my life consists of books and baking.' I shift my head so that I can see him properly and burst out laughing. 'Oh God, I can't believe I've just admitted to being so boring.'

'No, you haven't.'

'The truth is I rarely go out clubbing, I don't binge drink, smoke or take drugs – I've simply found something better to spend my money on. I know it sounds a bit wanky but from the moment I stepped into the teashop I felt at home. From then on it became . . . all I ever wanted.'

'So what will you change about it when you're the boss?'

'I'd like it to be even more of a haven for women.'

'What, more than flowery tablecloths and dainty china cups?' he asks with mock surprise on his face.

'Yes!'

'I didn't think that was possible.'

'Oh, it is,' I say, turning on to my front in excitement. 'I want to add a flower section to the shop – not an actual florist that makes bouquets, though. I simply want to have bunches of flowers available for people to pick and choose from so that they can go home and make up their own arrangements. Maybe have evening floristry classes once a week for people to attend.'

'Sounds nice.'

'I'd also like a gift section – where we can sell home-made signs and little trinkets . . . Pieces that people won't find anywhere else!' I suddenly realize that my mouth has started to run away with itself. I've never shared this dream with anyone before, so I've no idea why I'm blurting it all out now. 'What about you?' I ask, keen to take the attention away from myself, rolling back onto my back.

'What?'

'Ah, right. I guess being an actor is all you ever dreamed of.'

'No, actually. If I'm honest I never wanted to be an

actor in the first place. I wanted to be a plumber like my dad.'

'So what happened?'

'I was good at acting,' he says shrugging his shoulders.

'Nice that you're so modest,' I tease.

'Ha, ha!' he says slowly, poking me in the side and causing me to laugh. 'I used to be painfully shy, actually. I was fine at home but whenever I stepped out of the house I'd go really quiet, so my mum forced me to join our local drama group to build up my confidence.'

'And that's when they discovered you were a talented genius?'

'Something like that,' Billy says with a shrug. I hear him inhale deeply, as he hesitates before continuing. 'Once I started being offered more parts and earning good money from those jobs, it was hard to say I didn't want to do it any more. So I guess you could say I just fell into it without ever thinking if it was really what I wanted. Don't get me wrong, I love it, though!' he insists.

'I'm sure you do,' I say, taken aback by his honesty. 'I think it's funny how life can lead you down certain paths which you wouldn't have taken otherwise. Do you think you'll carry on acting forever?'

'I'm not sure,' he says, fiddling with a bracelet on his wrist. 'I've fallen into this teen pin-up type role and it's not where I wanted to be. I didn't realize when I took on that one role in *Halo* that everything else would change so drastically. I wanted to be viewed as a serious actor. Not someone people laugh at,' he admits with a weighty sigh. 'I'd like to be acknowledged for my talent and I'd like to be able to pick and choose my parts so I can be at home more.'

'Sounds nice.'

'Well, family means everything to me. I grew up in a family of seven.'

'Seven!' I exclaim, trying not to give away the fact that I already know this nugget of information from my Google rampage. 'I bet that was a noisy house.'

'Yeah, it was, but I always had someone to play with or someone to talk to.'

'How lovely.'

'Yep. But now I don't see any of my family as much as I'd like to.'

'How come?'

'Work. The stupid thing is, I flew them all out to LA when I was filming *Halo* so we could all stick together, but for the last year I've been in England on my own.'

'Do you think they'd move back here?'

'I doubt it. It's a different way of life over there and they're all quite settled. Do you have any brothers or sisters?' he asks, propping himself up on one elbow.

'Nope, it was just me, Mum and Dad. Tell me something . . .' I say, changing the subject as I concentrate on the twinkling above us.

'What?'

'Do you do this for everyone?'

'Do what?'

'Hang up fairy lights, bake scones and buy your date wellies?'

Waiting for him to answer, I find myself suddenly nervous of what he might say, and immediately start scolding myself for asking such a pathetically needy question.

'No,' he says slowly. 'Bizarrely, the girls I've dated in the past would have turned their noses up at this sort of thing.'

'Really?' I ask, not quite believing him. What sort of girl wouldn't approve of someone going to such romantic lengths to impress them?

'Yes, sadly they'd be far more interested in what exclusive restaurant or club I could get them into – wanting to go somewhere they could be seen.'

'Keeping up appearances?'

'Exactly. It's all about how you look and where you go. They'd run a mile if I made them get out of their designer heels and throw on some wellies and then brought them into a forest and made them sit on the ground to eat. But that's what I like about you. You're not at all prissy. You're real and lovely.'

'Oh God,' I squeal, letting out a chuckle. 'The fact I've been covered in flour since the day you met me is why you've brought me here, isn't it? Because I clearly don't mind a bit of dirt?' I cover my face with my hands as I let out a playful groan.

Billy sits up and grabs my hands away from my face, forcing me to sit up opposite him.

'No! That's not what I meant!' he says with a cheeky

smile as he tucks some of my hair away from my face. 'I mean you don't care about all that crap. Being in Hollywood and stuff, it's all about what designer brand you wear, what car you drive, what blooming ZIP code you live in – but that's not what really defines a person. None of that stuff actually means anything,' he says as he places a hand under my chin and lifts it up so that I'm looking directly into his eyes. 'The first day I saw you talking to the old lady in the shop, and making her day over a measly forty pence, I admired you for having your priorities right. Little moments like that are what make life worthwhile. None of that other stuff means anything,' he repeats.

I stop breathing as Billy slowly leans forward and plants his lusciously soft lips on mine. All other thoughts in my head are quickly swept away, as my mind and body are taken over by the intimately delicious moment.

A sudden urge to pin him to the ground and devour him completely swells through me, but I manage to suppress it . . . all in good time, Sophie May, I think to myself. All in good time!

6

The next few weeks whizz by in a blur with Billy and me spending as much time together as possible, which isn't easy when I work six days a week and his filming schedule is hectic and irregular. But we manage, and happily make the most of any time that does become available. If he has a busy day of filming ahead, and isn't required on set at the crack of dawn, he comes in before the shop opens to help with the daily baking session and so that we can work on his scripts. Surprisingly, he can now whip up a vanilla cupcake batch without any help or guidance from me; however, he still finds our chocolate and toffee layer cake a struggle. Other than that we've been surviving on late-night walks, proper dates on a Sunday (if he's off) and phone calls . . . of which there have been quite a few.

Despite him begging on numerous occasions, I have declined his offer of going on set with him. I already have to keep pinching myself over the fact that little reclusive me has bagged herself a boyfriend, so I think going on a film set and seeing people running around after him and pandering to his every need might be a little too much too soon. I'm happy just seeing him as the delightful Billy I happened to meet in the shop for a while longer.

It would be fair to say that we've been living in a bubble . . . a wonderful, shiny, bouncy bubble full of romance and sickly affection. But as everyone knows, bubbles inevitably do one thing – burst!

I stop in at Budgens on my way to work one day, a few weeks after our first date in the forest, to pick up some pink food colouring. Whilst walking to the checkout to pay, something from the newspaper stand catches my attention. My face. On almost every paper on the stand. My heart seems to sink into my stomach and I'm aware of my breathing becoming alarmingly irregular. I have to fight the urge to throw up on the spot as I slowly walk over and look closer at the image. It's of Billy and me kissing outside the shop, taken the previous day as he left to go to the set. I know that because of what I'm wearing; I have a pink scarf wrapped around my head and a pink spotty apron on.

I'm covered with flour and dough.

I look a mess.

I can remember following him out so that I could give him a quick peck without being watched by Molly and the customers as we're still trying to be discreet, even though most of the customers know, but now the whole nation has seen us.

How could we not have known someone was taking pictures? How can they just take pictures of me and print them without my consent? Are they even allowed to do that?

My eye wanders across the different papers as I take in their headlines, 'Billy's Sprinkle of Fairy Dust', 'Buskin for Love', 'Love in the Country for Billy Buskin', 'Billy Finds his Halo' and 'Bill's on the Love Bus.'

'Oh, it's you!' says Mr Tucker, the lanky, dark-haired manager, from behind the counter. 'I was going to walk a few of those up to you later on. I thought you'd want to see them.'

I turn and face him, not sure how to respond.

He beams back at me expectantly with his hands on his hips.

'Thank you,' I finally manage.

'Must be odd. Seeing yourself in the paper like that.'

I nod, still in a daze.

'Don't worry, they'll be moving on to something else tomorrow . . . chip paper wrappings and all that,' he says, sensing my uneasiness at the situation.

'Yeah . . .'

'Well, look, you take a copy of each,' he says as he hobbles around the counter with a carrier bag and starts to fold each paper carefully into it. Once he's finished he turns to me and proffers the bag, 'It's on the house. My treat.'

'Thank you.'

'Although, don't think I'm gonna be doing that every time or you'll cost me a small fortune,' he chortles. I give him a faint smile and leave as he continues to laugh at his own comment.

As I walk up the hill I can't help but look about me suspiciously as I try to spot any men with cameras hiding in the bushes – isn't that what paparazzi do, hide in bushes or in cars? Spying on their victims' every move, just waiting for their opportunity to snap? The High Street is, however, typically quiet, with only a few locals dotted around getting on with their own business, so there's nothing out of the ordinary to cause further concern.

Even though I know Billy had an early call time this morning, and won't be waiting for me outside the shop, my heart still sinks when I discover he isn't there. My guess is that he hasn't seen the papers himself yet, otherwise I'm sure he'd have come to check I was OK or at least called me . . . wouldn't he? Or will he be embarrassed being pictured with a normal girl with flour on her face, instead of some striking superstar?

As I unlock the shop door I'm welcomed by the sound of the phone ringing, and I hastily rush across the shop to reach it before it stops, hoping to hear Billy's voice.

'Hello. Tea-on-the-Hill, how can I help?' I say, my brain automatically giving the normal spiel.

'Is that Sophie May?'

'Erm . . .' This catches me by surprise. Nobody calls here to speak to me other than my mum or Billy, and they certainly don't ask for me by my full name.

Sensing my hesitation the caller ploughs on hopefully.

'This is Sarah Green calling from the *Daily Star*,' coos the lady, her voice sweet and friendly. 'I was just wondering if I could get a few words from you about your relationship with Billy Buskin.'

'Sorry, I –'

'It doesn't have to be much. Just, you know, how you met and that.'

'Erm . . .' unsure what to say I pull the phone from my ear and put back in its cradle. Within seconds it starts ringing again.

'Hello?' I say, picking up with uncertainty.

'Hello, can I talk to Sophie May?' This time it's a man's voice, much firmer and more direct than the polite caller before.

'No, sorry, she's not here,' I lie, as I secure the phone in its cradle once again, only for it to start ringing once more. This time I don't answer it and instead let it continue to ring, although once it's finally stopped it just starts to chirp again. On and on and on it sounds. I stand staring at it as it calls out to me with its manic, insistent cry.

I decide to pull the connection out of the wall, and as I'm doing so I hear Molly walk through the door. I turn to her, the panic rising once more.

'It's in the papers,' I say, holding up the plastic bag, before she has a chance to speak.

'What is, love?' she asks with concern.

'Me and Billy.'

'Oh . . . well, what do the papers say?'

I stare at her with a confused expression.

'I don't know . . . I've not read them.'

'Why not?'

I shrug my shoulders, unable to give an answer.

Molly stares at me for a moment.

'Come on, you don't even know what you're worrying over yet,' she says, as she takes the bag from me and sits at the table, pulling the chair out next to her for me to join her. She then grabs the papers out and lays them on the table in front of us. 'Oh well, that's a lovely picture, darling,' she coos, as we start reading the first article in the *Daily Dawn*.

BUSKIN FOR LOVE

Until now Billy Buskin has remained single since his split from his *Halo* co-star Heidi Black several years ago, with many speculating he was finding it hard to move on from their relationship. However, while filming his latest offering, on location in the Kent countryside, someone seems to have caught his eye.

Billy, who is currently filming an adaptation of the classic Jane Austen novel *Pride and Prejudice* in the little village of Rosefont Hill, has apparently been talking about the beauty (pictured above) non-stop on set, even hinting that marriage could be on the cards.

A source said: 'The last thing Billy was expecting to find in the country was a girlfriend, especially one who has nothing to do with the film. That's definitely what he finds attractive about her, that she's not a part of the showbiz bubble. She's just a normal girl, who works in a café. She's got good morals and she isn't caught up with the drama of Hollywood. In fact, she had no idea who Billy was when they first met.'

They continued: 'Billy hasn't been shy with his feelings at all. Sophie is all he talks about on set, and he regularly declares to us all that he has finally found love, as well as the girl he is going to marry.'

The new couple were caught sharing a tender moment yesterday outside Sophie's workplace, confirming that they are indeed an item.

Billy has dated a steady stream of celebs and A-listers in the past, earning himself our Womanizer of the Year award four years in a row, but could a true English rose be what he has been searching for all along? Watch this space!

Both of us just stare at the paper, allowing the words to sink in, then grab the next paper to read more.

After reading the other articles, all of which use the same source's quote and run almost identical stories, Molly turns to me.

'You feeling better now?' she asks as she gently strokes my arm.

'It's just so odd!'

'I know, love.'

'I hate gossip and now I'm the one being talked about.'

'Well, it's the nature of Billy's world, isn't it, darling? You just have to accept that this is going to come with it.'

'Yeah, I just hadn't even thought about it. I mean, I know he's in the public eye and that people take an interest in what he's up to, but . . . I don't know. I didn't realize I'd be a part of that,' I say, giving a little shrug.

'At least it's all positive. I wish I had someone going around saying lovely things about me!'

'True.'

'Now, we'd better get on with some work, or we're going to have quite a few grumpy customers. You still up for it today?'

'Of course! One thing, though.'

'What?'

'Can we keep the phone off the hook? It'll just keep ringing otherwise.'

'Oh yes, that'll be fine. Although I bet June's been trying to get through. She'll have read the papers!' Molly says with a chuckle.

Half an hour later the front door bursts open and in runs a red-faced Billy wearing what must be his Mr Darcy costume: black tailcoat, white breeches, white shirt and white cravat.

I was wrong when I thought Jude Law would make the perfect Mr Darcy: Billy is breathtakingly handsome in this get-up and I am momentarily transported into a different time and place – one where I'm Elizabeth Bennet, perhaps?

Out of breath, Billy spots me behind the counter and runs over to me with concern.

'I'm so sorry. Are you OK?' he asks, as he puts his hands on either side of my head, bends down and searches my face for signs of how I've taken the news splash.

'I'm fine. I was in shock at first but . . .'

'I've been trying to call you,' he says desperately.

'I had to take the phone off the hook because it

wouldn't stop ringing,' I say, still flustered from the sight of him in his costume.

'I was sat waiting to film a scene when I saw one of the crew reading the paper. As soon as I saw the headline I knew it was about us,' he says quickly. 'I tried to call you straight away but when I couldn't get through I was worried that you'd panicked, so I just left and came here.'

'You just left?'

'I didn't want anyone to stop me.'

I laugh at the absurdity of it all. The laughter increases and I can't stop, the more I tell myself that I shouldn't be laughing the more it comes out. The laughter causes more chuckling; even the odd unattractive snort manages to escape. I feel crazy, but the feeling of release soothes me after the whirlwind morning. When I finally stop, a perplexed-looking Billy is just staring at me.

'Are you OK?'

'Sorry. I think it's just the shock.'

'Right . . . I'm so sorry.'

'It's not your fault, Billy.'

'I know. But I should've warned you. It was bound to happen at some point. Promise me something: if it ever gets too much, or someone just turns up and you don't like it – call me,' he says, squeezing my hand.

'Seriously, I'm fine.'

'My manager's been on the phone.'

The serious tone of Billy's voice catches me by surprise. I wait for him to continue.

'They're trying to find out who the source is on set.'

'What for?'

'Well, it's not good to know that someone there's been repeating what I'm saying. I shouldn't have to censor myself. It can make life quite uncomfortable that way. I prefer to just trust everyone.'

'So you did say those things, then?'

Billy looks shyly at the floor, a sheepish grin spreading across his face.

'Perhaps,' he says quietly. 'I mean, perhaps you have been the topic of conversation once or twice. And perhaps I've been boring everyone to death telling them all how wonderful you are all the time … but just perhaps.'

'I see,' I say with a grin.

Once I've persuaded Billy that I'm not about to launch into a panic attack, and he has left to face the music back on set, Molly lets me wander down to the library to see Mum. I know she'll have seen the papers thanks to the library's new section full of newspapers and magazines, but she hasn't been down to see me. She could be rushed off her feet with library visitors, of course, or she might have tried to phone but couldn't get through. Either way, I take the short trip down to her.

When I walk through the library doors I notice that, except for a couple of lone readers, it's empty. Susan, Mum's colleague, who likes to keep conversation to a minimum, is slumped behind the counter. Her long brown hair hangs in front of her face, allowing just a couple of inches clear for her to peer through.

'Hello, Susan,' I say as I walk over to her.

'Hi,' she says in a clipped tone, keeping her eyes on the computer screen in front of her.

'Is Mum around?'

Susan looks up for a fleeting moment and registers that it's me, before returning her gaze to the screen.

'She decided to do some filing out back today.'

Mum is organizing. Cleaning. Something I know she does when she's got something on her mind that she doesn't want to face. It's her diversion tactic and has been for years.

'Is it OK if I pop back and say a quick hello? There's just something I need to talk to her about.'

Susan doesn't even bother giving a verbal reply. She just nods.

I walk into the library's back room to find Mum surrounded by piles of books, magazines and paperwork. Her forehead is covered with heavy frown lines.

'Gosh, be careful you don't get lost in all that!'

She jumps in surprise at being disturbed.

'Sophie! I didn't hear you come in!' she says, grabbing her chest.

'Sorry, Mum.'

She looks at me and smiles for a moment, but doesn't say anything.

'I take it you've seen the papers?' I say, deciding to kick the conversation off, rather than skirt around the subject.

'I have,' she says with a nod. 'Although it's not just the papers, mind, it's on the internet too, you know. All

over it. The schoolgirls were in earlier, on the computers as always. They all started shrieking their heads off.
I wondered what was going on.'

'It's weird, isn't it?'

'Just a bit,' she says quietly, looking at the floor.

'Mum?' I say with concern.

'I don't want to lose you, Sophie,' she cries. I watch as
her body crumples to the floor, melting into despair. I
go to her, wrapping my arms around her shoulders.

'Mum, you won't lose me,' I protest.

'I will, Sophie. I've always known that one day you'll
move away and that I'll be left on my own.'

'Mum . . .'

'It's not your fault. And it's not your dad's fault either.
But sooner or later I'm going to have lost two of the
most special people in my life and it'll be just me. In
that house. Alone.'

'Where do you think I'm going? Where has this
come from?'

'The papers, I guess. I always think of you as my
little girl, but I forget that you're a grownup now.
You're older than I was when I married your dad, you
know.'

'Mum, I haven't even known Billy that long! Don't
go marrying me off just yet,' I try and joke.

She looks at me sadly.

'Darling, you need to live your life. I don't want to be
the cause of you not doing the things you want to. I
don't want to be a burden.'

'But you're not.'

'Oh, I am. I'm the reason you didn't go to university. Admit it.'

'No, Mum . . . I mean, maybe at first I didn't want to go because of you, but then things changed. I found the shop and . . .' I can't formulate the words; instead I shake my head in protest.

'Baby girl, I want you to experience everything and I want you to have the kind of love that me and your dad had. You shouldn't be having to factor me into your decisions.'

We both sit in silence. I let the words circulate around my head and think of how different my life might have been. If only . . .

'You know, we used to dream up different lives for you,' she continues. 'With all sorts of different jobs and relationships and stuff. But we only ever had one real wish – and that was that you'd find love and happiness. I don't want to hold you back.'

'But you're my everything.'

'Yes, Soph . . . and I shouldn't be.' She plays with my hands, before she cups them both in hers. 'I'm sorry, love, it's just been playing on my mind a bit and then seeing all that in the paper today made it all the more real. You know?'

'Yeah, I do.' I think back to the night when Billy first asked me on a date, and remember my heart sinking as I saw the crumpled tissue in Mum's hand. I assumed she'd been thinking about Dad, but instead she's been worrying about losing me, while I've had my head in the clouds. Oblivious to her pain.

'I'm sorry I didn't realize you were upset, Mum.'

'Oh, shush, you. I want you to follow your heart and start the new chapter in both our lives. God knows we've grieved the last chapter long enough.'

She kisses me on the forehead and I wrap my arms around her skinny frame, holding her close.

7

Nine years ago . . .

Late September, towards the start of the school year in the upper sixth, we were all called into the assembly hall at the end of the day for a big energetic chat about our future prospects and all the wonderful things that life had to offer us.

Our Scottish headmaster Mr Hall stood before us and talked with great enthusiasm about the decisions we'd have to be making over the next year, 'I look at you all sat in here today and am reminded of your first day in those seats when I welcomed you to Rosefont High,' he bellowed, rocking backwards and forwards onto his toes as he did so. 'You were so eager to be part of the big school — to run around with the big girls and boys. And now here we are. You are the big girls and boys and we're getting ready to say goodbye in your last year with us. Looking around the room I can see that you're all just as eager as you were then — but now you want more. You want the world. And rightly so. The decisions you make over the next year are going to be the most important of your life because what you do will ultimately help shape your future,' he continued, giving a long pause to hammer his point home. 'So, as you start applying for university, seeking out those apprenticeships or maybe even planning your travels around the world, I hope you all realize that your future is limitless. I have high hopes for you all.'

The bell rang to signal the end of the school day, causing an intoxicating buzz to fill the room as people started to talk animatedly about their plans. Mary Lance, who was sitting next to me as usual, nudged me and gave me a beaming smile. The world is ours for the taking. What an exciting notion. I gave her a shy smile back and made my way to the exit.

On my way home, Mr Hall's words bounced around my brain – fuelling ideas of absent-minded travel around Australia with endless hugs from koalas or swanning off to university to study English where I'd be allowed to sit in peace and read all day long without a care in the world. The whole night I felt buoyed up about what my life could be like in years to come – how different it would be away from Rosefont Hill.

A few weeks later the reality of my life came and slapped me round the face. Shattering those illusions and confirming that, for me, life outside Rosefont Hill didn't exist.

I was asleep late one night when I was abruptly awoken with a shaking sensation. For a split second I was horrified that I was having another attack, but then I saw Mum's face in the darkness and realized it was her hands that were causing me to move so vigorously.

'Sophie, darling. Sophie, darling!' she voiced manically.

'Mum, what's wrong?'

She said nothing, but I could see her pursing her lips as she nervously started to twist her fingers around one another. She looked scarily timid and frightened.

'Mum?'

'I . . . I wanted to sleep. I wanted everything to stop. I just wanted to sleep. I . . .'

'It's OK, Mum. It's OK,' I cooed, trying to calm her down. 'What happened?'

She couldn't talk, she was in such a state. Instead, she held out her shaky hand and showed me the empty bottle of pills. The pills she'd decided to wash down with a bottle of whisky.

Obviously, I'd known that Mum hadn't been coping – the constant cleaning and agonizing over perfecting everything in sight, the fact that she couldn't be out of the house after dark and the sobs that still came from behind her closed bedroom door when she thought I couldn't hear her were all signs that she wasn't. However, I'd wrongly assumed that as time passed Mum would just get better. That she'd somehow learn to live again. I thought something would just click inside her and bring her back to me. Instead, what had clicked was the desire to get away from her heartache and the nightmares that plagued both her sleeping and waking hours.

Whether she'd actually meant to end her life is still a mystery, but one that I can't ponder too hard. I don't want to know the answer.

Mum was hospitalized for five weeks and diagnosed with depression.

I think she was relieved that there was something actually wrong with her, that there were others like her, that she wasn't just a freak. Obviously, that didn't make her experience with the illness any easier, but it did give her some comfort.

For me it was a wake-up call. A reminder of what our lives had become thanks to me.

Once again, the whispering started around school, but this time I didn't care. I'd cut myself off from everyone else years before and had done a good job of keeping them all at a distance ever since. I had many reasons to keep them out and, as far as I was concerned, none to let them in.

Any childish thoughts I'd had of being anywhere but at home vanished overnight. I needed to focus on getting my mum back and I didn't want to do anything that would cause her any more misery.

8

I expected the adventures of the day to wipe me off my feet and leave me exhausted, but I still find myself wide-eyed and unable to sleep at one in the morning. So I decide to reach for my laptop and let my curiosity run free. It doesn't take me long to type 'Billy Buskin Sophie' into Google and click on the news section. My heart stops as 243 separate articles pop up. TWO HUNDRED AND FORTY-THREE? It's even made the news in India, Australia and the States. It's surreal and mind-blowing.

I click on one link, and see that it's basically the same regurgitated story as before, but with a few details of Billy's previous relationships thrown in. Scrolling down I spot a section which allows readers to comment on the above story. My stomach tightens as I read their words.

What is wrong with Billy Buskin? He went from Heidi Black to that? She looks so . . . ordinary! Sort yourself out, Billy B!

She is in urgent need of a stylist! Quick, someone help her!

Yawn! Don't get too attached, Sophie. He'll be on to the next girl next week!

Talking marriage? What nonsense. The guy loves to sleep around. She looks BORING!

What?! Check out her stupid headscarf? As if someone like that could keep BB interested for more than 5 seconds. He's probably already dumped her and homed in on someone else on set!

Jeeeez . . . The thought of her naked makes me want to VOM! Put the cake down.

She looks like a rat! And what is it with all the flour? Look after yourself, girl . . . and lose a few pounds.

There are nice comments about being happy for Billy too, in fact there are more positive ones than negative, but I ignore those. They don't carry the same weight as the rest. The thing that hurts the most about all of these people's comments is that in some way I have felt the same. It's as if they can sense my insecurities and pick on each and every one of them, blowing them up and making them more truthful than when they were just niggling at me before our first date. I'm not pretty enough. I'm too normal. He'll find someone better, one of his fellow A-listers, and be off. I'm not good enough. I have nothing that would make him want to stick around. I'm not worthy.

Over the last month have we both been delusional? Billy has been outside of his glitzy world and thrust into a perfect little country life. But is there really any longevity in it? Seriously? Filming finishes in a matter of weeks, and with that Billy will pack his bags and head back to his previous life. Is there really a place for me in that world? Of course not. I've been foolish to think otherwise.

The next morning I don't get out of bed when my alarm goes off. Instead I just lie there, underneath a thick blanket of emptiness. My whole being aches. My face and head feel swollen and heavy. My eyes are still sore from the night of sobbing. I'm not a worthy human being and I just want to stay here, under my covers, all day, or for the rest of my life.

I phone the shop and leave a message for Molly saying that I'm feeling under the weather, my stuffed nose helping it to sound more convincing. Afterwards, I roll in a ball and pull the duvet up over my head, blocking out the outside world.

I'm woken up by a series of thumping bangs coming from the front door. I jump out of bed, my head still pounding, and wander down in my pyjamas, yanking open the door to stop the sound. Billy is standing there wearing a beaming smile.

'A little birdie told me you were too ill to get to work today – so I thought I'd come and be your nurse. I come bearing gifts – grapes, chocolate and some Sudoku puzzle thing,' he says brightly, indicating the plastic shopping bag by his side.

I'm rendered speechless as I hopelessly try to stop tears from forming once again.

'What's happened? Are you OK?' he asks, a trace of panic in his voice.

I lift up my arms and bury my face in the crease of my elbow as I begin, once again, to sob uncontrollably.

'Hey, hey, hey!' he says softly as he walks through the door and puts his arms around me, holding me tightly. 'What's happened?'

I can't speak, the tears are still choking me.

'Come on . . . calm down, Soph,' he says, shutting the door and walking me into the living room, where he sits down with me on the sofa. Billy cradles me and rocks me gently, soothing me, my face still buried in my arms.

'I'm sorry. It's nothing. It's just . . . I think we should stop seeing each other.'

'What? Sophie, what's brought this on?'

'It's nothing.'

'Don't give me that. What has happened?'

'I read –' my chest starts heaving again, forcing me to stop.

'Soph, what did you read? Tell me,' he urges.

'C-c-comments.'

'What comments? Wait a minute! On the internet?' he asks, as he tries to get me to let him see my face. With the amount of snot and tears I've been producing he has zero chance of that! 'Never read those comments, Sophie. Do you know who writes that stuff? Sad, lonely people who have nothing better to do than sit and write crap. They don't know you and they don't realize that they're talking about real people with feelings . . . None of them would ever actually say anything to people's faces. They just hide behind their computer screens spouting nonsense.'

'But their words are true!' I blurt out as another sob comes.

'Oh, baby . . .'

'I'm not good enough for you! I'm boring. I'm nothing. I'm just stupid old fat me.'

'There's nothing of you! Stop it!'

'In a few weeks, filming is going to be over and you'll be gone. Who knows where you'll be working next. You won't want me in your life then. You'll go back to your models. On to the next girl. You won't need me.'

'Sophie, I've never been as happy as I am when I'm with you! I honestly mean it. I know we've not talked about what happens after this but I just assumed you knew how I felt. We can make this work, it doesn't matter where I am. London is my home, I'm here most of the time, anyway.'

'But what about when you go back to LA?'

'You can come with me.'

'What? Just like that? Leave everything here?'

'If you want to.'

'It's not that simple,' I moan.

'It can be. I just mean that we can make everything as easy as possible. I want you with me. So please don't let them get to you. You know the truth, Sophie. Would I be here now if I didn't care?'

'I guess not.'

'Exactly. Come on. Let me see your face,' he says, as he tries to move my arms.

'No!' I shout as I resist his pull. 'I'm covered in snot!' I confess, laughing through the tears.

'I don't care.'

'Well, I do!'

Billy's arms let go of me and I hear him walk out of the room. He returns a few seconds later with a bundle of tissues.

'Here,' he says, as he hands them over.

I lower my arms but leave one hand on my face as I reach out for the tissues with the other.

'Thank you,' I say as I sort out the mess that is my face. 'Oh God, I must look awful. You're going to want to take back everything you've said now. Quick, run while I'm still blinded by this mountain of snot.'

Billy looks at me with intent as he leans forward and kisses me.

'I'm not going anywhere, Sophie. I love you. Completely and utterly love you.'

I can't help the smile that creeps across my blotchy face as his words engulf me. Years ago I'd have run a mile at such a declaration, but right now, with Billy, those words are more than comforting – because they mirror my own feelings towards him.

When Billy arrives at my house on Sunday to pick me up for our 'date day' there's a gleaming red sports car parked in the driveway.

'Erm, what's that?' I ask as I walk out of the house and pull the door closed behind me.

'My car!'

'I thought you didn't have a car here.'

'I didn't, but I wanted to take you somewhere so I got someone to drive it down here for me.'

'It's a bit flash, isn't it?' I tease.

'An impulse buy when I was younger and more reckless.'

'I see . . . Where are you taking me?' I ask, giving him a quick kiss hello.

'London.'

'What?' I know it might sound hard to believe, as we only live just over an hour away from the capital, but I've only been up to London a handful of times and those trips were with Mum and Dad when I was younger. I remember the excitement of waiting at the train station and watching all the other trains whizzing past at great speed, making my hair fly around wildly, before eventually getting on the train to London with my jam sandwiches and Worcester-sauce-flavoured crisps. Then when we got to London we'd walk down by the river, where I'd be allowed to have an ice-cream cone, with a chocolate flake sticking out of the top. We always ended up in Trafalgar Square, which is where Dad would place me on top of one of the gigantic statues of a lion and I'd sit there feeling extremely important because I was so high up.

'Can we feed the pigeons?' I squeak with excitement.

Billy fails to stifle a laugh.

'Sadly not. It's against the law now.'

'What? Since when?' I demand, failing not to show my disappointment.

'Dunno . . . years ago.'

'Why?'

'Something to do with them pooing all over the statues and disfiguring them, I think.'

'But that's ridiculous!' One of the things I loved more than anything about our trips to London was feeding the pigeons in the square. I'd squeal and laugh as what felt like hundreds of birds gathered around me in a quest to nibble on my hands full of seeds. Once all the seeds were dispersed evenly amongst them (there'd always be one fat one trying its best to scoff the lot), I'd run through my newly gathered friends and send them flying into the air. I'd twirl around underneath them, enjoying their flight as though I was some mad pigeon queen in charge of her flock. 'Please tell me you're still allowed to sit on the lions?' I say in desperation.

'Yes . . .'

'Well, that's something, I guess.'

'. . . but there has been talk of banning that as well.'

I stare at him in disbelief as he opens the passenger door for me to climb in. I do so in the most unladylike manner, as I've never had to get into such a low car before. I make the error of deciding to get in head first for some reason and then try to work out how to get my bum, which is left sticking up in the air outside the car, inside as well. I scramble around for a few seconds until

I'm finally in the seat. I look up to find Billy watching me with a smirk on his face.

'Anyway, I wasn't planning to take you to Trafalgar Square. I want to take you to my flat, to show you where I live.'

'Ah . . . so it's time to see the bachelor pad,' I say, closing the door on him.

Billy is still laughing when he opens his door, climbs in and pulls on his seatbelt. He presses a button in the middle of the dashboard and I jump, as a massive roar suddenly comes from the engine . . . no key necessary.

An hour and a half later we've parked the car in a private underground car park, full of cars that are probably worth more than our house in Rosefont Hill, taken the lift to Billy's floor and arrived outside his London pad as he unlocks the door and gets me to walk in first.

His home is beautiful, and nothing like the bachelor pad I was expecting – there's not a hint of black leather or glass anywhere. It's huge, but homely. Dark wooden flooring, exposed brick walls and chunky toffee-coloured furniture fill the apartment and make it feel more like a luxury country cottage than a city flat.

One side of Billy's home is a complete row of enormous sash windows, letting in an abundance of light. I walk over to them, look out and see that they overlook a huge park below.

'That's Hyde Park,' says Billy, without me even having to ask.

Looking back inside the flat I notice the framed

photographs which occupy the walls, not ones of him acting or on the red carpet, showing off his accomplishments as I might have thought, but action shots of him with the same group of people, laughing and playing.

'My family,' he offers, confirming my thoughts and proving to me again how close they must all be.

I turn to face him.

'This is beautiful. It's not what I was expecting at all.'

'What did you expect?'

'Seriously? I thought it would be ultra modern with all sorts of gadgets, like clapping to turn the lights on or voice control window blinds or something. I expected to see big black leather sofas or glass tables, awards on display or at least massive photos of you in the films you've been in.'

'Wow! I didn't realize you thought I was so self-centred!' he laughs.

'No, not at all! I just . . . this is so homely.'

'I'm glad you see it like that,' he says, before he slowly takes a deep breath, exhales quickly and continues. 'Sophie, I've got some news . . .'

'Right, what's happened?' I ask, taken aback by the sudden desperation in his voice.

'You know I've been going for loads of meetings in the last few weeks?'

'Yes.'

Even though Billy's filming schedule has been erratic and busy as usual he has had the added stress of coming back into London at any given opportunity for meetings about future projects.

'Well, I've lined up my next job.'

My heart plummets at the thought of him travelling back to LA to film his next blockbuster. I knew it would happen at some point, of course I did, I just didn't want to have to deal with it so soon.

'Oh, right,' I say, trying to sound more enthusiastic than I feel.

'I didn't want to tell you about it before, because I didn't want to get your hopes up and it's meant rejigging a few other projects around, but ... well, I'm doing a play in London,' he says, his face beaming with excitement.

It takes a few seconds for the words to land and for my brain to make sense of them.

'What? You mean you're staying here?' I ask slowly, needing clarity.

'That's right! I rehearse in London for a month and then the run is for twelve weeks.'

'That's amazing!' I squeal as I leap into his arms and plant my lips onto his. The relief of him remaining close by for at least another four months overwhelms me after being so certain he'd be jetting off as soon as filming had finished. My concern over what effect Billy's leaving could have on our relationship has been niggling away at me over the past few weeks. Those worries are immediately eradicated and replaced with excitement.

'I thought you'd be pleased.'

'I really am,' I say with a grin. 'So, what's the play?'

'It's a new piece by Simon Edwards called *Dunked*, at

the Duke of York's, near Leicester Square. You've been there, right?' he says as he guides me to the sofa, where we both sit down.

'Leicester Square? I can't remember. Possibly. Is it near Trafalgar Square?'

'Is that seriously the only place in London you can remember?' he asks, causing us both to laugh. 'They have a load of premieres at the Odeon in Leicester Square,' he explains.

'Oh, I see . . . So, what's the play about?' I ask, keen to know more about the wonderful project that is keeping Billy in the country.

'Well, it's a modern piece, with a really small company – I think there's only four or five of us. It focuses on this group of strangers and how their lives intertwine without them realizing. It's quite dark, but I think that's what I need to get further away from the whole teenybopper thing.'

'Sounds interesting.'

'It should be. I've never done any stage work professionally before and, although I know there's going to be a queue of critics waiting to bash me, I hope I can prove to people that I'm not a one-trick pony, you see? I needed to do something a little bit different.'

'I can't believe you're staying!' I gush, leaning in and kissing him again.

'Well, I thought it would make things easier for us, you know? I don't need to take on jobs that are miles away, but more importantly, I don't want to. I promise I don't ever want to be far away from you, Sophie May.'

I smile at him, drinking in his declaration.

Billy's dark chocolate eyes twinkle with excitement, as he continues to talk.

'I want you with me every day, Sophie – to know that my days will be starting and ending with you in my arms. I'd love it if you moved to London and lived here with me.'

My mouth turns uncomfortably dry.

I've only ever been to London on daytrips with Mum and Dad – is it really somewhere I'd be able to call home? It's so different from the slow, leisurely pace of Rosefont Hill – so loud and busy. So big! Could I cope with that day in, day out?

Having spent my whole life there, I feel so safe and secure with what I have in Rosefont Hill – Mum, Molly, all the locals and the shop. In London I only have one thing. Billy.

I look at his hopeful face and my head starts to spin. Could I really do this?

PART TWO

9

'Tall caramel macchiato, extra hot with whipped cream,' shouts Andrezj, my new Polish boss, who, before I even have time to pick up the cup he has just placed beside me, is already shouting out the next order.

'Grande sugar-free, soya vanilla latte.'

I falter for a second, breaking down the drinks' names, before picking up both cups and placing them under the espresso machine. At Tea-on-the-Hill the drinks menu was simple – white or black coffee, cappuccino, hot chocolate or any flavour tea you wanted (it's only boiling water and adding a teabag – hardly rocket science). Here it's a different story and it's taking me a while to get my head around it – there are just so many choices!

When Billy first asked me to move to London with him I thought he was mad, we'd only known each other a few months after all, but slowly he managed to win me round, somehow keeping me calm in the process, stopping me from freaking out over how fast things were suddenly moving between us. He'd made it sound so simple; if we wanted to see each other more and wanted to give our relationship a chance, then we'd have to live together, or at least closer. It would alleviate all the stress that not seeing each other would inevitably cause in the future. And yes, I realize that to the outside world all this might seem quick; it is! But Billy's view on waiting is that if we were to hold off for a few months then we'd only be doing so for those people who might judge us along the way, so why bother? One thing I've learnt is that Billy Buskin is a hard person to say no to.

Surprisingly, Mum was really calm about the news. I wasn't quite sure how to break it to her after her earlier outburst, but Billy decided to tell her with me. Billy and Mum had struck up a nice friendship, which was largely down to him joining us on our Friday nights in together, something we all looked forward to. Billy would be the perfect gentlemen around Mum – kind, caring and attentive – but he'd also have her laughing hysterically with his funny ways. It felt good to have that joyous sound filling our home once again. Something we've not had for years. It finally feels as though a new chapter might actually be starting for us, which Mum and I are both happily embracing.

Molly, however, was a mess when I told her the news. I've never seen her so distraught and it was awful to see the woman I thought to be so strong in such a state. She cried non-stop for my last few days at Tea-on-the-Hill, and has made me promise to call her every day, without fail. I'm happily complying.

No one has been more surprised than me at the sudden change in my life – leaving everything that I know and am comfortable with in Rosefont Hill to move somewhere new, where the only person I know is Billy. I didn't just drop everything carelessly and go running to

London – not quite. I had time to warn people, like Mum and Molly, and to think what would make the change easier for me. I decided that independence was key. I knew that I had to find a job, hopefully in a little boutique coffee shop or privately owned bookshop, so that I could continue to support myself and have some structure to my days. Billy hated the idea, especially as, in his own words, he can happily provide for the both of us – it was difficult to explain that the very thought of living off him and flying aimlessly through my days made me want to vomit. But he took it well, even if he didn't agree with it.

Even before moving here I started applying online for jobs, but heard nothing back. I was still searching for something by the time Billy handed over a key to his flat. Even after several weeks, not a single interesting job presented itself, meaning I had to take the first job that became available ... which is how I have come to be wearing a bright orange apron and baseball cap, with a great big commercial logo emblazoned on the front. That's right, folks, I'm now working at Coffee Matters. It's quick, it's frantic and there's hardly any satisfactory customer interaction, even though we have hundreds more visitors in an hour than we'd have had in a week back home. Therefore, it's basically the same job, minus the baking, polite chatter and any of the perks. I just have to keep reminding myself that it's a temporary measure that keeps me financially and physically independent. Obviously, I haven't told Molly about my new job. Not yet. I haven't plucked up the courage, as I know how disappointed she'll be.

'Sorry!' I say to the lady tapping her perfectly mani-cured fingernails on the counter top, letting me know that I'm taking longer than she finds acceptable to get her order to her. 'What are you waiting for?' I ask, politely, not letting her lack of patience irritate me.

She huffs and puffs out her lips in desperation.

'A grande sugar-free, soya vanilla latte?'

'Ah, righto! I'm on it,' I say as I pick up the carton of soya milk and flash her a smile. 'I'm new here, you see. It was my first day yesterday, so I'm still trying to get to grips with everything.'

'Right . . .' she says with a lack of interest, looking down to play with her watch, which immediately shuts me up and hurries me along.

Hours later, after feeling like a machine churning out drinks all day to ungrateful customers, I sigh with relief when I spot Billy outside, wearing a black trilby with dark glasses in an attempt to hide himself and blend in with the hordes of tourists on the streets. It's finally home time. I look in Andrezj's direction for confirm-ation that it's OK to go, to which I just get a nod of the head and a grunt. I grab my bag and leave.

'Ah, there you are!' Billy says, as he wraps his arms under mine and lifts me off the ground. 'So, how was it?'

'Absolutely fine!' I say, smiling, not wanting Billy to worry about me at work, especially as he wasn't keen for me to take on the job in the first place. He'd be mortified if he knew how miserable I actually was, and insist that I pack it in straight away.

'Really?'

'Absolutely! How were rehearsals?' I ask, changing the subject as I grab his hand and drag him in the direction of home. It has surprised me how close everything is in London; I always thought it was all so spread out but in actual fact, seeing as we live in the heart of the city, we can actually walk places with ease. I'm chuffed that I haven't been spending hours battling with the different tube lines and so on – I don't think I'd have been so keen on that.

Billy is now in his fourth week of rehearsals alongside Ruth Banks, James Arterton and Ben Drake. The mammoth difference between working on stage and film has alarmed him, which saw him majorly concerned last week as to whether it was something he was talented enough to do. I honestly thought he was going to walk, he was so down about the whole thing. However, after a big chat with the director he seems much more positive – apparently, Billy was experiencing some sort of 'actor's wall', which is similar to writer's block, I imagine, where nothing seemed to be working with his character. Once he knew it was common to feel crap at that point in the rehearsal process, he began feeling far more relaxed about it, making him much nicer to be around!

'Great, it's all starting to make sense at last.'

'That's good!'

'I'm quite looking forward to putting it in front of an audience now and seeing what they make of it.'

'There's not long to go!'

'Less than a week.'

'Blimey.'

'So, what shall we have for dinner tonight, Miss May?'

I'm about to answer when a guy with a huge camera jumps out twenty yards in front of us and starts snapping away in our direction. Billy's hand tightens around mine as we both slow our walking hesitantly, unsure what to do or which direction to turn in. I can feel my eyes widen as I make sense of the situation. He is a paparazzo and we're in the process of being papped.

I'm in my Coffee Matters uniform.

Before I can protest or even break into a smile to make light of the situation, the middle-aged man, wearing ripped jeans, scruffy trainers and a creased t-shirt, jumps on top of the motorbike sitting next to him and speeds off, leaving us to just stare after him.

'Shit!' I blurt out as Billy just turns to me, looking stunned. I hastily pull off my apron and cap. 'Why didn't I take these off before I left work? I was still in my apron, for God's sake! I look like the world's biggest loser!'

'No, you don't!'

I don't say anything, I just raise my eyebrows at him, letting him know that I know he is spouting rubbish. I look a state – this is far worse than being caught with some flour on my face.

'Seriously, Soph, you look cute. Anyway, they probably won't even use those pictures, they'll just end up clogging up the bloke's computer memory, forcing him to delete them,' he claims with a shrug.

'Billy, your girlfriend works in Coffee Matters . . .' I

explain to him slowly. 'As if that won't be turned into some sort of story? They're going to have a field day with that!'

Billy looks down at the floor and bites his lip. I knew he didn't want me to take the job on, probably for this exact reason, and he just didn't know how to say it without offending me or sounding snobby. Therefore, it's unfair of me to make him feel bad for something that is clearly not his fault.

I pull him to me and bury my head in his chest.

'I'm sorry. It's not your fault,' I say.

'Baby, you don't need to work!'

'Shush you. I do,' I say, as I pull his face towards mine for a kiss.

'But baby, it's not what you want to do. At least let me take care of you until something better comes along,' he pleads.

'I wouldn't dream of it!' I say, pulling away from him and tugging at his arm so that we can continue walking home. 'The hilarious thing is, of course, that Andrezj specifically said that staff are not permitted to take aprons or caps home with them . . . that'll teach me!'

The next morning when I leave for work I grab my mobile phone (something I've been using more than ever now that I've moved to London – it's my lifeline to my old life) and find I have five missed calls from Molly at the shop and one from Mum. I unlock it by swiping my finger across the screen and listen to the voicemails Molly and Mum have left.

Molly's is short and to the point. 'Orange doesn't suit you. That is all,' she says tartly, before hanging up.

Mum's message explains Molly's outburst, although, needless to say, I already know what she was referring to. 'Soph, just a little warning, Mr Tucker took the papers up to Molly this morning because you're in a couple. Don't think she was impressed with the whole Coffee Matters thing . . . I thought you were going to tell her? Anyway, don't worry too much about it. I think she's just still a bit down about you going. Plus she said the new girl Sally is useless. Give her a call. Speak to you later. Love to Billy. Love you. Bye!'

I decide to bite the bullet and call Molly straight back, knowing the longer I leave it the more agitated she'll get.

'Hello, Tea-on-the-Hill, how may I help?' says a voice I don't recognize, who I decide must be the Sally Mum mentioned.

'Hello, is Molly there, please?'

'Yep, can I ask who's calling?' she squeaks.

'It's Sophie.'

'Ohhh. I seeeee,' she says, elongating the words, letting me know she's aware of who I am. I wonder what Molly has told her about me. 'How are you finding London? Full of glitz and glamour?'

'Erm . . . yeah, it's great. Sorry, is Molly there?'

'Sure,' she sighs, seemingly deflated.

Molly is on the phone within seconds.

'Coffee Matters?' she squeaks. 'Coffee-blooming-Matters?'

I know I shouldn't, but I can't help but laugh.

'I know, Molly, but it's not forever. I tried all sorts of places, but nobody had any jobs going.'

'There must have been something else,' she insists.

'Honestly, Molly, do you think I'd voluntarily work there if I had any other option?'

There's silence from Molly on the other end. I know she won't stay mad at me, but she'll still want me to know that she's disappointed with the fact that I've left her wonderful, homely boutique of a teashop to work in what she sees as a heartless corporation which churns out loveless products.

'Is it as awful as I imagine?' she finally asks in a sympathetic tone, taking me by surprise.

'Far worse. No one cracks a smile and the only words exchanged are orders or complaints.'

'Complaints? Who's complaining about you, dear? Did I not spend eight years teaching you everything I know?' she says, stunned, making me laugh.

'There's just so much choice. Plus everyone is in such a rush.'

'Well, it's to be expected I guess, everyone just wants their early morning fix. They don't have the luxury of time.'

'Exactly, they aren't there to make friends and they've got places to be.'

'More fool them, then.'

'Yep.'

'I didn't mean it, you know,' she says suddenly.

'Mean what?'

'About orange not suiting you . . . you look lovely in the pictures. Tired, but lovely.' Typical Molly, I think, honest but fair.

Walking into work that day I'm asked thousands of questions by my colleagues thanks to the pictures in the papers. I think they all received quite a shock when they opened their *Metro* newspapers on the way into work this morning and saw the new girl's face inside. Therefore, I've abruptly gone from the new-girl-who-no-one-wanted-to-talk-to to the most-fascinating-person-who-ever-existed. It's alarming to see the change in them.

Surprisingly, Andrezj is the most intrigued by the situation and keeps firing questions at me throughout the day, regularly getting disgruntled with my answers as he starts to realize I'm still the extremely normal girl who he employed a few days ago.

'Your boyfriend is God, though, so why are you here?' he asks, in his thick Polish accent, while helping me to gather up dirty mugs from the tables (it was a one-person job yesterday, but suddenly requires two people now I've awoken their interest in me).

'Because . . .'

'Yes?'

'I want my independence.'

He tuts and rolls his eyes, wiping his long brown hair out of his face.

'What?' I ask.

Although part of me is cautious about what I say because he is a stranger, who hardly spoke to me before knowing about Billy, I still enjoy the feeling of talking to someone new, which, given my history, is a miracle. It's as though being with Billy has given me a topic I feel comfortable talking about; perhaps it has given me something to hide my own shortcomings behind, making me feel more confident.

'If it was me, I would be living the role – I'd get driven around in style by his chauffeur, and I'd buy everything from Harrods – even my weekly shop. I'd be off getting haircuts, facials and manicures all the time, getting ready for all the dinners and parties with his famous friends,' he says, snapping his fingers through the air with flamboyant flare. 'I'd be making the most of it, not picking up people's dirty tissues and chewed-up leftovers. That is not independence. It's stupidity.'

'I just don't see it like that, plus, Billy doesn't lead that kind of life. He's honestly as normal as I am – he just has a far more interesting job.'

'You can say that again.'

'I don't want to have to ask someone for money every time I do something.'

'Get him to give you an allowance, then.'

I stare at Andrezj in shock.

'I'd never do that!'

'Then you're foolish,' he insists, in such a matter-of-fact tone it makes me giggle. 'When I finally meet a rich man and get swept off my feet, I'll be out of here within seconds. Now, go grab the mop and give the toilets a quick wash.'

10

Over the next week I barely see Billy as the previews of his show start. Previews are when members of the public can buy discounted tickets to an unfinished show, while the actors try out new ideas and discover what works and, more importantly, what doesn't work within the piece. Each day the actors go in and are given notes from the director about the previous show and rehearse new changes before the next preview that evening. It's tough work and keeps Billy away from home all day and most of the night. I clearly hadn't thought my working hours at Coffee Matters through properly as we see hardly anything of each other. However, I always wait up for him to come home in the evenings so that we can spend a bit of quality time together – even if it is just half an hour.

The four or five hours spent in my own company at the flat drift by in a slow and painful manner as I try to find little tasks to do to keep my brain occupied. Reading and baking have continued to be the two things that successfully make the time go quicker, aside from speaking on the phone to Mum or Molly. Each night I whisk together a little treat for us to nibble on when Billy walks through the door. Sometimes it's a cheesecake, other times it's a batch of cupcakes . . . anything that tickles my fancy. I love it. The time spent mixing, concocting and whipping make me realize how much I miss this part of my old job. And the smell . . . wow! I love filling the flat with that homeliness that comes from home baking.

Tonight I have baked us a mini Victoria sponge, his favourite, which is sitting, perfectly dusted with icing sugar, on a cake stand in the middle of the kitchen table, ready for when he comes through the door.

'Hello, baby! That smells delicious!' he chimes from the hallway as he closes the front door behind him and walks into the kitchen, taking me into his arms.

'Why thank you, mister! Want a tea?' I offer as I pull away and make for the kettle.

'Actually, I'm going to have a brandy,' he says as he releases me and reaches for the drinks cabinet. 'It's been all I could think about on the walk home! Something to help me unwind.'

'OK,' I say, cutting two healthy slices of cake for us and putting them on plates.

'Are you going to have one with me?'

'No. Not when I've got to be up so early,' I say, taking the plates and snuggling into him on the sofa once he's poured his drink. 'So, how was tonight?'

'Bit of a quiet audience,' he says, screwing up his nose. 'It freaked me out because it's not what we've been used to, but they went berserk at the curtain call, so they must've loved it.'

'Well, that sounds good.'

'Yeah, just different,' he says, stuffing a piece of cake into his mouth. 'Probably best actually, Press Night audiences are notoriously bizarre with critics sitting in silence and friends and family getting into it, so it's good to have something like that before tomorrow.'

From what Billy's told me, Press Night is the most important night in a play's run. It's the night when critics, journalists and important people from the industry go to watch, and then tell the world what they think. It's seen as the play's official opening and so carries a huge amount of importance and pressure.

'How are you feeling about it?'

'I'm excited to have you there,' he says with a smile as he grabs one of my hands, giving it a squeeze.

'I'm looking forward to it!'

'Paul's going to be looking out for you when you get there,' he informs me.

Paul is Billy's manager, who I haven't met yet, but have heard a fair bit about. The two times Billy and I have been splashed across the tabloids Paul has been straight on the phone to Billy for more details of what's going on and to keep the journalists at bay. From what I can make out, Billy owes a lot of his success to Paul's tough negotiations and pool of wealthy contacts. Knowing he is such an important figure in Billy's life has left me nervous about meeting him.

'He's looking forward to spending a bit of time with you, I think … see what the fuss is about,' he adds, smiling. 'You're sat together, which is good. At least you won't be on your own.'

'Great. It'll be good to meet him at last.'

The next night I turn up at the theatre wearing the most glamorous dress in my wardrobe – a little black number with gorgeous red flowers printed all over it which hangs a couple of inches above my knee, opaque black tights and black patent stiletto heels – not killer heels, mind, just something to give me a bit of height and grace on Billy's important night. I did think about wearing something higher, especially as I know Billy's usual girlfriends wear tower-like heels, but I'm a nervous wreck as it is in this completely alien environment. God knows how I'd cope if I had to concentrate on not tripping over my own feet all night as well. So I've played it safe, choosing comfort and control over a broken ankle.

I walk down the tiny strip of red carpet that has been placed outside the theatre, and straight past the cameramen who are waiting for newsworthy people to arrive. Without Billy, people have no idea who I am and my picture is worthless, clearly, and rightly so as I am in fact a 'nobody'. A notion I've always been happy with.

Anxiety and fear of the unknown make my insides bubble in apprehension. I wipe the palms of my hands casually down my dress, trying to rid them of the sweat that has formulated, but they stay clammy, refusing to dry out.

With only twenty minutes to go until the show starts

I stand in the foyer waiting for Paul to arrive. My eyes scan the room, taking in the glamorous people arriving, wondering who's who. A lot of them seem to know each other as flamboyant greetings are exchanged and air kisses are being given everywhere I look.

I start to feel paranoid when a few girls walking by stare at me a bit longer than I find comfortable before turning to each other and whispering. They're younger than the majority of the gathered crowd and not your typical-looking theatregoers, so I assume they're fans of Billy. Feeling flustered, I bury my head in my programme in an attempt to hide myself. Out of nowhere the horrible comments on the website spring to mind – I wonder if any of them were behind the cruel remarks? As the thought occurs to me the girls continue to walk past. I breathe a sigh of relief.

'Sophie?' asks a man's voice a few minutes later. Standing before me is a man wearing a grey suit, white shirt and salmon tie, his blond hair gelled to the side in a sleek and tidy fashion, his green eyes piercing. He is groomed to perfection and looking at me with a tight and unconvincing smile.

'Paul?' I question.

He sticks out a hand for me to shake, which feels like a terribly formal greeting after spotting the air kisses that have been flying around the room since I arrived.

'Great to meet you at last after hearing so much about you from Billy,' he says.

'Likewise. It's good to –'

'Shall we go in?' he asks, interrupting me as he hands

me a ticket and starts to wander off into the auditorium. 'It's about to start, after all,' he adds, slightly turning back in my direction with another forced smile.

Shocked at being cut off so abruptly I follow in silence. Perhaps he didn't mean it – the show is about to start, after all. I'm sure the pleasantries will come later.

Paul leads us to our seats, squeezing past all those who have already made themselves comfortable in theirs, although they don't seem to mind as many of them appear to know Paul and stop him for a double air kiss, a quick hello, or to tell him how excited they are to see Billy up on stage at last. Paul doesn't introduce me, and so I just linger behind him uncomfortably, trying not to squash the person who either has my bum in their face, my boobs by their head or whose bags I'm straddling uncomfortably. By the time we get into our seats there's no time for us to talk further; the house lights dim slowly as the show begins.

My hand flies up to my mouth to cover the gasp that escapes it at the sight of seeing Billy onstage with his bum fully exposed, supposedly receiving oral sex from the naked girl on her knees in front of him (who swishes her long blonde hair all over the place with enthusiasm). Luckily, the rest of the theatre erupts in giggles at seeing Billy's bum, so my gasp is hidden, although I know Paul's heard me when he leans into me and quietly says into my ear, 'I hope he warned you about that. What an unnecessary shock that would be if he hadn't.'

Quite.

Why didn't Billy think it would be a good idea to warn me beforehand? Was he scared I'd overreact? Or didn't he see how it might make me feel to see that on stage while surrounded by a room full of strangers?

I somehow manage to put Paul's comment (and the vision of the play's opening tableau) out of my mind for the rest of the show, which is not an easy feat, but I get sucked into what's happening on stage and the intricate telling of the story. It's gripping, shocking and intensely heartfelt. Billy is every inch the wonderful actor I thought he would be – I'm amazed at his believable transformation into this moody and stern character. Honestly, I'm not just saying this because I'm his girlfriend, but I completely forget that it's him up there. As the cast come out to take their bow, I, as well as the rest of the audience, leap to my feet with cheers of praise and applause. I can't help beaming with pride in Billy's direction. He is magnificent – I'm surprised anyone has ever doubted that fact.

As soon as the curtain falls for the final time (the cast had to come out for three lots of bows, thanks to the relentless applause), Paul leads us to the stage door so that we can go up to see Billy.

On our way up the stairs Paul stops and turns to me with another one of his forced smiles.

'I wouldn't be too sensitive about certain elements of the play if I were you,' he warns as he purses his lips. 'It's his big night. Let's not ruin it,' he adds before turning and continuing up the stairs.

His unhelpful words manage to unleash my briefly forgotten feelings from the start of the show, and they start to niggle at me once more, causing me to feel dishevelled as we arrive at Billy's dressing-room door.

As soon as it's opened Billy excitedly jumps towards me.

'So, what did you think?' he asks.

The smile on his face says it all, he isn't aware of how that particular scene could have affected me, which is odd because that omission goes completely against the sensitive and caring character I know him to be. However, now would be the wrong time to broach the subject.

'You were brilliant,' I admit, because, bottom and oral sex aside, he really was.

'Better than Jude?' he asks with a cheeky grin. Will he ever let me live that down?

'Much better. Honestly, you were superb!'

'Thanks baby!' he says, leaning forward and kissing me.

A small cough from Paul reminds us both of his presence and we break away from each other.

'Paul!' welcomes Billy, giving him a hug. 'I hope you've been looking after my lovely lady.'

'I certainly have,' he says, putting a hand on my shoulder and acting friendlier with me than he has done all night. 'I've got to say, great feedback out there, mate. Everyone has stopped me to tell me they thought you were terrific. Fingers crossed for those reviews, hey?'

'God, don't remind me. Actually the other guys here were saying that they prefer not to see them, you know, so that it doesn't ruin your performance, or affect it in any way with their comments. They've known people to completely change their characters following them, throwing everyone else off. They don't even want the reviews to enter the building,' he says.

'That sounds like a good idea,' I say, glad that he has decided to take this approach after seeing him so nervous about tonight and what people might think. This definitely seems a more refreshing attitude to take towards something which is, arguably, just one person's opinion.

'But it's all about the reviews for you, Bill. That's why you're here, remember, to prove your worth as an actor!' Paul says with gusto.

'Yes, but if –' I start.

'Is that the time?' interrupts Paul, looking at his watch. 'We'd better get cracking and get you to the after party, there's a lot of people there who are eager to talk to you, Bill!'

I look in Billy's direction to see him giving me an excited wink, clearly oblivious to Paul's rude behaviour towards me.

Walking to the after party, which is being held across the street from the theatre in a trendy bar, we notice there's a line of photographers waiting outside. The nerves start to kick in again at the thought of walking into that crowded room on Billy's arm, knowing I'll be scrutinized and judged. This is my first proper outing with him, the first one I'm almost prepared for (well,

I'm flourless and wearing decent clothes), and I want to make a good impression – so far people have only seen the two sets of pap pictures, they haven't seen or heard anything else about me, so it'll be nice to get pictured when I'm looking my best and show that I'm not just some dowdy tea-girl. Although I still find the whole thing daunting, I'm proud of Billy, and want to be there with him on his special night, supporting him as a girl-friend should.

'Bill,' says Paul, stopping us both. 'I think it's really important that you do these photos alone tonight, the ones inside and outside. It's got to be about you and what you've achieved. It would be foolish to let some-thing else overshadow that,' he adds, taking time to slowly look from Billy to me so that he can hammer his point home. In other words, Billy should have no pho-tos taken with me, because that is what the press will focus on, thereby distracting from the purpose of the night, which is to show Billy's worth as an actor. I understand the point, obviously, but coming from Paul it feels more than a little bit unwelcoming.

Billy turns to me with concern.

'Is that OK?' he asks.

'Of course!' I say, not wanting to cause a drama on his special night by showing that I'm uncomfortable or disappointed that it has to be this way. 'It makes sense,' I say with a shrug.

'You sure?' he asks again, cupping my face with his right hand and rubbing my cheek with his thumb.

'She said yes, you soppy fool,' says Paul, while he

playfully pushes Billy towards the party. 'Go on, get in there, Bill! It's your night. Sophie will be safe with me. We'll see you in there.'

'OK, see you in there,' says Billy as he squeezes my hand, releases it and walks in to charm the awaiting press.

We watch Billy posing for the cameras and see him laugh as people shout things out to him about his pert bottom. Paul turns to me with another fake smile.

'I'm so glad you understand, Sophie. It could be quite awkward otherwise. You see, it would be different if you had a public profile yourself, it's hard to get past something like that, but well, it's still early days and things can change in a flash. There's just no point creating such a fuss over something that could dissolve as quickly as it was formed.'

His words ring in my ears as I break them down, slowly making sense of them.

'You don't think we'll last, then?' I ask him, as I look down and fiddle with a loose bit of black thread on my dress.

'Not at all, I didn't say that,' he says, putting his hand on his chest in shock, as if my interpretation of his words is pure madness.

'But that's what you meant, though. Right?'

'Sophie, don't be silly,' he says in a patronizing tone, resting a hand on my shoulder once again. 'I just think we should take our time – this is a lot for you to take in at once. It could be quite overwhelming, that's all. There's a lot to learn.'

Yes, I think, and the number one thing I've already

learnt is to be wary of the people I meet, even if they do work for my partner.

Billy spends the next hour doing a variety of interviews with press about the play and chatting up the important thespians and critics in the room. I, unfortunately, have been stood next to Paul during that time. Luckily for me, though, instead of continuing with the conversation he started outside, he has decided to ignore me completely and has continually failed to introduce me to whoever he is talking to, causing me to linger by his side while attracting odd glances from his showbiz pals. Although it aggravates me that he is being so rude, I'm actually quite glad that I'm not being included, because now, thanks to Paul, I'm no longer in the mood to make small talk with strangers.

When Billy finally finds his way over to us, an hour or so later, he has a woman in tow, her arm looped through his. She's wearing a little black dress, which she has partnered up with leopard print heels. Her bare, toned and tanned legs seem to go on forever.

'Sophie, this is Ruth Banks from the show,' says Billy, introducing us.

'Ah!' I say, recognizing her as the blonde with the enthusiastic hair-swishing talent.

'I just wanted to come over and say hello. Plus, OMG! So sorry about the whole blow job thing . . . how awkward?' she says, putting her hands to her cheeks in mock shame, causing Billy to laugh.

'Oh . . .' I say with a smile, swiping the air with my

hand as if brushing the subject aside due to its unimportance. Clearly this isn't actually how I feel about the whole thing, but I'm not entirely sure how one should react in these circumstances. I'd rather not have her mention it at all – especially seeing as Billy hasn't referenced it in the slightest.

'Seriously, they made us do that on the first day of rehearsals as well – talk about getting to know each other quickly. I just didn't know where to look!' she giggles.

'Ruth, you're making it sound like I've actually been swinging my bits in your face,' Billy says, bemused, while shaking his head, a flicker of annoyance in his voice. 'Don't worry, I've been safely under wraps, at all times!' he says to me, as he pulls me into him and kisses my forehead.

'Aww, you guys are so cute!' squeals Ruth. 'He talks about you non-stop!'

Paul, noticing that Billy has returned (and no doubt annoyed that he has his arm around me in public on his ever-so-important night), waves his hands in the air to grab his attention.

'Bill, you must come meet Clarissa Hall from *The Times*,' he calls, beckoning him over. 'She's been dying to hear about your process of finding the character and how you've coped under the pressure.'

'Sure!' Billy says, loosening his hold of me.

'You'll be ok with Ruth for a bit, Sophie. I'll bring him back,' Paul says as he hurries Billy along.

I look at Ruth, my designated babysitter, and smile.

We don't know each other.

This is uncomfortable.

'So, what do you do then, Sophie?' she asks, tilting her head to the side as though she's genuinely intrigued.

It's the question I've been dreading, but seeing as pictures of me in my uniform have been in the papers and the majority of people in this room have probably seen them, I can't really shy away from it.

'Actually I've not been in London long.'

'Oh, right?'

'So I've just got a little job to tide me over until I find something else more permanent.'

'So where are you at the moment?' she digs.

'Coffee Matters?' I don't know why I say the name as though she'll never have heard of it before, she clearly would have. I watch as a flash of pity and disinterest flicker in her eyes, before she manages to drum up her reaction.

'Oh, how lovely,' she says, unconvincingly.

'Not really, but it'll do for now,' I smile, hoping my honesty will banish the awkwardness that now sits between us.

'So many of my friends are in the same boat, having to do jobs they hate while trying to get somewhere in life. Oh gosh,' she says suddenly, grabbing my arm and looking over my shoulder at someone behind me. 'An old friend from drama school has just walked in, I've got to go and jump on him. Do you mind?'

'Not at all!'

'Great. Back in a sec,' she beams, as she literally runs

and catapults herself onto the unsuspecting man's back with whoops of joy.

I play around with the straw in my glass and look at the people around me who are making the most of this networking event. They're all laughing and talking excitedly to one another whilst occasionally giving quizzical glances at the girl in the corner, who is standing on her own.

Me.

Later that night, after hours of watching Billy circulate the room with Paul eagerly placed by his side, we both climb into bed. A small slice of light coming from the hallway illuminates the room gently, enabling us to see the room and each other. After a minute of silence Billy turns to me and runs his fingers through my hair.

'Did you really enjoy the show, baby?'

'I thought you were great, honey . . .' I say, putting on another smile and looking at him briefly before gazing back at the ceiling.

'But?' he says slowly.

I sigh. I'm acutely aware that I either let the whole thing slide by, not wanting to cause a problem, or I just say what's on my mind so that I can get reassurance of some kind that I'll be kept in the loop in future. As I'd rather not get the shock of my life again in a crowded room, I decide to be honest.

'Well . . . I wish you'd have warned me about certain moments.'

'Oh . . .' He stops fiddling with my hair and sits

up, leaning on his elbow. 'I said it was dark and dirty, didn't I?'

'I don't think you said dirty, but either way, it just would've been nice to know that you were about to expose your butt to the world,' I explain. 'And that you'd have someone so close to your bits pretending to, you know . . .' I continue, not able to look him in the eye.

We lay in silence for a few moments.

'You know Ruth never actually saw anything, right?' he says, rubbing his thumb along my cheek and chin, trying to soothe my thoughts with his actions as well as his words.

'Right . . .'

'Seriously, I think she was just feeling awkward about the whole conversation and just blurted stuff out. It's not easy doing scenes like that and then meeting people's other halves. Honestly, I've had my trousers on the whole way through rehearsals, it wasn't until we got in to the theatre for tech rehearsals that I actually had to pull them down and, to be honest, I was more concerned with getting my butt out and whether the audience could see the G-string up my crack – which I have to say was not very comfortable.'

'Lovely!' I say, at the grim image, although it's good to know he was properly covered up, of course. 'How do you even rehearse something like that? I mean, you must need to get into it or something. It must get you . . . excited.'

'Baby, I'm acting,' he says matter-of-factly. 'Plus, even

in rehearsals we had the director with us and all sorts, so I was always concerned about making it look right and standing at the correct angle or whatever. It's professional and it's just work. I'm not stupid enough to think what's happening at work crosses over into real life.'

'But yet you have dated your co-stars,' I blurt.

'What?' he says, pulling away from me as though my words have literally punched him backwards.

'Well, obviously at some point with them it became a reality . . .' I say meekly, instantly regretting having said anything about his past. I hadn't even thought of this earlier, so have no idea where the concern has come from.

'That was completely different,' he says dryly, looking away from me.

We sit in silence, unsure how to correct what's been said and erase the negativity between us, which has never been there before.

'I'm sorry . . .' I start.

'No, you've got nothing to be sorry for,' he says turning back to me slowly. 'I was single then, Soph. Everything was different back then. But baby, I'd never do anything to hurt you. You must know that?' His arms engulf me, making me feel safe once more.

'It was just strange for me, you know?' I explain. 'I'm not used to any of this.'

'I know. I should've told you what was happening right from the start,' he says with a pained sigh. 'I knew it.'

'Why didn't you, then?'

'I thought about it, I mentioned it to Paul.'

'And what did he say to do?' I ask.

'He said it was best not to worry you unnecessarily. That I'd make you think it was worse than it actually was.'

How interesting that Paul had queried the fact that Billy had chosen not to say anything about it, when he'd specifically told Billy not to tell me.

'I see . . .'

'How was it with Paul, by the way?'

'Fine. I'm not sure he likes me very much though.'

'Really? I'm sure he does. It was just a stressful situation tonight, lots of schmoozing to be getting on with. He was probably just preoccupied. I'm sure you two will get on like a house on fire soon enough.'

'Maybe,' I say, deciding not to tell him about the conversation outside and Paul's flippant behaviour towards me. Perhaps Billy's right and it was just a tense night for him, his keenness to get it right leading him to act bizarrely. Maybe . . .

11

Molly calls me on my way to work the next day, for her daily catch-up. I can't help but feel sorry for June Hearne as I've obviously pinched her early-morning gossip slot, although I have no doubt that Molly will be straight on the phone to her telling her anything interesting I've said, so it probably makes their calls more exciting.

'So, what was it like to see him up on stage?' she asks.

'Amazing! Honestly, Molly, I've never seen anything like it! The whole production was incredible.'

'Better than the local amateur dramatic group then?'

'Just slightly,' I laugh. 'There were some rather interesting parts, though . . .'

'Interesting?' she queries.

'Yeah.'

'That doesn't sound good.'

'No, it was fine, I just got to see a bit more of him than I thought I would.'

'Oh . . .' Molly says stunned.

'Just his bottom!' I say, feeling the need to clarify in case Molly starts telling the world that Billy got his willy out on stage.

'Oh, is that all? I thought you meant the front bit. Well, I wouldn't mind seeing that.'

'Molly!' I laugh.

'I meant the play . . . obviously!' she cackles. 'I can close my eyes for that bit if you like, although think before you ruin an old girl's little bit of fun. Anyway, how was the rest of the night?'

'Yeah, fine.'

'What were the people like?'

'Pleasant enough. I mean – everyone knows everyone.'

'Did you feel a bit out of the loop?'

'How'd you guess?' I laugh. 'It's all so cliquey.'

'Oh yes, but that'll change in time. They don't know you yet, duck.'

'I met his manager too.'

'What was he like?'

'I don't think he likes me.'

'Really?'

'Yeah, he's just a bit cold towards me. As though he's worried I'm going to corrupt his top act or something.'

'You? Corrupt him?' Molly cackles.

'I know!'

'I'm sure he meant nothing by it though, love. Billy's been with him quite a while, so he can't be that bad. Maybe he's just wary of new people. It's a tough business – just see how it goes, duck!'

'Yeah. I might have read a bit too much into it,' I say, wondering if that could actually be a possibility and if he's woken up this morning regretting his harsh words. 'I know it's stupid, but it also irritates me that he calls Billy Bill. It's not his blooming name and it sounds so . . . pompous!'

This causes Molly to laugh her head off as though I've gone mad.

I think about mentioning some of Paul's rude comments from before the party, but decide against it. It could be that he is just wary of people's intentions when they get close to Billy and is looking out for him. I'll give Paul another chance, I think.

That night, while I'm in the kitchen loading raspberries on top of a freshly made Pavlova, waiting for Billy to come through the door after the show, the phone rings.

'Hello?'

'Sophie!' booms Billy's voice.

'Hey! Where are you?' I ask.

'The guys suggested going out for a drink. You know, so that we can chill out together now that Press Night's out of the way.'

'Oh . . .' I say, looking disdainfully at the fruitful Pavlova in front of me that will no doubt go to waste now. 'That sounds like a nice idea.'

'Well, we've seen a few of the reviews and you'll never guess what – we've mostly been given five blooming stars!'

'Wow! Congratulations,' I cheer. 'But I thought you told Paul you weren't going to look at them,' I say, slightly agitated that Paul's won in some way.

'We weren't, but Ben's mum phoned him up when we were getting ready to go on stage. She was all excited, we could actually hear her squealing down the phone. Once we knew it was good news, we decided we might as well actually read them, so we looked a few up online. They're brilliant! That's another reason why we thought we should go out, so that we could celebrate the good news.'

'What did they say, then?'

'Basically, that they all loved the play and found it exciting, thrilling and sexy. Ooh, one said that I was a pleasant surprise and that the only disappointing thing was that I hadn't made the move to theatre sooner,' he says, proudly.

'Well, that's amazing! Congratulations,' I say. 'No wonder you want to celebrate!'

'Come out!' he asks suddenly.

'What?' I laugh, looking down at my purple pyjamas covered in little cartoon penguins.

'Come join us.'

'Oh, honey . . .' I hesitate, contemplating the idea. Should I run and change my clothes, put on a bit of make-up and meet him? Obviously, it would be nice to spend some time with him outside of the flat, and great to meet the cast properly after only speaking to them briefly last night as we were leaving, but I have work tomorrow. Plus, I've never been good at being spontaneous. If he'd asked me earlier, even in the show's interval, then I might have been tempted, but the thought of changing my plans suddenly makes me inexplicably nervous. 'Sorry, Billy, but I'm ready for bed.'

'Come in your pjs! You look cute in them!'

'Nah . . .' I respond, making up my mind. 'But thank

you. You just have fun with everyone. I've got to be up at seven for work, anyway.'

'Are you sure? I promise I won't be long. We'll probably only have a drink or two. I think everyone is still shattered from last night.'

'That's OK. I'll see you when you get in.'

When I put the phone down after saying goodbye, the flat feels emptier and quieter than before. I stand there rooted to the spot for a short time, feeling lost and unsure of what to do with myself. I don't feel like watching television or reading a book. I don't feel like doing anything. I feel deflated. I feel empty.

I look about the flat, at the objects that surround me. It's all pretty much still Billy's stuff, all placed where it was when I first came to visit. I did bring a few objects with me when I moved here, a reading lamp, a pile of books and a couple of photos, but I didn't want to intrude on Billy's space. I know that's silly, seeing as we were moving in together, but I simply didn't want to start moving his belongings aside to make space for mine. I didn't want it to look like I was taking over.

Billy did urge me to, though. He wanted it to feel like my home too, and not just somewhere I was staying. He thought it would help me to feel more settled here. Looking around the room now, I wish I had listened to him. Although would objects make me feel any better? I'm not sure even seeing my beloved Mr Blobby cuddly toy would be able to help muster a smile right now.

I put a glass cake dome on top of the Pavlova and leave it out on the side for Billy to see when he gets home. No doubt he'll have a slice before coming to bed. I pour myself a glass of water and go to the bedroom where I climb under the sheets and close my eyes, ignoring the loneliness that niggles away at my heart.

I'm woken by the sound of laughter. Loud. High-pitched. Laughter. Dragging me away from my dreams.

I open my eyes a smidgen, and take in the darkness of the room. It's late.

A mixture of voices starts to echo its way down the hallway and into the bedroom. Several people, all talking over each over in joyous animated tones.

What is going on?

Who are all these people that have interrupted my sleep?

Why are they here?

My sleepy mind can't quite cope with the unexpected commotion and is slow to piece together an explanation.

Billy.

He has decided to bring people back to the flat.

Why would he do that when I told him I needed to be up early in the morning? I roll over to find out the time; it's two in the morning. What is Billy playing at?

The bedroom door slowly opens, letting in bright light from the hallway, irritating me further. For some reason Billy decides to crawl on his hands and knees across the room, on to the bed and up to my face.

'What are you doing?' he asks in a childlike whisper – clearly having decided to have a few more than the one or two drinks he had promised.

'Sleeping!' I say, hoping my dull tone conveys the fact that I'm not impressed.

'Ha! No you're not!'

'Billy? What's going on?' I plead, wishing I was still asleep as my face refuses to relax its groggy frown.

'Oh, baby! You said you didn't want to come out so I thought I'd bring the party home. Now you can stay in your pyjamas!'

'But I have to be up in a few hours.'

'So?'

'So? So, Billy, I need to sleep!'

'But it's only Coffee Matters!'

I know he is right. I know that my job in blooming Coffee Matters isn't the best job out there, but nevertheless his words bother me. Why should my job be any less important than his?

'Come ooooooooooon . . .' he begs, tugging at my arm to try and get me to go with him.

'Billy, I said no!' I snap as I yank my arm back and tuck it under the covers.

'But you're being so boring! I just want us to have fun. Why won't you let us have fun together?'

I don't reply. Instead, I close my eyes and clamp my jaw shut, trying to block out his drunken words.

'Right. Don't worry about it!' he grumbles as he rolls off the bed and walks out of the door, leaving it wide open.

Have I gone mad? Is this a lovely thing for Billy to do so that I can join in the group? Or is it just selfish and inconsiderate when he knows I need to sleep? But then it is Billy's flat. I can't exactly moan about it and start imposing rules on the place. . . can I?

Judging by the sounds coming from the other room, Billy hasn't decided to ask everybody to leave. Instead, I listen to them all laughing, talking and singing, not caring that there's a person trying to sleep in the next room.

I lie there for a while, trying to block them out, but it's no good. I can't sleep knowing that there are other people in the flat – especially as they probably know I'm here and choosing to stay in the bedroom instead of going to see them.

Argh!

I climb out of bed, glance at my face in the mirror to check it isn't too horrific and puffy from being asleep, and make my way into the lounge.

Billy and four others are sprawled out across the sofas – their arms and legs draping all over each other like some sort of Renaissance painting. I recognize them all from the show. On one sofa James, tall and blond with the face of an angel, has a wine glass resting on his knee while he leans back against Ben, built like an athlete and with the poshest voice I've ever heard. Ben has his legs up across Fiona, the youngest of the group, who puffs away on a cigarette while wolfing down a huge helping of the raspberry Pavlova I'd left out on the side. I'm not sure which of her two activities I'm more annoyed at.

On the sofa opposite them is Ruth, the blonde girl who swishes her head in front of Billy's manhood at the start of *Dunked*. She has her head on Billy's lap, while he has his arm resting along her body and his hand placed on her thigh. Their closeness makes me inwardly squirm and feel uncomfortable. They look like a couple. I have a sudden urge to drag Billy back to the bedroom and ask him what he thinks he is playing at, but I don't. There are people here. I don't want to make a scene and appear like a bunny boiler of a girlfriend.

'Hey . . .' James says, noticing me, and causing them all to look in my direction.

Nobody jumps up to rearrange themselves – they all stay in their comfortable positions, as though there is nothing wrong or inappropriate with the affectionate way they're sitting. Perhaps there isn't. Maybe my awkwardness at it says less about them and their theatrical chummy ways and more about me and my inability to be so free and open.

Billy looks at me with a beaming smile – full of innocence, 'You decided to join us!'

'We didn't wake you, did we?' asks Ruth, rolling over and placing her hand on Billy's knee as she does so.

'Well –' I start.

'This cake is delicious!' squeals Fiona, stuffing in another mouthful. 'Honestly, I don't think I've ever had anything so tasty before in my life!'

I smile back at her. She might've eaten something I hadn't intended for her – but at least she's enjoying it.

I stand there with them all looking at me, not quite

sure what to do or say. Should I go over and lounge on the sofas with them all – perhaps cuddle up to James or Ben? Shuddering at the very thought of it, I do what I know best.

'Can I get anyone a drink? Tea? Coffee? Something to eat?'

12

Going out after the show becomes a regular occurrence for Billy and his cast mates, and one that is usually spontaneous. Being up on stage in front of a live audience gives him such a buzz he needs time to wind down afterwards before coming home to sleep.

The majority of the time he just stays for one or two drinks with the cast, or has a late dinner with Paul if he's been in to see the show with some bigwig casting director/producer/director, and comes straight home, rolling in at around midnight. But there are also nights when the party continues back at someone's house and he doesn't get home until a ridiculous time in the morning. I'm thankful that Billy hasn't invited everyone back to ours again, but nights like this are sleepless and restless ones nonetheless. Most of the time he calls and texts to let me know his plans, but sometimes he gets carried away and forgets. On those nights, I lie awake and wonder where he is, what he's up to and when he is going to come home.

Who he might be out with is the thing that worries me the most. Is he just out with Paul or the boys from the cast? Or is he with the whole cast and being overly affectionate with Ruth again? Or, and this is the thought that niggles at me the most, is he being propositioned by random girls? In London it's impossible to forget that Billy is such a heart-throb – he can rarely go anywhere unnoticed. I regularly witness the reaction from girls as they recognize Billy on the street. Their eyes light up and are instantly filled with desire – even if he has his arms wrapped around me, his girlfriend. I know, without doubt, that there are a whole bunch of women (and men) who would happily throw themselves at Billy if they had the chance. The thought of it happening while I'm sitting at home waiting for him makes me feel anxious and sick.

Sometimes, when I can feel myself starting to panic, I call or text him. Just once or twice, not the millions of times I'd like to try until he picks up. Although saying that, he usually picks up or replies straight away, immediately eliminating any fear that was mounting in me – making me feel silly for being dubious of the situation.

I don't join Billy on his nights out and am asleep (or pretending to sleep) by the time he decides to venture home. Even though we have a brief chat before I leave for work in the mornings, he is usually in bed, and occasionally still has his eyes closed, eager to fall back to sleep as soon as I leave. The conversation is hardly riveting and extremely one-sided.

One thing that Billy has started doing is meeting me after I finish work so that we can go out for dinner together – a quick bite to eat with a catch-up before he rushes off to the theatre for another show.

The evenings remain difficult. Those hours where I

feel lost in an unknown place. I become agitated and uncomfortable, unsure what to do with myself before it's a reasonable time to go to bed. I potter about aimlessly beforehand.

I've even stopped making cakes every night for us to munch on when Billy gets in – there's no point if he isn't coming home to actually eat them with me. Occasionally, I do make a batch of cakes for him to take in to share with the rest of the cast and crew – which I know Fiona (the raspberry Pavlova scoffer) enjoys. But that's it.

I won't lie, I find it all quite depressing and feel we'd have spent more quality time together if I hadn't made the move to London after all. I see less of him now that I've changed my life to be with him than I did when I was living a contented life in Rosefont Hill.

I keep reminding myself that a snippet of time spent with each other is better than none whatsoever. But it sucks.

I can't wait for this show to finish – then I might get my boyfriend back.

Sundays are usually our one day to be together, so we usually do nothing and completely chill out. However, today we have invited Mum and Molly over, so that they can see where we live at last.

Mum used to drive when I was younger, but hasn't for years, so, rather than them having the hassle of getting on the train and changing to get on the tube and so on, Billy decided to order them a car and chauffeur for the day. I thought it was an extremely sweet gesture and I knew they'd love it. I wish I could have been there to see the looks on their faces when the baby pink limousine turned up. It was Billy's idea to get one, playing on the whole movie star thing with an added girlie flourish. We know they found it funny because they used the built-in car phone to call us in hysterics straight away. Apparently, Molly was sticking her head out of the sunroof while the car was in stationary traffic, and trying to persuade Mum to join her, much to Mum's embarrassment.

I'm wiping down the kitchen surfaces, in a last-minute attempt to make the place spotless, when they knock, so Billy greets them at the door. I smile as I overhear a mixture of laughter and hellos as Billy welcomes them in and guides them to me in the kitchen.

'Oh darling, I've missed you so much,' squeals Mum, running in to give me a big squeeze.

'Oh, isn't this lovely!' coos Molly as she walks in behind her, looking around the flat.

'You've cut your hair off!' I say in surprise, noticing her new shorter do which is standing on end following her windy limo adventure.

Molly combs her fingers through it and shakes it about wildly, making it go fluffier.

'That's right! I've always thought about it, but never done it. So I just took the scissors to it one day and watched it all drop to the floor. It was wonderfully liberating.'

We all just stare at her in shock. I'm guessing Mum didn't know that she'd given herself the chop either, as she looks just as surprised as Billy and me.

'You cut it yourself?' I ask.

'Yes . . . it looks OK, doesn't it?' she asks, turning from side to side to give us all a better view.

'Yes, of course, gorgeous as always.'

'You, on the other hand, missy!' says Molly, as she walks over to me and grabs my waist. 'Where have you disappeared to? Is he not feeding you?' she says, glaring at Billy, causing him to laugh.

'Don't blame me!' Billy says, putting his hands innocently in the air.

'I think it's not having our cakes to nibble on every day,' I say with a shrug. 'The Coffee Matters treats aren't quite as tempting.'

'I bet!' squeaks Molly. 'But you'd better start eating them – you don't want scrawny arms!'

'I have told her,' says Billy, agreeing with Molly. 'She'll end up like a matchstick if she keeps going.'

'Hardly!' I argue, rolling my eyes.

'Men like their curves, madam,' says Molly, shaking her head at me. 'If they wanted to be with someone with the body of a boy then they'd have something wrong with them in the head.'

Billy laughs at Molly's inappropriate and extremely un-politically correct comment.

'Are you eating properly, Soph?' says Mum seriously, failing to hide the concern in her voice.

It makes me uncomfortable to have them all stood

around me and fussing over something I wasn't even aware was an issue.

'Guys, I'm fine. I'm just busy at work and not eating as much blooming cake as I used to.'

All three of them just gawp at me.

'What?' I demand, annoyed that the day together has not kicked off quite as I had planned.

'It's nothing, dear,' says Mum.

'Anyway,' I say, wanting to get the attention away from myself. 'What would you like to do today?'

Both Mum and Molly shrug at me.

'OK . . . how about a walk in the park? We could feed the ducks while we're there?'

'That sounds nice, love!' chimes Mum. 'Maybe we could feed the pigeons in the square while we're here, too?'

I look at Billy, who is trying to stifle a laugh. What is it with our family's need to feed the pigeons?

A little while later, the four of us stroll through Hyde Park with the warm sunshine beaming on our backs as we dodge the children, dogs and couples who have also decided to spend the day here. Billy and Mum walk slightly ahead of Molly and me, taking it in turns to play around with the camera we've brought out with us.

I slip my arm around Molly and squeeze into her, briefly resting my head on her shoulder.

'So, tell me about my replacement.'

'What, Sally?' she asks, taking my arm and linking it through hers.

'Yes. Where did she come from? What's she like?'

'Oh, well, she just wandered in one day looking a bit clueless,' she shrugs, raising her eyebrows.

'Kind of like I did, then?'

'You could say that. She was looking at the sign I'd put up about you sadly leaving and me needing new staff. When I asked her if I could help she was a little bit tongue-tied, so I realized she must've been interested in the position.'

'I see.'

'She's been absolutely useless,' Molly says as she releases a big sigh.

'Really?' I ask, laughing, enjoying the fact that the new girl isn't perfect and that I haven't been easily forgotten.

'Honestly, bless her little heart, but cooking, baking or anything like that isn't her forte. I've had to take over the entire morning baking session through fear of her burning the place down.'

'Oh dear.'

'Yes . . . but it turns out she's actually quite good with the customers. She loves talking to them and asking lots of questions and you know all the old dears love a natter. So, as long as everyone is happy, I don't mind being in front of the oven a bit more. You're just lucky you look all happy here, otherwise I'd be dragging you back with us,' she jokes, tugging at my arm.

'So, how old is she?' I ask, still curious about the girl who has replaced me.

'You know, I don't know. I think she's about your age,' guesses Molly.

'And where has she come from?'

'I think she said something about an aunt living nearby and staying with her for a bit. Actually, I guess, other than knowing she's a rubbish cook, I don't know much about her. She's so good at getting other people to talk about themselves it seems she hasn't had a chance to tell me much about herself yet,' says Molly, laughing.

'Smile,' calls Billy, as he points the camera in our direction, causing us to squeeze into each other and grin.

'But you must have got a CV from her?' I ask, once Billy has continued his conversation with Mum.

'Nope . . . I thought I'd just give her a trial, like I did with you.'

'Right,' I say, a little confused as to why Molly wouldn't have enquired about this girl a little more, especially as she's not from the village.

'She's much more confident than I thought she was at first, mind, but, quite frankly, she's not you.'

'Aw, Mol,' I say, leaning my head on her shoulder once again and putting my arms around her.

'Anyway, petal, how are you finding life here? Is it what you thought it would be?'

'In some ways, yes, but in other ways, not so much,' I say with honesty.

'What do you mean?' she asks.

'It's just different,' I shrug. 'I don't feel like I fit in

yet . . . I get up early and go to work, go back to an empty flat and potter about until it's time to go to sleep.'

'That doesn't sound too different from your life at home.'

'I guess broken down like that it's not, but I feel like I spend so much time alone. At least at home I had you and Mum with me.'

I look up at Molly and see the concern on her face. It makes me wish I hadn't said anything.

'Oh, you don't have to worry. I'm still settling in, that's all. Getting used to the busy streets and hectic lifestyles that surround me,' I laugh, suddenly realizing it's best for me not to worry either Molly or Mum with my doubts about having moved here – they'd only be anxious for me and I'd rather not burden them with it unnecessarily. I'm sure things will be different when I've managed to get myself a better job and when Billy has finished working on the play.

'Yes, I bet there's lots to get your head around,' she nods. Molly squeezes me tight before she continues. 'I hope you're enjoying it, though, duck, and not wasting all your time and energy in a thankless job. You've got to make the most of life and not let these little opportunities pass you by. Before you know it you'll be old and wrinkly like me and wishing you'd done more. Just make sure you're happy.'

An hour later, after walking several laps around the park, we're all spread out on a couple of picnic blankets, away from all the screaming children and men playing football. Molly and Billy seem to have dozed off in the heat, but Mum and I are still awake, soaking in the day.

Sitting talking to Mum in the sunshine, I notice that there's something different about her. Her cheeks glow a warm pink, her eyes sparkle and she laughs freely, looking comfortable. She doesn't seem to be caught up in the inner turmoil that she has had for over a decade and a half. She doesn't seem so fragile. I grab the camera from my bag and take a picture without her noticing.

'You look wonderful, Mum,' I say, looking back at the image.

'Thank you. I feel wonderful,' she says, as she takes my hand and squeezes it.

We sit smiling at each other. I feel choked up at how far we've come in just a few months, after years of being helplessly stuck in a rut.

'Actually, there's something I wanted to talk to you about,' says Mum, looking down at the ground, unable to stop a flicker of concern from appearing on her face, clearly finding it difficult to share whatever is on her mind.

'What is it? Are you OK? You're not ill, are you?' I say with panic.

'No, no, no, it's nothing like that,' she says, wiggling my nose like she used to when I was younger, which causes me to grin. She pauses, takes a deep breath and smiles at me as she says, 'I've met someone.'

I can actually feel the smile slide from my face as her

words hit me and I'm overcome with numbness. She continues regardless.

'It's nothing serious. We've just been out for a couple of dinners and occasionally we sit together and read, or go for walks. You know . . . I like the company. It's been so quiet without you at home.'

'I see . . .' I say, unsure of how to process the information. The thought that Mum would one day find someone new had never even occurred to me. It makes sense obviously and I'd hate for her to grow old alone, never feeling what she did with Dad again . . . but it makes it all so final. It's a mad thought, I know. Dad hasn't been with us for over fifteen years now and it's not as if that scenario will be changing any time soon. So surely it's only fair that she has company, right? Someone to listen to her thoughts and fears? Someone to make her laugh? However stupid it might seem though, I can't get rid of the disappointment growing inside me.

'It doesn't change anything, love,' Mum reasons, the earlier joy on her face slipping away, allowing me to see a glimpse of her vulnerability once more and the hurt that has overpowered most of our lives.

I don't want that Mum back, the Mum that was unable to function. The Mum I couldn't bear to leave. I'd be a fool to voice my thoughts or show any disappointment. I'd be selfish to expect Mum to live a life of solitude after so much hurt, when for years I wished her heart would mend – that I'd get my Mum back.

'Oh, I know it doesn't. It's just . . . a shock I guess,' I manage to say. 'You deserve to have someone though, Mum,' I add with a smile. 'I mean that.'

Mum squeezes my hand, causing me to look up at her face. It makes me so happy to see that warmth in her face once again.

'We'll never forget him, you know, love. No one can take away those special memories and the love that he gave us. He'll always be here, holding us two together.'

I nod, but remain silent, wondering if I'll ever miss him any less.

'Darling, what have you told Billy about what happened?' she asks quietly, making sure Billy and Molly don't overhear.

'Nothing,' I admit with a shrug.

'Really?'

'He's known all along that it's just you and me, but he hasn't asked.'

'He's never asked about your family?'

'No. There was a point early on that I thought he would, especially as I talk about Dad being around when I was younger, but he didn't. So I haven't told him.'

'Don't you think you should?'

'It's a bit late to bring it up now, isn't it? How do I just slip that one into conversation?'

Mum doesn't say anything. She reaches for my hand and squeezes it.

I know that at some point I'll have to open up about

the most painful time in my life, but right now I'm not ready for my past to taint my present. Not when I finally have a new life away from the tragedy that has loomed over me for so long. Burdening Billy with this and seeing that look in his eyes, that sorrowful, sympathetic look, is something I'm just not ready for.

The next day, Molly and Mum's visit plays on my mind. We had a glorious day in the sunshine, just lazing around, talking and laughing, but tiny things have niggled at me since: the fact that Mum is seeing someone, that Sally is supposedly a wonder with the customers and that I have talk to Billy about Dad is, of course, a huge part of it. But that's not all. I don't feel missed. It's as though I moved to London in the hope of living this joyous life with Billy, only to spend my days being belittled by vile customers and my nights walking around an empty flat alone, whereas they're back in Rosefont Hill and seem happier than ever without me.

It's these thoughts that lead me to being flustered, butter-fingered and confused at work – much to the annoyance of Andrezj and a few dissatisfied customers.

'Er, excuse me?' says a man's voice, deep and agitated.

'Yes? How can I help, sir?' I ask politely, as I look up to see a suited businessman looking at me in disgust. He holds his plastic cup out to the side, as if it's vermin in his podgy fingers, his round face flaming red and a hive-like rash appearing on his neck.

'I asked for an iced sugar-free coffee-based mint mocha frappuccino?' he spits, elongating each word and over-pronouncing them in that special way that English people do when they think they're talking to foreigners . . . or someone stupid.

'Ye-es?' I say, not quite seeing the problem and refusing to let him rile me.

'Coffee-based?'

I smile at him, hoping that he'll soon tell me my error so that I can get on with the orders from Andrezj, which are now piling up next to me.

His flaring nostrils tell me he doesn't appreciate the smile. Far from it. Now that I've played the nice card he's even more pissed off.

'There's no coffee in it?' he spits with rage. 'It's meant to be coffee-based!' his voice gets louder and causes a wave of silence to fall over the shop. 'Honestly, is it so difficult to get a fucking coffee order right?' he barks at me.

I just stare at him, hoping that he'll hear back in his head how he has just spoken to me and apologize, but his glare gets meaner and his jaw rocks from side to side as his anger continues to increase.

'I'm sorry, sir, let me take that back and I'll make you a fresh one,' I say as I grab the cup from his hand, feeling extremely uncomfortable and exposed, aware that everyone is staring.

'That's not the point is it, little lady. You should've made the right thing from the start. You might not have a proper fucking job, sweetheart, but the rest of us do and we deserve to get what we paid for.'

'I'm sorry, but I can't help thinking you're

overreacting –' I say, trying to reason with him before getting cut off.

'What?' he booms.

'It's only a coffee . . .' I explain.

'I've heard it all now!' he says in despair, raising his arms in the air, as if calling on the gods to come and shoot me down for my insolence. 'If a doctor went into work one day and decided to give a patient a nose job instead of, I don't know, a heart transplant, he'd be sacked.'

'Well, I think that's slightly different, isn't it? Look, I've said sorry, I can't do any more than that – so, would you like another coffee or not?' I say, as I pull the lid off of the discarded cup, ready to dispose of it.

'I don't want you to say sorry, I want you to acknowledge the fact that you're a useless human being and a waste of fucking space!' he shouts.

The cold drink goes flying through the air, landing on the guy's face and suit, before I even have a chance to think about my actions. The gathering crowd of customers and staff (who decided to simply watch and not interject while I was being verbally attacked) gasp in shock.

Silence falls over the shop.

Oh crap!

A loud clap starts up from somewhere in the shop, causing a few more people to join in, adding wolf-whistles and cheers.

'I'd have done that five minutes ago!' declares a woman at the back of the queue.

'What a twat. Well done you!' shouts out a burly builder.

'Who does he think he is?' a teenager asks loudly, tutting at the businessman in disdain.

Regardless of their support, I know I'm in trouble.

While my unhappy customer wipes the creamy drink away from his face and looks down at the mess I have made of his (no doubt designer) suit, I decide enough is enough. I turn to Andrezj and give him an apologetic shrug as I whip off my apron and baseball cap, leave them on the side, grab my bag and calmly walk out of the door.

13

The journey home is quick as I battle to keep my composure, the shock and adrenaline causing my body to shake uncontrollably. As soon as I walk through the door I stop in my tracks and sob. Big fat tears spill out of me. I cry so hard my breathing becomes erratic.

Billy arrives by my side in the hallway, looking dishevelled from another night out. He doesn't say anything, he just holds me as the tears continue to fall.

'I want to go home,' I wail. 'I hate London. I want to go home!' The words get caught in my throat, making me sob harder.

When my tears start to subside Billy guides me to the kitchen and sits me down in one of the swivel chairs at the counter. In silence, he makes us both some tea, then sits in front of me and takes my hands in his.

'OK, baby. What's happened?'

'I've been an absolute idiot.'

'What? How?'

Slowly I tell him about the morning's events – the horrible man at work and the vile things he shouted at me before I lost my rag and drenched him in sloppy brown liquid.

Billy sits in silence, his mouth wide open in disbelief.

'So you just left?' he asks, a smile creeping across his lips.

'Yeah . . . I figured that I was going to get sacked anyway. There's no way Andrezj could keep me on after that, even if he wanted to.'

Fresh tears threaten to fall at the thought of it. How could I have been so reckless?

'Baby, I'm so proud of you,' Billy says, kissing the back of my hand.

'What? Why?'

'Because you stood up for yourself.'

'Hardly! I just saw red.'

'I think there's more to it than that. This guy . . . was he the only one to treat you this badly?'

'No,' I admit sheepishly, taking a gulp of my tea.

'What? Seriously, baby, if I'd known that you were being treated so badly I'd have stopped you working there. I can't believe you've not told me this stuff.'

'It's not like everything about the place was bad,' I try and reason. 'Besides, I thought something better would come along quickly. I didn't realize I'd be stuck there quite so long.'

'Why didn't you tell me, Sophie?' he asks, as a frown appears on his face.

'You've got a lot on,' I shrug.

'That's a rubbish excuse.'

'What? You've been busy with the show – I haven't wanted to bother you with my nonsense.'

'Why didn't you tell me you were so unhappy?'

'I'm not unhappy,' I lie.

'I think crying and saying you hate being in London and that you want to go home kinda constitutes being unhappy.'

'Billy . . .' I say, burying my head in my hands. 'I'm just not very good at saying I need help!'

'Why not?'

I look at his loving face and think about spilling my guts. Getting everything out there and telling him exactly what has happened to make me resist depending on others for the majority of my life.

But Billy starts to speak again before I get the chance.

'Admit it, you've hated it here, haven't you?'

'No!'

'I dragged you to London so that we can be closer, but then stay out late every night while you have a shitty job and spend your nights alone,' he pauses to let out a heavy sigh. 'I'm so sorry for being so selfish.'

'No, no, no. It's not your fault.'

'I could've made things better.'

'It's not you. I guess it's just not been what I thought it would be like. If I'm honest, I've been lonely.'

Billy stares at me, silently, allowing me to continue.

'Back at home I spent so much time on my own, but never once felt lonely. Here, even though I see hundreds more people each day, I've never felt lonelier. Sitting at home each night, I don't have a clue what to do with myself. Outside the streets are buzzing with excitement and I'm not a part of it. But you are.'

'That's why I've tried to get you to come out with me, so that you could make some friends here.'

'It's not about friends, Billy. Not really. I've never really had many of those,' I say honestly. 'It just doesn't feel like home.'

'Yet,' Billy adds.

I look up at him, his eyes big and hopeful.

'Molly said something interesting to me yesterday, about grabbing the opportunities life throws your way,' he says.

'She said something similar to me.' Perhaps, I think, she's been more tuned in to how unhappy I've been than I thought.

'Well, I think we should take that on board and not waste time doing something one of us hates . . .'

I sigh, knowing what he's about to say.

'Will you please stop being so proud and forget the idea of getting another job?' he asks.

'But –'

'Just for a little while? I've only got a couple of weeks left on the show anyway and after that, well, who knows where we'll be. But I want you in my life. Actually in it. With me.'

'It would make things easier if we actually spent time together,' I say, giving the idea some thought.

'Exactly.'

'And I do have my savings, so I could dip into those if I needed to.'

'Well, we'll see about that, shall we?' he says, raising his eyebrows at me.

Billy's always been amazed at the fact that I'd managed to raise so much simply from working in a teashop, so I know he'd hate to see me dwindle it away now.

'I just want you to realize that what's mine is yours,' he continues. 'You don't even have to ask – just take one of my cards and keep it with you.'

'No! I couldn't do that!' I protest.

'Of course you could. Seriously, we're a team. I hate the thought of me eating out at The Ivy or somewhere and you stressing over whether you can afford a sandwich from M&S. It's stupid.'

'M&S? Do you realize how much their sandwiches cost?' I ask with a laugh – Billy's understanding of money and how much things should cost are so different to mine. 'Look, it's a very nice offer but I've not had to rely on anyone else for money for a long time. There's no way I can just start now,' I explain.

'You won't be relying on me. Just take one of my cards and act like it's yours,' he pleads.

'But what would I do with all that free time?' I ask.

'Spend it with me? Or walk around London? Visit museums and do all the touristy things you've not done yet?' he says with a grin. 'Come on. Surely anything is better than working in a place where you're not valued?'

'I guess so.'

Could there be a way of this actually working without me feeling like I'm taking the mickey and sponging off Billy? Is there a way of keeping some independence and maintaining some sort of structure?

'What about if I clean and do all the washing?' I offer.

Billy raises his eyebrows at me, not sold on the idea.

'No, listen. If I do that then at least I'd feel like I'm earning my keep. I won't feel like I'm just scrounging off you.'

'So you'd rather fill up your time with cleaning and washing?'

'Billy, it's a two-bedroom flat – there honestly won't be much to do. I can do it all while you're at work. I've never understood why you had a cleaner anyway!'

'All right, then,' he finally agrees, even though he doesn't seem thrilled to do so. 'This means that at the moment we'll be together in the days, all day long . . .'

'Yep,' I say excitedly.

'And with no job to wake up for in the mornings you can come and meet me out for dinner or whatever after the show.'

'If you like!' I say, trying to hide the fact that I'm not overly keen on the idea.

'But most of the time I can come and meet you back here and we can just chill?'

'Sounds perfect!'

'You know the only reason I've not come back is because I've known you'd be asleep and I haven't wanted to wake you. You know that, right? It's never been because I haven't wanted to spend time with you,' he says earnestly.

'I know . . .'

'Promise me that if ever you feel low or unhappy you'll tell me, OK? I don't want there to be any secrets between us.'

'I promise. Actually, Billy, there's something –'

His mobile starts ringing, drawing his attention away from me as he pulls it out of his pocket.

'Ah, it's Paul. Is it ok if I get this? He left me a message earlier on but I haven't called him back yet.'

'Of course!'

Billy gives me a kiss before turning away and picking up his phone.

'Paul, mate! So sorry – I've only just got up,' he says, walking into the bedroom.

That was my chance.

I could have told him about Dad and what happened all those years ago. Explained the struggles that have turned me into the person I am today.

Argh!

Billy yelps with joy in the other room – Paul has obviously given him some good news.

The moment has now passed.

'You are not going to believe it!' Billy says, running into the lounge where I'm curled up with a battered copy of *Jane Eyre*.

'What's happened?'

'Honestly, I've never been so excited!'

'Come on! Out with it!'

'That was Paul . . .'

'Yeeeees . . .'

'Right, well, there are two bits of information actually,' Billy says, ruffling his hair and making it stand up on end like a mad person. 'OK, the first thing – I read this script a few months ago and loved it. It was this semi-biopic about a crazy rock star in the seventies – really gritty and miles away from anything I've done before.' The words are gushing out of his mouth with such enthusiasm that I can't help but beam at him as he continues. 'I really wanted to be considered to play the rock star but the producers weren't too sure about casting me in it because of *Halo*, they kept saying I was too clean for it or whatever – but Paul brought them in to see *Dunked* the other night and, well, it looks like they want me for it!'

'That's amazing!'

'I know! One look at my backside and they were gripped!' he laughs. 'The best bit is it's filming just outside of London, and so I'll be able to push for us to stay here and have a car and driver every day instead. I think that will be nicer for us.'

'That's brilliant!' I say. Pleased that he won't be leaving home on this job either. 'What's it called?'

'At the moment it's called *The Walking Beat*, but that might change.' He takes a deep breath before continuing. 'But enough about that . . . the second thing is just a little bit more exciting.'

'More exciting?' I repeat.

'Yes . . . I can't believe I'm saying this,' he says, a smile spreading across his lips.

'Go on!' I urge him as he pauses for dramatic effect.

'I've been nominated for a BAFTA award!'

'What?' I squeal.

'A bloody BAFTA! For Best Actor!'

I jump on him, screaming with excitement.

'That's incredible!' I gush.

'I know . . . I never thought this day would come. I've always been told, "Once a teen star, always a teen star," but this proves them wrong. I've been nominated for a bloody BAFTA . . . I can't believe it!'

'For *Halo*?'

'God, no! You must be joking. It's for this one I shot last year called *Twisted Drops*, all about a soldier in the First World War who gets captured by the French. Gosh, I can't believe it!'

I just sit, smiling at him, unsure what else to say.

'And I've decided I want you with me on the red carpet,' he says decisively. 'By my side. I don't want you shunted off somewhere in the corner waiting around for me. Like I said earlier, I want you with me. Next to me.'

'What? ' I say in shock. 'Are you serious?'

'Deadly.'

Paul's words on Billy's opening night start replaying in my ears. He'll hate this.

'Have you mentioned this to Paul?'

'Not yet,' he says with a shrug.

'I have a feeling he's not going be too impressed with this idea . . . it's going to be a big night for you *and* your career, Billy. It's far bigger than your Press Night and we both know that he didn't want me anywhere near you then!'

'I don't care. I want to share the night with you and I

want to show the world how beautiful the love of my life is,' he says, kissing me and pulling me close.

'You really think it's going to be that simple?'

'Of course . . . I'll talk to Paul.'

Later that day, after lounging around on the sofa for most of the morning while Billy calls his family to tell them the good news, he plucks up the courage to phone Paul and tell him that he'd like me to join him on the red carpet. Well, I say 'tell' but the pleading, whining and endless discussion that I can hear from Billy in the bedroom suggests he's having to work hard to get Paul to agree.

He is on the phone for two hours.

'All sorted,' announces Billy, when he finally walks back into the room and joins me on the sofa.

'Really?' I ask hesitantly.

Billy looks drained. I've never seen him so pale. His tone might be upbeat but the look on his face is one of deflation. I've no doubt that Paul has spent the whole conversation trying to get Billy to uninvite me.

'Look, if it's a problem I really don't mind watching from home.'

'What?'

'I'll be fine.'

'No way!' says Billy, scooping me up and sliding me onto his lap. 'I want you with me, remember?'

'And what did Paul say about that?' I prompt.

'He was fine with it,' he says with a shrug as he starts to stroke his hand along my thigh.

'Billy?'

'Well, OK . . . once he knew I wasn't going to back down he was,' he says with a cheeky grin.

'That sounds more believable.'

'It's all good, though, he gets it now. He's even offered to help you find a dress.'

'What? Why?'

The thought of traipsing around shops with Paul does not fill me with delight. Yes, I know I said that I'd be willing to give him another chance in case I was wrong about him and his condescending ways – it was an important night – but does that chance really have to occur while I'm in a heightened state of paranoia dress shopping?

'It's a special night, so you need a special dress. Paul's good with stuff like that.'

'But I've already found a dress!' I blurt.

'You have?'

'Yep. I saw a lovely dress in Warehouse a few days ago.'

Actually, this is true, it was a lovely black ruched number with a swooping cowl neckline – simple but dressier than I would normally go for.

'Baby,' he says with a chuckle as he squeezes me closer to him. 'That is exactly why I love you.'

'What is?'

'Thinking you can go to something like this wearing something from the high street.'

'Why can't I? It's what I can afford,' I say, honestly.

'Plus I don't really fancy going on a shopping trip with Paul.'

Billy cracks up with laughter.

I look at him in bemusement. 'What's so funny?'

'I wondered why you looked so confused and put out about the whole thing.'

'I don't get it.'

'Paul won't actually be taking you out shopping, there's not going to be a *Pretty Woman* moment where a snobby woman in some posh shop ridicules you for just walking in there.'

'Well, that's good,' I say, getting even more confused.

'All Paul is going to do is send an email out, or make a few calls, to a few fashion PRs and see whether they'd like to dress you for the event. They'll then send him dresses in your size to try on and wear if you want to.'

'But I don't want that . . .'

'Why not?'

'Because I won't be able to afford those clothes and I don't want you to pay for something so extravagant.'

'No, they don't send them expecting you to pay for them.'

'Huh?'

'Whatever you decide not to wear, you just send back. And usually what you do wear you get to keep – depending on the designer and whether they're tight or not. The stingier ones will ask you to send it back unwashed in case you shrink it. At least, I think that's how it works for girls.'

'So, basically, I don't have to go out to shop because all these dresses are going to come here for me to try on, and then whatever I do wear I don't have to pay a penny for?' I say, trying to get my head around this bizarre arrangement.

'That's right. The biggest question you'll be asked on the night is, "Who are you wearing?" That's why they do it. It's good publicity for them – especially if you're standing with someone who's nominated for Best Male Actor,' he says with a cocky grin.

Once Billy has left for work I jump straight on the phone to Molly, to fill her in on the news.

'Guess where I'm going!' I blurt out as soon as she picks up.

'Where? Tea with the Queen?'

'Not quite,' I laugh.

'Off to Barbados with Simon Cowell?'

'No!'

'That's a shame – he always looks like he's having so much fun on those jet skis. Where then?'

'The BAFTAs!'

'Noooooooooo!' she says in amazement. 'With all them fancy people in those nice dresses?'

'Yes!'

'That'll be lovely!'

'Annnd . . .' I tease.

'Yeees?'

'Billy's up for the best actor award!'

'No!'

'Yes!'

'Well, that's blooming exciting, isn't it, love! You must be over the moon!'

'It's all a bit bizarre!'

'How are you going to have your hair?'

'I haven't thought about that, I don't even know what I'm wearing yet, Mol.'

'I think you should have it up in that plait style you did once – was it at Christmas? I thought that looked very pretty.'

The hairstyle in question was to try and disguise a ghastly fringe I'd decided to give myself. It looked awful. A plait working its way along the top of my head was the only way I could get rid of it.

'Actually, I think someone's coming over to do all of that.'

'Really?'

'Yes, this team of people are coming over apparently, to make me look like a star,' I chuckle.

'You already are a star, love. No amount of make-up or hairspray is going to make you more so. What about a dress? Oh, there are some great sales on at the moment. I saw a lovely purple number in Monsoon the other day . . .'

'Actually, Mol,' I say, interrupting her before she runs away with herself. 'Paul's sorting it all out.'

'Paul? The manager who doesn't like you?'

'You said not to read too much into that!'

'Did I?'

I can sense that Molly is disappointed.

'Don't worry, he's just asking a few designers to send me dresses to try.'

'Why would they do that?' she asks, equally as confused by the idea as I was.

I fill her in on the dress-loaning thing, which seems even more of an alien concept now I'm saying it out loud. It lifts her mood.

'So that's how it's all done!' she says, impressed that she now has some insider knowledge into this bizarre world. 'Ooh, if anything turns up in a size fourteen and you don't have to send it back, send it my way!'

'And what would you do with a designer frock?' I ask, giggling.

'I don't know, I've never had one before . . . it can be my new uniform. Or maybe I'll get buried in it.'

'Molly!' I shriek in shock. 'Don't be so morbid.'

'Well,' she sighs. 'Oh, you'll look stunning on that red carpet, duck. I can't wait to see you on it. Is it shown live? Yes, I think it usually is! I'll have to ask your mum over to watch it with me, or maybe I could do something in the shop. That'll be nice.'

'No, Mol, don't go to all that trouble, they probably won't even show me.'

'Of course they will, you'll be with Billy!' she argues.

I give up, knowing that once Molly has an idea in her head there's no getting through to her.

'I've got some other news that you'll be pleased to hear,' I say, changing the subject.

'Yes, dear?'

'I no longer work at Coffee Matters,' I declare, feeling extremely relieved to be able to say it.

'That's brilliant!' she chimes. 'What made you decide to leave so suddenly? Yesterday you were on about sticking at it for a while longer.'

'Actually, I had to quit before they sacked me,' I admit truthfully.

'What?' Molly shrieks, enjoying the shocking news. 'What did you do?'

'I may have chucked a drink over some rude man's head.'

The laughter that booms through the phone continues for the next five minutes, causing me to break into hysterics myself. Every time we try and speak again the laughter bubbles up and we land up in a fit of giggles once more. Eventually we both give up trying and decide to talk tomorrow instead.

That night I agree to meet Billy at the theatre after the show so that the two of us can go for a celebratory dinner at J Sheekey – a place known for its posh fish and chips.

I'm standing at the stage door waiting for him to come out when Paul arrives with what can only be described as a leggy blonde. Paul is dressed in another smart suit, this time in a dark green, and his companion is in skin-tight jeans, a baggy t-shirt, a fluffy jacket and boots. On me the outfit would look like I hadn't bothered to make an effort – but on her it looks simply stunning. Her bouncy blonde waves and perfect red lips add to the glamour.

Even though I'm sure Paul has spotted me he doesn't say anything, so, rather than pretending I've not noticed him, I walk over, reminding myself that I've decided not to hold the last time we met against him.

'Paul?' I say.

He looks up at me in confusion, as though he doesn't recognize me.

'I'm S–'

'Oh my gosh, I'm so sorry. We don't usually see you here,' he says in surprise.

'No, I'm usually tucked up in bed by now,' I agree with a smile. 'We're off for dinner to celebrate.'

'How lovely.'

I *was* wrong about him, I think, as I take in his warm and friendly smile.

'Coco,' he says, turning to the woman by his side. 'This is Billy's latest girlfriend, Suzy.'

'Oh!' I say, embarrassed that he's called me by the wrong name. Should I correct him? Would that make us both feel stupid and uncomfortable? And what's with his use of the word 'latest'?

'Suzy, it's a pleasure to meet you,' Coco says in an American accent as she holds out a long slim hand to shake before leaning in for a double-cheeked kiss. I'm quite taken aback by the gesture. She is spellbinding.

Out of the corner of my eye I spot Billy walking out of the theatre with his arm draped around Ruth's shoulders. Spotting me, he says his goodbyes and gives her a kiss on the cheek before coming over. She waves to me before walking off in the opposite direction.

'Don't you look gorgeous,' Billy says as he approaches me and leans over to kiss me.

'Great show tonight, Bill!' says Paul, slapping him on the back.

'Paul, I didn't expect to see you here!'

'I'd completely forgotten that I had two tickets booked for tonight. I was going to cancel them but Coco rang to say she was in town.'

'Coco?' he says, turning to the blonde beauty. 'Coco!' He grabs her in a tight embrace. 'How long's it been?'

'Too long, darling!'

As the two of them talk about the last time they saw each other, Paul leans into me and quietly informs me, 'Billy and Coco go way back – both of their careers took off at the same time, although Coco's in modelling. I always hoped they'd hook up, it would've been headline heaven – but Billy had his own ideas.'

'Right,' I respond flatly, miffed as to why he would share this information with me.

Billy looks at his watch. 'I'm so sorry, guys, but we have a table booked for dinner at J Sheekey.'

'Leaving poor Coco so soon? Oh, I wouldn't stand for that, my dear,' Paul stirs, giving her a little nudge and causing her to pout at Billy.

Billy gives them an apologetic look and turns to me with a shrug. 'I'm sure we can get a bigger table . . .'

'Great!' beams Paul. He takes Coco by the arm and starts to guide her towards the restaurant.

'Sorry,' Billy mouths at me as we start to follow our meal-crashers along the pavement.

If at the start of the night I was in any doubt that Paul had engineered the whole evening in a bid to try and sabotage our romantic meal, I'm not now. He has somehow managed to work it so that I'm stuck next to him, in some tediously awkward conversation, while we look across the table at Billy and Coco who are engrossed in chatter about their mutual friends. All of whom I've never heard of.

'So, I'll get someone to phone or email a few places tomorrow to see about getting some dresses sent to you,' says Paul, as he dabs the side of his mouth with his napkin.

'Thank you, that's kind of you.'

'Not at all. If Billy's insistent on taking you we can't have you going in any old thing. You have to make a good impression,' he smiles tightly – the warmth disappearing slightly. 'You'll be amongst people like Coco here . . . although, saying that, she'd look good in a bin bag. Not everyone would.'

'Are you talking about me, Paul?' Coco drawls from across the table.

'Only nice things!'

She raises her eyebrows at him before turning her attention back to Billy.

'Just look at her. That face, that body, that smile. She just oozes charisma. The sort of girl anyone would be lucky to be seen with.'

He isn't directly saying anything nasty about me, in fact he hasn't referenced me at all, he is simply gushing about Coco, but it's as though he is listing all of her finer qualities to show me exactly what I lack.

'I've always been amazed by the chemistry between these two,' he continues.

'What are you saying now?' asks Billy with a tinge of irritation in his voice.

Paul flounders for a moment at being overheard.

I enjoy seeing him squirm, even if it is just for a nanosecond.

'That I can't believe you've not been cast opposite each other yet.' He says, recovering himself. 'You're a natural fit!'

'Oh, Pauly!' says Coco, blushing.

'You know me, my dears, always thinking business.'

'But you're a model, aren't you, Coco?' I ask, a bit confused.

'Yes, Suzy,' she starts, while leaning across and patting my hand.

The wrong name causes Billy to turn to me with a quizzical look.

'But I can't do that forever. Looks fade,' she says with a sad shrug.

'Not yours,' chimes in Paul.

'Oh, Pauly, you are sweet to me. No, I've just started to have a few meetings to see where that takes me,' she explains to Billy and me. 'Actually, Billy, I was almost cast opposite you in *The Walking Beat*.'

'No way!' Billy exclaims. 'That's the film I was telling you about today.' He says to me.

'Yeah, it would've been fun, but I just got word this morning that it didn't go my way. I'm bummed. I'd have loved to have played your leading lady.'

I'm secretly relieved. The thought of Billy going to work in the presence of Coco every day would be too much to bear.

'Can I interest anyone in desserts or coffees?' asks the waiter.

'Ooh ... yes please!' I start, salivating at the gorgeous gooseberry crumble on the menu.

'No thank you,' answers Paul. 'Perhaps just a pot of green tea?'

'Same for me,' echoes Coco.

'Double espresso for me,' says Billy.

They all turn to me to see what I'll order. There's no way I can order the crumble now they've all decided against one.

'Yes, a pot of fresh mint tea for me please,' I smile.

'Are you sure you don't want a dessert?' asks Billy. 'I'll share if you like?'

'No, no . . . I'm good. Thank you.'

As the waiter leaves, and Coco turns to ask Billy a question about another mutual friend, Paul leans in towards me.

'Good idea,' he whispers. 'All that fatty cream?'

Again, nothing is actually said. It seems Paul has decided to go for a new approach with me, and that's to leave the unsaid words to linger in the air suggestively.

14

It's a very surreal experience when, two weeks later, dresses of all shapes, colours and sizes get dropped off for me to try on, as well as shoes, bags, bangles, necklaces and earrings to complete the look. Paul has decided to come over and assist Billy and me in picking out the perfect ensemble. I did try and suggest I'd be more comfortable trying on the dresses alone, but neither man took the hint.

The good thing is that Paul decided to bring his PA Samantha with him to help me get in and out of the dresses with ease. I must admit that, although I wasn't keen on having her here (and seeing me in my underwear), she's been a godsend. I'd have had no idea how to put on half of these outfits without her, with all their clasps, wraps and fancy lacing – in fact, even the weight of some of them has been a struggle for us both to deal with. I'd never have coped.

Samantha hardly speaks as she changes me from one dress into another, and doesn't walk out with me when I show Billy and Paul what I'm wearing. Instead, she stays in the bedroom preparing the next outfit for me to try on and hauls the dresses around the room, which is no easy task for her tiny five-foot-one frame.

'Bill, I think this is too much,' says Paul, shaking his

197

head at the heavily beaded cream dress I'm currently wearing, as he walks around me to take in the whole vision.

At the start of the afternoon I felt self-conscious every time Paul walked around me like this, examining every detail with a frown on his face – but now, after trying on twenty or more dresses, I'm starting to get used to his scrutiny.

'But she looks perfect,' exclaims Billy.

'Oh yes, she looks great, gorgeous even, but it's too attention-grabbing,' Paul says, shaking his head at me and the dress. 'People will assume that she is purpose-fully trying to steal the limelight from you and it could backfire on her. You don't want that.'

I didn't realize picking a dress to attend some awards-show thingy would be so political – if a dress is too revealing or eye-catching then it's perceived that you're trying to pull a Liz Hurley and making it 'all about you'; if it's nothing special then you're unsupportive and a sap. You've got to strike a balance and this is obviously why Paul felt we needed his insight.

'But I want her to have the limelight. I want people to notice her,' argues Billy.

'Actually,' I say, butting in on their discussion and reminding them that I too have an opinion. 'I'm not so sure about this one. I like it, but I don't love it.'

'Well, in that case, take it off, my darling,' says Billy with a theatrical finger snap in the air, becoming more like Franck Eggelhoffer from *Father of the Bride*. 'If you "like" it you take it off and we never speak of it again. If you "love" it, you wear it!'

I laugh as I head back into the bedroom.

'It's coming off!' I shout to the men as I turn around and let Samantha unhook me from it.

I peel myself out of that tight number and turn my attention to the rails of dresses lined up in front of me, which Samantha has kept in order so that we know how far we've got. I've already tried on at least half of them, but nothing has stood out to me yet. They're all gorgeous, of course they are, but I want to wear something that keeps me looking like me, and just turns me into a glammed-up version of myself. All of these dresses dazzle on their own, but I want to be the thing that dazzles. Quite simply, I don't want the dress to overpower me.

Samantha pulls out the next one for me to try; a dark teal, strapless dress. Figure hugging to the knees, it then flicks out dramatically with a trail. It's a real statement piece. I squeeze into it and breathe in as Samantha does up the corset at the back, followed by a trail of tiny buttons leading from my shoulder blades to just below my bottom. I look at myself in the mirror, letting out a little sigh, finding the tight fit extremely over-exposing and restrictive. Even though I know I've lost weight lately, to me, my hips are my worst feature still and this dress accentuates them and draws attention to that problematic area. I notice that even Samantha is frowning at it slightly. I decide to let the judges have a look anyway and so waddle out to Billy and Paul, feeling like a mermaid gone wrong.

I've got my tongue stuck out of the side of my mouth and am frowning heavily as I concentrate on how to walk in this difficult fishtail design – it's not easy. The only way that seems to work is to flick my feet with each step, helping to move the heap of material lying on top of them. It's too much effort for someone like me who likes her comfort.

I can't help but laugh when I look up to see the men gawping at me. They look as confused as I feel.

'Gosh, we definitely don't want that face on the red carpet,' declares Paul with a mortified expression.

'Not my favourite . . .' admits Billy, although he looks pained to say anything negative.

'Yep, I agree. Awful!' I tut. 'I don't want to have to worry about how to walk in the blooming thing. I'm going to be nervous enough as it is!'

As I turn to leave I hear Paul say quietly to Billy, 'Good job. Did you realize it's quite similar to the one Coco wore to the Oscars last year – when she looked sensational? It would be horrific if people compared the two.'

Horrific for me, I think. What normal girl would want to be compared to a model, after all?

I don't bother waiting for Billy's reply. I just want to get out of this dress as quickly as possible.

I huff my way into the bedroom, ready to try on what feels like the millionth dress, to find that Samantha has the next one laid out on the floor, ready for me to step into. It's what I would call vintage pink. Not so pink that it screams at you in a sickly sweet Barbie type of way, instantly making you look like a three-year-old – it's more subtle than that and less garish against my skin tone. The actual design is floaty and free, with one piece of fabric going over one shoulder, leaving the other shoulder bare. It's fitted at the waist – without the need of a corset – and then has multiple layers of fabric in various lengths making up the lower half of the dress, like waves, making it free and whimsical. It's stunning, elegant and feminine and makes me feel like a princess the moment I slide into it.

Before walking out to show it off to Billy and the dragon that is Paul, Samantha stops me and hands me a pair of light grey shoes from a box beside her. Surprisingly, they don't look too high, and, once she's helped me into them, they're comfortable enough to make me think I might get away with staying upright in them. Looking at the complete ensemble in the mirror I can't help but smile at my reflection.

This is the one.

I won't have anyone else tell me differently.

I feel extremely beautiful and special in it.

I quickly glance at Samantha, who's standing behind me, and notice she's also smiling. Catching her eye, I give her a wink and a little giggle before walking out to Billy and Paul with pride.

'That smile says it all!' beams Billy. 'It's perfect!'

'Nice,' says Paul.

'Thank you,' I say, not caring that he doesn't sound

overly enthused. 'I love it,' I gush, unable to remove the grin from my face.

'You "love" it?' queries Billy, using his weird Franck accent again, causing me to laugh and nod my head. 'You wear it!' he booms.

I can't help flinging my arms around in the air with excitement.

'And I must say, you have remarkable taste for some-one who supposedly knows nothing about fashion – it would've been the most expensive of the bunch,' Paul informs us. 'It's designed by none other than Vera Wang.'

'Ooooh! Good choice!' says Billy, knowingly.

I smile at them both, without a clue who this Vera lady is . . . although I do love what she's done with this dress!

One evening the following week, I'm at home cleaning out Billy's food cupboard of the various cans and jars that are past their use-by dates when the house phone rings. I pick it up to find Paul on the other end.

'Billy's at the theatre, I'm afraid,' I say, trying my best to remain cheerful and friendly even though I know he's not my biggest fan.

'Yes, I know that,' he says with a hint of annoyance. 'I was calling to speak to you actually.'

The fact that he has waited for Billy to be at work before calling is not a good sign. Neither is the fact that he is calling me when he never has done before.

'Oh, OK. What's up?'

'Nothing . . .'

The silence that comes from the other end of the line unsettles me. While I wait for him to speak I start to peel the label off a jar of pickles, trying to distract myself from how uncomfortable I feel.

'Is there something I can help you with, Paul?'

'No.'

OK . . .

'But I thought we could have a quick chat about next weekend.'

'Oh?'

'I had a call to say you can keep hold of your dress as a thank you for choosing to go with the Vera number,' he says flatly.

Although I'm delighted that I'm allowed to keep it, I've already been told by Paul and Billy that I can only wear the dress once – so, what am I meant to do with it? Wear it to clean the house? Do the weekly shop in it? Or perhaps float around in it on my walks around the park? Nope, the reality is that it'll just sit in my wardrobe, sadly gathering dust.

'That's great! Thanks for letting me know,' I say, hoping to get off the phone as soon as possible.

'I'm sure it'll make quite a classy addition to your current wardrobe,' Paul adds.

Deciding to ignore the dig, I remain silent.

'Also, you might want to wear your shoes around the house.'

'To stop them from rubbing? Yes, I've already been doing that.' I say politely.

'And to practise being elegant.'

Ahh . . .

'Is there anything else, Paul?' I ask, my patience deserting me.

'Yes. There is,' he says, his voice failing to hide a sour tone. 'I just wanted to tell you that there's nothing to worry about. It'll be busy, loud and manic there – but try and enjoy it. Billy should be with you every step of the way. But then, obviously, for him this is work. It's not all fun.'

'I know that, Paul.'

'Good. It's an important night.' He sighs before changing his tone to a seemingly warmer one. 'Sophie, I know you have a tendency to feel self-conscious and to *panic* – you shouldn't worry. On Sunday all eyes will be on the A-listers around you. Not on you.'

'Right.'

'Obviously, I would love to say that I'd be there if anything were to go wrong but, well, as you've taken my ticket – you're on your own.'

'I'm sorry, Paul, but is there a problem here?'

'Not at all, Sophie. But one thing . . .'

'Yes?'

'Don't fuck up,' he says, before hanging up.

Later that night when we're crawling into bed I decide to talk to Billy about the conversation.

'Paul phoned tonight,' I start.

'Yeah, he said.'

'He did?'

'Yeah. Great news about the dress! I bet you're thrilled.'

'I am . . .' I turn to face him. 'Billy, have you told him about my panic attacks?'

'Not really – just about how we met,' he says with a shrug.

'Why did you tell him that?'

'Why shouldn't I? He's my manager. I tell him everything.'

'But this isn't your thing to tell, Billy. It's personal to me. I really don't want Paul knowing that sort of thing about me.'

Billy's top lip curls up under his nose, clearly confused.

'I don't understand what your problem is with Paul. He's nothing but nice about you. Why are you so off about him?'

'I'm not!'

'You are. Sophie, you have to understand how important Paul is to me.'

'I do.'

'Paul phoned to check you were OK and comfortable with the plans for the weekend – that's the kind of decent guy he is.'

No, he didn't, I think to myself. It seems that Paul's main purpose was to make me aware of what he knows and to rile me enough so that I would say something to Billy – ultimately causing friction between us. How clever.

'I was just shocked he knew,' I say, trying to alleviate the tension between us.

'To be honest, Sophie, I don't even know much about your panic attacks – only what I saw when we first met. Every time I ask you about them you clam up.'

'I don't like talking about them.'

'Fine,' he says with a huff as he rolls over, facing away from me.

'Billy!'

'It's fine, Soph – but just know that all any of us want to do is be there for you. We love you.'

'I know.'

There is absolutely no way that I want to open up now with this horrible atmosphere surrounding us. I curl up under the covers and wonder how the conversation spiralled out of control so quickly.

15

I fiddle with the waves of my dress with one hand and hold on to Billy's hand with the other as we make our way, in the back of a blacked-out Rolls Royce Phantom, to the BAFTA awards. My stomach is in knots and my breathing shallow as the nerves kick in.

'You OK?' asks Billy, squeezing my hand.

'Not really,' I laugh. 'You?'

Billy already knows the outcome of this night could have a huge effect on his career, and thanks to that knowledge he has hardly slept over the past few weeks.

He takes a deep breath, closes his eyes, tilts his head backwards and sighs quickly, causing his lips to blow a raspberry.

'I'm crapping myself,' he says shaking his head.

I can't help but laugh at the pair of us getting ourselves in such a state, wondering if the other guests are as petrified as us.

'We've just got to keep thinking, "What's the worst that could happen?"' I try and reason.

'Well, I could faint and wet myself,' he says, without cracking a smile. 'Or swear, or look like a bad loser.'

'If you lose . . .' I say, emphasizing the 'if'.

He shrugs at the correction.

'I'll be fine once I get there. It's only the journey that

gets me anxious,' he says, taking another deep breath and looking in my direction, taking me in. 'You look so beautiful.'

I can't help but grin back at him. I feel beautiful. I have had a full glamour makeover, which started yesterday with a spray tan, manicure and pedicure – the best bit being that I didn't even have to leave the flat for the luxury. Two delightful beauty therapists came to the house and did the whole thing there.

The spray tan was possibly the most bizarre thing I've ever done, with me standing in a pop-up tent in the en-suite bathroom, embarrassingly wearing the tiniest underwear I own, as a lady literally sprayed cold orange liquid onto me as I put myself into different unflattering positions. I won't lie, at first I looked like I'd been tangoed, so I was petrified at what I might look like when I woke up, having been warned that the colour would darken overnight ... but luckily most of the brown came off in the shower, leaving me with just the sun-kissed look they promised. Phew!

Today the makeover continued with a hairstylist and make-up artist arriving at nine o'clock this morning. My hair has been cut, blow-dried and set in massive rollers by the hairstylist, to give me big bouncy waves, sadly not the plait style Molly had suggested, but I'm sure she'll love this look when she sees it.

The make-up artist has inspected my face so closely that I've spent the majority of the morning holding my breath so that I don't breathe on her. She has hidden the flaws, accentuated my cheekbones and made my skin glow. Even I think I look angelic. I am, however, acutely aware that this is the result of several hours in a make-up chair. I'll be back to looking like me again in the morning.

'It's a big upgrade from being covered in flour or wearing a Coffee Matters uniform, that's for sure!' I say to Billy. 'But will I stumble in my shoes and fall arse over tit, making a fool of myself? Only time will tell,' I smile.

Billy lets out a booming laugh – one I'm aware I haven't heard in a while.

'I'll keep a hold of you!' he promises.

'You'd better . . . and what about you, Mr Handsome?' I say, admiring his smart black tux and the way his hair is slicked up in the quiff style he had when we first met. He looks simply divine and every inch the Hollywood movie star.

'What, this old thing?' he smiles, tugging on the cuffs of his shirt the way men always do in films.

I can't help but beam at him as I take in his gorgeousness. I know that my move to London hasn't been easy so far, but being here with him, on his special night, makes it all worthwhile. I wish I could bottle the feelings of love inside me and save them for a rainy day – to remind myself of their magnitude in those moments of doubt.

'I love you, Billy,' I say, taking his hand to my lips and kissing it gently.

He smiles back at me with a look of utter love and devotion.

'Then nothing else matters,' he says with a shrug.

We both fall silent as our car turns a corner and we spot the commotion outside the Royal Opera House.

A wide red carpet has been laid out, with metal barriers standing around it, to keep the public and fans under control. They're squeezed together against the partitions, standing at least ten people deep the whole way up the walkway. It's rammed. Even from inside the car we can hear them screaming out the names of the other actors who are walking up and down the carpet, giving autographs and posing for pictures.

The car takes us halfway up the red carpet before stopping to let us out, in the prime position in front of the waiting crowd and world's media. I take a deep breath, not entirely sure if I want to get out at all – perhaps just staying at home watching this on television would have been a lot simpler. However, before I can express my concerns to Billy, the doors either side of us are being opened by the footmen outside, and Billy slides out. I'm offered a hand by the footman on my side of the car, which I take hold of. He helps guide me from the safety of the car on to the red carpet, where I face the expectant crowd.

The screams for Billy are insane. I'm actually rooted to the spot as pandemonium seems to be breaking out around us. A couple of passionate girls manage to get over the barrier somehow and fight their way to Billy, only to be removed by security within seconds. Paul was right: it's loud and scary. I turn to see the car we've just left pulling away, leaving us behind. There's no way out now. Billy comes over to me and takes my hand.

'It'll be fine, baby. Just smile and relax. We can get through this,' he whispers in my ear, cupping my face, causing the crowd watching to go crazy. I look up into his eyes and see the nerves and excitement there.

I'm so proud to be stood with Billy on this important night. I wink at him and feel myself stand a little taller.

'Yes, we can,' I smile.

'Excuse me? Billy?' asks a woman wearing a rather official looking headpiece. 'I'm Heather from BAFTA. I'll be looking after you until you get inside. Could I ask you to make your way to the photo line-up?'

'Of course!' says Billy, as we follow the lady further down the carpet, where a big metallic structure has been erected for photographers to work from. They stand in rows set at three different heights, all leaning forward, eager to see who the next arrival will be.

''Ello, Billy!' shouts one of them.

'Who's the pretty lady?' shouts another.

'Billy Buskin and Sophie May,' says a man in a suit, stepping forward, who I'm guessing has to announce every person who arrives to avoid confusion among the photographers. 'Billy is nominated for Best Actor for his role in *Twisted Drops*.' A few of the cameramen repeat the names and the nomination details into their cameras before picking them up and aiming them in our direction.

'There are so many of them,' I whisper to Billy. 'Which lens do I look at?'

'Let's start at the left and work our way along, then just go to whoever shouts the loudest.'

'Shouts?' I ask.

Billy squeezes my waist and winks at me with a grin before turning to the photographers. I place one arm under his, around his waist, and let the other dangle by my side, squeezing my diamante clutch bag. Once I'm ready I look up at the photographers who start noisily snapping away instantly. I smile as I look from camera to camera and try to keep in control of my face, which has decided to twitch and shake with nerves in a way I've never experienced before.

Once we've held eye contact with each camera lens the shouting increases.

'This way, Billy!'

'Excuse me, love, could you just turn into Billy a bit, show us the back of your dress?'

'Billy! Billy! Billy!' shouts a man at the top of the structure, waving.

'Do you think you'll win, Billy boy?'

'Can you get a bit closer to each other? Don't be shy!'

'Over here!'

'Show us your teeth!'

'Your bird scrubs up well, Billy!'

'Didn't feel like wearing your apron tonight, darling?'

'Are you nervous?'

'Thanks, everyone,' Billy says, holding up his spare hand as we turn to leave.

'You still working in Coffee Matters, love?' one of them shouts after us.

'I'll have a tall hazelnut latte!' chimes another, while letting out a menacing laugh.

'Can't believe the mutli-millionaire would make you do that. Billy, give the pretty girl some pocket money!'

I squeeze Billy's hand a little tighter. All I can compare the sensation to is what I expect it would feel like to have a gang of thirty wolf-whistling builders shouting whatever they fancied at you. It's rude and intimidating and I'm glad to be moving away from them.

'Just ignore them,' he says to me, continuing to walk away.

'Why do they shout out stuff like that?'

'To get a picture of me running towards them losing my rag.'

'Seriously?'

'Yep . . . it would be worth a bit more than me standing there smiling like everyone else, that's for sure. You OK?' he asks, stopping and turning to me with concern.

'It's all a bit bizarre,' I admit. 'Don't you worry about me, though, mister!'

'Billy, Sophie, if you'd like to come with me,' says Heather. 'We'll do a bit of press but then we'll get to your seats fairly quickly due to the time,' she explains.

Billy continues to hold my hand as we walk further down the red carpet, but when he has to talk to various radio stations, TV programmes, magazines and tabloids about the evening ahead I decide to stand back with Heather, rather than standing gormlessly by his side, knowing nothing about the other nominated films. Even though I'm not next to him he still points me out proudly to every interviewer he's with, leading them to look in my direction with intrigue – to which I give a smile and a little wave, not sure what else to do.

While waiting on the red carpet for Billy, I take the time to look about me and take everything in. It's still absolute chaos, but my ears have started to adjust to the sound at least. All around me famous people (I can tell they're famous thanks to the crazy crowd desperately screaming after them) wander up and down the carpet, greeting fans, having their photos taken and talking to the press. I gawp at them all, taking in the madness of the whole situation, wishing I knew who these import-ant people were.

Eventually, we get to our seats in the gigantic auditor-ium of the Opera House, after being stopped by almost everybody we pass along the way – all wanting to wish Billy good luck with his nomination.

I'm mesmerized as we sit in our luxurious seats in the beautiful red and gold theatre, with its incredible high ceilings and architecture, looking at the glamorous people walking about us. It feels surreal to be here sur-rounded by such class and prestige.

'How's my loser face?' asks Billy, grabbing my atten-tion as he tilts his head to the side in earnest whilst nodding and clapping with a knowing smile.

'You're going for the "Ah, well-deserved, he's the rightful winner" look?'

'Correct! With a touch of, "I thought so, I'm just happy to be here."'

'Well, it looks good. Very convincing. Erm, just a thought, though – have you written an acceptance speech at all?' I ask, suddenly realizing that I've not seen him practising, writing one out, or anything of that nature, which I'm guessing must mean he has omitted to write one.

He looks back at me with a sheepish shrug while raising his eyebrows.

'But what if you win?' I ask. 'You might actually win! Why haven't you prepared?'

It dawns on me that Billy doesn't think he is going to get his hands on that award after all. For him, it actually is all about the being nominated and being put in the same bracket as the other worthy nominees after battling against his teen-star image for so long.

'Don't panic,' he says, tapping the top pocket of his jacket. 'Paul gave me a list of people that I'd need to thank, in case. I'll just ad lib around that if I need to.'

'Right,' I say, taking hold of his hand and kissing it.

'Have I told you how beautiful you look yet?' he asks, changing the subject.

'You might have mentioned it.'

'Good,' he says with a smile.

'Time for some finishing touches,' I say, picking a strand of hair from his suit jacket and straightening his tie.

'Ladies and gentlemen, please welcome your host, Bernard Sharland!' booms an invisible voice around the theatre, causing people to cheer, as an extremely tall man with thick-framed glasses makes his way out onto the stage, waving. Billy widens his eyes at me in anticipation and shakes my hand in excitement as we snuggle into each other and get ready for what lies ahead.

'Good evening, all,' says the presenter, a well-known comedian and chat show host. 'Welcome to the BAFTA Awards at London's Royal Opera House. I am your host, Bernard Sharland, and I will be escorting you through tonight's proceedings, where we will be celebrating this year's greatest films and awarding those who have been outstanding in their field. Now, I know what you're thinking – has Billy Buskin got confused and found himself here instead of the *Nickelodeon* awards?'

My insides curdle as laughter spills out around us. Billy had warned me earlier that this was going to happen; being a former teen star there's no doubt that he'll be an easy target for jibes like this. I look at Billy and see him smile and salute the presenter, who returns the gesture before continuing.

'Well, don't worry, folks, he has actually been nominated, and deservedly so, I might add, for his performance in *Twisted Drops*. But Bill,' he says, directly to Billy, as if talking to a small child, 'I do have to warn you that this is a prestigious affair . . . there will be no heckling, no stunts and no green slime. I understand this could be confusing, but if at any moment you find it all too much, just locate your nearest adult, and they'll be able to guide you through the proceedings.'

The audience laughs further, some choosing to clap at the joke too. A few of them look in Billy's direction to see if he sees the humour in the whole thing, before allowing themselves to laugh.

'No, seriously, it's good to see you, Billy!' Bernard concludes before continuing with the rest of his opening speech.

'Well, I thought I got off lightly there!' he whispers in my ear. 'It could've been far worse. I actually thought it was quite funny.'

We sit through several awards being dished out before a cameraman runs to our side, sticking his camera lens in our direction, letting us know that Billy's category is next. He clasps my hand even tighter and turns to give me a kiss.

'Here goes nothing,' he whispers.

'I believe in you!' I encourage, as we both turn our attention back to the stage.

'Next tonight,' announces Bernard. 'To present the award for best male, we have last year's outstanding winner. Please welcome the delightful Mr Andrew McGreal.'

The crowd gives a raucous applause of appreciation as Andrew walks onto the stage and over to the podium, clutching the BAFTA award in one hand and the gold envelope, containing the winner's name, in the other.

'Good evening all!' he says to the crowd with a beaming smile, his broad northern accent instantly making him friendlier than most of the other presenters who have been on stage with their stiffer RP accents. 'The question I have been asked the most since winning this award last year is "Where do you keep it?" Is it on my mum's mantelpiece, or in my downstairs loo? Well, if I'm honest, I keep mine with me at all times and whip it out any time I'm in auditions, important meetings or stressful situations, reminding people that I am the best . . .' He unbuttons his suit jacket and pulls out his own BAFTA, placing it in front of him on the stand, causing us, and the rest of the audience, to laugh loudly. 'That's just to remind you all,' he smiles, looking down at the envelope in front of him. 'Let's crack on with it, shall we? The nominees for this year's BAFTA leading actor award are: Tom McLean for *Bad Mind*, Russell Mode for *Into the Dark*, Sam Watts for *Tinker* and Billy Buskin for *Twisted Drops*.'

I rub Billy's hand in support, although if I'm honest the action is more to settle my own nerves than his, as the tension causes adrenaline to rush through me unexpectedly.

Short clips of each actor in their nominated film roles are played on the screens on stage, each receiving a short burst of applause from the appreciative audience.

Billy turns to me with a smile, letting out a small sigh. 'This is it!'

He continues to look at me, even though we're aware that Andrew is opening the winning envelope on stage.

'The winner of this year's BAFTA for best leading

actor is . . .' Andrew pauses, before continuing. 'Well, well, well! It's Billy Buskin!'

The room erupts in cheers as I watch Billy's face drop with shock and his body fold into his chair with disbelief. He takes a few seconds to compose himself before eventually looking around at the people surrounding us who are patting him on the back and shouting words of congratulation. I'm sitting motionless by his side, my hand clamped over my mouth, feeling in awe of the moment. I'm filled with so much pride that I want to burst into tears. Billy looks at me and pulls me into his arms, burying his face in my hair.

'I can't believe it,' he mutters, shaking his head.

'You better go get your award, baby,' I whisper, aware that the applause is starting to die down from the expectant crowd and that they'll want to hear from their winner.

He nods, looks up at my eyes, grabs my face with both hands and kisses me, before running up to the stage and embracing Andrew, who gives him his trophy.

'Wow,' starts Billy with the award firmly in his grasp as he stands in front of the microphone. 'I really wasn't expecting this. At all,' he confesses, shaking his head in amazement. 'I didn't even write a speech . . . I don't think I'm meant to admit to that, though, am I? Very helpfully, my manager did hand me a long list of names telling me it would be rude not to thank them all if this outcome were to occur – well, I ended up leaving that list at home. It felt presumptuous, almost, to carry it around with me. So, if you're on that list I will thank you properly once I've woken up from this crazy dream.' The room responds with scattered laughter. 'But there is one person here who I would like to thank . . .' he continues. 'The better half of me, that is, Miss Sophie May. I feel like I've already won the biggest prize of all having her beside me. It's thanks to her that my life is now complete.'

Tears fill my eyes as Billy leaves the podium, and against all efforts from the ushers for him to exit the side of the stage like all the previous winners, he strides back down the front steps and up the aisle. He scoops me up and embraces me, holding me tightly as though there is nowhere else he would rather be. We ignore the clapping and cheering around us and focus on this special moment together.

16

I thought Billy was popular before his win but the party after the awards shows me that things are about to get even crazier. It feels as though everybody comes over to Billy to congratulate him on the film and his award, meaning we can barely walk two steps without being stopped by someone new. A buzz of excitement surrounds him and it feels as though all eyes are focused in his direction.

'And what about you, dear?' asks an elderly woman who has been speaking to Billy for the last few minutes, whilst keeping eye contact with the both of us, therefore making me feel included in the conversation. I never realized before how rare an occurrence this actually is, but the fact that it makes an impact on me means that it must be. 'You're no doubt incredibly proud?'

'Yes, I am,' I declare, enjoying her warmth.

'And that speech!' She squeals while clutching her chest. 'I haven't seen something as romantic as that for a while. You make sure you look after this one, Billy,' she winks.

'I sure will!' he says with a smile, tightening his grip around my waist.

'Right, I'd better be off. These parties tend to get a bit wild and I'm too old for that now. Congratulations again, the pair of you,' she says, before turning and shuffling towards the exit.

Watching her leave, my heart stops as I spot a familiar face walking towards us. Noticing that I've suddenly tensed up, Billy looks at me to see what's wrong. When he looks in the direction of my eyeline I hear him laugh quietly as it all becomes clear.

'Billy? Jude. I just wanted to come over and congratulate you on your win,' says Jude Law (yes, my flaming crush!) as he offers Billy his hand to shake. He is much taller than I imagined. That's not to say he is massively tall, he's probably average height for a man, but I've heard so many people tell Billy that he looks smaller off the big screen that I just assumed all actors were a little shorter than they seemed. I notice Jude's teeth are pearly white as he gives Billy one of his trademark wide grins, almost causing me to melt with delight. I take the opportunity of being so close to him while he is preoccupied with Billy, to continue to inspect his face in detail: his perfectly ruffled hair – although, yes, slightly balding (I don't mind), his sexy five o'clock shadow coming through (making him appear rough and rugged), and his electrifying green eyes (splashes of heaven). He is simply intoxicating, without a single imperfection – none that I can spot anyway . . . although I even find the thin wrinkles around his eyes intriguing.

'Thank you so much, it's quite bizarre,' answers Billy.

'I'll bet. It'll take a while to sink in. This must be your wonderful lady,' he says, turning his attention to me and shaking my hand. 'Miss Sophie May, was it?'

I nod and smile with enthusiasm, suddenly losing the ability to speak. He said my name . . . he's remembered it from Billy's speech.

'Excuse me, guys,' says a bald man, who holds up his huge camera in explanation of the interruption. 'Is it OK to get a snap?'

'Of course,' says Jude.

'Let's get Sophie in the middle,' says Billy, with a cheeky grin in my direction, as they each stand either side of me facing the camera. Billy lays his arm around my waist while Jude rests his hand on my shoulder. I stop breathing as I put all my focus into smiling for the camera and not falling to the floor in awe of Jude's greatness.

'Cheers, guys,' the cameraman says after a few clicks, heading off and looking about for his next photograph.

'Actually,' says Billy, going after him. 'Is it OK to get your email address so that I can get a few stills of some of the photos you've taken today?'

As he does so, Jude removes his arm from my shoulder and smiles at me. I look at the floor shyly, not sure what to say.

'I love your dress, by the way,' he says politely, filling the silence between us.

'Thank you. It's by Vera Wang,' I manage, although I'm not sure he needed to hear that information.

'Well, you look stunning in it,' he says with a sparkling smile.

Luckily, Billy comes back at this precise moment, folding a piece of paper into his pocket.

'Well, it's been a pleasure to meet you both. Enjoy the rest of your night!' he adds, before shaking Billy's hand again, squeezing my arm, giving me a wink and wandering off.

He winked at me.

Jude Law winked at me.

Billy gives me a gentle nudge, bringing me back into the room and making me aware that I'm just staring in Jude's direction.

'Earth to Sophie . . .' he quietly says in my ear.

I turn to him, open-mouthed, still agog from what has just occurred.

'I can't wait to tell Mum and Molly about that!' I suddenly say.

'I thought so . . . luckily you'll have some photo evidence to show them too!'

Throughout the night people continue to come over and congratulate Billy, although as time goes on and more alcohol is consumed people are less respectful about butting in on his conversations with others. They become even more focused on him, with any earlier social barriers having tumbled down.

Interestingly, they become more aloof towards me. I, obviously, am not successful or the star of the evening so am of no importance to them whatsoever. I'm amazed at how many people come over and ignore me entirely. Even if I try and start up a conversation with them, they're quick to direct their attention back to

Billy as soon as they can. It's wondrous to observe, even if it does leave me feeling slightly perturbed.

'Darling, I must say that I have tipped you from day one to achieve great things!' slurs one lady who has been saying the same lines of admiration to Billy for the last five minutes, while tapping his chest.

'Thank you, Lorraine,' Billy says again, smiling shyly.

Although we've been taking it steady with our celebratory glasses of champagne (neither us wanted to get too giddy on such an important night), it appears, as we look at the chaos surrounding us, that others are making the most of the night – and the free bar. Billy currently has five people gathered around him, all of them talking in his direction and none of them seem to care that Billy's attention is torn between the lot of them. He looks quite happy amongst them, so I decide it's a good time to freshen up in the loo and get us both another drink. I make the obvious hand signals and mouth to Billy, over the heads of his entourage, and head off.

After waiting forever at the toilet, the structured designer dresses making it impossible for anyone to pee quickly, I stand at the bar waiting to be served.

'Is he enjoying himself, then? Making the most of being everybody's best friend for the night?' someone asks to my left. I look over to see Russell Mode, one of the actors who were also nominated for the best actor gong earlier. He is swirling his drink around in his hand, causing the ice to bang on the side of the glass as he does so. From the sight of him I imagine he has been sat here a while; he has a floppy, intoxicated way about him and he struggles to hold eye contact.

'Hello. Russell, isn't it?' I ask politely, to which he nods silently while pouting his lips. 'Well, yes, he is. It's not quite sunk in for him yet,' I say, repeating what I've been overhearing Billy say all evening.

'Oh, it will do, soon enough. And then his life is going to change forever,' he says dramatically, focusing on the drink in his hand. 'I'd make the most of him while he's still the Billy Buskin you know and love,' he continues with a frown. 'Soon enough he'll be the star of Hollywood, in the big boys' league, I mean, not just in some crappy little teen thing which mindless girls fantasize over. And to do that, to be one of them in the big league, he needs someone just as dazzling as him on his arm.'

'Now, Russell,' I say, placing my arm on his shoulder in a friendly manner, acting more confident than I feel. 'I've worked blooming hard to look this good today, well, a whole team of people have, in fact, it took them hours. Are you trying to say I'm not dazzling enough?'

'You're the one that works in Coffee Matters, right? I mean, no offence to you, I'm sure you're lovely . . . but to give you that extra va va voom, you need to be part of a power couple. Maybe that can happen with a girl who works in Coffee Matters. Maybe you'll be able to prove me wrong. I hope you do. But don't say I didn't warn you,' he explains with a hint of malice, making me feel uncomfortable. 'If I was you, I'd run while you've still got your pride and dignity, before he can run off with his leading lady, leaving you without a second thought.' He leans forward, his voice deeper and slower, adding more weight to his words. 'It's a game, and he is now the key piece. From this moment on every girl in the industry is going to be batting their eyelashes in his direction, doing everything they can to get his attention. Do you really think you can hold them off? It's only a matter of time.'

'Well . . .' I say with a sigh, still managing to wear a smile. 'Thank you for that, Russell. Enjoy the rest of your evening.'

I turn back into the crowded room, wipe away a single tear, throw back my shoulders, clench my jaw to steady myself, and head straight towards Billy. He looks up at me from the current group that have accosted him, as though he can sense me walking towards him. A big grin fills his face. I watch as he makes his escape from the group and walks in my direction.

'Can I just say, I am definitely the luckiest person here tonight, and it is nothing to do with that blooming award.'

I smile at him, trying to forget Russell's words that niggle away at my brain, trying to remember that I know Billy better than he does. Surely Russell's words were uttered purely out of spite, to put doubt into my mind and get some sort of revenge? Billy wouldn't conform to such an old stereotype, would he?

'Hey, did you get those drinks?' Billy asks, noticing my empty hands.

'No, I couldn't get to the bar,' I lie.

'You know what? I've had fun, but I think I've had my fill, anyway,' he says, looking around the room.

'Honestly?'

'Yes! Take me home, Princess!' he says, using his award to point towards the exit.

Getting in the car on the way home, Billy answers a call from his excited mum and dad, then speaks to Paul, so I pull out my own phone to discover I have dozens of missed calls and messages, not only from Mum and Molly, but from a whole heap of numbers that I don't recognize.

I decide to listen to the one from Molly first. 'Hello, duck!' she starts, calling from what sounds like a very busy room, full of people talking loudly. 'Well, who'd have thought you'd scrub up so well, eh? I was sad you didn't go for the plaits in your hair, mind, but I can see why, it wouldn't have worked – the down-do was much better with that dress. Congratulations to Billy on his win, we all screamed our heads off when his name was read out, and what a speech! Oh, your mum's here . . . I'll pass her over.' I chuckle at the thought of them handing around the phone just to leave a voice message; it's not as if I was there to speak to either of them.

'Hello, love,' says Mum. 'You looked so pretty. Say well done to Billy! I'll try and call you later, but I expect you'll be off celebrating. Have fun.'

I wonder what it would have been like for them all

sat round watching me on the TV. I can imagine them huddled together in the shop, passing round the teapot and cakes, chatting away as they wait to see if they can spot me on the screen. The thought of it makes me smile, before a pang of homesickness grabs hold of me suddenly. What did they think when my face popped up? Not just Mum and Molly, but people like Mrs Sleep and Miss Brown – did they cheer with delight? Did they think I'd changed from the Sophie they used to know when I was serving them in the shop? I hope not. I hope they realize it's still me, just a glamorized version . . . a version which took lots of time and effort from other people to create, but will disappear in minutes when I get ready for bed shortly.

The next message I listen to is from Mum; I'm guessing she decided to call again later on when she got home from the shop. 'Hello, love. Me again. I know you're probably out, but I just wanted to call again and tell you how beautiful you looked tonight. I'm so proud of you. Speak to you later if you're not home too late, or in the morning. Night, night. Love you.'

I look at the time and notice it's one in the morning. She'll be fast asleep by now, so instead of calling her back I listen to the other messages on my phone. One is from Andrezj, my former boss at Coffee Matters: 'Looking hot, lady!' he shouts down the phone. 'Let's do lunch sometime – somewhere fancy, baby! Get Billy to book us a table somewhere splendid. Definitely not Coffee Matters!' he laughs before hanging up.

The other voicemail is from my old school friend Mary Lance, who I haven't spoken to for about seven years.

'Hi, Sophie! It's Mary Lance here from school. I've just switched on the television to see your beautiful face. What a lovely surprise. I called Molly for your number, hope you don't mind. It sounded crazy in the shop, like she's having a party or something. Anyway, I'd love to catch up with you if you're free, maybe grab a coffee?' I'm surprised at how thrilled I am to hear her voice, even though it's been so long. It would be nice to see her again, now that we're older, with a few less social boundaries surrounding us.

Next, I flick through my text messages,

> Hello, Sophie-soph. It's Carla Daily, I used to be in your class back in the good old days, remember? Mary just gave me your number – we ended up at Sheffield together. Needless to say, I wasn't doing dentistry. Ha! Anyway, oh my god, look how you've grown! Amazing! Mary mentioned about us all meeting up and having a night out. Sounds fun. Get in touch. Let's sort it! Going home next week to see the 'rents. You about? I'll pop in the shop. Xx C xX

I remember Carla from primary school. She hung out with the popular girls in our class, as I did at one point. Seeing as I went through school in a bubble of avoidance, I can't recall ever actually speaking to her once everything had changed for me. Although maybe I did before that. It's strange to think of her and Mary as friends now, but then I still think of them as the eighteen-year-old girls that left school with me all those years ago. I've changed, so no doubt they have too.

The next few messages all follow the same lines. It seems that Mary is now part of the popular crowd, thanks to Carla's help, no doubt, and has decided to pass around my number. I decide to delete the lot without reading them, my earlier thrill at Mary getting in touch subsiding.

'Who are they from?' asks Billy. Having finished his telephone call from Paul, he is now reading over my shoulder.

'Oh, it's nothing. Just some people I used to go to school with,' I say, realizing that that's all they were and ever will be. They weren't ever really friends who I shared things with – I made sure I had none of those, preferring to keep them all at a distance, not wanting to be asked questions. They're strangers to me now, only getting in touch because they've seen me on television.

'Your old school friends? We should have them over to the flat!' Billy says with enthusiasm.

I grimace at the thought of it.

'What?' asks Billy, looking confused.

'They haven't spoken to me in years. They've just watched the awards and that's why they they've got in touch, not because they seriously want to know how I am. In fact, they probably want to know more about you,' I explain, feeling deflated by the truth of my words. 'They've never tried to contact me before now.'

'But they're your friends . . .' he offers.

'Not really,' I admit. 'So, what did Paul say?'

'He's chuffed, obviously.'

'Not angry that you forgot to write your speech, then?'

'The opposite. Apparently, people from *Twisted Drops* have been calling him all night in hysterics, finding the whole thing hilarious. So I don't think I've managed to seriously offend anyone. He also said that he thought you looked incredible, as did my mum and dad by the way.'

I look at him questioningly. I highly doubt that Paul would've found it within himself to say something nice about me – not that I'm going to say that out loud, though. Not after the last chat we had about him.

'They did. Paul said he's even had a few calls from people wanting to know more about you. Some asking if you're an actress or model yourself.'

'Shut up!' I say, whacking his arm gently.

'I'm serious! I'm sure you could get into it all if you wanted.'

'No chance. What else did he say?' I ask, feeling embarrassed.

'The producer for that rock film *The Walking Beat* has been on the phone to him, too. They want to announce me as their lead as soon as possible and get the ball rolling while there's such hype about the win.'

'Do you still want to do it?'

'Definitely. Although I think it's going to be a crazy experience.'

'Great, I'll have the flat back to myself then!' I joke.

'No, you won't. You'll be coming with me.'

'What? To the set?'

'Yeah, of course I want you there. We're a team, remember? Besides, I want you to see how boring it all actually is. I'm telling you, you'll feel so sorry for me once you experience the early morning starts, the never-ending days and see the way I'm bossed around like a moving prop.'

'You poor, poor thing!'

'I know . . . it's so tough.'

We sit silently for a few moments, letting the quiet sink in after our manic day.

'Ahhhhh!' squeals Billy, clenching his fists with excitement. 'I still can't believe I won! It's crazy. I always dreamed I'd get a pat on the back for my work one day – but this is bonkers.'

'You deserve it.'

Billy flashes me a cheeky smile. 'It's made me realize how much I love it. Wait, does that make me sound egotistical?' he asks with a grimace. 'Moaning about acting when we first met and now that I've won an award I love it?'

'Not at all.'

'It's like it's awoken a fire in me. Paul is so geared up. He has such massive plans. There's all sorts of meetings being set up, over here, in LA and New York . . . who knows where we'll be in a few years' time. I feel like our future has just been thrown wide open. It's so unbelievable.'

I'm thrilled for Billy because he really does deserve the praise that is being sent his way, but this talk of the future scares me. Not because I'm not being included – I am. Billy is always careful to say 'we' and 'us', but because our world is about to be dictated by Billy's career. Putting Paul in the driver's seat. I'm not sure how I'd be able to cope having Paul's input into every decision we make.

I can't sleep. A mixture of excitement and nerves swirls through me, keeping my mind active and alert. It's been an amazing night for Billy and I'm delighted that I was able to be there to watch and support him. It was such a rush to be by his side – I actually thought I'd be left on my own again, looking like a lemon as I was on the Press Night, to be honest, but Billy kept me close to him as promised.

Even though I'm largely ecstatic about how the evening went (that I didn't fall over in my heels or make a fool of myself in front of Jude), I can't seem to shake off Russell Mode's comments or the feeling that things are about to snowball so fast that I won't be able to keep up.

When it comes to women, I trust Billy. I honestly do. It's hard not to trust someone who has never really given me any reason not to. Yes, I know he is popular with the ladies and I know he likes to be affectionate with Ruth, but that's just his way. Right? And yes, the whole inappropriate thing with the play was a problem, too, but that was just his naivety about how to handle the situation. Having spoken about it I'm sure that scenario will be handled differently next time around. Although will I ever get over the distress of watching Billy fool around with someone else – even if it is in the name of work? I know I'll deal with that when I have to, but thanks to this new film that time might come sooner than I'd have liked. Rock stars are, after all, notorious for their bad-boy behaviour. I'd be foolish to think there'd be nothing risqué in it.

If Russell is right and it's only a matter of time before he runs off with a co-star or some glamorous model he meets on a night out, then what am I doing here? Why am I actually sitting around waiting for him to crush and humiliate me? Because I love him, I guess, is the obvious answer. From day one I've always said that I can't compete with those types of women, powerful and glamorous, but I believed him when he comforted me by saying he wasn't interested in the changeability of girls who would be all over you one minute for the cameras and then drop you the next. He wanted something more meaningful. I do believe that in me Billy has found someone he can have a normal life with – as normal as he can have, being an actor and having parts of his life on display for all to judge. I know I give him stability in an otherwise unpredictable lifestyle – but am I just a phase in his life? Billy's way of trying to fight the urge to become a part of the actor's world that he'll inevitably succumb to eventually anyway?

In reality, it's not Billy that I'm worried about, I don't believe he would purposely go out to cheat or find someone new. I honestly don't think it's in his character. What unnerves me is the scores of women who will now be on his case, trying to tempt him. Doing all they can to win his trust and lure him in their direction, not caring that he has a girlfriend. In fact, in some twisted way, I predict my presence in his life will make him even more of a challenge for them, making him even more desirable. I can't sleep as the image of these seductive lionesses walking around their prey fills my mind.

I suppose only time will tell if he'd be stupid enough to fall into their traps, but for now I have to keep faith in Billy and stand by him, until he gives me cause to do otherwise.

As for Billy's future glittering life and my presence in it? Who knows. I just wish I could get rid of this feeling of grief that has clamped hold of my heart.

PART THREE

17

The flashing of my phone causes me to stir. I always sleep with it on silent when I've decided to have a lie-in the next day, knowing that Molly or Mum will call me at the crack of dawn otherwise, forcing me to wake up earlier than planned.

It's a couple of weeks since the BAFTA awards. Billy has finished working on *Dunked* and is waiting for filming to commence on *The Walking Beat*, so we are making the most of having nothing planned and have been enjoying waking up when we want to, napping if we fancy it and being spontaneous with our days without the need to rush back home for anything. It's been glorious just being a couple again with no outside interference.

The screen of my phone is so bright I can't open my eyes properly to see who is trying to get hold of me, so I miss the call. I close my eyes again, turn over and extend my arms above my head whilst flexing my feet, revelling in the sensation of my muscles stretching after being curled up in a ball all night. I cuddle into Billy, enjoying the warmth of his body underneath the fluffy duvet, and continue to doze.

A little while later I force myself to wake up and get

out of bed, even though Billy is still sound asleep. I grab my phone and walk into the kitchen, fill up the kettle and flick it on. As it starts to grumble, letting me know that a well-needed coffee is on its way, I have a look at my phone. Sixty-seven missed calls and ten voicemails. Panic grabs me, instantly knowing that something has to have happened for people to be trying to get hold of me so urgently before ten o'clock in the morning. I go straight to the voicemails.

'Oh Sophie, I'm so sorry!' cries Molly's voice, causing a lump to form in my throat. I've never heard Molly cry as hard as this before. She sounds heartbroken. 'I didn't know, I honestly didn't. I wouldn't have told her anything if I had. But she kept asking me questions about you. I thought she just admired you, or realized how much I was missing you . . . I –' she tries, before breaking down in sobs. 'I didn't mean to tell her about you. I didn't know she was a journalist, Sophie.' My chest tightens as I make out her words through the sobs of regret. Eventually, she has to put the phone down because she can no longer speak.

There are seven more voicemails from her, each of them offering more of an explanation as to what's happened, which I start to piece together. It turns out Sally, the girl Molly decided to employ as my replacement, without even seeing her CV, is a freelance reporter. She hadn't just randomly turned up in Rosefont Hill to see her aunt, she was there to see if she could persuade me, face to face, to do an exclusive interview with her about my relationship with Billy. Instead she managed to get a job in the shop and worm my life story out of the clueless customers, fitting little pieces of information together until she had a story she could sell.

Once I've heard enough from Molly, I pull the phone away from my ear and discard it. Taking deep breaths, I steady myself on the kitchen worktop, wondering what to do. My mind feels empty, offering me no answers. Eventually, I walk into the hallway, grab my coat and walk to the corner shop, not caring that I'm obviously still in my pyjamas.

The sight of the front pages grips me by the throat, restricting my breathing. Each contains two pictures, one of me and Billy at the awards and one of me when I was younger, with my arms flung around my dad, kissing him on the cheek as he laughs at the camera. I know the picture well – after all, I've gazed at it long-ingly for years. It's also the one they used back then when it all happened.

I clench my jaw and push away the tears that threaten to spill out of me. Quickly, I grab one of the papers and pay for it at the counter, ignoring the idle chat com-ing from the young shopkeeper serving me, wanting to be back home as soon as possible.

Back at the kitchen table I put the paper in front of me and stare at my dad's beaming face. I sit down and slowly absorb the details of my life that someone I have never met has decided it's fair to share with the world, without my knowledge or consent, or giving me any warning.

SECRET HEARTACHE FOR BUSKIN'S GIRL

She's won over the heart of former lothario Billy Buskin, as he displayed in his acceptance speech at last month's BAFTAs, but behind Sophie May's dazzling smile hides a bitter heartache, which led her to shut herself away from those around her throughout her teenage years.

Speaking to friends close to Sophie it has been revealed that the tragic death of her dad, when she was just eleven years old, has understandably had a huge impact on Sophie's life.

Carla Daily, who grew up with Sophie, said, 'At primary school she was friends with everyone. She was always dancing or prancing around and found everything funny. She was such a lovely girl, always bubbly and kind. Everybody wanted to be her friend. She was the popular one who all of us flocked to.'

However, Sophie changed dramatically when her father, Dean May, was killed instantly in a hit-and-run accident, just minutes away from their family home in Rosefont Hill.

Carla continued, 'Obviously, there were rumours about what had happened flying around the playground, and I can still remember the school assembly when the headmaster called us all in to tell us about what had happened to Sophie's dad. At that age none of us had had to deal with news like that before, we didn't really understand death. We all just sat there looking confused, knowing that it was a terrible thing that had happened, but not quite sure what we were meant to feel or how to react. A lot of us cried, imagining how we'd have felt if it was our own dads and feeling bad for our friend's loss.

'It was so sad, but what shocked us the most was the state of Sophie when she finally came back into school. She looked ill. Her rosy cheeks had disappeared along with her smile. Her hair, which was always long and free-flowing, was now pulled back in a painfully tight bun. She looked awful.

'She no longer wanted to talk to anyone either, no matter how much anybody tried to comfort her. Whenever you tried to talk to her you'd see her shaking, as if she was scared of us. It was terrifying. She'd become a closed book; literally an empty shell of the girl that she once was. I tried on many occasions to talk to her about it, but seeing her wither away like that made me frightened to go near her, I didn't want to upset her further. So I gave up eventually, we all did.'

According to the source, Sophie's mum Jane May suffered from severe depression following her husband's sudden death, leaving Sophie to care for them both.

'I think a large part of that was having to look after her mum, who I heard had a breakdown as a result of the accident. It must've been a lot for Sophie to cope with, especially at such a young age. Very stressful, I imagine.

'We all moved to secondary school a few months after the accident. My mum thought the new environment would make Sophie better, give her a fresh start away from everyone who knew about her dad, but it made her worse. Somehow she managed to isolate herself even further. They didn't know what she had been like before, so they just accepted her as this quiet girl, meaning no one bothered with her.'

When at eighteen Sophie's peers were making plans for their futures, she shrugged off the idea of going to university or travelling, preferring to stay at home.

'It was pretty obvious that Sophie wouldn't leave her mum,' the friend continued. 'It's like the guilt of escaping their despair ate her up. To be honest, I never spoke to her about it, but from the moment her dad died, the Sophie we knew disappeared.'

Sophie never reformed the bonds with her former friends. Instead, it was working in her local teashop, at the end of sixth form, which brought her back into the community, thanks to her friend and former employer, Molly Cooper.

Looking back at the day Sophie first walked into the shop, she said, 'I knew who she was as soon as she walked through the door. All of us in the village had heard about what had happened to her dad, of course we had, but I didn't expect to see her looking so fragile so long afterwards. I wanted to do all I could to help her move forward, but obviously the death of someone so close, when they're just suddenly snatched away from you like that, is heartbreaking. I don't think anyone fully recovers from it. Ever.

'She still has the odd shaky day, you know, when things get brought to the surface. But her main concern is, and has always been, her mum.'

Speaking of the night the accident occurred, Molly said, 'Something like that, a death, in a village as small as this, hits the whole community hard. For days, it felt wrong to laugh or feel any joy. A black cloud had washed over us, so

I can only imagine how that must have felt for poor Sophie and her mum. Dean had only popped out to grab something quickly from the shops. He was literally a few hundred yards from home when he got knocked over. He died instantly.

'It wasn't just the death that Sophie had to deal with of course, it was the knowledge that people were whispering about her behind her back. That's what she really struggled with, and that's why she became a closed book, I think. No one was doing it to be mean, we were all just concerned, but as a child she viewed that differently. She just wanted to disappear. I think working here [in Tea-on-the-Hill] helped her see that, sometimes, calling on those around you is a good thing. Sometimes life is too tough to face alone, no matter how much you want to shut everybody out.'

It appears that, with the help of Molly and the customers in the shop, Sophie started to come out of her shell, after years of hiding away.

It was in this comfortable environment that she met Billy for the first time.

'I knew straight away that she'd caught Billy's eye,' continued Molly. 'Sophie's always shied away from any kind of attention, so she was completely oblivious to his affection for her. But I could see him watching her, being amused by her little ways. I knew he'd taken a shine to her.

'They have a connection which makes her feel safe in a world that has been full of so much uncertainty, whilst giving him the normal relationship he craves.'

Billy stated in his BAFTA acceptance speech that Sophie has completed his life, saying, 'There is one person here who I would like to thank . . . the better half of me, that is,

245

Miss Sophie May. I feel like I've already won the biggest prize of all having her beside me. It's thanks to her that my life is now complete.'

Well, it seems, in some way, that Billy has completed hers, too, by filling the void left by the sad death of her beloved father.

'What's that?' I hear Billy ask from behind me, causing me to jump in fright. I'd been so consumed by the article I hadn't heard him come in. 'What's wrong?'

I stay silent, aware of the tears and snot running down my face. Not sure what to say, I close the paper and slide it across the table in his direction, by way of an explanation. I hide my face, unable to look at him as he reads the front page, cringing as he turns the pages over and reads more. I sit motionless and wait.

'Where has this come from?' he says softly. 'Who did they tell all this to? Molly wouldn't talk to a journalist.'

'Sally . . .' I squeak.

I feel his hand on my back, moving in a gentle, rubbing motion. He leans into me and kisses the top of my head, staying close. I hear him make a few sounds with his mouth, taking breaths as if about to say something, but, like me, I guess he doesn't know where to start.

'Why didn't you tell me?' he asks, sadly.

'There was never a good time,' I answer truthfully.

'I knew something was wrong. Whenever you've talked about your childhood it's always been the memories that include your dad – but, obviously, I knew he wasn't around. I just didn't want to ask.'

246

'No, I know I should've told you. I almost did a couple of times,' I say, sighing. 'Losing Dad was the hardest time of my life. I've always felt that by telling you I'd be lifting the lid and making it all real again, having to relive it. It's taken me so long to want to move on with my life. I wanted to keep it in the past. I didn't want to taint what we have. I didn't want you to feel sorry for me. I don't want to see the pity in your eyes, too.'

'I can understand that, baby, but it's a huge part of who you are. OK, I promise to give you no pitiful looks,' he says, squeezing me into him once more before sitting beside me. 'It's out there now, though, so take your time and tell me about it. Tell me what happened,' he pleads. 'Tell me your version of what happened.'

It was the day after the three of us had painted my bedroom pink. Coming home from school I found Dad banging nails into the walls and hanging up photo frames, full of pictures of him, Mum and me. It looked wonderful. Looking at that wall made me feel so happy, wanted and loved. The three of us always had such fun together – we were a real team.

It was then that Mum decided to come in and sit me down on the bed with a big smile on her face, telling me she had some news to tell me. I honestly thought they were taking me to Disney World. Giddy excitement rose within me as I sat waiting for those words to come from her lips.

'I'm pregnant,' she announced, with a huge grin, glancing at Dad who was also beaming with joy beside her. 'You're going to have a little brother or sister to look after, aren't you a lucky girl?' she added as she wiggled my nose in her fingers.

I guess I was in shock, or disappointed that I wasn't going to meet Cinderella or Minnie Mouse; it wasn't usual for me to act up with my parents or be spiteful . . . but I just went berserk. I can remember screaming at them, telling them I hated them for destroying us. Asking them how they could be so mean. It was meant to be just us three. Wasn't I enough for them? I couldn't understand why they had done this awful thing. I told Mum she was too old to have a baby, that it would be disgusting when my friends spotted her walking around the village with an ugly bump, that she was an embarrassment.

I was only eleven years old, of course, but even then I knew better. I knew what I was saying was spiteful and malicious. I knew I was hurting them. The words still haunt me now along with the hurt expression on Mum's face. How could I have been so selfish to the two people I loved most in the world?

At first they tried to calm me down, but in the end they left me on my own in my room – letting me scream, shout and sob until I found myself exhausted into an angry silence.

A little while later I heard my door open and someone creep into my room. The sigh told me it was Dad. I was curled up under my duvet in bed, hugging Mr Blobby, pretending to sleep. He perched next to me on the bed, causing the whole thing to wobble.

'Soph, you will always be so special to us,' he said, pulling the duvet down slightly to reveal my face and stroking my forehead.

I stayed silent, still feigning sleep with my eyes shut.

'Do you want to know a secret? You'll always be my number one,' he persisted. 'I cried so much when you were born, I couldn't get over how much love I felt for this tiny little thing who was squawking her head off. I don't think I could love anyone as much as I love you.'

'That's what you say now, but wait until the baby comes along,' I shot back, opening my eyes and giving him a sulky pout. 'You won't love me as much then, I won't be your favourite any more.'

'Oh yes, you will,' he said, planting a kiss on my forehead, leaving his face right in front of mine on the pillow.

I looked into his eyes and I saw the sincerity.

Dad would never lie to me. Would he?

I bit my bottom lip, mulling over his worlds.

I needed to be sure.

I needed a guarantee.

'Pinkie promise?' I squeaked sadly, holding out my little finger.

'Pinkie promise,' he laughed, grabbing my little finger in his and shaking it wildly in the air, sealing the deal and making me chuckle. 'Now,' he added, his tone changing to a more serious one, letting me know that what he was about to say was important. 'Mummy is downstairs and she's a little bit sad that you're upset,' he said, as he brushed my hair away from my face. 'We have to take extra special care of her from now on. We can't be shouting at her and making her sad. She needs you.'

'I'm sorry, Daddy,' I mumbled, my lower lip starting to quiver.

'Hey, baby girl . . .' he cooed, kissing me again on the forehead. 'I know you are. Why don't you go downstairs and see Mummy? Give her a hug and tell her you're sorry?'

I pulled a face at him, needing further encouragement to take the walk of shame and apologize for my appalling behaviour.

'I'll make you one of Daddy's extra special hot chocolates if you do.'

'With cream and marshmallows?' I begged – making the most of the offer.

'Yes! And we can drink them in front of the fire if you like. Now, off you trot,' he said, lifting me off my bed and guiding me to the door.

I leapt down the stairs and ran into the living room to see Mum, who was lying on the sofa. I could see she had been crying and I felt terrible.

'I'm so sorry, Mummy,' I cried, bursting into big sobs at the thought of upsetting her.

'Oh, love . . .' she said, grabbing me and laying me down next to her on the sofa, giving me a big hug. I held her back, so tightly.

'I didn't mean the things I said.'

'I know, love. I know,' she whispered, kissing the side of my head.

'Is it going to be a girl or a boy?'

'We don't know yet.'

'If it's a little girl, can we call her Ginger?' I squeaked.

'As in the Spice Girl?'

I nodded in reply, as I looked at her with pleading eyes.

'We'll see, love. Although you already have a goldfish called Ginger, you don't want to upset her by stealing her name . . .'

'True,' I said sadly, wishing I hadn't given such a good name away to a boring fish.

We were still curled up on the sofa when Dad came in and said that we were out of marshmallows.

I moaned. It wouldn't be a real hot chocolate without marshmallows.

Anger rose within me again – had Dad known we were out of them and tricked me into coming downstairs? Had I been lied to? The tears that had only just left me threatened to spurt out once more.

Wanting to keep me calm and to stop another outburst, Dad decided to run down to the shops quickly to pick up some more.

Phew. Crisis averted.

'Do you fancy coming with me, Soph?' he asked, nudging me gently.

Lying there next to Mum on the sofa, all snuggled up in front of the fire, the thought of going out in the cold wasn't appealing at all. I didn't even answer him; I just closed my eyes and shook my head, holding on to Mum a bit tighter.

We dozed off.

It was the sound of sirens blasting by and the blue lights flashing past the front of the house that woke us with a start, causing us both to jump up off the sofa.

Mum's eyes were instantly full of fear. Looking back, it was as if she knew that something serious had happened. As if she knew it was Dad.

'Soph . . .' she said, coming down to my level calmly. 'I'm just going to go out and find Daddy. You stay here all wrapped up, OK?'

I nodded and watched as she walked out of the front door and into the cold, dark night.

She didn't even bother putting her coat on.

She left in her slippers.

Unsure what to do, I just stood in the same spot. Looking at the front door. Waiting for them both to come back home.

When I heard a knock on the door quite a while later I knew it wouldn't be either of them, they wouldn't have needed to knock – Dad had his keys with him.

I opened it to find a policewoman standing on the doorstep. She had a very kind face. She was sort of smiling at me, but it was a sad smile. A troubled smile.

'Sophie?' she asked.

I said nothing. I just nodded my head slowly.

'Hello, Sophie, I'm PC Wallis. Your mummy has asked me to pick you up so that we can go meet her. Is that OK?'

I can remember thinking to myself, 'She didn't mention my daddy. What about my daddy? Why aren't you taking me to him?' But I said nothing. I walked upstairs to get Mr Blobby and then followed PC Wallis to her car.

It felt so strange to be in the back of that police car behind PC Wallis and her partner — a young man who didn't even turn around and say hello. I can recall the route perfectly; I know the traffic lights that let us drive by without pausing and those which stopped us with their menacing red glare, where we were joined by other vehicles on the road and where we drove in solitude through the empty streets.

I didn't say anything to the two adults in front of me on that journey, and they didn't say a word to me. They barely spoke to each other, in fact. The only noise in the car was the constant bark of the police channel, '. . . any cars in the area can you make your way there immediately and report back. Over,' '. . . suspect on foot, heading west on Brucknell Road,' and lots more police jargon that I didn't understand. I listened carefully, though, trying to hear if there was any mention of my dad at all. There wasn't.

Once at the hospital, I was taken to Mum who was slumped on a chair in the middle of a busy corridor. Walking towards her I could see her puffy red face and could tell she'd been crying. I knew that wasn't a good sign.

I felt more scared than ever.

'Mum?' I said meekly, when I was finally standing in front of her, the short walk through the corridor seeming to have taken hours.

She looked up with a pained expression, her face and body crumpling as she slid off the chair on to her knees, grabbing hold of my waist and burying her head into my body.

Then she started wailing.

The noise was like nothing I'd ever heard before, loud and animal-like. It sounded as if she was in so much pain.

I stood there as her sobs vibrated through both of us, causing us to shake.

I can remember not knowing where to look as people around us began to stare at the broken woman on her knees, gripping hold of me. I wasn't embarrassed, though. I was numb.

Nothing made sense.

Mum never did tell me that Dad had died. Those actual words were never uttered from her mouth. The wailing, which lasted for months, told me everything I needed to know. That and the fact that Dad wasn't there to make her stop.

I didn't join in. I didn't shed a single tear when my dad died, because there was one thought that kept hammering around my head – it was my fault. If I hadn't been such a spoilt little cow, Dad wouldn't have been out in the dark on his way to buy a stupid packet of marshmallows. He wouldn't have been in the middle of the road as a car, going twice the national speed limit and driven by a drunk, whizzed around the corner and ran straight into him. Killing him instantly.

I'd done it.

It was my fault.

It was wrong for me to cry.

I'd look at Mum with her tortured faced and I'd be consumed with guilt.

Going back to school and seeing other people was awful. I couldn't bear the looks on their faces as I walked into a room — the stares, the whispers. I couldn't stand their kind, pitiful, empty words. Or how their eyes would well up as they spoke. I could feel their pain adding to my own, increasing my guilt and weighing me down further.

I was convinced that one day someone would find out the truth and declare me a murderer. That they'd all turn on me in disgust.

I withdrew into myself. My body language changed. I was so sunken, shoulders rounded, chest concave, head dipped. It was like I was trying to make myself as small as possible, so that nobody would notice me. I hated their attention.

At first, people did try and help me, to get me talking about what had happened, like my teacher Mrs Yates and the girl who had previously been my bestest friend, Laura Barber, but after a while they gave up and left me to my own devices. No longer sure what to say to try and tempt me to talk, or unable to understand that I hadn't 'gotten over it' already. Their desistance suited me fine. I didn't feel like I deserved their time. I had done a terrible thing. I had killed my dad. I didn't want them talking to me, or about me. I wanted to disappear.

That's when my panic attacks started — although I never had the courage to ask anyone for help. It was embarrassing. In some way I thought it was a punishment for being such a bad person.

Things went from bad to so-bad-she-wondered-what-there-was-left-to-live-for for Mum. She suffered a miscarriage just weeks after Dad's death.

The doctors weren't sure whether it was her age, stress-related, or simply one of those things – either way, she'd lost her husband and unborn child in a matter of weeks. She might have had me, but it seemed her unborn child had been her glimmer of hope – another connection to Dad that had disappeared.

She quickly became a shell of her former self. Nervous and twitchy, constantly cleaning anything and everything, she obsessed over it and became panicky if things weren't done her way.

Our relationship at that time was strained to say the least.

She never blamed me. Never mentioned the fact that if I had only let Dad give me a blooming hot chocolate without marshmallows, then he'd still be with us, but I knew that's what she thought. I'd robbed her of her husband and her unborn child.

A light in her eyes had gone out – as though part of her had died too. She didn't love me as much. She would sometimes still hug me and talk to me like a mother does but it would be rigid and stiff, her mind was elsewhere. She was empty. Cold. Distant.

She kept working through her grief. She had to. With Dad gone she was the only one able to bring money home. She spent as much time as she could at the library, hating being at home. I wasn't sure whether that was because Dad's belongings were still scattered around the house as a constant reminder that he was no longer with us, or so that she could spend as little time with me as possible.

When I was old enough, I decided to get a job in the local flo-rist's to help Mum with the bills at home. I wasn't getting much, £15 for a full day's work on a Saturday, but it all helped. I was their 'bucket girl', the one who had to clean out all the slimy buckets at the end of the working week. I liked the job because I was secluded, able to hide away in the back room not talking to anyone while I got on with the cleaning. I also liked it because the owner would let me take some bunches home with me if they were past their best. There was something about the life of a flower and its brief beauty that had me transfixed — all its energy went into blooming. For that one moment they'd be beau-tiful and close to perfection — but as soon as that moment had passed, they'd start to shrivel away almost instantly. I saw my life in those rotten petals. My family had bloomed to its peak, but now we were withering away.

All I wanted was my mum back. I'd lie awake at night lis-tening to the sobs coming from behind her bedroom door. Sometimes, especially if I'd had an attack in the night, I'd want nothing more than to go to her. To be held by her. On those occa-sions I would take Mr Blobby and tiptoe across the landing. I wouldn't go into her room. I wouldn't even knock. I'd just sit outside hugging my toy. Longing for my mum but feeling too ashamed to reach out for her. I didn't want to add to her worries when she was already so fragile.

For six years we lived under a cloud of doom, not really com-municating or expressing how we felt. Life had stopped. We walked around our house in silence, unsure how to move for-ward, not wanting to move too far away from what was.

Mum's close call with the pills was the start of our recovery. She promised that she hadn't meant to take them. She just wanted to end her recurring nightmares so that she could sleep. She wasn't thinking straight. Hadn't thought about how her actions could've left me all alone in the world. It was a horrific time, especially as it took us back to the emergency ward at the hospital – back to that horrific place.

It was after her stay in hospital that things started to become more bearable. We began to talk, not about Dad or anything important, but about silly things – books we'd read, or something we'd seen on the news. It allowed a relationship to be rebuilt between us.

I made sure I was there for her, whether she needed me or not. I'd cook when I got home from school, making sure we'd sit down together and eat – something we'd stopped doing when our unit had been blown apart. I started doing more around the house so that Mum had less to worry about, although her obsession with cleaning and for things to be precise continued, so there was only so much I could do. I was there more, choosing to sit downstairs with her instead of being cooped up in my bedroom alone, blocking out the world. I watched TV or films with her. Sometimes we'd just sit and read together. We even did the odd puzzle.

I think that's when she started loving me again. I don't think she had anything left inside her to give before that.

With Mum on her way to coming back to me, there was no way I could think of leaving Rosefont Hill to go travelling or to university. How could I swan off and live another life when I had done this to Mum?

The guilt still clung to me, making me doubt myself and keeping me away from other people. All my energy and time went into keeping Mum safe and well. I still didn't think I was worthy of anyone else's love or affection.

It was Molly who made me see that I was. She never asked questions about that time that had obviously had a massive impact on my life and she never looked at me with pitiful eyes. To others I felt like the walking personification of my dad's tragic death, but to Molly I was simply Sophie May, a quiet little girl who was willing to learn.

Molly's husband Albert had died a few years earlier from a heart attack, so she knew what it was to grieve the loss of someone you loved more than anything else in the world. We had something in common. She never tried to force information out of me, but she did talk about Albert a lot. She was forever telling me stories of the pair of them and their son Peter. I admired her for doing so. I saw that by speaking of the man she loved she was keeping his spirit alive, that he was as much a part of her then as he was when he was living. So, I did talk to her about Dad, about how he used to make me laugh and how much I missed him. She was the only one I've ever opened up to. I couldn't bring him up at all at home — even after years had passed it felt too raw, I wasn't sure how Mum would react. I couldn't cope with the thought of seeing more anguish in her eyes when she was on her way to getting better.

In time, I spoke to Molly about the actual night of Dad's death, Mum's miscarriage, and how guilty I felt. How, in my eyes, I was just as guilty as the drunk driver who ran into him. She was aghast that I'd been carrying those feelings around with me for so long. Shocked that it was guilt that had driven me to cut myself off and feel unworthy. Eventually, she made me realize that what had happened was a tragic accident, and one that I'd punished myself for long enough.

It wasn't as if I transformed my life and turned back into the carefree, larger-than-life character I was before my dad died — I don't think she'll ever return — but I started to let people in a bit more. I started to feel human again.

Obviously, as an adult, looking back I can see that I didn't actually kill my dad, some intoxicated moron, who was too drunk to realize that he'd even knocked someone over, let alone killed them, had. I can see that I didn't actually cause my mum to miscarry either; events like that are out of our control. However, somewhere deep inside me that eleven-year-old girl still picks away at me occasionally, causing me to doubt myself. After all, the chain of events did start with me, and my appalling behaviour . . .

I stop speaking, suddenly aware that tears have been streaming down my face whilst filling Billy in on the details of those morbid years.

'I'm sorry,' I say, taking a few deep breaths to calm myself down.

'Baby, you don't need to say sorry,' says Billy softly, his forehead lined with concern.

'I worry that I'm forgetting him . . .' I blurt. 'I don't remember his face any more. Well, I do, but the image in my head is from the pictures of him I've had surrounding me, not of him moving around and actually living. I can't remember his laugh, his voice . . .' I admit, shaking my head.

'That's only natural, but it doesn't mean you love him any less.'

'But I never really knew him. Not in the way adults know and understand each other, you know? I knew him as a child,' I explain. 'I heard somewhere that when people die, those around them have a desire to turn them into some sort of saint, to put them on this unrealistic pedestal, which is far from the reality of who that person actually was. Maybe I've done that. Maybe he wasn't a great man.'

'And maybe he was.'

'Maybe . . .' I mutter, looking at the floor, trying to gather my thoughts. Surprised that I've allowed myself to voice this fear, which I've kept to myself for so long. 'Oh, I'm so angry with Molly!' I groan.

'But she didn't know what Sally was up to. You know that.'

'No, Billy, that's not the point. I didn't think she'd ever share what I told her with anyone else.'

'But she didn't. Can't you see that she didn't share any of the details you've just told me? You don't know what Sally said to get those words out of her or how she's twisted her sentences to fit the piece. This Carla person must've mentioned the whole thing first; it wouldn't have been Molly, that's for sure.'

I think back to the text I'd received from Carla on the night of the BAFTAs; she did say that she'd be back in Rosefont Hill to see her parents the following week, and that she'd pop into the shop while she was there, so no doubt that's when she would have spoken to Sally. Carla probably went in declaring that she was once my best friend or some nonsense like that. She'd have loved passing on information and acting in the know, probably feeling a little bit vindictive because her message to me had gone unanswered. My guess is that, after getting wind of the story, Sally would have turned to Molly for clarification of what she'd heard or simply to fill in the blanks.

'I just wish she hadn't said anything. I know she loves a gossip, but this is . . .' I shake my head, at a loss for words.

'Has she tried to call you?' Billy asks calmly.

'Yes. I've had more than sixty calls from her,' I say sheepishly.

'Don't you think you should call her back?'

'No! Not yet . . . I can't yet. I have to think about what I'd say first.'

'What about your mum?' Billy asks with a sigh.

I hadn't even thought about Mum. I don't remember seeing any missed calls from her, but she's bound to have seen the papers today in the library.

'I'll call her!' I say, rushing to get my phone from the kitchen counter, ashamed at not having phoned her sooner.

'Hello, Rosefont Hill Library. Susan speaking. How can I help?' Susan asks in her usual bored tone.

'Susan, it's Sophie here.'

'Oh, hello,' she says, perking up at the mention of my name.

'Is Mum there at all?'

'No, she's taken the day off.'

'Oh.'

'Although she did open up first thing. She was here when the papers arrived but then asked to leave when I got in. Said she wasn't feeling well,' she says dubiously, letting me know that there was more to it.

'Right, I'll try her at home, then. Thanks, Susan,' I say before putting down the phone and dialling mum's home number, shooting Billy a worried glance.

'She left when she saw the papers,' I say, shaking my head, listening to the continuous ringing of the phone. 'There's no answer.'

I look at Billy in a panic.

'Don't worry . . . let's just drive out there.'

'Are you sure?' I ask, already running to the bedroom to change out of my pyjamas so that we can leave.

'Of course!' he says, following me, throwing on some clean clothes. 'It's not as if either of us is going to relax until we know she's OK, are we?'

I don't bother knocking when we arrive home. I use my key instead and let us both in. We walk through to the living room, where we find Mum sitting on the floor, surrounded by boxes. Straight away I feel sick at the thought of her obsessive cleaning again; however, before I can react I spot what's in her hand and scattered on the floor around her: photos of Dad. Tears instantly prickle at my eyes.

'Mum?'

'Oh,' she says, startled, clearly deeply immersed in the photo she was looking at. 'Hello, you two. What are you doing all the way out here?' she asks, before lifting the photograph to her face, a smile forming as she takes in the image.

'I tried to call you.'

'Oh, was that you? I thought it was one of those cold callers,' she says, distractedly.

'Mum?' I plead, knowing that she's seen the papers, and that she knows why we're here.

'I'm fine, love,' she says, lowering the photo in her hand and letting out a sigh, looking up at us both.

'Really?'

'Yes . . .' she says slowly, looking back down at the pictures on the floor. 'I saw that photo in the paper and had a sudden longing to see more of them. I can't remember the last time I had a good root through all of these. I don't think I have since . . .' she breaks off sadly.

'Do you want a cup of tea?' asks Billy, gently rubbing her shoulder.

Mum places her hand on top of his and pats it as she nods.

'Thank you, darling.'

With Billy out of the room I go over and kneel beside Mum, looking down at the scattered photos.

'I don't think I've even seen most of these!' I say, as I pick up photos of Mum and Dad looking extremely young and funky.

'No, you won't have done, because you're not in them,' Mum says with a chuckle.

'What do you mean by that?'

'You used to have this obsession about it being the

three of us . . . I don't think your little mind could quite grasp back then that your mummy and daddy had a life before you were born. It was as if we were leaving you out and you'd go off and sulk. You were only interested in seeing pictures that involved you in some way.'

'Such a spoilt brat,' I mutter.

'No, you weren't . . . you just had some funny ways about you, that's all. Your dad used to find your little quirks so endearing. He used to argue that it was charming and that your need for inclusion was beautiful. You were never needy, love, you were a giver. His little lovebug.'

I can't help the lump that forms in my throat or the tears that fall at hearing this new piece of information.

'I'm so sorry . . .' I say, instantly feeling guilty, wiping the tears away.

'There's nothing wrong with crying, love,' Mum says, putting her hand on my knee. 'I used to worry about you not letting your emotions out.'

I just nod, biting my lip, not sure what to say.

'Sometimes I just lie in bed and think about what must go through his head as he looks down at us,' she confesses. 'I know he'd be so proud of you, Sophie.'

'Really?' I ask meekly, not sure that I understand why he would be.

'Oh yes, moving to London like that was a big decision, driven by love, he'd have liked that bit. He was such a romantic thing. Although, I don't know what he'd have been like around Billy.'

'Don't you think he'd have liked him, then?'

'Oh, he'd have loved him. But your dad was so protective of his little angel. I think he'd be keeping Billy at arms' length, letting him know that if he were ever to cross the line and hurt you that he'd be in for it.'

'I'd have won him round in no time!' declares Billy as he comes back into the room carrying a tray with three mugs.

'I don't doubt that,' grins Mum.

'What on earth are you two wearing in this one?' I ask, laughing, as I spot a photo of the pair of them, Mum wearing a yellow chequered dress and Dad in a flower-patterned shirt, unbuttoned to reveal a tad too much chest hair, with high-waisted orange hipsters.

Mum takes the photo, peers closely at it and just smiles.

'That was our first date at the cinema, one of his friends took it, I think.'

I look at Mum as she absorbs the image and remembers a happier time. A bubble of love and warmth engulfing her as she enjoys the feeling reminiscing gives her, after blocking out those memories for so long.

The doorbell rings, causing us all to look at each other. I notice Mum's cheeks turn a bright shade of pink.

'Erm . . . I'll just go and get that,' she says, before shuffling towards the front door.

Billy looks at me questioningly. I shrug in response, not sure who it could be and what could cause Mum's sudden change of behaviour.

When we hear Mum's muffled conversation at the

door, it's immediately apparent that she is trying to get rid of whoever has arrived. It's a man. I assume it's the male company she's been keeping. Without thinking I jump to my feet and head towards them.

I spot Mum hanging out of the front door talking quickly to an ashen-faced man in front of her.

'Hi, I'm Sophie,' I say, peering over Mum's shoulder at the visitor. 'Do you want to come in for a cuppa? The kettle's still hot.'

Mum turns to me, her jaw slackened in shock, not quite sure how to deal with the situation.

'Erm . . . is that OK, Jane?' the man asks, looking at Mum hesitantly.

She looks at me before she answers, studying my face to see if it's a good idea.

'Yes . . . yes, that would be nice. Sophie, this is my friend Colin,' she says, stepping out of the way to let Colin enter.

'Hello, Sophie, a pleasure to meet you finally. I've heard so much about you,' he says, reaching forward and giving me a kiss on the cheek.

I smile back at him, taking in his rounded face and neat grey hair, his voice soft and kind. Yes, I can see why Mum would like spending time with him; so far he seems very friendly.

'Shall we go into the kitchen?' I ask, aware of the photos of Dad still on the floor in the living room and not wanting this to be even more uncomfortable than it already is.

'Good idea,' says Mum, giving my hand a quick squeeze, before leading the way.

'I'll bring in our teas,' offers Billy loudly from the other room, letting us know he's been listening in.

'I brought this round for you, Jane,' Colin says, pulling a 550-piece puzzle of baked beans out of the plastic bag he has been carrying. 'It's called an impossipuzzle, or something like that. Aaron, my son,' he says for my benefit, 'gave it to me last Christmas.'

'Oh?' questions Mum.

'It's highly frustrating as it all looks the blooming same, but I guess that's what makes it all the more satisfying when you finish it,' he adds sheepishly. 'It took me days.'

'Well, thank you,' says Mum, as she takes the box and studies it.

I'm drawn in by the innocence of the exchange, happy that Mum has someone in her life to make such simple, yet thoughtful, gestures.

Silence falls on the room as we all stand awkwardly looking at the floor.

'Oh, sorry! I'll get you that tea!' I blurt, turning to the kettle.

Before we head back to London, I walk up to my old bedroom and pack some of the photo frames and pictures from my wall, deciding to hang them up in Billy's flat instead – his idea. It feels strange to take them down from the spot where Dad hung them all those years ago, but I know I'll benefit more from having them with me and being able to look at them every day.

Mum walks in on me and wraps her arms around me.

'Thank you,' she whispers.

'Don't be silly. You couldn't have left him out in the cold,' I smile. 'He seems nice.'

'He is.'

Mum sits on the bed and sighs heavily, letting me know she's about to say something I don't want to hear.

'You really should call Molly, love.'

'I will,' I say with a shrug, not really wanting to talk about Molly now, happy to ignore the situation.

'Petal, I spoke to her earlier and she feels awf—'

'Mum!' I moan, stopping her.

She sighs again, clearly disappointed that I don't want to discuss the matter – but unable to leave it there.

'Just remember everything she's done for you. This isn't her fault.'

'I know, Mum. I know. I promise I'll call her later.'

'Well, don't make her wait too long. She's a good lady who is distraught at having let you down. Don't make her suffer,' she pleads. 'She's really done nothing wrong.'

I try to focus on the photos in front of me, as I pack them into a box, blocking out Mum's words. I don't want to speak to Molly yet. I know she'll be feeling terrible, and I hate that Sally has used her in this way, but I'm just not ready to tell her it's fine and that it doesn't matter. Not yet. It's already been such a heartrending day, I'm exhausted, and I don't think I could cope with another big chat right now.

Sitting in the car on the way home Billy takes my hand and kisses it.

'You OK?'

'Bizarrely, yes,' I say, smiling back at him. 'What a strange day.'

'It's been an emotional one for you.'

'Yeah. I feel quite drained now.'

'I bet.'

'It's good to see Mum looking happy with Colin, though.'

'Did you find it strange to see?'

'Not really, actually. They seem more like friends than anything else, don't they? But even if they're more than that, I think it's made me realize how lonely this has been for her. I'm glad she has someone to talk to and look out for her.'

'He seemed very caring.'

'Yeah, I liked him.'

'He's widowed too, you know,' Billy reveals.

'Really?'

'His wife passed away in her sleep two years ago.'

'Oh . . .' It's tragic that they've both lost their significant others, but it comforts me to know Mum has someone to share that pain with now. Colin has clearly been the reason behind her new outlook and being able to look back at her life with Dad with joy, so I'm grateful to him for that.

'Paul called when you were upstairs with your mum,' continues Billy. 'He's been trying to get hold of me all day. I had a brief chat with him.'

'What did he say?'

'Nothing much, just checking that you're OK.'

'That's nice of him.'

'He's had a few editors approach him to see if you'd like to share your side of the story. But he's told them that seeing as they didn't have the human decency to contact you before running the story, you have no desire to speak to them now. I think that was the right thing for him to say.'

'Yeah! Definitely,' I say.

'He's really fighting your corner.'

What's this? Paul showing some kindness towards me? He has a business mind when it comes to Billy, always striving for him to reach the dizzy heights of stardom, but maybe somewhere in there he actually does have a heart. Maybe . . . or perhaps he just wants Billy to think he does.

18

'Right, I just want you to read it,' says Billy, a few days later, coming out of the bedroom with the script of *The Walking Beat* in his hands.

I look at him questioningly.

'Why?'

'So that you know what to expect . . .' he says, biting his lip.

'In what way?'

He shrugs, guilt flickering across his face.

'Is this your way of telling me there're a few scenes I won't be thrilled about?'

Billy sighs, sitting down next to me on the sofa.

'I just want you to read it all in context, if I tell you what's in it without you seeing it you'll just freak.'

'Your words are so comforting right now,' I say sarcastically.

'I'm sorry. Just remember it's an amazing script with a brilliant director, who will film it in an arty way. It's going to look more classy and less like porn.'

'What?'

'Argh! See? I'm not good at explaining it,' he moans, covering his eyes with his hands. 'I just want you to think of it as more of a mechanical thing, rather than something with feelings involved. Just read it, please?'

'Fine!' I say grumpily, turning the first page, irritated as Billy continues to just sit on the sofa, staring at me as I go to read it. 'Are you just going to watch me?'

'Sorry,' he says, breaking away and getting up off the sofa. 'Actually, Paul wanted me to drop by and sign some papers. I might as well go do that quickly while you read this.'

'OK.'

'Love you,' he shouts as he walks out of the door.

I don't have to read very far into the script to find the first 'love' scene, in fact the film opens with one, and it makes me want to vomit.

APRIL, 1971, LONDON, ENGLAND
INT. STAN'S HOTEL ROOM

The door of a hotel room bashes open, in wades STAN BAR - A DANGEROUSLY SEXY ROCK STAR IN HIS LATE TWENTIES - with a woman - MEGAN REACH, EARLY TWENTIES - wrapped around his waist. He carries her into the room and slams the door behind them in haste. The pair grab at each other longingly, exploring each other's mouths, writhing around in excitement.

Stan throws Megan on to the bed, away from him, slowing down the process. He picks up a packet of cigarettes from the side, pulls one out and lights it, taking a deep drag. The pair hold eye contact throughout, as though this is part of the foreplay. Stan unbuttons his shirt and lets it drop to the floor, revealing his toned body. He takes another drag and watches Megan and waits for her as she does the same. Stan looks at Megan's bra, raising his eyebrows slightly, telling her to take it off. She does so, freeing her breasts. She looks at him expectantly, nibbling her lip in excitement at what's to come. With one hand Stan unbuckles his belt and unbuttons his trousers causing them to drop. Without waiting for Megan's next move he lowers his pants. Close-up of Megan's eyes as they widen with delight. She quickly removes her skirt, leaving her in just her knickers. She leans back on the bed, arching her back, her eyes begging Stan to come to her. He walks towards the foot of the bed, takes another drag and removes the cigarette, holding it in his hand. Using his one free hand he slides his palm up Megan's leg, stopping occasionally to tease her, their breathing gets more laboured the higher he goes. Holding eye contact still, he lowers her knickers, inch by inch. Once they're off he discards them on the floor and puts out his cigarette. Stan lifts one of Megan's legs and rubs his bottom lip in the arch of her foot. With his tongue he traces his way up her body again, ignoring where she wants him the most and finding her neck. As he sucks on her ear lobe Megan moans with pleasure.

I clench my jaw as I read through the rest of the script, each rub, lick, kiss and grind resonating through my brain, giving me a headache. I place it on the coffee table in front of me, resisting the urge to chuck it across the room, and grab the cushion next to me for comfort, hugging it into me tightly.

Despite the presence of all these detailed scenes, I can see why Billy was so drawn to the script – it's intense, dark and electrifying. Essentially, it follows a rock star as he reaches the height of his fame and has everything: all the money he could wish for, groupies at every venue, and the critical acclaim – however, as booze, drugs and sex take over his life, he becomes self-destructive, paranoid and increasingly violent, which results in him killing his wife. Although he is cleared of the charges, thanks to a back-hander to the judge, his reputation is in tatters. The uncertainty of his future sees him increasing his drug use, causing him to see his wife's face everywhere, as though she's haunting him. It's thrilling and gripping, and miles away from the teenage drama of *Halo*, so I can understand why it's a great project for Billy to be involved in . . . but even so, that doesn't make it any easier to read or accept.

I'm not sure whether to be pleased that Billy has handed me this to look at or not, although I'd have been in for a big shock if I'd have turned up to the set, ignorant of what was about to take place, as I watched him roll around with some girl and pull her knickers off.

The reality is that this is his job, though, right? No matter how different Stan Bar is from Mr Darcy,

I knew what he did when we got together, so I can't start throwing my weight around now, making demands. But the thought of him on set, licking, stroking and thrusting various naked girls makes me feel heartbroken – no matter how innocent the filming of the scenes might be.

Reading the script, it makes sense that actors usually date other actors. To those outside of the profession, the notion of sending your partner off to work every day where he'll be fondling someone else is just plain barbaric. At least with two actors they each have to do the same thing, sharing some sort of mutual understanding.

I sigh heavily as Russell Mode's words trickle into my brain . . . 'Every girl in the industry is going to be batting their eyelashes in his direction now, doing everything they can to get his attention.' If ever there were a time for a girl to be close enough to tempt Billy and demand his attention, it would be when she's got her naked body wrapped around him, while he's nibbling on her ear.

I know my reaction to this script is pivotal. If I react badly, blow up and go nuts at the stupidity of someone doing scenes like this when they're in a committed relationship, I'll push Billy away and drive a wedge between us. I'll be giving these girls the advantage of things not being rosy at home. Allowing them to wiggle their way through the cracks and come between us. However, if I stand by Billy and realize it's work, nothing more, turn up on set and be as nice as pie to everyone, becoming friends with them all, there's no way they'd cross that line. Not if I show I'm an actual figure in Billy's life, who he loves and respects. Right?

I have to remain calm and rational, no matter how tempted I am to scream and shout, declaring the whole thing ridiculous. It's only for eight weeks, after all, how hard can that be?

'I have to tell you something,' says Billy, striding through the front door an hour later, puffing in distress.

'OK . . .'

Having read the script I still feel a bit queasy – the fact that Billy is obviously in a state over something else does not fill me with confidence.

'Paul . . .' he says, scratching his head as he screws up his face in angst. 'While I was there he found out who'd been cast opposite me in the film.'

'And . . .?'

'It's Heidi Black.'

I repeat the name in my head for a while, knowing that it sounds familiar, but not being able to place it.

'Heidi Black? I know that name . . .' I say in confusion. That's when it dawns on me. 'She's your ex.'

'Yes,' says Billy, biting his lip and looking uncomfortable.

'Ah . . .'

'I don't want you to panic,' he says, taking my hands and rubbing the backs of them with his thumbs.

'You're going to be doing these sex scenes with your ex?'

'I know this is going to be really odd, but trust me, it'll all be so professional and above board. It's literally a case of putting what where for the camera, anyway.'

'Right . . .' I say, trying to get my head around this new development. I remember back to the time I sat Googling Billy before our first date and Heidi came up with her luscious blonde hair and toned body. Clicking through those photos led me to feel worthless. How will I cope when Billy is around her and her perfection every day?

I have to play this carefully, especially as Billy has been open about everything, and not left me to discover it for myself this time.

'She's more like a friend now, anyway. Well, a friend I never speak to. Plus, she's engaged to this producer, they're getting married at the end of the year. It's not as if either of us is still in the place we were. It's been years . . .' Billy stops and lets out a sigh. 'I'm babbling on.'

'You are!'

'I'm so sorry. I've no idea why they've cast her. The whole way through casting they've been banging on about getting me as far away from *Halo* as possible, so it doesn't make sense.'

'Billy, it's fine.'

'It's not.'

'Yes, it is,' I say, putting my arms around him.

'I want you there, so you can see it's all above board, that it's all about hitting your markers and making it look right. It's technical, nothing else.'

'Baby . . . I trust you with all my heart,' I say sincerely, knowing that I do and thankful that he's taking such care over the matter, rather than expecting me to take it in my stride.

'Good! The last few weeks have really made me realize how much I love you, Sophie. I want to protect you from being hurt for the rest of my life. Honestly, you don't need to worry about me doing these scenes. They mean nothing, so I don't want you to panic.'

There's no stopping that, I think to myself, wondering how I'll manage to keep calm when I see him kissing Heidi Black on screen.

The new Heidi Black development makes me phone Molly. She is the only one I want to talk to about the matter. The only one I know won't judge me if I moan or vent. I need her.

I've been so wrapped up in my own torment and misery that I selfishly blocked out how Molly must've been feeling during that time. In the eight or more years that I've known Molly I've never gone a day without speaking to her. It's been a week – far too long – and I know I should have phoned her sooner.

I wait until Billy is out and I know Molly will be at home and able to talk without prying ears. I crawl into bed and dial her number.

My heart thumps as the phone rings and I wait for her to pick up.

'Hello?' she eventually answers, sounding out of breath.

'Molly, it's me.'

'Oh, my darling! I'm so sorry.'

'You don't have to be, Molly. It's not your fault.'

'No, but . . .' she says, flustered over where to start. 'Sally started up a friendship with Carla, you see. She'd come to me and asked these questions about you – I didn't want to say anything but I had to put her straight. Carla had said all sorts of rubbish.'

'Molly, honestly you don't have to explain.'

'She didn't even tell me,' Molly continues. 'She just didn't turn up for work on the Saturday, she didn't call or anything. I spent the whole day worrying. And then on the Sunday I saw the papers and knew exactly what she'd been up to.'

'That's awful.'

How could someone trick such a kind lady as Molly in that manner? Does this Sally have no shame whatsoever?

'Everyone in the village is outraged!' she continues. 'Everyone had been so nice to her.'

Suddenly I realize it's not just me who needs to vent some anger and get things off her chest. Likewise, it's not just me that has been wronged.

I listen as Molly continues, clearly eager to share her version of events.

'A few of the ladies came to me because they were worried about the things that they'd told her – I had a right panic at what else that little toerag knew. Miss Brown was in a complete state about the whole thing. But when I asked her a few questions it turned out it wasn't anything about you, she'd only sung your praises. No, she was worried that she'd admitted to lying to her family about baking the cakes we make for her every time they visit.' At this Molly starts laughing hysterically. 'Oh, I know I shouldn't . . . but as if the nation would really care about that?'

'You never know, "Granny Brown's baking frown" has quite a ring to it,' I chuckle back.

'Oh my sweetpea, I'm really am so sorry. I know that must've hit you hard.'

'You know what, Mol, it did but I'm glad it's out there now.'

'Really?'

'Yeah. I should've told Billy months ago.'

'Probably explains a thing or two about your hermit behaviour!'

'Oi! I've only just forgiven you,' I laugh.

'You said I didn't need forgiving!'

There are certain people in life who can tease you about your idiosyncrasies without you getting seriously offended. For me, Molly is the only one who can joke about my shortcomings and get away with it. I imagine that's because we know each other so well.

'I'm so sorry it's taken me so long to call you, Mol. It was stupid of me to leave it this long.'

'Don't be daft.'

'No, it was childish of me. I should've called you straight away.'

'You're calling now, love, that's all that matters!' she coos. 'How is everything there anyway?'

'Fine . . . except you'll never guess who Billy's new leading lady is.'

'Who?'

'His ex.'

'Noooooo!'

'Yep.'

'Crikey. You're not worried, are you?'

'I'm not overjoyed about it!'

'That's hardly surprising, dear. It's just another part, though – like all the rest.'

'Yes, Mol, but this script is so . . . explicit!'

'In what way?'

'Sex. And lots of it.'

'Oh dear.'

'Seriously, I wouldn't even be able to read a single scene to you without blushing.'

'What are you more worried about? Him being with his ex or filming naughty bits like that?'

'To be honest, both fill me with dread,' I say, as I ponder the question. 'What if all his old feelings for her come flooding back? I can't compete with her, Molly, I know I can't.'

'But you don't have to!'

'I just can't bear the thought of losing him.'

'You know what, I never once thought about life without Albert. Not once did I think to myself, "How will I cope if he's no longer here?" But then he died and I learnt how to cope. Even when Peter decided to leave me and move halfway across the world, I coped,' Molly says. 'My point is, there's no point worrying about losing Billy when you still have him. Where's the sense in that? All you'll end up doing is tainting everything with your doubt.'

'I guess . . .'

'My girl, just remember that it's you he comes home to every night.'

'Yes, but is there any point in him coming home if he'd rather be somewhere else? There's so much happening at the moment, opportunities being offered every day – it's all so exciting for him. But for me it's just . . .'

'Overwhelming?'

'Yeah. I guess. I've got nothing exciting to give him.'

I hear Molly sigh down the phone. 'Don't let your doubts get into his head – nothing will push him away faster. That boy loves you, Sophie. You've got to start believing you're good enough.'

19

Billy meets his fellow cast members for *The Walking Beat* at rehearsals a couple of weeks before filming, with the director wanting to warm them all up so that they don't waste time on set. Following his first day with them all, I don't ask Billy too many questions when he first comes through the door (I don't want him to know I'm trying to size up the situation), but when we're sitting down for dinner a little later I try to delicately ask a few questions about the cast. Trying to prise information out of him without making it known that I'm worried the girls are maneaters, ready to pounce on my man at the first opportunity they're given.

'So, what's everybody like?' I ask innocently, twirling my spaghetti round my fork.

'Really nice, actually. I didn't really get a chance to talk to people that much, there's so much to do. The guys in the band are awesome. Literally they just sit there jamming any time there's a break. It makes me wish I knew how to play something.'

Billy's character Stan is the band's lead vocalist and frontman. Whereas the rest of the band were cast for their musical abilities, with the director wanting them to be able to function as a band, the role of Stan needed someone with charisma, charm and sex appeal as the driving force . . . so ego over musical talent.

'You feeling left out?'

'Kind of . . . and talentless,' laughs Billy. 'I've made it my mission to be able to play a song on guitar by the end of filming.'

'Which song are you going to learn?'

'God knows . . . an easy one!'

'So, what's everyone else like? Are all the girls nice?' I ask, placing a big forkful of pasta into my mouth to stop myself asking more questions.

'You mean my groupies? They seem nice,' he says with a shrug. 'All really welcoming and just as nervous about the whole thing as I am.'

'I bet they are. What are their names?'

'Erm . . .' Billy says as he struggles to remember them. 'God, this is bad. There's Holly, Rebecca, Karen and Sarah. I can't remember the other two, I didn't see that much of them. It's good to have a bit of rehearsal time, it helps to get rid of that awkwardness of being touchy-feely with someone you've just met. This way, when we get on set we'll just be able to bash out scenes easily rather than having to be wary of upsetting each other.'

'Right . . .'

'They're looking forward to meeting you.'

'Really? I thought you didn't get a chance to speak much?'

'We didn't, but you're always on my mind,' he says, with a laugh and a wink.

It's good to know Billy's been talking about me, that I'm not banished from his mind the moment he steps into a room full of girls. However, I wonder if he has mentioned me because he's looking forward to having me on set with him, or because someone's been getting too close for comfort?

'How were things with Heidi?'

Billy screws up his face.

'What does that mean?'

'She's been a bit off with me. A bit . . . frosty.'

'Why?'

'I've got no idea, I thought things were fine between us. Although she's been like it with everyone else, too, not just me, so something must be going on with her.'

'That must be strange for you, after being so close.'

'A bit, but as long as she's OK in the scenes and does her job, which she seems to be doing, that's all that matters.'

I find myself happy that Heidi has placed some sort of barrier between them; I'd rather that than them being overly close and familiar, remembering the good old days.

On the morning of the first day on set we get picked up by a driver at five am. It's painful to see that time in the morning, no matter how excited I am to join Billy at work. I clamber around the bedroom trying to make my brain function enough to get dressed, not sure what to wear. Seeing Billy lazily put on his comfies, I end up throwing on a pair of jeans, a woolly jumper and a pair of Ugg boots Billy bought me for Christmas (I'm pretty sure they're the comfiest thing ever invented).

When we eventually get into the car, we fall straight back to sleep.

As soon as we arrive at the studio, an hour later, we are ushered into Billy's dressing room, which is basically a caravan in the car park. It's simple, cute and very warm. It has a little kitchen/living/bedroom area all rolled into one, with a brown sofa-bed in the bay of the window, TV, kettle and fridge in the one space. It has its own bathroom attached to the side of it with a toilet, sink and shower inside. It's not the most glamorous place in the world, but it's exciting, nonetheless. For me it is, anyway, Billy has obviously been in various different versions of the same thing many times before.

We barely have a chance to put our bags down when there's a knock at the door.

'Come in,' calls Billy.

The door opens and a man wearing a red knitted hat and black bomber jacket walks in carrying a clipboard under him arm.

'Hello, Billy!' he says chirpily.

'Stephen, good to see you, buddy!' Billy says, as they share a man hug. 'This is Sophie.'

'Hey!' he says, turning to me and shaking my hand.

'Hello!'

'I've heard a lot about you. I'm Stephen, I'm the Second Assistant Director. Basically it's my job to make sure Billy is here and happy with everything that's going on.'

'He does an awful job,' mocks Billy.

'Oi!' laughs Stephen as he playfully punches Billy in the arm.

'See? If I'm bruised the make-up ladies are going to be so mad at you!'

'You're such a peach. Right,' he says, turning his attention back to me. 'If there's anything you need at all while you're with us just give me a shout or simply stop one of the runners or anybody with one of these,' he says, gesturing towards a walkie-talkie-like contraption in his back pocket.

'Thank you,' I say with a smile.

'Right, first things first, guys, what can I get you for breakfast?' asks Stephen, rubbing his hands together.

'Seeing as it's Sophie first day on set, let's go for the works!' suggests Billy.

'It would be rude not to,' chuckles Stephen.

After we've sampled almost everything catering has to offer – cereal, bagels, pastries, full English breakfast and French toast – we're stuffed.

When Stephen knocks on the door again he finds us curled up on the sofa watching *Daybreak*.

'Billy, are you ready for hair and make-up?'

'Yep!' he says, getting up off the sofa and having a good stretch.

'Do you want to go with him, Sophie? It's a bit of a squeeze in there with everyone running around, but he shouldn't be too long.'

'Not with a face like mine!' jokes Billy.

They both turn to me to see if I'm going to join Billy

or not for his first trip out of the trailer. I'd quite like to if I'm honest, but the way Stephen phrased the question, as though he was discouraging me from going, makes me think it's probably best for me to stay here.

'Erm . . . if you won't be long and it's tight for space then I'll just meet you back here,' I shrug.

'BillyBillyBillyBillyBillyBilly Buskin,' sings a girl's voice while she bangs on the bottom of the door, before flinging it open. 'Oh!' says the girl in shock at spotting me on the sofa, as she stays at the bottom of the trailer's steps. 'I'm so sorry,' she says in confusion, checking the sign on the door to make sure she hasn't gone to the wrong dressing room.

'Don't worry, he's just off getting his hair and make-up done. He shouldn't be too long now, though.'

'Oh,' she says, wrapping her long fluffy coat around herself.

'I'm Sophie,' I say as I walk over to the door, eager to introduce myself to this girl who is clearly close to Billy.

'Sophie? Oh! You're his girlfriend! Of course! He has been so excited about you joining us here. It's lovely to meet you. I'm Holly,' she says as she offers me her hand to shake, instantly becoming friendlier now she's made sense of the situation.

'Holly!' booms Billy's voice. I pop my head out to see Billy walking towards us both. He's wearing a light brown wig, with long straggly hair hanging around his face and over his shoulders. He looks ridiculous.

288

'Heeeeey! Billy Bear! Nice hair!' she laughs as she runs over in his direction, throwing her arms around him. Billy laughs back as they both start walking towards me.

'So you've met Sophie already, then!'

'Only just,' I say.

'I've been here for hours. I'm already bored!' she chimes. 'Stephen told me you were in so I thought I'd hunt you down.'

'You already had hair and make-up?'

'Can't you tell?' she asks, flicking her red hair off her shoulder. 'I've even dressed!' she says, opening her coat to reveal a tiny mini dress. She kicks out a foot behind her in a cutesy Marilyn Monroe way, and lets out a girlie giggle.

Despite knowing it's only a costume, I instantly feel underdressed in my comfy clothes. Even though Billy also arrived in his comfy attire, I hadn't thought about the fact that he'd be spending most of the day in his costume. I make a mental note to make more of an effort tomorrow, especially if all the girls look as gorgeous as Holly.

'She was nice,' I say, once Billy is back in the trailer and Holly has gone to say hello to someone else.

'Holly? Yeah, she's sweet.'

'You seem quite close.'

'Not really, I probably speak to her a bit more than the other girls, that's all. They all get a bit funny about just coming over and talking to me, whereas Holly doesn't seem fazed by anything.'

'I think she might have a bit of a thing for you.'

'Nah! Don't be daft,' he says, as he takes his shoes off and sits back down on the sofa beside me.

'She seemed quite smitten.'

'It's nothing like that, she's honestly like that with everyone, goes round hugging anybody. It doesn't mean anything.'

I don't know why Billy is so quick to dismiss the possibility. Could it be that he is blind to her obvious affection for him? Or is he just trying to shut me up and extinguish my fears?

There's another knock at the door, which Billy opens to find a woman in her late fifties carrying hangers full of clothes, which appear to be weighing her down.

'Hello! I'm Judith, your dresser,' she says,

'Pleasure to meet you. I'm Billy and this is Sophie,' says Billy as he grabs the clothes from her.

'Thank you, could you just pop those into that wardrobe for me?' she asks, brushing her fringe away from her eyes. 'Ah, yes, someone said you had company,' she says, looking at me. 'That's a good idea. There's so much waiting around on these jobs. It can get quite lethargic. Hello there,' she says, sending a warm smile in my direction before pulling a notepad from her pocket and squinting at it.

'What was your name again?' asks Billy.

'Judith,' she says, looking up from her pad. 'Sorry, just checking I've got everything. As I said, I'm your dresser. So I'll be bringing you the costumes you need for the scenes each day and getting you in and out of them . . . not because we don't think you can dress yourself, it's just for my personal enjoyment,' she chuckles, causing us to laugh with her.

Walking into the studio with Billy for the first time, I feel nervous and tiny as I look at the enormous space around us, which resembles a big factory warehouse. With its steel walls, mountains of scaffolding holding up bright lights, and various pieces of expensive-looking equipment dotted around, all encircling the set, which has been pitched up in the middle of the vast space, it all seems pretty daunting. Bizarrely, it's colder than I thought it would be, in both temperature and atmosphere.

The room is incredibly busy, with crewmembers dressed from head to toe in black, rushing everywhere and barking out orders to other crewmembers in a bid to get things organized quickly so that they can get started as soon as possible. The occasional person might look up and see Billy and say a quick hello, but largely they're all so focused on their individual tasks they don't register us.

Actors arrive in full costume, immediately helping themselves to tea and coffee, which has been laid out for them on a big wooden table, despite the fact they would have already had copious amounts of tea in their dressing rooms – my guess is that it gives them something to do while they're waiting to be told what's happening and that they're allowed on set. Everyone is in their own little world, psyching themselves up for the scene ahead. Sensing the nerves in the room, Billy and I stand quietly to one side, deciding it's best to do introductions later when everyone has had a chance to settle in.

Today they're filming some of the club scenes from earlier in the film, where Billy and the band are performing and are at the height of their fame. With nearly all of the actors in it, it's meant to be full of energy and excitement, like one big wild party. From what I can see of the set from where we're stood, the club has red leather sofas lining the mirrored walls with matching stools at the white bar, and black-and-white tiles patterning the floor. It sounds as though it should all look gorgeous, but it actually looks like it could do with a wash; the floor has been streaked with dirt and the furniture has been battered and worn in, making it all appear dark and grimy, adding to the rock and roll vibe the designers have been creating.

In today's scenes Billy's character Stan will be the ultimate showman, strutting around the club with more than an air of self-importance and arrogance. Every time I look at Billy I get the giggles thanks to his long hair and costume, which is an unbuttoned cream shirt, low-slung jeans held up by a chunky buckled belt and big black boots. He really does look like a seventies rock star, so it feels quite surreal to be snuggling in to him.

'How are you feeling?'

'All right,' Billy says with a nod and shrug. 'Today should be more fun than anything else.'

'Where's best for me to stand?'

'Well, anywhere that you're not in the way and not in shot would be good.'

'No, you don't say.'

'You'd be surprised how many visitors have wandered into shot without realizing it on past jobs.'

'Seriously? OK, I'll stay alert then,' I promise, hoping I don't manage to embarrass myself by making such a stupid blunder.

'Stephen knows you're here anyway, so I'll just tell him where you are. He'll keep an eye on you and check you're happy.'

I stop listening as a woman in a thick, white floor-length fur coat struts into the room. She wears it open to show her black knee-high boots, tiny denim hot pants and crop top, exposing her slender tanned legs and skinny midriff. Her blonde hair, straight and silky-looking, cascades down to her waist. I watch as she casts her eye around the room, inspecting the scene around her, demanding her presence be known, which, judging by the fact that most of the room has fallen silent and is looking straight at her, it is. Eventually, a young guy carrying a walkie-talkie runs over to her, asking if he can get her anything.

Billy turns to see what's caught my attention.

'Ah . . . Heidi.'

'Wow!' I exclaim, surprised at how stunning she is in the flesh.

'Hmm . . .' Billy grunts with a frown.

'Is she still being off?'

'Yep.'

'That's a shame.'

'It's her problem,' he shrugs.

'OK, everyone,' booms a male voice, although with so many people around I have no idea who is speaking. 'Now that everyone is here, can we have all the actors on set, please?'

'Right, stay here and avoid those cameras. Help yourself to tea and coffee, and if it gets really boring, feel free to chill out in the dressing room if you like,' offers Billy, before giving me a kiss and running over to Stephen to point out where I'm standing.

It's a long morning, with long gaps between takes where everyone lounges around on set waiting to be told what to do next. The director Max Rossini chooses to talk to each actor individually, perfecting all the minuscule details that will be picked up by the camera.

I am now, thanks to Stephen, sitting in front of a small monitor, so I can see what's being filmed, rather than trying to make out what's going on over people's shoulders. Despite being nicely tucked in a corner, out of the way, I feel like a spare part. Everyone else, all those hundreds of people flying around the floor, has a purpose and a role to play in the grand scheme of things, even if it's just holding an actor's coat during takes, or getting people water in the breaks. However, as a girlfriend, and the only one on set, I seem to have spent the majority of the morning getting in the way, and consequently being shoved around, which is why Stephen has plonked me here with my own monitor. So now I'm sitting here, watching, whilst drinking gallons of tea and scoffing down biscuits. I'm sure that once I get to know everyone as the days go by I'll feel less awkward, though. Plus it's interesting to see Billy at work and, as he kept insisting, it really is far less glamorous than it's perceived to be.

While Billy is talking to the director, I notice Holly looking at me with a massive grin and waving frantically. I can't help but laugh as I give her a shy wave back, not wanting to draw attention to myself. It's such a small gesture from her, but it's a sweet one and makes me feel included, somehow. Perhaps I've completely misjudged her, I think. Maybe she is just nice to everybody, without there being any hidden agenda.

Billy surprises me on set. Even though he's told me he doesn't really know any of the cast, they all seem more than friendly with each other, Heidi aside, of course. In the scene he's obviously playful with the female cast members as his character Stan is a real babe magnet. This leads to them whispering in his ears or whatever, but it baffles me when it continues after the camera stops rolling. I watch as nearly all of the girls, at some point, make their way over to him during the breaks and toy around with his new long hair, touching his bare chest, posing in their revealing outfits and laughing at everything he says, clearly flirting with him. I'm irked when, every now and then, they'll be cut off during filming and remain in their seductive positions, lingering over Billy longer than necessary.

It irritates me, but that isn't what surprises me as I

assumed I'd see girls behaving this way around him; what surprises me is seeing him flirt back. Now, obviously, Billy is a friendly guy who oozes charm – that's what attracted me to him and won me over. It could be that he is just returning their gestures and wanting to build an onscreen rapport, not thinking about how it might appear. I don't think he would callously behave in that manner in front of me, he's not that sort of person. But he does seem to enjoy having that physical closeness with other women – like Ruth. I found his relationship with her a tad too familiar for my liking – I'm sure any girl who saw her partner nuzzling up to another girl would. This make-believe acting world is such a weird one to get my head around. What's real and what's not?

In his defence, Billy has pointed me out to a few of the girls, blowing kisses in my direction in a sickeningly sweet, yet cute, way – so he isn't acting like I don't exist. But what is he like when I'm not around if he's like this when I am?

I know, I know. I shouldn't look into everything too much and overanalyse. I can't afford to get jealous or overprotective now, not when there's so much to come during filming which I will have to bite my tongue over.

However, as I watch in silence, I start to feel increasingly disheartened.

During the afternoon, when Billy has gone to have his make-up retouched and I'm back in the trailer, I get a call from Mum, who is extremely excited about her daughter being on the set of a film.

'So, tell me all about it?'

'If I'm honest, Mum, there's nothing to tell.'

'What?'

'It's all moving quite slowly.'

'There's got to be something you can tell me. What's she like?'

'As gorgeous as I feared.'

'I bet she's not a patch on you.'

'Do you think you're biased, by any chance?'

'Never,' she insists.

'Billy was right about her, she's really cold towards everyone. It's unbelievable how much she changes when the camera is on her, though.'

'She's good, then?'

'Very!'

'No rude scenes yet?'

'Not yet. But it's only the first day. All that is yet to come.'

'You dreading it?'

'I'm not looking forward to it, that's for sure,' I admit.

'I don't know how you can watch it, love. I wouldn't be able to.'

'Billy's asked me to,' I say, although now I'm doubting if it's such a good idea to watch after all, especially knowing how much it affected me just seeing him interact with the girls earlier.

'You're a stronger woman than me. If I'd had to watch

anyone so much as look at your dad in the wrong way I'd have given them what for.'

'Mum!' I squeal, shocked at her fighting talk.

'Well . . .'

'What are you up to tonight?' I ask.

'I'm off to the theatre!'

'Really?'

'Yes. Colin found some tickets for half price to go see the musical version of *Brief Encounter*.'

'It's been turned into a musical?' I laugh.

'I think so . . . or perhaps it was *Breakfast at Tiffany's*,' she chuckles.

'And how's it going with Colin?'

'Oh, he's a good man. Nice to have him around.'

'Good.'

'He knows he'll never replace your dad,' she says quietly. 'But likewise I know I'll never replace his wife.'

'Would you want to?'

'Not replace her. No. It's just lovely to have someone treat me like I'm special again.'

'You are special.'

'Thank you, my love . . . but I think I need to hear that from someone other than you for a change.'

Lying in Billy's trailer, a week into filming, we're curled up under the covers, waiting for Billy to be called to set. So far we've been sat here for two hours, and are bored stiff. Judith wasn't joking when she said there was a lot of waiting around, and thanks to Billy being in costume and having to be prepared to go on set at a moment's notice, we can't just disappear off for an hour or so. We, or at least Billy, must remain in the dressing room or close by at all times.

'So, if you had to date one of the girls here, who would it be?'

I don't know what makes me ask, and I don't really want to know the answer, but seeing Billy every day amongst the girls and seeing him act so confidently around them keeps the idea of him wanting to be with women like that at the forefront of my mind. It just keeps niggling away at me, no matter how much I try to calm my own concerns and keep them away from Billy.

'I wouldn't want to. I have you,' he says with a shrug.

'OK, but what if I was no longer here?'

'Why aren't you here?'

'I don't know, I just don't exist.'

'Well, that would be sad . . . I'd have to just live a life of solitude.'

'Come on, honestly, which one?'

'I don't want to play this game.'

'Why not?'

'Because I don't like any of them like that!'

'Oh, come on. They're all super hot, and they all fancy the pants off you!'

'Sophie!'

'What?'

'They don't.'

'Oh, of course they do. They're all over you like a rash any chance they get.'

'Sophie, you're being silly,' he says with a hint of irritation.

'It's only a game,' I say in a mock sulk.

'Really? Or will it make you wonder if I actually fancy someone and start you getting all paranoid on me? Look, Sophie,' he says with a sigh. 'I love you completely. There's nothing I wouldn't do for you. I need you to just believe that. I know this is all strange for you, but I promise I'm doing all I can to make it as easy as possible for you. OK?'

I nod, feeling stupid for even asking such a ridiculous question. I cuddle into him and close my eyes, pretending to go to sleep. Not wanting to discuss the matter further.

20

It's not long before the director schedules the filming of the opening sequence with Billy and Heidi, which is the first of a long list of love scenes to be filmed. My heart plummets when I see it on the call-sheet for the following day, which has been left in Billy's dressing room at the end the day's filming.

Noticing me sighing, Billy comes and peers over my shoulder at the page in front of me.

'Ah . . .' he says, rubbing the sides of my arms.

'Ah, indeed,' I nod, turning to face him.

'I know I've said that I want you there, but I'm not going to force you to sit and watch it if you're not comfortable.'

'Well, it's not going to be the most wonderful day of my existence, that's for sure.'

'Mine neither. I'm pretty nervous about it,' he says, fiddling with my hands.

'Why?'

'Despite what you might think, it's not something I'm used to.'

I hadn't even thought what it might be like for Billy to perform love scenes. Thinking about it now, it must be extremely exposing and embarrassing, depending on the actor, of course. I'd hate to put extra pressure on him by watching.

'I don't want me being there to make it harder for you,' I say.

'It won't. I want you there to see there are no secrets being kept from you. That it's nothing sordid.'

'I know it's not,' I say, letting out another sigh.

'I don't know what I'd be like in your position. I think I'd drive myself mad over it.'

'Well, I think we can safely say that I won't be rolling around a bed half naked with another guy any time soon, so you can keep hold of your sanity for a little while longer.'

'Good point,' he leans down and kisses me, resting his forehead on mine. We stand with our eyes closed and our arms wrapped around each other.

'I'll come and watch . . . I want to support you and be there for you. I'm trying my best not to turn this into some weird thing between us.'

'I know you are, and I admire you for that,' he says, taking my hand and kissing the back of it.

'Knock, knock! It's time for the old granny to see you naked!' calls Judith from outside, causing us to break away.

As I walk on to set with Billy the next day, I feel anxious about what I'm about to witness, worried how it will affect me and how I'll keep a check on my emotions. I want to be OK with this, but, even now, the very thought of it makes my skin crawl as I look at the mock-up hotel room the set designers have created. It's dark, shabby and dingy, with orange curtains, brown wallpaper and a heavily patterned carpet. Again, it all looks like it could do with a wash.

I've been told scenes like these usually call for a 'closed set', where only the crew members needed to shoot the scene are present. From what Billy's told me, it's so that the actors don't feel uncomfortable when doing something so intimate, enabling them to lose their inhibitions and focus on the task at hand. I'm here because Billy's asked the producers for me to be, which they allowed after speaking to Heidi, who apparently agreed to it without any fuss.

I wonder what it must be like for Heidi, first of all, to do a scene like this, secondly, to do a scene like this with her ex, and thirdly, to do a scene like this with her ex when his current girlfriend is watching. I haven't said a single word to her; Billy was right when he described her as 'frosty'. The only people she seems to whip up a smile for, when the cameras aren't rolling, are the director and the producers – or anyone in a powerful position. To those types she is friendly, warm and giggles like a little girl, but when they aren't paying her attention she is steely faced as she sits watching everyone else around her like a hawk.

Most people have learnt to let her sit in silence if they're next to her on set in between takes. However, I've watched as Holly has tried, on numerous occasions, to strike up conversations with Heidi only to be completely ignored as though she has said nothing.

Seeing Holly's happy face fall in a deflated way every time she tries is uncomfortable to watch.

With all her beauty I should be more worried about Heidi, but because of her attitude, which Billy assures me is miles away from the girl he once dated, I'm not as worried as I should be. This mentality wavers slightly, though, when I spot Heidi walking on to set wearing her knee-high boots, a see-through blouse and the tiniest black skirt I've ever seen. She looks incredibly sexy, and I instantly feel dowdy in comparison.

'OK, can we have you on set straight away, please, guys?' Stephen asks quietly to Billy and Heidi, his tone highlighting the delicate nature they want to tackle the scene with.

'I love you,' Billy says with a wink and a squeeze of the hand, before walking over to the set.

I sit in my usual spot, watching the monitor as Max, the director, who has worn the same brown leather jacket, denim shirt, jeans and trainers for the past week, goes over and starts talking to them both. He speaks so softly I can't hear what he is saying, but spotting Billy with his arms crossed I can tell he feels uncomfortable already.

Suddenly Max breaks away and talks to Stephen, who informs everyone how the morning is going to run.

'Right, we're going to take it from Stan throwing Megan on to the bed, fitting the door sequence in later,' he says. 'Can we start, Billy, with you chucking Heidi, just so that we can get the cameras where they need to be?'

'Yep,' Billy says, walking to the middle of the pretend hotel room.

The morning doesn't go smoothly. Even though Billy and Heidi are breaking a huge heap of personal boundaries with their touching, writhing and licking (which actually causes my heart to shrivel up painfully like a prune), they aren't comfortable and appear awkward and clumsy on screen. They've now completed the striptease section, and have moved on to the start of the lovemaking, with Billy having to lick his way up Heidi's naked body before kissing her neck.

It's been gut-wrenching to watch, and at times I have had to look away, preferring not to watch as the person I love gets his ear nibbled by this vixen woman, who has her pert boobs out on display, or watch him slide his way up her. Surprisingly, I've managed to hold it together. So far.

Each time they go for another take, a distressed Max cuts about a minute into the scene, before walking in and talking to Billy and Heidi, trying different tactics to get what he's after, unhappy with the lack of steam and passion being created. Although he has remained gentle with them so far, I've watched him getting increasingly irritated with each failed take.

'CUT! This isn't working!' screams Max, as he walks towards Billy and Heidi, holding his hands in the air in desperation. 'It needs something more. It needs to be sexier. Guys, come on, you're not giving it to me. This is setting the tone for what's to come. Stan is meant to be a sex god, so play with her, use her, tease her. Manipulate her body like you're the master of it. Megan is gagging for it. She wants him and she wants him now. She's got to show him what she's got, entice him with her body. They're wild. Wild! You're both too in your heads, it needs to be all about the physical,' he says, pounding his fist against his hand to hammer home his point. 'Just for one take, can we try it so that . . . I don't know, could you suck on her nipple or something? Or tweak it? Is that OK with you both? It needs to be more dangerous, on the edge of explosion. I need desire!'

Billy and Heidi look at each other, uncomfortably, making me feel mildly relieved to see they've both recognized Max's request as ridiculous. I know in Billy's earlier scenes I've been highly sensitive to the smallest of glances from one of the girls, but this is bordering on the insane. It's too much to ask these two people, who are actors, to do. They play characters, yes, but their bodies are their own. In my eyes, and I'm sure millions would agree with me, it would certainly be taking this ludicrous situation a step too far.

Sensing their reluctance, Max keeps going with his encouragement.

'You both want to get away from *Halo*, don't you? Away from that squeaky-clean image, opening up the chance for grittier roles. Well, let's cause an uproar, then. Let's grab it by the balls and go for it!'

His words hang in the air.

'It's fine by me,' huffs Heidi, as she gets back into her

starting position on the bed, pushing her hair over her shoulders, sticking out her breasts.

I watch as Billy hesitates, looks at the floor and taps his foot on the ground.

He doesn't turn to look for me.

He nods his head slowly and stands at the end of the bed with his back to me.

'We can try that,' I hear him mutter.

Something in me dies.

On the monitor I see sadness in his face, I can see that he doesn't want to be doing this, however, his frown quickly fades away when somebody shouts, 'Ready . . . camera rolling . . . action', and he jumps into the role of Stan Bar – fiery and intense.

I look around helplessly as they start to film the shot again, not able to believe that I'm actually about to witness this.

No one notices me.

Everyone is wrapped up in the scene, all busy doing their jobs.

I squirm as I look at the monitor, holding my breath in disbelief. I watch as the camera pans with Billy as he moves up Heidi's body, his tongue gliding along her shiny legs, over her toned stomach, leading up to her nipple. He stops. For a second I think he's seen sense – that he's not going to go through with it. But instead, he looks up at Heidi, her face eager and wanton, begging him. He smiles at her, lets out a deep chortle and flicks her nipple with his tongue playfully, before taking it into his mouth.

A wailing sound causes everybody to stop.

On the monitor, Billy looks up in shock, as confusion and anger flicker across his face. People start looking in my direction, which is when I realize the sound is coming from me. I cover my mouth to stop it, frozen to the spot as everyone glares in my direction.

In shock, I run from the room.

I'm back in Billy's dressing room by the time he catches up with me. He slams open the door.

'What was that?'

'That's the same question I've been asking myself, Billy, "What was that?"' I ask, flinging my arm in the direction of the studio. 'Don't worry, I'm going – so you can carry on without interruption from your stupid girlfriend,' I blurt, getting my coat and bag from the sofa.

'What do you want me to do? I can't just ignore the director. Do you want me to quit? Is that it?' Billy shouts. 'Do you want me to just walk away because you feel uncomfortable?'

'What?' I stammer, not understanding how I'm suddenly in the wrong – did he not see what he was doing back there?

'I have done everything I can to make you feel welcome. I have spent hours talking you through every little detail, making sure you feel included and a part of this whole thing.'

'I know . . .'

'Hours when I should've been getting to know everyone so that it's not awkward when we're on set together.'

'I've never said you couldn't spend time with them.'

'No, you haven't, but any time I do spend with them you make me feel bad about it. I can feel you seething, bubbling away the minute one of the girls comes over to me.'

'I don't do that.'

'Any girl I chat to, straight away you're saying they fancy me – making everything awkward because I don't want you to think I'm egging them on in some way.'

'I've never stopped you talking to anyone . . .'

'But you have! Can't you see that?'

'Billy! I have had to sit there quietly, with a smile on my face, and watch you kiss other girls as they've had their legs wrapped around you, while you talk dirty to them. To be honest, if I have the odd moment of paranoia it's hardly surprising, is it?'

'But it's acting, I'm playing a character. That's all it is. Why can't you understand this is work and not the filthy thing that you've built up in your head?'

'How can you not see this the way I do?' I shriek.

'I can, but you're being overly sensitive about it. It's not about you and me, it's about the character.'

'Overly sensitive? Billy, you had another woman's nipple in your mouth!'

'And?'

'And?' I scream back at him, unable to see how he can't comprehend where that might be a problem. 'Your ex-girlfriend's nipple? Do you really not see what's wrong with that?'

'It's work!'

'It's disgusting!'

'It's what the director asked for. I didn't have a choice.'

'Yes, you did,' I shout firmly. 'You could've thought how that might affect me and realize that asking someone to do something like that is far from normal, it's sick, and you're stupid for going along without questioning it. For just doing it because the director told you to. Do you know how ridiculous that sounds?'

'But I was acting. That's what I do.'

'Then you're pathetic,' I spit.

Billy stares at the floor silently, his face red with rage.

'I won't come here any more,' I say quietly, stopping myself from shouting further. 'I didn't realize me being here was such a problem or that I was being such a burden.'

'Sophie . . .' he says softly.

'I'll see you at home,' I say, cutting him off and walking out of the door.

I walk past the trailers, past the studio and catering, and off the site. Once outside the gates I look around in desperation, realizing Billy's not come after me. For some reason I thought he would.

I wander over to a nearby bench and sit down with my head in my hands, taking deep breaths, hoping it'll help calm me down.

My phone starts vibrating in my pocket. Thinking it might be Billy checking where I am and wanting to put things right, I pull it out. It's not him, though. It's Molly calling from home.

I look at her name flashing on the screen and desperately want to answer it, to sob down the phone and complain about Billy. But something stops me. I'm not ready to talk about anything yet, not when I haven't been able to make sense of any of it.

Am I to blame for being so paranoid? Have I really been giving the girls daggers every time they go near Billy? If I have, then in doing so I went against Molly's advice and have made a complete mess.

I stare at the phone until it stops.

'Sophie?' I look up to see an anxious-looking Holly walking towards me. 'Judith told me what happened. Are you OK?'

'Not really!' I admit, forcing a smile.

'This has all got to be so strange for you,' she says, joining me on the bench, putting her arm around me.

'It is a bit.'

'God knows how I'd feel if I were in your position.'

'Stupid?'

Holly holds me tighter as I let out a groan of frustration.

'I'm sorry.'

'You know Billy really loves you, right? He has literally spoken about you non-stop since the first day of rehearsals.'

'I doubt that.'

'No, he has. I reckon that might be why Heidi has been such a sourpuss from day one.'

'Do you think?'

'Definitely. Think about it, she's working with an ex . . . what's worse than working with an ex? Working with an ex who doesn't want you.'

'Maybe.'

'Definitely!'

'I just didn't think it would be like this. He really went crazy at me.'

'He's under a lot of pressure.'

'But he was in the wrong! What can't he see that?'

'You know he can. He probably doesn't want to admit it knowing that he's got to go back in there and reshoot it.'

'Do you think he will?' I ask, looking up at her face, hoping there's some chance that he wouldn't be such a fool.

Holly raises her shoulders sadly, giving me a pitiful smile.

Ahh . . .

'Thank you for coming to find me,' I say, standing up. 'I think I should go home now.'

'Do you want to come in so that Stephen can get you a car home?'

I screw my face up at the thought of walking back into the studio, knowing that people will still be talking about my outburst, and knowing that Billy will be preparing to go back on set and resume his position.

'I tell you what,' begins Holly. 'I'll go back in and tell Stephen where you are – just so that he can send out a car to take you home. How does that sound?'

'Thank you!'

She gives me another big hug before walking back through the gates.

21

I bash my way around the flat for hours, keeping myself busy with the washing and cleaning, waiting for Billy to come home. In all honesty, I feel like ripping up all of Billy's clothes and breaking everything in sight, still fuming at the situation. I'm annoyed that Billy would be so cold about the whole thing and beyond angry at the fact that he'll have gone back on set to retake the disgusting shot as though my feelings don't matter.

We've never argued, not like this. In fact, I don't think I've ever argued or shouted at anyone in the way I did today since I was a child. At least this time I know I'm right and not just being 'overly sensitive', as Billy so kindly put it.

At times, during the afternoon, when I feel myself wavering on whether I was right or wrong, or calming down, a fresh thought pops into my head, reminding me of what an arse Billy has been and how much of a fool he has made me look, refuelling the anger and fire within me.

I'm ready for him to walk through the door, and for us to have a mammoth confrontation where I tell him the millions of things he has done wrong and how much he has hurt me.

My phone bleeps at me, interrupting my rampant thoughts.

It's a text from Billy.

> Been asked out for dinner by Max. I'm
> sorry, but have to go. Be home later. I
> want to sort this out. x

After such a horrendous day, one that could potentially spell the end of our relationship, he has chosen to have dinner with his director, rather than coming home as soon as possible and rectifying the situation with me. This says so much about Billy's current state of mind. Over the past few months, especially following his BAFTA win, I have watched as Billy's priorities have changed. No longer has the emphasis been on a happy home life and our future together, and keeping Billy grounded in a fickle industry. Instead, it's all been about his career, and how to build on his success and make people respect him more. His thirst to be desired and admired taking over his thoughts.

Playing the character Stan, and channelling into such a huge ego, has no doubt added to that, making him selfish and narcissistic. Perhaps it's been difficult for him to switch off from the character at the end of the day, but the notion of taking a pretend life that far is ridiculous to me.

As the hours tick by without him returning home, my new-found feisty attitude starts to dissolve. My anger gives way to fresh waves of paranoia and fragility, making me feel alone and nervous.

Where is he?

I already know that he has an early call time tomorrow, so what would make him stay out so late? Perhaps something has happened to him . . . the thought sends a chill through me as I remember what happened the last time I had an explosive argument. With my mum and dad. I feel sick.

Around 2am I try to call him. It rings through with no answer. When I call again a few minutes later it goes straight to voicemail.

Unable to keep my thoughts occupied with anything else but what could've happened to him, I sit in the living room, clutching a pillow, watching the clock hands slowly move, second by second, longing for him to come home.

I must have nodded off at some point, because I'm woken by the sound of my phone ringing. I snatch it up, hoping to see Billy's name, but instead it's Paul's. He is the last person that I want to speak to right now, but the fact that he is calling means that he must have some information on where Billy is. I pick up.

'Hello?'

My voice is hoarse and quiet, the tension having built in my throat overnight.

'Sophie?' Paul says, as clipped as ever.

'Do you know where Billy is?' I blurt out.

'Yes.'

'Has something happened to him? He didn't come home last night.'

'It's OK, he's fine.'

'Where is he?'

'He stayed here last night.'

'Why? I thought he went out to dinner?'

I hear Paul sigh down the phone line. Is he annoyed that he has to deal with me? Exasperated to be dealing with this pesky matter rather than planning Billy's next big deal? Am I really that much of a bother?

'He did, but . . . Look, Sophie, I have a million things to be getting on with. Billy will explain everything when he gets home tonight. He just asked me to call you to say he'd be back at nine. What's happened is nothing to do with me.'

'What do you mean, Paul? What has happened?' I ask, starting to panic.

'Sophie. I work for Billy, which means that I have to do what he says. That is why I called. After your attitude yesterday, I personally wouldn't have bothered.'

'What?'

'I can't say any more. I think all this is best coming from him.'

'But –'

'It's not my job to deal with matters of the heart – just to make Billy the best he can be. A job which your very presence makes difficult.'

'Paul?'

He hangs up.

My face crumples in pain as fresh tears tumble down my cheeks.

Something has happened.

Something has happened which led Billy to go to Paul's rather than come home. Unless he didn't go to Paul's and went somewhere else instead . . . Paul could just be covering for him.

It hits me. Hard and powerful.

Billy's cheated.

Away from the cameras and the film sets, and hiding behind the guise of a stupid character, where it seems anything is acceptable, Billy has done the thing I've feared he would.

Billy has cheated.

The hours trickle by as I sit and wait. I don't keep myself busy like I did yesterday. I don't have the energy. I sit in one spot on the sofa. Staring at the wall. Waiting. Slowly becoming numb to the pain that is eating me up inside.

I get call after call from Molly. Perhaps Billy has called her and explained the whole thing, said I could do with a friendly voice . . . I ignore her calls. I listen to the silence.

Eventually I hear a key slide into the lock as Billy returns home, aware of him hesitating before turning it and letting himself in. I'm still sat on the sofa when he walks into the living room; his posture is stooped, his face red and blotchy. He looks drained, as though in shock, which catches me by surprise – I didn't expect him to look so bad. He glances at me, takes one look at my face and bows his head into his hands in shame, before sinking to the floor as he releases thick, heavy howls. Resting his head on the carpet and pounding the floor with his fist.

I don't go to him.

I remain on the sofa unable to move, as each one of Billy's wails confirms my earlier thoughts; words being deemed unnecessary.

I listen to his self-pitying sobs, wanting them to stop as they bang around in my brain. My heart cracks at the sound, my world caving in around me. I clench my jaw in a bid to steel myself, trying to block out the pain.

'I'm so sorry,' he cries, slowly scooping himself up from the floor, trying to control his breathing, his head still buried in his hands. I flinch as he moves closer to me, but he doesn't even try to touch me or seek comfort; instead he sits next to me. He stares at the floor in front of us, shaking his head. 'I'm so sorry,' he repeats.

'I think it's a bit late for that,' I say flatly, looking directly at him.

'Let me explain!' he whimpers.

'Will it all disappear if you do?'

'No . . .'

'Well, then, I don't think I want to hear it.'

'Please . . . I need you to understand.'

I don't say anything, but my silence allows Billy to continue.

'Just let me tell you everything, before . . .' he takes a

few deep breaths, trying to compose himself as he starts to describe the events which have led him here, to this sofa, in such a mess. 'After you left yesterday I felt terrible, all I wanted to do was come home and be with you. I was useless in the scenes, I couldn't get you out of my head. I hated knowing I'd upset you so much . . . Max took Heidi and me aside at the end of the day, and asked if it was OK for him to take us out for dinner, saying he wanted to talk to us in a more relaxed environment, away from the studio. I had to go and see Paul briefly, so said I'd meet Heidi and Max at the restaurant a little while later. When I turned up only Heidi was at the table. I thought about leaving, knowing how it would look if I stayed, but she told me Max was on his way, said that he'd just had to nip home quickly but he'd insisted that we start dinner without him. I should've known then. I should've left . . .' he reflects, with a sigh.

'Carry on,' I say, feeling sick. Wanting Billy to hurry up and just tell me what's happened.

'I sat down. I could see that Heidi was immediately more relaxed than she has been on set – she was much more like the Heidi I used to know, smiling and friendly. It was actually nice to see her like that instead of her being cold towards me. She kept bringing up little things that had happened on *Halo*, funny little jokes and moments.'

'How lovely!'

'Please . . . don't,' Billy begs, pausing before continuing. 'Realizing it was getting late I went to send Max a text, to ask where he was, but Heidi stopped me. It

319

turned out she'd known all along that he wouldn't be joining us,' he says with a heavy sigh. 'When I challenged her about it, she said, "I just wanted to have a nice night together. Away from all the distractions." I thought about leaving again, but our main courses arrived.' Billy hesitates before continuing, hopefully realizing the lunacy of his justification for staying longer. 'That's when the mood started to change. She started saying how I was often in her thoughts, how she regularly thinks about what we'd be like together now, being older and wiser, talking about how much press attention we'd get if we were to get back together. I laughed it off, not wanting to indulge in ridiculous talk like that with her. I'm so happy with you, she knows that, plus as far as I knew she was getting married, so I took it as just hypothetical rubbish that wasn't worth getting into. I started to chat about other stuff, but I could see that she was unnerved by my rebuff.'

'Poor thing,' I say sarcastically.

'As soon as the meal was finished I asked for the bill and we left,' he continues, not letting my interruption stop him. 'I must've drunk more wine than I thought, though, making my reactions slower. Once we were outside she just pounced on me. Literally, pounced. Before I could even register what was happening her mouth was on mine and she was grabbing at me. Cupping my bits,' he says, shaking his head.

'And then you went back to hers, how lovely,' I say, suddenly wanting the conversation to be over, not wanting to hear any more.

'No! I pushed her away from me. It ended there, but . . .'

'But what?'

'There was a photographer there who caught the whole thing.'

I laugh, with what must be shock, but don't say anything.

'I looked at Heidi, confused at what had happened, but she had this big smile on her face, she said something like, "Say hello to the new Brad and Angelina," and winked at me. She'd set it up. I couldn't believe it. I went to go after the pap, but he'd already disappeared. Heidi tried to put her arms around my neck, but I pushed her away again, told her how much she disgusted me and walked off. I could hear her screaming after me . . . I wanted to come home, I wanted more than anything to hug you and –'

'But you didn't, so what did you do?'

'Called Paul and went over to his.'

'Letting me wait up all night worrying about you, thinking something awful had happened to you.'

'I'm so sorry, we've been trying to find out who the photographer was and what actually happened. It turns out that the meal was Heidi's idea from the start. She'd suggested it to Max after I'd followed you out. He was never actually going to be joining us. It was just a ploy to get me there. Obviously, Max didn't know what she had planned, he thought she just wanted to clear the tension between us and make things less awkward.'

'So who was the photographer?'

'Don't know. Paul's been frantically on the phone to various editors trying to see who might have the photos, but they're all staying pretty tight-lipped. They know they've got a news splash on their hands. I'm just so sorry,' he sobs, breaking down once again.

'You've been trying to stop it from going to print?'

Billy doesn't say anything, but nods. The news makes me want to gag; once more my heartbreak will be splashed across the news pages for all to read and judge unfairly.

'Did you kiss her back?' I ask flatly.

'What?'

'Did you kiss her back? It's a simple question.'

'I don't know. No. It all happened so fast. I wasn't thinking.'

'Do you fancy her?'

'What? No!'

'Do you still have feelings for her?'

'No! Right now I hate her and can't believe I might lose you because of that wicked bitch!'

'It's not just her fault though, is it?'

'What do you mean?'

'It's everything. All the girls on set, the way I've had to sit and watch you, the way you spoke to me yesterday . . .'

'I know and I feel awful about all of that.'

'Really?'

'Yes!'

'You've changed, Billy. When we first met you had a grasp on reality, what was important in life, but I think you've lost your perspective on all that.'

'Please, Sophie, I'm so sorry.'

'And I've changed, too. I was so happy to move here, to be a part of your life, but the thing is, there actually isn't space for someone like me in it. Your world is all about you, and I think I need something to be about me for a change.'

'But this is about you, I want to do anything I can to make you happy. It hurts so much that I've hurt you! I'm sorry I've acted so badly. I know I didn't say it at the time, but I do understand what you were talking about with the nipple thing. You were right, it's absolutely sick. I can't believe I justified it, let alone tried to turn it around and act as though it was your problem. I was just so frustrated, and not with you . . . but you're the one I took it out on, and I shouldn't have. I'm so sorry.'

Fresh sobs sound from Billy's mouth as he breaks down again. This time he falls into my lap, throwing his arms around my waist, locking me there.

'I love you so much, you're the most important thing in the world to me. Please don't leave me,' he begs.

At some point, after hours of tears and hearing more apologies from Billy, we decide to go to bed, agreeing to talk about it more in the morning when we've both calmed down and can be more rational about the matter.

I don't sleep. Various thoughts run through my head, stopping me from switching off.

I have an overwhelming urge to leave, to escape Billy, London and his pathetic showbiz world and go back to

Rosefont Hill, where I feel loved and secure. The thought of being home with Mum right now fills me with such longing, and I want, more than anything, to talk to Molly, to bury myself in her arms as she coos away at me. Happy to have me back.

I look at Billy, and see that he is dead to the world. Sound asleep, looking like he doesn't have a single worry or concern.

I don't want to be here, the thought is loud and clear.

As the new day begins and light starts to filter through the curtains, I climb out of bed. Careful not to wake Billy, I quietly get dressed and fill a small suitcase with my belongings. Luckily, I don't have many things here still, and, other than my photos of Mum and Dad, anything I leave behind is replaceable or, like my Vera Wang dress, no longer needed.

Knowing that Billy is likely to follow me to Mum's to try and persuade me to come back with him or to sort things out; I take a notepad and write him a short message.

Billy,

I can't stay here. I need to go home and think things through properly on my own. It's not just the one incident that's made me want to leave, I've actually felt low for a while, but haven't quite been able to pinpoint why.

I can't carry on when I'm so unhappy. I need time to concentrate on me, and chase my own dreams, rather than just watching others fulfil theirs without a second thought for what I

*might want. I'm sorry to just leave like this, but I couldn't face
more heartbreak. Please give me time and space.*

Sophie X

I place the note on the side in the kitchen and walk out
of the flat.

Once I get to the station, I have fifteen minutes to spare
before my train leaves. Curiosity gets the better of me
on seeing a WH Smith. I walk in and grab the newspaper with Billy on the front, not daring to even look at
it in detail before getting on the train, knowing that if I
do I'll collapse to the floor and never get up again.

'Oh yes, this is terrible, this . . .' says the girl at the
checkout as she scans through the paper. 'Who'd have
thought Billy could be such a rat, hey? Especially when
just a little while ago he was parading that normal bird
around! It's her I feel sorry for. It's just awful.'

I block out her words, pay, grab the carrier bag and
head straight to the train, sitting myself in a corner,
away from the other passengers.

I stare out of the window, in a daze, wondering
where it all went wrong. Did I play the whole thing
badly by making myself too readily available by moving in with him and quitting my job so soon after getting
together? We'd eliminated the thrill aspect of dating
because we were worried the relationship wouldn't sur-
vive if we weren't in close proximity. And I'd given
myself over to Billy completely, even though I knew

he'd never be able to do the same for me, causing my life to seem uninteresting and losing myself somehow.

Eventually, when the train starts moving, I pull the newspaper out of the plastic bag and study the front page. The picture is exactly how Billy described; Heidi has one hand around the back of his head pulling him closer, the other on his crotch, her lips are locked on his, her face intense and passionate. What's more interesting in the image is Billy; his hands are by his side with his fingers flexed, not touching her, although they could be about to push her off, his head is pulled back into his neck, trying to get away and his face is grimacing. He's clearly uncomfortable and distressed, in shock at what's happening. I can see that, but anyone else looking at it would think Heidi and Billy were caught in the throes of passion, especially with the headline that's attached, and the story beneath it.

BILLY'S BUSK-SINFUL FOR BLACK

Billy Buskin and Heidi Black look set to rebuild their romance after years apart, thanks to sexual tension building between them on the set of their new film *The Walking Beat*.

Just months ago, Billy Buskin was gushing about his love for girlfriend Sophie May when accepting an award for best male actor at the BAFTAs. However, it seems the pair have now split following hefty rows, causing him to run back into the arms of his ex, Heidi Black.

Billy and Sophie were still together earlier this week, with insiders claiming that the increased sexual tension on set between Billy and his ex led to the couple arguing constantly.

An insider has said: 'Billy and Heidi have been trying to keep apart when at work, but the sexual tension has been apparent from the start, so it was only a matter of time before something happened.

'[Billy] had been bringing his girlfriend Sophie into work with him, in a bid to put a barrier between him and Heidi. However, the intense sex scenes caused them to have a massive bust-up on set earlier in the week, bringing filming to a halt as the couple argued loudly in his trailer.

'It didn't surprise us when Sophie finally snapped, in fact, we're surprised it didn't happen sooner. She'd have to be blind to miss the chemistry surrounding Billy and Heidi.'

The source continued: 'Heidi was clearly embarrassed by the drama and felt awful that her actions could have such a negative effect on their relationship. She was seen comforting Billy when he returned to the set a little while later, even managing to raise a smile from him. They continued to whisper to each other for the duration of the day.'

It seems in this exclusive photo that Billy has put the arguments with Sophie behind him, happily turning to Heidi for support. The old lovers were caught in a passionate clinch after a romantic meal in Mayfair's dark and overtly sexy restaurant, Hakasan, where they headed straight after filming their raunchy scenes together.

A friend of Heidi's spoke to us, saying: 'It's early days, and obviously Heidi is keen for Billy to deal with his split first, before taking things further with her, but she really thinks it could last this time, now that they're more mature and able to understand the pressures of the job.

'At the start of filming, Heidi was going through heartache of her own, after breaking off her engagement with film producer Roger Szams. Billy noticed she was quiet and became her rock, reigniting their friendship.

'I personally can't believe they've managed to keep apart for this long, the bond between them was always so strong.'

The pair last worked together on teen film *Halo*, which led to them being a couple for several years. They split amicably, saying distance and hectic work schedules were to blame.

Even though I know it's a pile of rubbish and that the 'friend' is probably Heidi feeding the paper lies, it pains me to know that everyone else reading this will see it as the truth without questioning it. It also angers me that more of my personal sadness has been shared with the world, turning my life into a spectacle once again. Seeing as I spent the whole of my teens shying away from people, preferring they knew nothing about me, it's crushing to know my life is being laid out for everyone to judge. I feel ridiculed.

I ring the doorbell when I arrive home, not having the energy to root through my bags and find my keys.

When Mum comes to the door, I watch as her expression turns from delight to worry as she sees my face.

'Love, what's the matter?' she asks, stepping out of the house towards me.

'Oh, Mum!' I whine, as I fall into her arms and sob.

22

Wanting to be alone, I go up to my old room and shut the door as soon as I'm inside. Standing there, I can't help but feel disappointed as I look around at the pink walls and little-girl décor, exactly as it has been for the past fifteen years. Everything that was once familiar is now strange to me, uncomfortably so. After finally allowing myself to leave Rosefont Hill behind to experience what else life had to offer, my room feels tiny and dingy. I feel as though I've worked my way backwards – it's humiliating.

But I'm safe here, I remind myself.

Dumping my bags on the floor, I shut the curtains – irritated by the sunlight that filters through, making the world seem bright when it obviously isn't. On the bed, I throw myself under the duvet and find Mr Blobby waiting for me. I bury my face in his belly.

I want to do nothing but hibernate here for the rest of my life. Lying in the darkness, not wanting to face the world.

My earlier tears have finally stopped flowing, seeming to have dried up for now. Instead numbness surrounds me as I continue to reflect on where it all went wrong.

Looking back, I never felt enough. At first that feeling

didn't stem from Billy, not at all; for a long time I did feel like his world, but it came from the people in Billy's life who couldn't comprehend him falling for a 'normal' girl when he could have so much more, people like Paul and Heidi.

On that first Press Night, when I stood alone, looking at the clique around me, I felt like such an outsider; I felt like I didn't match up to the greatness that surrounded me. Even after that, when I was included more, no one genuinely wanted to talk to me, they wanted to talk to Billy. I was just someone they were lumbered with if he happened to be talking to someone else. Many people feigned an interest, if they were polite enough, and the odd few blocked me out, preferring to stand in silence next to me, just looking in Billy's direction, waiting for an in. On those occasions, I would question myself as to why these people would choose to talk to me anyway, and no doubt that came across as I stood awkwardly at Billy's side, looking a little out of my depth in my surroundings. You could say I'd made myself 'not enough' from the start. It was always in my thoughts, eating away at me.

I'd pushed my own dreams and ambitions aside, and happily so, to try and make our relationship work – Billy is a superstar, who has succeeded in doing great things and gaining critical acclaim; his job and dreams were always going to be more important than mine, because his success was on a much bigger scale. Whatever I manage to achieve in life would always pale in comparison to his successes – it's thoughts like that which made our life together very one-sided. The emphasis was always on what Billy was doing, and how I could fit in around his plans to make his life as easy as possible. My purpose was to make Billy happy, to lovingly welcome him back into a warm, clean home of an evening. It all sounds very quaint and sweet, but I ended up living my life for him and having nothing of my own; nothing to take pride in. I'd lost myself.

Occasionally, I think certain thoughts and I wonder if they're real, or if my brain finds it easier to look back and see all the faults in a bid to get over the heartache I feel. After all, I didn't always feel bad, I wasn't always made to feel like nothing; that occurred in only a handful of tiny moments; however, the feeling they caused lingered, because I always saw the truth in them. They helped to feed my own insecurities.

I miss Billy.

If Billy was plucked out of his life and able to exist as the man I first met and fell in love with, I know we'd be happy together, if the relationship was more balanced. However, I know that equality could never be struck with him staying in his profession. Quite frankly, he has too many people blowing hot air up his arse, telling him how wonderful he is and what he should be doing with his life. He's never able to live just for himself.

Billy hasn't turned up at Mum's, he has been respectful of the fact that I asked him not to, although he has left me a barrage of texts and missed calls. Every time I look at my phone there is some sort of message on there from him, along with a missed call or two from Molly, although even she seems to have stopped trying for a couple of days. I know she'll have read the papers and that she'll be worried about me, but I haven't had the energy or enthusiasm to talk to anyone. I'm surprised she's not turned up at the door, bringing cake to mend my broken heart. Perhaps Mum has told her I'm not up for visitors just yet.

I stare at the photos on my pink bedroom wall, having hung them up as soon as I got back, and think of Dad, trying to block out all the other thoughts that niggle at my brain, concentrating on his beaming smile, his kind brown eyes and the love which encompasses every image.

For five days I have stayed under my duvet in bed, the time passing in a blurred mixture of tears, snot and never-ending cups of tea and toast. So far, my desire to block out the outside world has been honoured and I've been left to stew in my own sorrow, but I know Mum won't let me continue in this way forever. Over the past two days, each time she's come in she's lingered by my bed, eager to say something, but always deciding against it at the last second and shuffling away. We've never been in this situation before – one where she's the giver, trying to find the right words to say to pull me out of my stupor. I can't help but feel sorry for her and her efforts.

As Mum knocks on my bedroom door, for the fourth time this morning, I hear her muttering to herself and

I know this time she won't leave without trying to get her words out.

After letting herself in, Mum places another cup of tea on my bedside table, next to the mountain of snotty tissues I've created, and sits down next to me on the bed. She turns to me, pulling a sad face – one that is full of sympathy and possibly mirroring my own expression.

'Love, you can't just stay in bed and mope about here for the rest of your life,' she says softly, as she concentrates on sweeping stray bits of hair away from my face.

'Why not?' I sulk.

'Because . . . you can't.'

Unsatisfied with the answer I stay quiet and just stare back at her.

'Soph, I know how it feels to want to shut yourself off from the world, but it won't do you any good.' She sighs and looks away from me, taking in the room – my dolls, teddies and books. Her eyes rest on the photo frames in front of us. 'I did a really bad job, didn't I? After your dad died.'

'No!'

'Yes, I did. It's OK,' she says calmly, 'I can easily admit that myself. I know I was rubbish. I just couldn't function, you know?' she says, glancing at me before turning her attention back to the photos. 'I didn't see the point in getting up in the morning. I just couldn't get past the fact that he'd gone.'

'It was hard for you, Mum,' I say, as I pull myself up into a sitting position.

This isn't the conversation I thought we were going to have – I thought she'd fluster her way through talking about boys and heartbreak. I didn't expect her to talk about Dad, especially not his death.

'It was, but I should've remembered that I had an eleven-year-old at home who needed her mother,' she continues calmly. 'I didn't even think about how the whole thing was affecting you. I forgot that you'd be hurting too. That's awful.'

'Mum, you don't have to –'

'But I do, Sophie. I was so absorbed in my hurt that I didn't console you in yours. You should've been my top priority but I was selfish. '

'But you had so much to deal with and –'

'Sophie, I'm not looking for you to make excuses for me. I'm trying to explain,' she says softly, cutting me off. 'I felt like I didn't know who I was any more. I'd lost my present and my future – the only thing I wanted to cling on to was the past – but the past was too painful to think about. We were so happy, and then suddenly it was gone,' she pauses and looks down at her hands as she rubs them together. 'He was so young – it was so unfair. I couldn't understand it. All I could think about was the life we'd lost. I couldn't bear the thought that I had so much of my own life to live without him. That he had missed out on so much.'

I don't say anything, choosing to let Mum voice these feelings she's never been able to share with me before. I lean forward and hold her hand, giving it a gentle squeeze. Letting her know I'm here. Listening.

'And then I think of your little brother or sister that we never had. I failed him. I failed your dad because I wasn't able to do that right.'

'Mum, that's rubbish!' I protest, suddenly feeling a tightening around my throat at the mention of that other life.

'And then there's you . . . my biggest regret is that I let life stop for you.'

'But it was my fault,' I blurt.

'What was?'

'Dad's death . . . everything.'

'Why do you think that?'

'Because of our argument. Because of me being a spoilt brat and demanding marshmallows. Because if I hadn't done that, then Dad would still be here.'

'If you want to go down the blame route I could say that it was my fault for not realizing we were out of marshmallows when I did the shopping.'

'That's just stupid.'

'And so is you thinking it's your fault,' she says sternly, before turning away and shaking her head. 'I should've insisted we both got help straight away – therapy or whatever. I can't believe I let us plod along like zombies for so long – that I let you stay at home and look after me instead of living your life.'

'But I didn't want to go anywhere else, Mum.'

'And why not? Tell me honestly why you stayed at home,' she says, squeezing my hand.

I pause before responding. To share the thoughts in my head could be upsetting for Mum, but is it better for us to have those unsaid words out there at last, so long after the events that have unquestionably shaped our lives?

'I was scared,' I say matter-of-factly, not letting emotion take over – ensuring that my words can be heard. That we can communicate at last. 'Scared of what you might do to yourself if you didn't have me around to look after you.'

Mum looks at me with a sad nod.

'I never begrudged it, Mum.'

'But you stopped your life to look after me.'

'What life?' I say with a laugh. 'I had no real friends at that point anyway. It's not like I was itching to leave your side to be with them. By the time your breakdown came, Mum, I was so relieved to have a glimpse of the old you back that I'd have given anything to stay with you. Yes, it was hard. Yes, it was painful to see you in such a state. But there was no way I was going to go and leave you.'

I look down at our entwined hands as memories of my childhood and the little girl I once was flicker through my brain.

'I sometimes wonder what my life would've been like if Dad hadn't died – and not just because he'd have been here with us, but I look at who I am now and I wonder who I would've been if I hadn't had to go through all that loss.'

'Before that you were such a bright young thing – a bubble of energy.'

'See, I see myself as two separate people – before and after, you know?'

Mum nods.

'Not only did Dad get snatched from us, but I felt as though my childhood got taken from me, too. I was so different to everyone else. I knew things that I shouldn't about how cruel life can be and how quickly it can be crushed.'

'You were forced to experience so much so young.'

'I was . . . and I think that is partly why I cut myself off from everyone.'

'Do you think it's had a knock-on effect? With your relationships as an adult?' Mum asks. I'm surprised at the frankness of the question, of the whole discussion we've been having, but it feels good to share. Good to get the niggling thoughts out of my head.

'Definitely. I'm better now than I was, but it's still there sometimes. The fear of getting close to someone in case they leave me.'

'You let your guard down with Billy, though.'

'Yes, and look where that got me.'

'Soph, don't you think you're being a bit quick to act on this whole thing?'

'What do you mean?' I snap suddenly, pulling my hands away from hers and instantly shattering the ease of our conversation by getting defensive. Inwardly I cringe at my tone – I know Mum is trying to help. 'I'm sorry,' I grumble quietly.

'That's OK, love,' she says as she stands up and picks

a few stray bits of cotton from my duvet cover off her skirt. 'Locking yourself away in your room isn't going to do you any favours, though . . .'

'I know, Mum. But I'm just not ready to face anyone yet. I need time.'

She leans over and plants a kiss on my cheek. 'Just remember that we're all waiting for you to come back to us.'

She leaves and I lie back and bury myself under the duvet once again.

After a few more days of solitude I finally muster up the energy to walk downstairs to the kitchen, needing something other than the copious amounts of tea and toast my mum has been bringing me. I'm halfway down the stairs when I overhear her and Colin talking in hushed voices. I'm about to turn and sprint back upstairs, not being in the mood to see Colin, when Mum's words stop me.

'I can't believe it,' she says. 'They said she's quickly getting worse.'

'You have to tell her now.'

'But she's still so fragile herself, Colin. I don't know how she'd cope.'

'Jane, she has a broken heart. That's all.'

I want to shout in protest, tell Colin I think he's an idiot for being so flippant about what I'm going through, but I don't, because I need to know what they're keeping from me.

'Can you imagine how she'd feel if she dies without

her having said goodbye?' he continues. 'That would be devastating for her. You need to tell her so that she can go and see her.'

'Tell her what?' I say quietly at the door. Afraid of what I'm about to be told.

They both stare at me for what feels like hours, before speaking.

'Love . . .' says Mum finally, worry lines appearing on her forehead, clearly pained by whatever news she has to break to me.

'Just say it.'

'Molly's not well.'

'What's wrong with her?'

'It's cancer.'

My heart stops beating at the word. I don't respond. Instead I stay quiet as Mum fills me in with more details.

'It seems she's known for quite some time, since before you moved to London, in fact. That's when she first found a lump in her breast, which turned out to be malignant. It was only when she went in for more tests that they found it was also in her lungs and spine. She was told then that it was terminal.'

My jaw drops in shock. She was riddled with it and has kept this a secret from me for months.

'Why didn't she tell me?'

'She didn't tell anyone. I think she didn't want to be a burden.'

'But we could've helped,' I squeak, not able to understand why Molly would have chosen to go through this alone. 'Where is she?'

Silence falls on the room, Mum hesitant to tell me, her hand covering her face in sorrow.

'Where?'

'At the hospice.'

'What?' I gasp.

I don't know much about hospices, but one thing I do know is that they're the places extremely sick people go to die.

Molly is about to die.

My best friend, the person I love more than anything, is about to die.

The person I love but have ignored over the past week or so because I've been so self-absorbed, is about to die. She hasn't been calling to see how I am. She's been calling to tell me of her own heartache.

'I'll drive you there, if you like,' offers Colin. The first time he has spoken since I entered the room.

I nod my head at him, still trying to make sense of the news.

'Can we go now?' I ask, not caring that I've been cooped up in my room for days without washing, that I'm wearing my pink-and-white-striped pyjama bottoms with a massive grey jumper and that I look like crap.

'Of course,' he says. 'But . . .'

'But, what?'

He looks down at the floor, pursing his lips together in hesitation.

'There's a photographer parked outside.'

'What?'

'He's been here for days.'

'Oh love, we haven't wanted to worry you, especially as you've been up in your room with no plans to go outside anyway,' explains Mum. 'We thought he'd eventually get bored of sitting there.'

I shake my head at the vulgarity of the situation.

'So, basically, he is waiting for the first shot of me since the break-up, preferably with me looking like shit.'

'Sophie!' reprimands Mum, never having heard me swear before.

'Let's give him what he wants shall we? Then he can bugger off back to wherever he came from and leave me alone. Come on,' I command, striding to the door and chucking on my boots.

Mum and Colin sheepishly follow behind me, no doubt taken aback by my feisty attitude.

As soon as I open the door, I spot the scumbag as he hastily scurries out of his white van, wearing a baseball cap and leather jacket, and leaps towards me. He instantly holds his camera up to his face and starts snapping away.

'Lovely to see you finally, Miss May. I was beginning to think I had the wrong address,' he shouts, running backwards in front of me. 'So sorry to hear about you and Billy. Do you have anything to say on the situation? Have you heard from him at all? Has he begged for your forgiveness yet?'

With my eyes concentrating on the pavement below, I clench my jaw to stop myself from biting back and swiftly make my way to Colin's silver Ford Mondeo, choosing to ignore him. I know he's after a reaction of some sort, although I'd have thought a photograph of me in this state would have been enough to satisfy his needs!

Sensing my reluctance to reply, he continues.

'We've all felt ever so sorry for you. It must've been awful watching him all over Heidi like that. Apparently he is back at work already, acting as though nothing has happened, that must be painful for you to hear – thinking of him back on set, with her. All over her again without a second thought for you. They've not been pictured out together any more, you'll be happy to hear. Doesn't mean anything, though, they're probably shacked up in bed together, making up for lost time.'

Before slipping into the car, I do the unthinkable; I flip him the birdie.

I don't speak in the car. I'm annoyed that the media would be so callous as to come after me so that they can write a stupid article on how heartbroken and devastated I am without Billy, but to be honest, I don't care. The fickleness and the unimportance of that world hold no significance next to the knowledge that Molly is leaving me.

I look out of the window and take in the world around me. Watching as people go about their daily business, not aware that one of the kindest people I know is at death's door.

I think back to all the calls I've missed, the times she's tried to get me to listen to her, only to be ignored.

I try to remember the last time she tried calling . . . was it yesterday, or the day before? Why didn't she leave a message telling me the truth? Although what would she have said? 'Hi Sophie, Molly here. Just wanted to let you know I'm dying. And that you're being a crappy friend.'

Oh, Molly . . .

When we pull into the hospice car park, Colin parks the car and switches off the engine. Both he and Mum take their seatbelts off but stay in the car.

'You OK, love?' Mum asks, swivelling in her seat so that she can see me.

I nod hesitantly.

'Is it OK if I go see her on my own first?'

'Of course it is, Sophie,' she says, as she leans over and takes my hand in hers, rubbing it. 'You go in and then I can see her afterwards. How does that sound?'

'Thank you.'

'Do you want me to walk in with you? Or would you rather we stayed here?'

'No, you stay here,' I say, stepping out of the car.

My footing is unsteady as I make my way towards the entrance sign along the pebbled pathway, nerves causing my body to convulse involuntarily.

When I get to the reception desk, a round-faced lady with a blonde bob and heavy fringe is there to greet me.

'Hello, darling. How can I help?'

'I'm here to see Molly? Molly Cooper?'

'Can I take your name, please?' she asks, filling in a form in front of her.

'Sophie May.'

She looks up and inspects my face before smiling at me.

'So you're Sophie! She's been asking after you ever since she got here.'

'Really?'

'Yep. She'll be thrilled you've come.'

I smile back at her, unsure what else to say.

'She's in room seven, which is just down the corridor to your left.'

'Thank you,' I say, turning to leave.

'Molly's is the only closed door – she's been complaining of the noise the other patients have been making. I think she's frustrated that she can't get out of bed and see what's going on,' she smiles warily. 'I must warn you, she's very weak and tired. Don't let that scare you. And don't take offence if she falls asleep while you're talking to her, she's done that to me a number of times, so I'm hoping she means nothing by it. She'll be so happy to see you.'

I can't speak, already feeling the emotion gathering in my throat. I give her a pained smile and start to make my way to Molly's room.

Walking through the green hallway I hear cries of pain and weeping pouring from every room I pass, causing me to glance through the open doors as I walk by, even though I know I shouldn't. Some of the cries come from the patients, who call out in pain or confusion, wondering where they are or what's happening to them. Others are from their families or loved ones who are standing by their bedsides, looking devastated at seeing someone they love so close to death. It's terrifying to see and causes my insides to curdle in trepidation.

My walk becomes slow and heavy as I near Molly's closed door, fear taking hold of me. Outside her room, I pause before going in, trying to steady my breathing, which has become erratic and keeps catching in my throat.

Knowing that what I see on the other side is going to shock and upset me, I try to prepare for the worst, telling myself to expect Molly to look gaunt and ill, but it doesn't seem real or possible for her to be on the other side of this door. I'd love to run away and pretend none of this is happening, to block it all out, but I could never do that to Molly, knowing that she needs me, that she's been asking after me, and that I've added to her recent anguish by ignoring her calls.

Terrified, I quietly twist the handle and open the door. As I walk in the sight in front of me instantly sends heat prickling at the back of my nose and deep in my chest. I clench my jaw and hands, trying to hold off the tears that are already threatening to pour.

I'm unaware of anything else in the room other than Molly: sweet, kind, wonderful Molly. Lying in a hospital bed, looking tiny and frail. Propped up by pillows and smothered in white sheets.

Her face is thin and grey, almost transparent, enabling me to see every vein that lies underneath. Her eye sockets seem to have sunk into her face, and her chin

345

seems to have disappeared completely due to her extreme weight loss. Her cheekbones, however, stick out sharply, making her seem more alien than human. I watch as her chest rises and falls dramatically, showing her breathing to be heavy and laboured.

Slowly, Molly opens her eyes, aware of someone in the room with her. My whole body tenses in shock as her once-sparkling blue eyes look back at me, now glassy and grey. An emptiness lies behind them, as though she's already disappeared.

'Hello, duck!' she says, her voice raspy and weak, yet somehow managing to sound cheerful. 'You made it!'

She lifts a shaky hand for me to take, my presence seeming to give her a sudden burst of energy. I quickly move towards her and gently take hold of the offered hand, marvelling at the thinness of it, the fragility of these bony fingers, which were once so strong from baking all day, the skin so thin and delicate; so futile.

'Hello, you,' I say warmly, cursing myself as tears manage to escape from my eyes.

'I'm so happy you're here, pet. So happy,' she says, making an effort to lift my hand and kiss it, the action causing a lump to form in my chest and throat. I watch as she closes her eyes briefly, looking peaceful and content.

Words fail me as more tears roll.

'Oh, Molly,' I weep, emotion taking hold of me.

'No point crying now, duck,' she says, opening her eyes and looking at me with concern.

'You should've told me.'

'I didn't want anyone to know.'

'Why?'

Molly doesn't answer, she just screws her face up, closing her eyes again.

'You're my oldest friend, Mol! I haven't been there for you and I should've been. I should've been looking after you, Mol. Instead, I've been so self-absorbed.'

'You've done more than you know, just by being here now,' she says quietly, keeping her eyes closed, holding my hand to her chest. 'My best friend. My girl.'

With my free hand, I grasp her other hand and kneel close to her, watching as she flitters in and out of sleep. At times her face is a picture of calmness, at peace with what's to come, maybe dreams of seeing her Albert again filling her with joy. However, there are also moments when it flickers with confusion and pain, which I struggle to watch.

I feel so useless knowing that it's only a matter of time and that I can't do anything to stop her dying, no matter how much I want to.

She keeps trying to wake up and talk to me, but doesn't have the energy, so instead, she'll take a deep breath, open her eyes slightly to check I'm still with her and close them again. I can see she's tired and that she needs to rest, but I know she won't if she knows I'm still here.

Remembering that Mum wanted to come in and see her too, I straighten up, wanting to leave before I wear her out further.

'I'm so proud of you, Sophie,' she says, opening her eyes and looking at me.

I feel unworthy of the comment, sure that there is nothing about me to be proud of. Especially as I appear to be making a mess of everything lately.

I lean over her and give her a kiss on the cheek, before resting the side of my face on hers and whispering into her ear.

'I love you, Molly. Thank you for turning my life around. I have no doubt I couldn't have done it without you. I love you, Mol,' I say, squeezing her hand and turning towards the door to leave.

'I love you, Sophie,' Molly says, opening her eyes again. 'Love you, Sophie. I love you, Sophie,' she repeats again and again in a coarse voice. I struggle to keep control as I walk out of the room and shut the door.

I barely take two steps before I have to hold on to the wall to steady myself. Leaning against it, I slide to the ground and grab my knees, hugging them into me. Molly's last sentence rings in my ears, causing me to feel an abundance of love and a painful amount of grief all at once. It was a mutual understanding that we'll never see each other again. That was it. Our years of friendship building up to that final farewell.

I'm stunned at her transformation and distraught at her weakness.

How can life be so cruel to someone so giving?

Needless to say, I don't sleep. All I can think about is Molly, lying in her bed at the hospice. All alone.

I wonder what's going through her head. Is she frightened of what's to come? Is she worried that at some point she's going to close her eyes and never open them again? Or, after months of knowing this was to be the outcome, is she relieved the end is so close? Putting an end to her pain and torment.

When the phone rings early the following morning, I know straight away. I curl up in bed and listen as Mum runs down the stairs to answer it. Moments later she knocks on my door, walks in and sits on my bed, looking distressed as she puts her hand on my side.

'Soph, that was the hospice calling. Molly passed in her sleep last night.'

Although I knew the words were coming and although I knew, without a doubt, that this would be the reason for the phone call, the shock still hits me hard.

'They said that she wasn't in any pain, that she was very peaceful. Oh love, I'm so sorry,' she chokes.

Her tears spark off mine, as uncontrollable sobs fly out of me, my whole body shaking with heartache. My beloved friend has gone. I feel relief at having seen her, enabling me to say a proper goodbye, but sad that I hadn't managed to say everything I should have done. Now I never would be able to.

I have so much to be thankful to Molly for and I'm not even sure if those feelings could ever actually be broken down and expressed in words. I just hope she knew how special she was to me, how much I adored her and how grateful I am to the woman who taught me so much and stood by me with patience and kindness as she tried to mend my broken being.

One thing that pains me is that, having seen her, I

can't get her grey face and glassy eyes out of my thoughts. When I think of her now a knot forms in my stomach, as it's that version of Molly that appears in my head, not the kind-faced Molly I have known and loved for years. The sight of Molly looking so fragile and empty on her deathbed seems to be etched in my brain, refusing to budge, filling me with despair.

23

A couple of days later, I'm attempting to read in the living room, my mind refusing to take in any of the information on the page. I must have read the same paragraph at least twenty times, but again and again my thoughts manage to worm their way through, overriding the written words in front of me and deleting their meanings; turning them into shapes that my eyes glance over indifferently. It's highly frustrating, especially as I'm trying to read so that I can give my mind a break from those worries. No matter how hard I try it seems nothing can stop Billy, Molly and my lack of future plans from leaking through into my consciousness. Giving me something to agonize over, as they demand my attention.

An unexpected knock at the front door halts my efforts.

Although I'm still housebound and feeling fragile, not wanting to go out and face people yet, I have been getting out of bed and pottering around the house. I'm no longer sticking to the confines of my bedroom as I realized I'd slowly start to go mad if I sat staring at my pink walls any longer. For the moment, forcing myself into the shower each morning and stopping myself from wearing pyjamas in the daytime seems like a gigantic personal achievement. This means that, despite looking a mess, with my hair bundled on top of my head in a messy bun, my clothes baggy and mismatched, the arrival finds me clean, at least.

I answer the door to find a man in his late thirties standing on the doorstep. I know who he is instantly. His sun-kissed hair, ruffled and messy, and his tanned hands, with which he is rubbing his equally bronzed face, give him away.

'Hello,' I say, not sure of the best way to greet him.

'Sophie?' he asks, looking exhausted.

'Yes.'

'I'm Peter. Molly's son.'

I've never met Molly's son, as he'd left for Australia before I started working at Tea-on-the-Hill, but she talked about him and her late husband Albert non-stop. I'd always thought she'd shut up shop and move over to Oz one day, although that day never came.

'I've heard so much about you,' I say, unable to stop myself from beaming at him.

'Likewise,' he says with a sad smile. 'Is it possible to come inside?'

'Yes, of course.'

I let him in, leading him into the kitchen, where I brew a pot of tea for us both.

'How long have you been back?'

'Just a few days. Luckily, I got to see her before she . . .'

'Yes.'

'I hear you did, too?'

I nod as I place cups and saucers on the table, along with the biscuit tin.

'That's good,' he continues. 'The nurses said it was as though she was holding on. Wanting to say proper goodbyes.'

'Did you know?' I ask, pouring out the tea and offering him the sugar.

'No, but I should've guessed.'

'How?'

'She was calling more, talking a lot about my dad and the trips we'd been on and stuff,' he says, pausing to take a sip of his drink. 'She was getting really sentimental about things.'

'So when did you hear?'

'When she went into the hospice. She called me her first night there, and I got the earliest flight I could.'

'I guess, being there, she knew the end was in sight and that she couldn't put off telling people any longer.'

'Not that it would've changed anything of course, if we had known sooner,' he says in a matter-of-fact tone. 'It would've been nice to have been prepared, that's all. It all seems so sudden this way.'

'Not for her, though.'

Peter takes another sip from his cup while I fiddle with the handle on mine.

Poor Molly, I think. I wonder what was going through her mind over those last few months. Did she really think she would be saving us from heartache by keeping the truth from us? Preferring us to find out when she was on the verge of dying, rather than when we could be there for her and comfort her? Or could she really not bear the thought of being the one who had to be looked after for once? She must have suffered from horrendous pains for months and simply ploughed on regardless.

'How long are you staying over here for?' I ask, breaking the silence.

'Not long, a week or so, probably. There are some legal things that I need to sort out, regarding her house and the shop. But once that's done I'll head back to Sydney.'

'I see.'

'I'm actually here because she made something very clear to me, and, well, it's in her will,' he says, putting down his cup and looking up at me. 'You're to have the shop.'

I stare at him, gobsmacked, frozen in shock as I try to take in his words. Is Molly really giving me Tea-on-the-Hill?

'What?' I blunder. 'That can't be right. What about you? Surely she'd want you to have it?' I ask, confused that he isn't up in arms over the fact that his mum is giving away his inheritance to someone he's never met before, but instead he seems calm and pleased with the decision.

'No, Sophie. It makes complete sense, really. There'd be no way of me keeping check on it from Oz, even if I had someone in to manage it. Sooner or later I'd be forced to sell it, and can you imagine if I sold it and it got turned into a fish and chip shop or something? I'd feel awful and Mum would probably come and haunt me for letting it happen. Plus, tea has never really been my thing,' he jokes, reaching across the table and placing his hand gently on top of mine, offering me a sympathetic smile. 'You loved it as much as she did, Sophie. To me it was just a place that sold tea and cake; I never really understood what was so special about it. But you did.'

'I just never expected this. Why has she done it?' I ask, failing to comprehend the news.

'She can tell you that herself,' he says, pulling an envelope from his pocket and sliding it across the table towards me. 'She wrote you a letter and asked me to pass it on. No doubt she explains it all in there.'

'When did she write it?'

'I'm not sure . . . I'm guessing before she went into the hospice, though. I don't think she was up to doing much in there,' he says sadly.

I stare at the envelope with my name on the front, written in Molly's hand, unsure what to do or say. Should I pick it up and rip it open so that we can both take in Molly's words? Or should I leave it where Peter has placed it until he leaves so that I can devour it alone?

'It's a bit eerie, really, getting a letter from a dead person,' says Peter, before inhaling deeply and standing up, clapping his hands on his sides awkwardly. 'Right, I'd better be going.'

Once Peter has left, I pick up the envelope and take it upstairs, retreating back to the safe haven of those four pink walls once again. Sitting at the bottom of my bed, I stare at it in my hands for a few moments, trying to brace myself for what it contains, before turning it over and opening it.

My hands shake as I pull out the paper inside and unfold it, taking in the page full of Molly's last scribbled words to me.

My dear girl,

I'm writing this not knowing how long I have left . . . How's that for dramatic? I was hoping to see you one last time, but it seems time isn't on our side.

I know you'll be angry at me for not telling you. I didn't tell anyone. You'll probably think it was my pride stopping me from telling people – so that I wouldn't be seen as an invalid by Mrs Sleep and co. while they fussed around me. But it wasn't. At first it was because I didn't want to admit what was happening. Quite simply, pet, I wanted to block it out. Sadly, I didn't realize how quickly I would deteriorate.

So, the purpose of this letter? It is to tell you how much I love you, and how our time together has given me some of my fondest memories. You are a breathtaking young woman and watching you blossom and grow into such a wonderful human being has been one of the highlights of my life. I say that with absolute sincerity and hope that one day you'll believe in yourself as much as I believe in you. You deserve to have so much happiness.

The shop means as much to you as it does to me, it gave us both a purpose and healed our hearts. Therefore, I'd like you to have it. I don't expect you to put your life on hold so that you can run it, or to feel tied down to it, mind, but it is yours to do whatever you wish with.

Billy came to see me today. What a fool he has been. I have no doubt that he loves you as much as I do. What you must remember is that love, as powerful as it may be, is never simple or straightforward. I know you and Billy are going to have a lifetime of happiness together, just like me and my Albert did. He loves you so very much. Remember that. Believe that. Nothing else in the world matters — something Billy has finally realized.

Oh my darling Sophie, catching a glimpse of you again would fill my heart with joy. You are forever in my thoughts.

I love you,

Molly
Xxx

I sit on my bed for hours, reading and rereading it, taking in her words, grateful to have something so special from her to keep, cherish and savour.

There's one thing that niggles at my brain and irritates me, though, and that is — when did Billy go to see Molly? How did he know that she was ill? Had he known she was ill before I did?

It feels so strange to know that he would have driven out all this way and not even attempted to come and see me. Not that I would've wanted to see him, obviously — I'd told him to give me space — but I'd have thought he would have tried, given the circumstances.

With curiosity getting the better of me, I find myself grabbing my phone and texting him. Conscious of the fact that I don't want to engage in conversation, I decide to keep the message short, succinct and devoid of any emotion.

> How did you know about Molly?

No pleasantries, just straight in there with the point.

Once I press the send button I regret it immediately. Any control I thought I'd gained instantly leaves me as all I can do is sit and anxiously stare at my phone, waiting for a reply.

Within minutes it bleeps with a response.

> Hello! You OK? It's so good to hear from you, Sophie. Molly called here. I thought she was about to give me a bollocking, but it turned out she was looking for you. I could tell something wasn't right, in the end she told me where she was and I drove over. She agreed to let me call your Mum when I was there. Are you OK?

That explains how Mum and Colin discovered the news after months of being kept in the dark like everybody else. Mum never mentioned speaking to him, but that isn't so surprising.

Before I even decide whether I want to send a reply or not, my phone bleeps again with another message from him.

> I was going to stop by and see you but I
> had to get back to London to sort a few
> things out, I couldn't get away for long.
> Plus, I guessed you wouldn't have
> wanted to see me anyway. That's why I
> phoned instead. How is Molly?

Part of me wants to bite, to say something about how good it is to see he's still putting his work first, but I don't. Because I know I have to tell him about Molly passing. It would be wrong of me to include anything scathing while writing those words.

> She died Tuesday night. In her sleep.

I respond, sadness engulfing me as I send it.

> Oh Soph, I'm so sorry to hear that. Are
> you OK?

> Not really. It's such a shock. I can't
> believe she's gone.

I write honestly, suddenly wanting to feel his love.

> I know. It's awful. Helps to put things
> into perspective though, doesn't it . . .?
> Oh Sophie, I wish I could hug you. I miss
> you so much. Can I see you?

Even reading the words causes me pain, letting me know how much I miss him, too. I want him here to hug me and comfort me, to tell me that everything will be all right and to reassure me that Molly is in a happier place now. I love him so much. I need him.

Feeling betrayed by my own heart, I'm suddenly angry at myself for letting my guard down and allowing him in. Crushed that my heart has leapt in anticipation of his messages and caved in when it needed to stay strong. I have an urge to shun him, to push him away and make him see that he can't text me caring and tender messages after what he has done. It's his fault we aren't together.

No.

Simple. Unyielding. Decisive.

> Please? I have so much to tell you.

> I don't want to know, Billy. I'm getting rid of this phone. There doesn't seem much sense in having it seeing as I'm back home and you're now the only person who calls me on it. Plus, the last thing I want to hear about is how amazing your flipping life is. Goodbye.

I hastily switch the phone off and throw it at the wall opposite me, which feels good for a split second, but turns out to be a stupid idea as I put a big dent in the wall and the screen of the phone cracks. Not that I have any intention of using it again any time soon – it's not as though I have millions of friends to call.

*

When Mum comes home later that afternoon I'm sitting on the stairs waiting for her, hugging one of the wooden spindles.

'When were you going to tell me you'd spoken to Billy?' I ask, once she's walked into the hallway.

'Oh, love,' she says, putting down her bag and removing her coat. She turns to face me, letting out a little sigh. 'Come on, that really doesn't matter, does it? What matters is that we found out about Molly before it was too late.'

'I know,' I say sulkily.

'No one knew. Not even June Hearne,' she says, leaning on the banister and taking my hand.

'But she looked so ill, Mum! Why didn't people notice that?'

'People assumed she was stressed out because she was running the shop on her own. It was a lot for someone her age to be doing.'

'So after Sally left she didn't get anyone else in?'

'No. I think she was worried to . . .'

'Because of me?'

'Don't be silly,' she says, sitting down next to me, and putting her arm around me. 'You can't blame yourself for any of this. She'd already been told she had cancer before you left. So, please don't think that.'

'Why didn't she tell me as soon as she found out, though?'

'Because she knew that you wouldn't leave her.'

That's true. There would be absolutely no way that I'd have gone swanning off on a whim if I'd known.

Seeing as the whole thing turned into such a mess, with hindsight, I'd have preferred it if she'd told me and made me stay.

'There's one thing I really don't understand though, Mum . . . when she eventually got too weak to run the shop, where did everyone think she'd gone? She just disappeared. Didn't anyone think that was strange?'

'She left a note on the window saying she was taking a break – which, because she'd been running the shop alone, seemed plausible. Everyone thought she'd gone to Australia to see Peter.'

'Without telling anyone?'

Mum doesn't say anything, but looks regretful at not having questioned it at the time.

'So, instead of soaking up the sun in the company of her loved ones, like people thought, she was only a few miles away, dying alone.'

'Sophie, she could've told people but she chose not to. It's obviously what she wanted and –'

She stops speaking as the phone in front of us starts to chirp. Patting my knee as she stands up, Mum goes and answers it.

'Hello? Oh!'

I watch as a frown appears on her face and she starts to smooth back tiny wisps of her hair with her free hand before fiddling with the frames of her glasses. She is clearly feeling uncomfortable. It doesn't take me long to realize it's Billy, who has decided to call the house phone now that I've switch off my mobile. I can faintly hear his voice as he asks if he can speak to me.

I shake my head at Mum profusely.

'No, no, no! I don't want to speak to him!' I whisper to Mum as she places her hand over the mouthpiece so that he can't hear me.

'Soph, I really think you should listen to what he has to say. He really –'

'No, Mum! I don't care.'

She sighs deeply and holds the phone to her chest.

'Are you sure?'

'Yes. I've got nothing to say to him.'

She looks up at my face sadly, before turning away from me.

'I'm so sorry, love,' she says politely down the phone. 'I'm afraid she doesn't want to talk. I know you do, love . . .'

I run up the stairs and go back to the safe haven of my room, wanting to get away.

24

The next day, I receive an envelope in the post, with my name and address written in Billy's handwriting. I think about not opening it and just burning it straight away or shredding it, but curiosity gets the better of me.

I open it to find a black and white photograph of Billy, Molly, Mum and me, taken in Hyde Park on the picnic blanket the day they'd come to visit late last summer. We're all huddled closely together, as Billy stretches out his arm to take the photo, allowing our faces to fit in the frame. Billy has one eyebrow raised and is flashing his teeth, looking incredibly cheeky. Next to him, Molly is debuting her short crop and has the tips of her fingers combed through the front of her hair, leaning on her hand slightly, which covers her right eye. I'd never noticed before, but she looks pained in some way. Exhausted. But perhaps someone else could look at the image and say she looks happy and peaceful, quietly content. It might be that looking at the image with hindsight is leading me to read too much into it. I know she was happy on that day; I was there, I saw her laughing and making jokes as usual. How were we to know she was keeping such a devastating secret from us all?

I think back to our chat that day, where Molly had

talked about grabbing opportunities and not letting life pass me by like they had her. At the time, I thought she was talking about my job in Coffee Matters. I thought she was trying to get me to quit so that I didn't waste my life in a thankless job when I could be enjoying life. In reality, though, was she hinting about the end of her life? How self-obsessed of me not to even question that something might have been wrong with her.

In the picture, I'm sat in between Molly and Mum, with my arms around them both, squeezing them into my body. My eyes are closed tightly, all screwed up, and I have a stupidly massive grin on my face. Mum has been caught laughing, showing the glow that surrounded her that day and has done ever since. It's a beautiful photo, which has captured a blissfully perfect moment.

There's no note included in the envelope, but on the back Billy has written:

There is no happiness like that of being loved by your fellow creatures, and feeling that your presence is an addition to their comfort.

I know the quote straight away. It's from Charlotte Bronte's *Jane Eyre*, my favourite book, taken from the moment Jane returns to Thornfield Hall after spending a month nursing her despicable aunt. Does this mean Billy has taken the time to read it after admitting to never having read a book in his life on our first date? Surely not. I doubt he'd find time in his busy schedule to do something as dull as reading . . .

Although, as for his choice of quote – it couldn't be more fitting to the picture.

I sit on my bed for hours, looking at the photo, taking in every single detail, making sure that I don't miss a thing and feeling the warmth that bounces from it.

I'm surprised when another envelope from Billy arrives the following day, this time containing a photo of the two of us, taken in a pigeon-free Trafalgar Square, on the day he'd first driven me to London to see where he lived. Once we'd got over the excitement of possibly moving in together, Billy had decided to take me to the square to prove that he wasn't lying about the no-feeding thing. I was very disgruntled when we arrived to find he had been telling the truth, but Billy grabbed hold of me and dragged us both to one of the lion statues where we decided to snap a series of silly photographs. We took it in turns to scramble our way on top of it or to stand beside it as we pulled ridiculous faces – pretending the bronze lion was about to eat us. It was stupid and fun and caused us to laugh raucously.

This picture is one of the calmer of the bunch, one that we asked a passer-by to take of us, when we were poised between the lion's paws. I'm sat looking at the camera smiling sweetly, with a hand placed on Billy's thigh, while he is sat with an arm around my waist and his forehead resting on my head, looking at me. There's something enchanting in the way Billy gazes at me, as though nothing else in the world matters.

Turning the picture around, I find another *Jane Eyre* quote on the back:

I have for the first time found what I can truly love — I have found you. You are my sympathy — my better self — my good angel. I am bound to you with a strong attachment. I think you good, gifted, lovely: a fervent, a solemn passion is conceived in my heart; it leans to you, draws you to my centre and spring of life, wraps my existence about you, and, kindling in pure, powerful flame, fuses you and me in one.

PART FOUR

25

Black. That is all I see looking in the mirror on the day of Molly's funeral. Black, black, black. Black dress, black shoes, black tights, black coat and a black ribbon holding my hair in the plaited style Molly loved.

But it's not just my clothes that ooze the darkness. It's everything. I can see the blackness under my eyes from the lack of sleep and the general doom that surrounds my existence.

'Are you ready, love?' my mum asks, as she knocks on my door.

'Yeah,' I say, fiddling with my coat buckle as I try to do it up. 'I don't think I can face seeing everyone, Mum. I want to say my goodbyes but –' I stop, choking on my own words.

'It's OK, darling,' she says, walking in as she takes the buckle from my hand and fastens it up for me, holding my hand in hers once she's finished.

Not only will the whole village be out in force today at the church, but they'll also be gathering at Tea-on-the-Hill for Molly's wake, something Peter and Molly's friends at the WI have grouped together to organize. All I had to do was give them my permission to use it now that I'm its new owner. It's a lovely idea, and one that Molly would have loved, but I don't think I'll be able to cope with being in the shop yet without Molly's presence.

'It's too much, Mum.'

'I know,' Mum says, as she pulls me in for a hug. 'Why don't we go to the church and wait until everyone is seated and busy before going in? Hey? We can sneak out before the end if you like?'

I nod. Going unnoticed is exactly what I want to do today.

We sit at the back of the church and are the first people to catch a glimpse of Molly's coffin as it is carried in. The sight is heartbreaking.

Suddenly, the realization that this is all very real hits me.

Molly is in there.

She's gone.

I'm never going to see her again.

The service goes by in a blur as questions and thoughts fill my brain. Why Molly? Why now? She'd given so much to everyone she'd ever met . . . how could such a slow and painful death happen to someone like her?

It's not long before Mum is leaning into me, saying we should leave if we want to get out before being stopped.

I nod and allow her to guide me out of the wooden doors of the church.

We walk home in silence – both absorbed in our own thoughts.

*

When we get home we notice Colin in the garden, bending over a firepit lighting some wood. Unsure what he is doing, we both go out to him.

'Colin?' calls Mum.

'Oh!' he says, startled. 'I thought you'd be a bit longer.'

'What are you doing?' Mum asks, gesturing towards the fire.

'I, erm . . .' He turns to the fire and then back at us sheepishly. 'When my wife Pauline died I wasn't too sure what the best way was for my kids to be able to say goodbye. I wanted them to be able to express what they felt, but thought going to her funeral would be too hard on them.' He stops and picks up a stick, poking the burning wood, making the flames dance wildly. 'So I lit a fire in the garden and we all sat round and spoke about their mum. Talked about all the little things that made her the wonderful woman she was. I wanted them to remember the good times. We ended up writing these letters to her, which we read out and then threw onto the fire – the smoke taking the words up to her in heaven. I . . . I thought we could do that for Molly.'

What a remarkable man, I think, as I take in this thoughtful gesture.

'That's lovely, Colin,' says Mum.

'I mean, we don't have to read them out if you don't want to,' says Colin, looking at me. 'I don't want any of us to feel uncomfortable. I just thought it would be nice to send up our thoughts.'

'Thank you,' I say.

'Let's get out of these clothes first, shall we? Get into something more comfortable,' says Mum, as she starts to walk towards the back door.

I smile at Colin and then follow Mum inside.

My dearest Molly,

I wake up and I think of you.
I see a teacup and I think of you.
I see a cake and I think of you.
I see a flower and I think of you.
I taste a scone and I think of you.
I see a smile and I think of you.
I hear a laugh and I think of you.
I feel a hug and I think of you.
I go to sleep and I think of you.
I will never forget you, Molly, for you are part of everything around me – every object, every thought, every feeling, everything I do – EVERYTHING.

I hope that one day I am able to touch the lives of others in the way that you have touched mine. You turned my life around and put the sunshine back into my world.

I will love you forever.

Your girl Sophie. Xxx

26

Almost two weeks have passed since Molly's death and the shop has remained closed during that time while I try to recover from the loss of two important people in my life in close succession, pondering on how to move forward.

The photos are still arriving daily from Billy, still with a simple quote written on the back, nothing more. It seems he has been making his way through some of the classics that I'd mentioned to him when we were together. *Wuthering Heights, Sense and Sensibility* and *Jude the Obscure* are just a few of the books he's been quoting. I still can't imagine him finding the time to sit down and read them, or having the concentration to do so, but something tells me he must be.

The latest offerings bear quotes from *Pride and Prejudice*, making them even more poignant as they bring back memories of when we first met and used to run through his scenes together in the shop.

I know I probably shouldn't open them, I should probably dispose of them straight away, but the happiness that fills my heart, especially if the photos are of moments with Molly and Mum, cause me to indulge. I haven't even found it in myself to throw them away once I've devoured them. I can't. Instead I've been keeping them in a box under my bed, in order of when they arrived. Every time I pull the pile out and look at them I see the visible love they display and feel a warm comfort. Momentarily my heartache is eased.

Needless to say, I've never written back, so I justify opening them by telling myself that Billy will keep sending them regardless, blind to whether I'm looking at them or not.

Despite their not seeing me, the support from the community has been unwavering. Quite a few of the customers from the shop have left meals, cards and flowers with Mum at the library, checking to see how I am and sending me their best wishes. I'm touched by their kindness, yet dubious as to whether I deserve it. Thankfully, none of them have tried to stop by the house, choosing instead to give their offerings to Mum whilst still giving me the space I need at this complicated and messy time . . . although I'm hardly using the time productively. I've been trying to do all I can to keep my mind occupied so that I don't have to think too much about the past or future – but I can't concentrate. Thoughts keep finding a way of flooding in, no matter what I try doing.

Several days after Molly's funeral I'm sitting in the kitchen, quietly immersed in the impossipuzzle Colin brought round for Mum all those months ago, identical pieces of orange surrounding and infuriating me. I'm about to swipe the whole lot on to the floor in frustration when a knock at the door stops me.

Peter is on the doorstep, rhythmically tapping his legs impatiently as he waits.

'Peter, hi!'

'Hello, Sophie! How are you?'

'Getting there, I think, although I'm not too sure where "there" is exactly yet.'

'I know the feeling,' he replies, with a glum smile.

'Do you want to come in for a tea or coffee?'

'Actually, I can't – I'm on the way to the airport,' he says, gesturing to the taxi which has its motor humming behind him. 'It's time to head back home at last.'

'Oh, I see.'

'I just wanted to drop these round. I know you probably still have your set of keys, but these were Mum's,' he says, handing them to me, along with a brown envelope. 'There's some more legal jargon in there, too, but I think everything's sorted now. It's all yours,' he adds.

'Wow . . . thank you,' I say, looking down at the keys in my hand.

'Any idea on when you're going to reopen it?'

I look at him wearily, pulling my bottom lip through my teeth as I decide on the best way to answer – I don't want him to think Molly made the wrong decision in passing it on to me, that I won't honour her wishes.

'Soon, I think.'

'Good. Mum would want that. It's been lovely to meet you at last, even in these crappy conditions. Bye, Sophie,' he says, leaning towards me and giving me an awkward side hug with a few light pats on the back.

'Thank you, Peter. Have a safe trip.'

He pivots to leave, but turns back to me straight away.

'Mum always said to me it's a place that heals hearts. Don't leave it too long.'

I watch as he jumps into the taxi and it pulls away.

I look down at the keys in my hand and cup my fingers around them.

Hours have passed since Peter called round. The sky outside has faded to black, bringing with it a new sense of calm, despite the owls hooting from their nests.

It's now one in the morning. For the last couple of hours I've been sitting on my bed, staring at the keys on my bedside table, wondering what to do and knowing that I can't continue to hide from everyone for much longer – I reacted in that way after Dad's death, locked myself away and didn't speak to anyone. It didn't help. Instead, it ended up prolonging the agony. I know this time round that I won't be able to move forward if I act in that way again; this time I have to give myself the time to grieve, but know when to pick myself back up again.

Impulsively, I throw on a pink hoodie and grey jogging bottoms, snatch up the keys, head downstairs and chuck on my boots. I make my way out into the cold night air and briskly head for Tea-on-the-Hill, walking through the alleyway and on to the empty High Street. With fire pumping through my body the journey whizzes by, making it feel as though I'm outside the shop within seconds.

The wind is knocked out of me when I spot the messages and drawings stuck to the windows and door, and bunches of flowers left underneath by people paying their respects. I notice they're not just from the customers, but from other people in the village, whom Molly had made an impact on, too. They're wonderful messages of love and thanks, showing how much Molly meant to everyone within the community.

Once I've read them all and absorbed their warmth, I put the key in the lock and let myself in. I don't switch on the light; instead, I close the door behind me and simply pull up a chair and sit in the darkness.

I instantly feel the love oozing from all around me as I remember how much devotion and joy was poured into the place every day, and not just by Molly and me, but by all the elderly women, mums and schoolgirls who chose it as the place to visit as they mulled over their lives. The thought makes me realize that it's not just me that has experienced a loss – everyone has. I've been selfish to think otherwise.

Molly had told Peter that this place heals hearts. Well, I know it does. So for that reason I know it can't stay closed for much longer; people need it in their lives. Now more than ever.

I once had a dream that I'd run my own teashop and that I'd fill it with little gift ideas, flowers and books; it's the dream I told Billy about on our first date in the woods. But like so many of my dreams, something else came along for me to push it aside and change my focus. I was wrong to let that happen again after years

379

of secretly saving and planning. Maybe this time it's not too late to turn my dream into a reality.

I sit in the dark for hours, smiling at the memories of the woman and the place that brought me back to life and wondering how I can repay them both.

I leave as the sun starts to rise, walking home unnoticed.

Even though I stayed in London for months, I never once dipped into my savings – and that's not because I let Billy pay for everything, not at all; it's because I was frugal and kept an eye on my outgoings. Knowing, when shopping, what was a necessity for me to have and what was a pointless splurge. That means I still have a hefty sum of money to put into the business. Even though, thanks to Molly, I no longer need the money to purchase a shop of my own, I still need the money to make changes to Tea-on-the-Hill and put my stamp on it.

Sitting on the sofa the following day with a notepad and sketchbook, I think up little gift ideas, some that I could make and others that I could perhaps source locally: things like candles, little signs, cards, plaques with inspirational quotes on, and wooden photo frames. My mind churns out ideas with excitement, feeling inspired by the future for the first time in months.

I'm still on the sofa hours later, mapping out some of my home-made gift ideas, when Mum walks in and sits next to me, having a good nose at what has motivated me suddenly.

'What are they?' she asks.

'Just little ideas . . .'

'They look pretty.'

She sits and watches me as I continue to sketch.

Right now I'm thinking of different wall hangings, like plaques or chalkboards. I was thinking that a chalkboard in the shape of a big star or heart would be quite pretty as a gift – it could work for a woman of any age; for a young girl it could be something to doodle on or write their crush's name on a million times, and for an older person it could be a place, more pleasing to the eye, where they could write up their shopping list or important notes to themselves.

'I'm thinking of what to do with Molly's,' I tell Mum after a few minutes, keeping my eyes on the pad in front of me.

'That's good, love. What have you been thinking?'

'I still want it to feel like hers. I think it would be awful to take away the things everyone loved about the place. But I also want to introduce a few new things. Like little home-made gifts.'

'Are you planning on making them all yourself?'

'Most of them. Or is that being a little too hopeful?' I ask, doubting the idea.

'I don't think so.'

'I guess I'll just have to wait and see how they sell first and take it from there.'

'When were you thinking of reopening?'

'I'm not sure yet, but I thought I could spend a bit of time making bits before then. It might be a good thing to focus on. Although, God knows how I'll turn what I'm drawing into an actual thing.'

'You should ask Colin to help.'

'Colin?' I ask, screwing up my face in confusion. What could he know about making delicate home-made gifts?

'Well, he used to be a carpenter, love. I'm sure he wouldn't mind doing some bits for you . . . or teaching you how to make them yourself?'

A huge smile spreads across my face as I pull Mum into me, giving her a big kiss on the cheek, thrilled there's a way my plans might actually become a reality.

27

The day of the reopening of the shop comes quicker than I'd expected, the days leading up to it having whizzed by. Inside, it looks relatively the same as before, although it's been spruced up with a lick of paint and there's now a big cabinet made of weathered white wood against one of the far walls, where some of the home-made gifts are displayed.

Hanging off the outside of it are some of the heart-shaped blackboards Colin and I have been sawing together over the last couple of weeks, and inside the cabinet's glass cupboard are the rest of our creations.

On the shelves of the cabinet I have placed some of my favourite books, mostly classics, with a little sign saying, 'Devour me'. The idea being that people can just pick them up to read while they're drinking their pot of tea or coffee.

The only thing I've not managed to incorporate yet is my idea of having flowers available, too, and that is due to the lack of space. I'm sure I'll find a spot for them at some point, but for now, I'm happy with what we've already managed to create.

Seeing as the shop has been closed for a couple of months, I decided to make a celebration of reopening it. One night last week, I dropped leaflets into the other village shops and to the old regulars, announcing that I'd be having a mini street party to welcome the shop back into all of our lives and that I'd be delighted if they would join me for tea and cake.

So, here I am, standing outside the shop, with the new sign above me covered up for its grand unveiling, which will be the first noticeable difference the villagers will see in the shop. In front of me I've laid out a huge table, which is laden with cakes of all shapes and sizes, as well as dozens of big teapots, for everybody to help themselves to – at first, I thought I might've been being too hopeful and made too much, but now, as a crowd has started to gather, I'm slightly worried that I might run out of it all rather quickly.

It feels as though everyone has turned up in support. Looking around me I spot Miss Brown, Mrs Sleep and Mrs Williams standing in a huddle sipping from their teacups and happily nattering away; they're mirrored by the schoolgirls Janet, Ella and Charlotte. June Hearne, Mrs Woodsman, Mrs Wallis and Mrs Tayler stand at the table in front of me, all deciding what cake to nibble on first, knowing full well they'll be coming back for more. I'm surprised at how happy it makes me feel to see all of their faces smiling back at me once again.

Mum and Colin wander over to me after working their way through the crowd, topping up cups with more tea.

'Are you ready, love?' whispers Mum.

'I think so.'

'You'll be great,' winks Colin.

I've always liked Colin, but over the last few weeks he has proven himself invaluable. His help has been priceless. I've enjoyed getting to know him a little bit better and understanding why there has been such a huge change in Mum. I have a lot of time for him.

'OK ... here goes nothing,' I say, as I squeeze Mum's arm.

I pick up a spoon and teacup from the table and tap the metal against the china, grabbing everyone's attention.

'Hello, everyone,' I say, taking a deep breath before continuing. 'Firstly, I just want to say a huge thank you to everybody for your continued support over the last couple of months and for coming up here today. You have no idea how much this means to me. I'm so sorry it's taken me a while to pluck up the courage to do this but –'

I stop as a lump forms in my throat, threatening blubs if I continue. I look down at the ground in front of me and clench my jaw as I try to take hold of myself and my emotions.

'Go on, Sophie! We're right behind you!' shouts a merry Mrs Sleep from the crowd, sparking further cheers of support.

I look up and smile at the group in front of me who have walked up here to join me today, and hear the truth in her words – these people are behind me, as they always have been, giving me nothing but encouragement. I inhale slowly and continue.

'Thank you. Sorry about that ...' I say, once I've

composed myself with a few deep breaths. 'Just one month ago we lost a woman with one of the biggest hearts any of us have ever known. I have no doubt that at some point in each of our lives Molly extended her hand of kindness to us. There was little that Molly would not do for people. In fact, I think in all my years of knowing her I never heard her say no to anyone. Nothing was too much for her, especially if she felt she was helping someone in need. She taught me so much and gave me, as well as you, a place to hide when life felt too tough to deal with. For me, the heart of this shop will always be hers, and that is why I have come to the decision to change its name. Ladies and gentlemen, I present to you . . . Molly's-on-the-Hill,' I say, tugging at the sheet to reveal the new sign Colin and I have been working on – a white-polka-dotted pink background, with the name going across it in swirly black writing.

As the sheet falls I hear a number of surprised gasps from the crowd.

'Oh my!' says Mrs Sleep.

'Woooow!' says Janet. 'It's beautiful!'

'She'd have loved that!' calls June.

Miss Brown is the first to start the clapping, which spreads across the group.

'To Molly!' shouts Mum.

'To Molly!' we all chorus back, holding our teacups and cakes up to the heavens.

28

Sprawled out on the living room floor with pots of glitter, rolls of ribbon, bows, pipe cleaners, glue, buttons and pens surrounding me or resting on my lap, so that it's all within hand's reach, I'm putting together some more home-made gifts.

I'm currently working on the heart-shaped plaques Colin and I have been carving lately, decorating the edges of them before carefully writing some of my favourite quotes on the front. Now, in the most beautiful handwriting I can muster, I'm adding one from *Little Women*, 'I'm not afraid of storms, for I'm learning how to sail my ship,' which is exactly how I have felt for the past week of Molly's being open again. It has been wonderful standing behind that counter and greeting people once again. At times, it has felt a bit daunting having to deal with the whole thing alone, but I feel like I'm getting there.

Amazingly, the gifts have been selling as well as the hot cakes (ha-de-ha), which I'm delighted about, as I always believed they would. Overall, the customers are pleased with the little changes I've made, although I did have to cheer up a disgruntled Miss Brown when she realized her favourite spying spot had been moved slightly to allow space for the cupboard, meaning it had gained a few blind spots. I sent her home with a special lemon drizzle cake to apologize and that seems to have done the trick as she hasn't moaned since. She has now found a new spot in the corner by the window where she can spy on the customers in the shop and those passing by – a double whammy.

One of the highlights of the week for me, though, was when Janet, Ella and Charlotte ventured in after school and picked up a book each and decided to sit in silence for an hour and a half whilst reading. I couldn't contain my joy at the sight in front of me and decided to give them all muffins (skinny ones, of course) on the house. I promise those are the only occasions on which I have given away free food ... actually, there was Mr Tucker's birthday cupcake too!

'Want a tea, love?' Mum asks, getting up off the sofa.

'Yes, please,' I smile, watching as she changes the television channel before leaving the room.

Bernard Sharland, the presenter of the BAFTA awards, appears on the screen, hosting his own chat show. He is at the end of cracking a gag, which eventually causes the audience to laugh hysterically.

'Now, ladies and gentleman,' he says, trying to calm down the rowdy audience. 'My next guest has had a whirlwind career. He was plucked from obscurity when he was just a boy and whisked to LA where he took on a life-changing role in *Halo*. Since then he has won the hearts of millions of teenage girls and scored big time at this year's BAFTAs. Here tonight to promote his latest role in a new film adaptation of *Pride and Preju-dice* – please welcome Billy Buskin.'

'Muuuuum!' I shout, quickly moving everything off my lap and running around looking for the remote to switch it over.

A quick glimpse at the screen stops me.

I watch Billy walk into the television studio, looking pale and fraught. His face is noticeably thinner with gaunt shadows darkening his features. He looks unchar-acteristically sad and downbeat. I'm shocked by the change in him, at how fragile and unconfident he seems. I drop to my knees and crawl closer to the telly.

'Billy, welcome,' Bernard says, shaking his hand before they both sit down on adjacent leather sofas.

'Hello, Bernard. Thank you for having me on,' Billy says, rubbing his hands on his thighs with nerves.

What is going on? This isn't the Billy I know . . .

'Not at all. Now, the last time I saw you, which was at the BAFTAs for those viewers who don't know, you seemed to be on top of the world – you'd just won the award for best male actor!'

'Yeah . . .' Billy replies in a disinterested manner. 'Crazy.'

'And you've been incredibly busy since with the film-ing of *The Walking Beat*, right?'

Billy doesn't speak. He just nods keeping his eyes to the ground.

'OK . . .' says Bernard, with a frown. 'Shall we move on to why you're here? You filmed *Pride and Prejudice* last year – can you tell us about that time? There were some amazing actors on set with you. What was the experience like?'

Something in Billy's eyes twinkles at the question.

'It was the best time of my life,' he says with a smile, as though he is remembering it as he speaks. 'I'd wake up in the mornings full of excitement and anticipation at the day ahead.'

'It is great when you land a job like that – it doesn't feel like work,' agrees Bernard.

'No, not that,' Billy declares, looking up at the host. 'It had nothing to do with the work.'

'Oh?'

'It was all about my time in that quaint little village; the lack of worry, the constant warmth that I felt every day from the people there.'

'And one person in particular? Sophie May?' prompts Bernard.

I gasp.

'Yes,' Billy says, eagerly. 'Every day I'd look forward to seeing her and catching a glimpse of her smile. She can light up a room just by entering it – but she has never been able to grasp how special she is.'

'Are things still on between the two of you? I thought Heidi Black was back –'

'Don't even get me started on her,' Billy snaps, his face darkening once again. 'I don't want people to think the version of me that's printed in the papers is who I am, because it's really not. Absolutely nothing has happened between Heidi Black and me.'

'You're referring to the splash in the papers a few months ago? When you were caught, supposedly, in the midst of a passionate embrace?'

'Yes, but we weren't. I was set up and pounced upon. There's absolutely no way I would be so disloyal to Sophie. I'm still hurt that Heidi put me in that position and used me in that way.'

'It must've been tough working alongside her afterwards.'

'I didn't work alongside her. I quit.'

My jaw drops. He pulled out of the film? When did that happen?

'Really?'

'Yes. The most important thing in anything I do is being able to trust the people around me,' he continues. 'I didn't feel I could work in those conditions. It wasn't an easy thing to do – I had to go through endless meetings with my lawyers because there are so many legalities involved. In fact, there's only so much I'm allowed to say because of that.'

'I see. Where does this leave you now?'

'If I'm honest, I don't know,' Billy replies with a sigh, his face twisting in confusion as he crosses his legs and starts to shake one nervously. 'I'm not blameless in this whole thing. I played my part, too. I became selfish and egotistical. I got carried away with my acting roles, blurring the lines of what was appropriate and not, without a second thought for anything else. I allowed myself to become absorbed in my work and sucked into a life that is neither real nor satisfying. I ignored the views of someone I really love and . . .' he stops and covers his face.

'It's OK, Billy,' comforts Bernard as he pats Billy's uncontrollable leg.

'When I was with Sophie, everything started to make sense,' he says, raising his head to show his blotchy eyes. 'I realized that a lot of the things in my life were worthless. It was all just pointless. Sadly, since then, and especially since winning the BAFTA, I found myself getting more wrapped up in the whole thing. I reignited a spark for acting but that spark took over. I listened to more and more people big me up and tell me what a huge success I could be if I did this or that. I followed their advice, never stopping to question how my actions might affect others or what Sophie wanted.'

'What did she want?'

'Stability? To be made to feel like she was my world . . .? All the things she should've got from me without asking.'

'And what do you want?'

'Sophie,' Billy answers simply.

My heart seems to jump into my throat, as a guttural sound leaps from my mouth.

'When I met Sophie, I watched as she gave herself over to people – offered her time, patience and kindness and never once asked for anything back. Whereas with acting, what do we do to deserve the admiration of all those people? Nothing. I've acted selfishly during my career, thinking largely of myself and nothing else, as most actors do.'

'Surely you're being hard on yourself, Billy,' offers Bernard.

'Maybe, but I don't think so,' Billy says, shaking his head. 'I think I'm seeing myself honestly for once.'

'You're not thinking of chucking it all in, are you, Billy?' laughs Bernard with a wink, trying to make the mood of the interview brighter.

'Not forever, no. But I've worked solidly from such a young age – I think it's time to take a break. Perhaps a year or two to experience the normal things in life.'

'Oh!'

'I think it's time for me to refocus. Growing up I was so close to my family. They meant the world to me. But, succeeding in this business has meant that I have no time to see them. It's made me think it's acceptable to just chuck money at them. Does it make up for my absence or ease any guilt? No, it doesn't. Love makes life worth living, not money.'

'I'm sure a lot of the viewers would agr–'

'Sophie was a far better person than I'll ever be, because she has always put love first and I forgot to give her credit for that. Now she's gone and she won't even take my calls.'

'If you could speak to her, if you could make her listen to you, what would you say?'

I watch, breathlessly, as Billy dips his head and rubs his face while he thinks. He looks up with uncertainty, biting his lip.

'I would tell her that my world is colourless without

her in it, and that, from the moment I met her, she was all I ever wanted.'

'Well, isn't that romantic? I hope she listens to you, Billy,' Bernard says, as he reaches across and grabs his hand. 'Good luck with everything. Enjoy the break and be sure to come and see us when you decide to return to the big screen . . . please don't leave it too long! Billy Buskin, ladies and gentlemen,' Bernard says, encouraging the audience to applause, before moving on to his next guest.

I switch off the television and curl into myself, burying my face in the carpet. My soft whimpers turn into mournful moans within seconds.

I miss Billy so much, how did we manage to get ourselves into such a mess when everything should have been so perfect?

I feel a warm hand spread across my back as I lie on the floor howling with despair. The hand slides up and down my spine, trying to calm me.

'Sophie. I'm so sorry.'

Was that . . .?

I hold still.

Waiting to hear the voice again.

Wanting to be sure.

For a moment, there is silence. Nothing, as I try to make sense of what is going on.

'I mean it. I know now. You are all I ever wanted,' he says softly.

He's here.

He is actually here.

Even though I've ignored him for weeks and told him I don't want him to come after me, he is here. Confusion fills my brain. Small sobs seep uncontrollably from my mouth. Yet, something inside of me is glowing – expanding with happiness.

What do I do now?

'Baby?' he pleads, as his hand comes to a stop on my back.

I take a deep breath and slowly uncurl from my foetal position. I take him in – checking this is real, that my mind isn't playing some mean trick on me. First, I see his feet, wearing the same purple Converse trainers he was wearing the first day we met, then his legs, his torso, his hands that used to soothe me, his arms that used to wrap around me. His mouth. His beautiful mouth . . . I stop here, unable to bring myself to look into his eyes.

'How?' I ask shakily, gesturing at the television.

'Filmed it yesterday,' he says with a dismissive shrug. The how is unimportant, what matters is that he is here in front of me.

He takes one of my hands and rubs the back of it with his thumb.

Not knowing what else to say, I look down at my hand in his as I try to make sense of the feelings stirring inside of me.

'The shop,' he says, breathlessly. 'You did it. It looks incredible. She'd be so proud.'

The mention of the shop and Molly causes a further influx of emotion and a swelling of pride in my chest. I've come so far. I've done something for myself for the first time in my life. And I achieved this even though I felt lost and heartbroken. I did it.

'I'm so proud of you.'

For once, I feel as though I am worthy of the comment.

I look up into his eyes, his big, honest, chocolate swirls, and find a smile creep onto my face.

'I've been a complete idiot, Sophie. I'm so sorry for not –'

I pull Billy towards me and kiss him.

I've had my fill of blame, sorrow and hurt. I don't want to hear any more. Likewise, I've had enough of having to live without the people I love beside me every day.

Molly once said to grab every opportunity that comes my way – on this occasion, I think I'll take that advice literally . . . she'd have liked that.

Acknowledgements

I'd like to send a gigantic thank you to:

My agent Hannah Ferguson, who not only believed in me from the start, but also guided me through this whole adventure with a friendly smile and lots of cake.

Claire Pelly, for turning my creation into an actual book for others to enjoy!

Beatrix McIntyre and Fiona Brown for making the copyediting and page-proofing process so painless! Plus everyone on the sales, marketing and publicity teams who have supported *Billy and Me*.

Dorothy and Karen, for unknowingly prompting me to sit down and actually write – it was time to stop thinking and start doing!

Scabby, Savvy, Emma, Hayley, Lauren, Kara and my other gorgeous friends, for letting me get on with this and not being too annoyed with me when I couldn't come out to play.

Izzy, for being open and honest and helping me fit together the pieces of the puzzle, and to the rest of the McFamily.

The Falcone/Fletcher gang – Mum, Dad, Giorgie, Mario, Debbie B, Debbie F, Bob and Carrie . . . The most encouraging family I could ever wish for. You're the best!

My husband Tom, for letting me talk his ears off about characters and situations. For giving me endless advice and support . . . and for not minding that I've been sat around the house for most of the past year.

To all my Twitter, Tumblr and Facebook followers who have kept me entertained along the way – you've never failed to put a smile on my face!

And finally, Molly, for teaching me so much and making such a huge impact on my heart – I love you too.

Q&A with Giovanna

Billy and Me looks at the price of fame and having a relationship in the spotlight. What made you decide to write about this subject? Did you draw from your own experiences?

Thanks to the media, people have certain ideas of what dating a celebrity must be like – some girls even claim that it's all they want from life. All us 'WAGs' just shop and eat lettuce leaves all day, don't we? Erm, no. In *Billy and Me* I wanted to capture a more rounded version of that supportive lifestyle. There are incredible highs, but there's also the hurt, the insecurities and the loneliness to contend with. And yes, I'd be lying if I said I wasn't inspired by my own experiences at first, but that was only when I started. The novel had a life of its own after those initial ideas.

What made you decide to set the majority of *Billy and Me* in a tiny village in Kent? Do you have a particular connection to this area?

I have lived in Kent – I studied there for three years – but I don't think Sidcup can be compared to Rosefont Hill. With Kent known as 'The Garden Of England', it seemed fitting to set my idyllic village there. Also, I wanted somewhere small and safe for Sophie, with a close-knit community, somewhere vastly different to the busy streets of London.

One of the main themes of *Billy and Me* focuses on keeping hold of your dreams and not losing sight of who you really are and what you want out of life. What is it about this theme that made you want to write about it?

Being an actress it's important to keep focused and positive, which is hard when there's so much rejection out there. I think of it like being on a bucking bronco – you sit there holding on for as long as you can, trying not to get flung to the ground. It's inevitable that you will be at some point, what's important is how you handle it when you do. You get up, get back on and keep striving towards your goal. I've had my fair share of setbacks and it's so easy to get sidetracked and lose sight of what you cherish and value – but it's those little things that make everything worthwhile! That's where the magic happens.

How and where do you write?

First, I create a big summary, letting me know where I'm going with the plot and helping me focus my thoughts. Then I just get cracking. I aim to write 1,500 words a day. On a good day I'll do double that, on a bad day I'll do half. I write in my office at home, which is like my little den – it's full of posters, Venetian masks, inspiring quotes, books and photos of almost everyone I know and love. I usually write in there but sometimes, if my room becomes a distraction (there's so much to look at), I sit in the garden room looking out at the greenery – just me, my laptop and a glass of water. Oh, and a cat, or two, or three, or four . . .

Who or what was your biggest influence in deciding to become a writer?

A couple of people said they thought I should do it – my husband and my friend Karen. I knew I'd love to, but had no idea where you start with something like that. Then I met Hannah, an agent, who told me she thought I'd be good at it . . . again, where do you start? Then, I was out for lunch with author Dorothy Koomson one day and she told me her biggest piece of advice to aspiring authors was, 'do it'. So I did!

What are your favourite books?

I have so many – I'm a real bookworm. Three books that I read years ago that have stuck with me are *Jemima J* by Jane Green, *My Best Friend's Girl* by Dorothy Koomson and *Playing Away* by Adele Parks. *Jane Eyre* by Charlotte Brontë is my absolute favourite though.

How do you most love to spend your time when you're not writing?

I'd love to say lying in bed while eating chocolate, but I don't want to appear like a complete slob. In my down-time I read anything I can get my hands on, see my friends and remember what it's like to have a life, and go on great walks in the country.

Where's your favourite place to escape to?

I'd have to say my bed!

What would you do if you fell in love
with both your best friends?

Giovanna Fletcher

You're
The One
that I want

Read an extract of
You're The One That I Want now . . .

Maddy

Only fifty-two feet stood between me and my husband-to-be. All that was left for me to complete the transformation from Miss Maddy Hurst to Mrs Maddy Miles was to walk that fifty-two feet and say my vows. Then I'd be able to leave the past behind and look to the future with security, dignity and the love of a good man, knowing that I deserved to be receiving it.

But even though I knew it was what I wanted, it was still the most difficult fifty-two feet I'd ever had to walk. I knew I was walking away from someone who had the potential to take me to new dizzying heights with his love – a love that was mine for the taking, but never truly within my reach. Perhaps if the circumstances were different we'd have had something magical. It pained me to be walking away from those feelings, from him, but I'd said all I needed to say. He knew I loved him and that my love for him was unconditional, as it had always been.

'Give me Joy in my Heart' started playing inside the church, tearing me away from my wandering thoughts, and letting me know it was time for my entrance. One by one the bridesmaids calmly walked through the giant wooden archway. Pearl, the last of the bunch, turned to give me a big wink before following suit, the little train of her mint chiffon dress floating behind her.

'You ready?' asked my dad, who looked incredibly cute in his light grey suit, and emerald-green tie – which I noticed was slightly wonky. His salt-and-pepper-coloured hair was mostly covered up by a big top hat, which bizarrely made him appear shorter than usual, even though it gave him extra height. He looked as nervous as I did – something I wasn't prepared for!

I straightened his tie and gave him a little nod.

He checked over my veil in the way Mum had clearly instructed him to – so that it creased at the sides and not in front of my face. Then he stood beside me and lifted my arm before hooking it through his.

'You look beautiful, Maddy,' he whispered.

'Thanks, Dad,' I managed to say, the nerves seeming to have taken hold of me.

'Feeling nervous?'

Another nod.

'You'll feel better when you see him. Come on, grip hold of your old man. It's time for your groom to see his bride,' he said, firmly squeezing my arm into his side.

At our cue, we started to walk at the steady pace we had agreed on – not so fast that we were almost running to the altar, but not so slow that people started yawning with boredom either. We'd practised it that morning to ensure it wasn't a complete disaster.

I found myself clutching tightly on to Dad's arm as we turned into the church and walked through its doors. A sea of faces welcomed us – all of the congregation were on their feet, looking at me with the broadest smiles I'd ever seen. And there were so many of them! It was a wonder to think we even knew that many people.

During my wedding dress fittings I was told numerous times to enjoy that particular moment, to look at those faces, the ones of the people we both loved and admired, and bask in their warmth. Their love that day was for us. I'd been told to embrace it. But as I took in their faces, their happy smiles, filled with joy, they made the feeling that had been mounting in my chest for weeks tighten further.

That was it.

There was no going back.

A surge of happiness bolted through me as I spotted him, staring back at me from the altar, looking simply divine. My wonderful man, Robert Miles – strong, reliable and loving. My best friend. I pursed my lips as my cheeks rose and tears sprang to my eyes at the very sight of him, looking more handsome than ever in his grey suit. His tall muscular frame visibly relaxed as his dazzling green eyes found mine, his luscious lips breaking into a smile that I couldn't help but respond to.

And then I stole a glance to the right of Robert, to see my other love, Ben Gilbert – kind, generous and able to make my heart melt with just one look. But he wasn't looking back at me. Instead, he had his head bowed and was concentrating on the floor in front of him; all I could see was the back of his waxed brown hair – the smooth olive skin of his face and his chocolate-dipped eyes were turned away.

His hesitance to look up struck a chord within me, momentarily making me wobble on my decision.

Suddenly, something within me urged him to look at me. Part of me wanted him to stop the wedding, to show me exactly how much he cared. Wanted him to stop me from making a terrible mistake ... but is that what I thought I was actually making? A terrible mistake?

I loved Robert, but I loved Ben too. Both men had known me for seventeen years – each of them had seen me at my worst, picked me up when I'd been caught in despair, been my shoulders to cry on when I'd needed to sob. They were my rocks. Plural. Not singular.

Yes, I'd made my decision. I'd accepted Robert's proposal, I'd worn the big white dress and walked up the aisle – however, if Ben had spoken up, if he'd even coughed suggestively, then there's a possibility I'd have stopped the wedding.

Even at that point.

But, as the service got underway, as the congregation was asked for any reasons why we should not have been joined in matrimony without a peep from Ben, it started to sink in that he was not about to start fighting.

He was letting me go ...

He just wanted a decent book to read ...

Not too much to ask, is it? It was in 1935 when Allen Lane, Managing Director of Bodley Head Publishers, stood on a platform at Exeter railway station looking for something good to read on his journey back to London. His choice was limited to popular magazines and poor-quality paperbacks – the same choice faced every day by the vast majority of readers, few of whom could afford hardbacks. Lane's disappointment and subsequent anger at the range of books generally available led him to found a company – and change the world.

'We believed in the existence in this country of a vast reading public for intelligent books at a low price, and staked everything on it'
Sir Allen Lane, 1902–1970, founder of Penguin Books

The quality paperback had arrived – and not just in bookshops. Lane was adamant that his Penguins should appear in chain stores and tobacconists, and should cost no more than a packet of cigarettes.

Reading habits (and cigarette prices) have changed since 1935, but Penguin still believes in publishing the best books for everybody to enjoy. We still believe that good design costs no more than bad design, and we still believe that quality books published passionately and responsibly make the world a better place.

So wherever you see the little bird – whether it's on a piece of prize-winning literary fiction or a celebrity autobiography, political tour de force or historical masterpiece, a serial-killer thriller, reference book, world classic or a piece of pure escapism – you can bet that it represents the very best that the genre has to offer.

Whatever you like to read – trust Penguin.